"ONE! TWO! THREE!"

The two boys — th███████████████████████ ██ —
moved toward each ot██████████████ Martin understood
what they were going to do.

"No!" he shouted. Emilio, dark eyes wide, turned toward
him. The blond boy turned too, his eyes flaring bright sapphire blue. He snatched at Emilio.

Martin threw himself at the dark-haired boy, sending him
sprawling across the floor. For a second, he felt an extraordinary pull on Emilio, as forceful and demanding as if he
were being sucked out of a depressurized airplane.

When it subsided, and they were lying on the floor in cold
and darkness, Martin realized the boy was crying.

"I wanted to go," Emilio sobbed. "I wanted to *go.*"

GRAHAM MASTERTON

A TOM DOHERTY ASSOCIATES BOOK
NEW YORK

MIRROR

Copyright © 1988 by Graham Masterton

First printing: April 1988
First mass market printing: June 1989

A TOR Book
Published by Tom Doherty Associates, Inc.
49 West 24 Street
New York, NY 10010

Cover art by Jim Thiesen

ISBN: 0-812-52202-8   Can. ISBN: 0-812-52203-6

Library of Congress Catalog Card Number: 87-51393

Printed in the United States of America

0 9 8 7 6 5 4 3 2 1

À François Truchaud
Merci, mon ami!

One

MORRIS NATHAN LIFTED his folded sunglasses up in front of his eyes like a lorgnette and watched in satisfaction as his fourth wife circled idly around the pool on her inflatable sunbed. "Martin," he replied, "you should save your energy. Nobody, but nobody, is going to want to make a picture about Boofuls. Why do you think that nobody's done it already?"

"Maybe nobody thought of it," Martin suggested. "Maybe somebody thought of it, but felt that it was too obvious. But it seems like a natural to me. The small golden-haired boy from Idaho state orphanage who became a worldwide star in less than three years."

"Oh, sure," Morris agreed. "And then got himself chopped up into more pieces than a Colonel Sanders Party Bucket."

Martin put down his drink. "Well, yes. But everybody knows that, I mean that's part of the basic legend, so I haven't actually shown his death in any kind of graphic detail. You just see him being driven out of the studio that last evening, then fade-out. It's a bit like *Butch Cassidy and the Sundance Kid*. You remember the way that ended."

Morris lowered his sunglasses and squinted at Martin thoughtfully. "You know something, Martin? I used to deceive myself that I married for intellect, can you believe that? Conversation, wit, perception—that's what I wanted in a woman. Or at least, that's what I *kidded* myself I wanted in a woman. My first three wives were all college graduates. Well, you remember Sherri, don't you—my third? Who could forget her, I ask? But then one day just after Sherri and I were divorced, I was looking through my photo albums, and I realized that each one of my wives had one thing in common that wasn't anything to do with intellect."

He turned and looked fondly out at the twenty-nine-year-old titian-haired woman in the tiny crochet bikini circling around and around on the breeze-ruffled surface of the pool.

"Jugs," he said, "that's what I married them for. And I was being a fool to myself for not admitting it. I was like the guy who buys *Playboy* and tells himself he's buying it for the articles." He wiped his mouth with his open hand. "It's infantile, sure. But that's what I like. Jugs."

Martin shielded his eyes with his hand and peered out at the woman in the pool. "You made a good choice this time, then?"

"Well, sure. Because Alison has the figure without the brains. If you subtract her IQ from her bra size, you get a factor of eleven. And, believe me, next time I meet a woman I take a shine to, that's going to be the only statistic I'll ever want to know."

Martin paused for a moment before getting back to the subject of Boofuls. He didn't want Morris to think that he wasn't interested in Alison, or how small her mind was, or how enormous her breasts. He picked up his vodka-and-orange-juice, and sipped a little, and then set it down on the white cast-iron table.

"I have the treatment here if you want to read it," he said, clearing his throat.

Morris slowly shook his head. "It's poison, Martin. I can't think of a single producer who isn't going to hate the idea. It has the mark of Cain. All the sickness of Fatty Arbuckle and Lupe Velez and Sharon Tate. Forget it. Everybody else has."

"They still show *Whistlin' Dixie* on late-night television," Martin persisted. "Almost anybody you meet can remember at least two lines of 'Heartstrings,' even if they don't know who originally sang it."

Morris was silent for a long time. A pair of California quail fluttered onto the roof of his Tudor-style poolhouse and began to warble and look around for dry-roasted peanuts. Eventually, Morris said, "You're a good writer, Martin. One day you're going to be a *rich* writer, that's if you're lucky. But if you try to tout this particular property around Hollywood, you're not going to be any kind of writer at all, because nobody is going to want to know you. Just do yourself a favor and forget that Boofuls ever existed."

"Come on, Morris, that's ridiculous. That's like trying to say that Shirley Temple never existed."

"No, it's not. Shirley Temple wasn't brutally hacked to death by her grandmother, now, was she?"

Martin rolled up his screenplay into a tight tube and smacked it into the palm of his hand. "I don't know, Morris. It's something I really want to do. It has absolutely everything. Songs, dancing, a sentimental story line."

Alison had paddled herself to the side of the pool and was climbing out. Morris watched her with benign possessiveness, his sun-reddened hands clasped over his belly like Buddha. "Isn't she something?" he asked the world.

Martin nodded to Alison and said, "How're you doing?"

Alison reached out and shook his hand and sprinkled water all over his shirt and his screenplay. "I'm fine, thanks. But I think my nose is going to peel. What do you think?"

"You should use sunscreen, my petal," said Morris.

Alison was quite pretty in a vacant sort of way. Snub nose, with freckles. Pale green eyes. Wide, orthodontically immaculate smile. And really enormous breasts, each one as big as her head, barely contained in her crochet bikini top. By quick reckoning, Martin worked out that her IQ was 29, give or take an inch.

"Are you staying for lunch?" Alison asked him. "We only have fruit and yogurt. You know—my figure and Morry's tum-tum."

Martin shook his head. "I only came over to show Morris my new screenplay."

Alison giggled and leaned forward to kiss Morris on his furrowed scarlet forehead. "I hope he liked it, he's been *so-o-o* grouchy today."

"Well, no," said Martin, "as a matter of fact he hated it."

"Oh, *Morry*," Alison pouted.

Morris let out a leaky, exasperated sigh. "Martin has written a screenplay about Boofuls."

Alison made a face of childish disgust. "Boofuls? No

wonder Morry hated it. That's so *icky*. You mean a horror picture?"

"Not a horror picture," Martin replied, trying to be patient. "A musical, based on his life. I was going to leave out what happened to him in the end."

"But how can you do that?" asked Alison innocently. "I mean, when you say 'Boofuls,' that's all that anybody ever remembers. You know—what happened to him in the end."

Morris shrugged at Martin as if that conclusively proved his point. If a girl as dumb as Alison thought that it was icky to write a screenplay about Boofuls, then what was Paramount going to think about it? Or M-G-M, where Boofuls had been shooting his last, unfinished picture on the day he was murdered?

Martin finished his drink and stood up. "I guess I'd better go. I still have that *A-Team* rewrite to finish."

Morris eased himself back on his sunbed, and Alison perched herself on his big hairy thigh.

"Listen," said Morris, "I can't stop you trying to sell that idea. But my advice is, don't. It won't do you any good and it'll probably do you a whole lot of harm. If you do try, though, you don't bring my name into it. You understand?"

"Sure, Morris," said Martin, deliberately keeping his voice flat. "I understand. Thanks for your valuable time."

He left the poolside and walked across the freshly watered lawn to the rear gate. His sun-faded bronze Mustang was parked under a eucalyptus just outside. He tossed the screenplay onto the passenger seat, climbed in, and started the engine.

"Morris Nathan, arbiter of taste," he said out loud as

he backed noisily into Mulholland Drive. "God save us from agents, and all their works."

On the way back to his apartment on Franklin Avenue he played the sound track from Boofuls' last musical, *Sunshine Serenade*, on his car stereo, with the volume turned all the way up. He stopped at the traffic signals at the end of Mulholland, and two sun-freckled teenage girls on bicycles stared at him curiously and giggled. The sweeping strings of the M-G-M Studio Orchestra and the piping voice of Boofuls singing "Sweep up Your Broken Sunbeams" were hardly the kind of in-car entertainment that anybody would have expected from a thin, bespectacled thirty-four-year-old in a faded checkered shirt and stone-washed jeans.

"Shall we dance?" one of them teased him. He gave her a tight smile and shook his head. He was still sore at Morris for having squashed his Boofuls concept so completely. When he thought of some of the dumb, tasteless ideas that Morris had come up with, Martin couldn't even begin to understand why he had regarded Boofuls as such a hoodoo. They'd made movies about James Dean, for God's sake; and Patricia Neal's stroke; and Helter Skelter; and Teddy Kennedy's bone cancer. I mean, that was *taste*? What was so off-putting about Boofuls?

He turned off Sunset with a squeal of balding tires. He parked in the street because his landlord, Mr. Capelli, always liked to garage his ten-year-old Lincoln every night, in case somebody scratched it, or lime pollen fell on it, or a passing bird had the temerity to spatter it with half-digested seeds. Martin called the Lincoln "the Mafiamobile," but not to Mr. Capelli's face.

Upstairs, in his single-bedroom apartment, his coffee cup and his breakfast plate and last night's supper plate were stacked in the kitchen sink, exactly where he had left them. That was one feature of living alone that he still couldn't quite get used to. Through the open door of the bedroom, he could see the rumpled futon on which he now slept alone, and the large framed poster for Boofuls' first musical, *Whistlin' Dixie*. He walked through to the bare white-painted sitting room, with its single antique sofa upholstered in carpetbag fabric and its gray steel desk overlooking the window. Jane had taken everything else. She and her new boyfriend had simply marched in and carried it all away, while Martin had carried on typing.

The boyfriend had even had the nerve to tap the desk and ask Jane, "You want this, too?"

Without looking up from the tenth draft of his *A-Team* episode, Martin had said, in his B.A. Baracas accent, "Touch this desk and you die, suckah!"

Jane's departure had brought with it immediate relief from their regular shouting contests, and all the tension and discomfort that had characterized their marriage. It had also given Martin the opportunity to work all day and half of the night without being disturbed. That was how he had been able to finish his screenplay for *Boofuls!* in four days flat. But after three weeks he was beginning to realize that work was very much less than everything. Jane might have been demanding and awkard and self-opinionated, but at least she had been somebody intelligent to talk to, somebody to share things with, somebody to hold on to. What was the point of sitting in front of the television on your own, drinking wine on your own, and laughing out loud at *E.R.* with nothing but a lunatic echo to keep you company?

Martin dropped his rejected screenplay onto his desk. The top of the desk was bare except for his IBM golf-ball typewriter, a stack of paper, and a black-and-white publicity still of Boofuls in a brass frame. It was signed, "To Moira, with xxx's from Boofuls." Martin had found the photograph in the Reel Thing, a movie memorabilia store on Hollywood Boulevard: he had no idea who Moira might have been.

The wall at the side of his desk was covered from floor to ceiling with photographs and cuttings and posters and letters, all of Boofuls. Here was Boofuls dancing with Jenny Farr in *Sunshine Serenade*. Boofuls in a sailor suit. Boofuls in a pretend biplane in a scene from *Dancing on the Clouds*. An original letter from President Roosevelt, thanking Boofuls for boosting public morale with his song "March, March, March, America!" Then the yellowed front page from the *Los Angeles Times*, Saturday, August 19, 1939: "Boofuls Murdered. Doting Grandma Dismembers Child Star, Hangs Self."

Martin stood for a long time staring at the headlines. Then, petulantly, he tore the newspaper off the wall and rolled it up into a ball. But his anger quickly faded, and he carefully opened the page out again and smoothed it on the desk with the edge of his hand.

He had always been entranced by 1930s Hollywood musicals, ever since he was a small boy, and the idea for *Boofuls!* had germinated in the back of his mind from the first week he had taken up screenwriting (that wonderful long-gone week when he had sold a *Fall Guy* script to Glen A. Larson). *Boofuls!* had glimmered in the distance for four years now, a golden mirage, his one great chance of fame and glory. *Boofuls!*, a musical by Martin Williams. He couldn't write music, of course, but he didn't need to. Boofuls had recorded over forty original songs, most of them written by Glazer and Hanson, all of them scintillating, all of them catchy, and most of them deleted, so they wouldn't be too expensive for any studio to acquire. *Boofuls!* was a ready-made smash, as far as Martin could see, and nobody had ever done it before.

Morris Nathan was full of shit. He was only jealous because *he* hadn't thought of it and because Martin had shown his first signs of creative independence. Morris preferred his writers tame. That's why people like Stephen J. Cannell and Mort Lachman always came to him for rewrites. Morris' writers would rewrite a teleplay four hundred times if it was required of them, and never complain. Not out loud, anyway. They were the galley slaves of Hollywood.

Although he never worked well when he was drinking, Martin went across to the windowsill and uncorked the two-liter bottle of chardonnay red which he had been keeping to celebrate Morris Nathan's enthusiastic acclaim for the *Boofuls!* idea. He poured himself a large glassful and drank half of it straight off. Morris Nathan. What a *mamzer*.

He went across to the portable Sony cassette recorder which was all the hi-fi that Jane had left him, and rewound it to the beginning of "Whistlin' Dixie." Those gliding strings began again, that familiar introduction, and then the voice of that long-dead child started to sing.

> *All those times you ran and hid*
> *Never did those things you should have did*
> *All those times you shook in your shoes*
> *Never had the nerve to face your blues*
> *You were—Whistlin' Dixie!*

Martin leaned against the side of the window and looked down into the next-door yard. It was mostly swimming pool, surrounded by bright green synthetic-grass carpeting. Maria was there again, on her sunbed, her eyes closed, her nose and her nipples protected from the morning sun by paper Sno-Cones. Maria worked as a cocktail waitress at the Sunset Hyatt. Her surname was Bocanegra, and she had thighs like Carmen Miranda. Martin had asked her for a date one day, about fifteen seconds before a huge Latin bodybuilder with pockmarked cheeks had appeared around the corner of her apartment building and scooped his arm around her and grinned at Martin and said, *"Cómo la va, hombre?"*

Martin had blurted out a quick *"Hasta luego,"* and that had been the beginning and end of a beautiful relationship.

He sipped wine and thought about getting back to the *A-Team* rewrite, but it was pretty hard to get into Murdock's latest outbreak of nuttiness when he was feeling so down about *Boofuls!* He whispered the words along with the tape. *"You were—Whistlin' Dixie!"*

Just then the telephone rang. He let it ring for a while. He guessed it was Morris, more than likely, wanting to know when the rewrite was going to be completed. The way he felt at the moment, January 2010. At last, however, Martin turned away from the window and picked up the receiver.

"Hello? Martin Williams."

"Hey, Martin!" said an enthusiastic voice. "I'm real glad I got in touch with you! This is Ramone!"

"Oh, Ramone, hi." Ramone worked behind the counter at the Reel Thing, selling everything from souvenir programs for the opening night of *Gone With the Wind* to Ida Lupino's earrings. It was Ramone more than

anybody else who had helped him to build up his
unique collection of Boofuls souvenirs.

"Listen, Martin, something real interesting came up.
A lady came into the store this morning and said she
had a whole lot of furniture for sale."

Martin cleared his throat. "I could use some furniture, sure. But actually I was thinking of taking a
trip out to the Z-Mart furnishing warehouse in Burbank. I can't afford anything antique."

"No, no, no, you're not getting my drift," said
Ramone. "This lady bought some of the furniture from
Boofuls' old house. There was an auction, you get it,
after the kid was killed, and everything was sold.
Drapes, tables, knives and forks. They even sold the
food out of the refrigerator. Can you imagine what kind
of a ghoul would want to eat a murdered kid's ice
cream?"

"But what happened? This woman bought some of
the furniture?"

"Maybe not her personally, but her husband or her
father or somebody. Anyway, she has, what, lemme
see, I made a list here—she has two armchairs, a liquor cabinet, a sofa, four barstools, and a mirror."

"Are you going to sell it for her?"

"No, not my scene, furniture. And—you know—
apart from you, nobody's too keen on Boofuls stuff. I
told her to advertise in the paper. Maybe some sicko
will want it."

"What are you trying to say? That I'm a sicko, too?"

"Aw, come on, man, I know you're legitimate. You
should see some of the guys who come in to look
through Carole Landis' underwear, stuff like that."

Martin said, "I'd like to see the furniture, sure, but I
really don't have too much spare cash right now."

"Well, that's up to you," Ramone told him. "But if you're interested, the lady's name is Mrs. Harper, and she lives at 1334 Hillrise. There's no harm in taking a look, is there?"

"All right, I guess not, thanks for thinking of me."

"No sweat, man. Whenever I hear the name Boofuls, I think of you."

"I hope that's a compliment."

"*De nada*," said Ramone, and hung up.

Martin finished his wine. He knew what he ought to do: and that was to sit down dutifully at his typewriter and zip another sheet of paper into the platen and carry on writing the *A-Team*. However much he disagreed with Morris; however chagrined he felt by Morris' reaction to *Boofuls!* Morris was an industrious agent with matchless contacts, and he made his writers money. If Martin didn't finish this rewrite by tomorrow morning, it was quite conceivable that Morris would never be able to sell him to Stephen J. Cannell Productions ever again.

But, damn it, he was so dispirited, and so damn sick of writing slick and silly dialogue. An expedition to Hillrise Avenue to look over some of Boofuls' original furniture might be just what he needed to lift his spirits. Just to *touch* it would be something—to touch the actual furniture that little Boofuls had sat on himself. It would make him seem more real, and Morris Nathan more imaginary, and just at the moment Martin couldn't think of a better tonic than that.

Hillrise Avenue was a steeply sloping street up by the Hollywood Reservoir. The houses had been avant-garde in 1952; today they were beginning to show signs of shabbiness and wear. Hillrise was one of those areas

that had never quite made it, and was resignedly dete-
riorating for the eventual benefit of some smart real-
estate developer.

Martin parked his Mustang with the rear wheels
cramped against the curb and climbed out. From here,
there was a wide, distant view of Los Angeles, smoggy
today, with the twin tombstones of Century City rising
above the haze. He mounted the steep concrete steps to
1334, sending a lizard scurrying into the undergrowth.

The house was square, strawberry pink, with Spanish balconies all the way around. The garden around it
was dried up and scraggly. The paths were overgrown
with weeds, and most of the yuccas looked sick. The
roof over the front porch was heaped with dead, desiccated vines, and there was a strong smell of broken
drains.

He rang the doorbell. It was shrill, demanding, distant, like a woman shrieking in the next street. Martin
shuffled his Nike trainers and waited for somebody to
answer. *"All those times you shook in your shoes,"* he
sang softly. *"You were—Whistlin' Dixie!"*

The front door opened. Out onto the porch came a
small sixtyish woman with a huge white bouffant hairstyle and a yellow cotton mini-dress. She wore two sets
of false eyelashes, one of them coming wildly adrift at
the corner of her eye, and pale tangerine lipstick. She
looked as though she hadn't changed her clothes or her
makeup since the day *Sergeant Pepper* had been released.

Martin was so startled that he didn't quite know
what to say. The woman stared at him, her left eye
wincing, and eventually said, "Ye-e-es? Are you selling
something?"

"I, uh—"

"I don't see anything," the woman remarked, peering around the porch. "No brushes, no encyclopedias, no Bibles. Do you want to clean my car, is that it?"

"Actually, I came about the furniture," said Martin. "You're Mrs. Harper, right? Ramone Perez called me from the Reel Thing. He's kind of a friend of mine. He knows that I'm interested in Boofuls."

Mrs. Harper stared at Martin and then sniffed, pinching in one nostril. "Is tha-a-at right? Well, if you're interested in Boofuls, you seem to be just about the only person in the whole of Hollywood who *is*. I've taken my furniture to every auction house and movie memorabilia store that I can *find*, and the story's always the same."

"Yes?" said Martin, wanting to know what it was—this story that was always the same.

"Well," pouted Mrs. Harper, "it's *macabre*, that's what they say. I mean, there's a market in motion picture properties. The very coffin that Bela Lugosi lay in when he first played Count Dracula. The very bolt that went through Boris Karloff's neck. But nobody will *touch* poor little Boofuls' furniture."

Martin waited for a moment, but Mrs. Harper obviously wasn't going to volunteer anything more. "I was wondering—maybe I could come in and take a look at it."

"With a view to purchase?" Mrs. Harper asked him sharply; then fluttered her left eye; then squeezed it shut and said, "Darn these lashes! They're a new brand. I don't know what you're supposed to keep them on with. Krazy Glue, if you ask me. They will . . . *curl up*. I've seen centipedes behave themselves better, and live ones at that."

She led Martin into the hallway. The interior of the

house was sour-smelling and gloomy, but it had once been decorated in the very latest fab 1960s style. The floor was covered with white shag carpet throughout, matted like the pelt of an aging Yeti. The drapes were patterned in psychedelic striations of orange and lime and purple, and white leather chairs with black legs and gold feet were arranged around the room at diagonal angles. There was even a white stereo autochange record player, which reminded Martin so strongly of the Beatles and the Beach Boys and his high school dances that he felt for one unnerving moment as if he were sixteen years old.

"I'm a widow," said Mrs. Harper, as if she felt a need to explain why the interior of her house was a living museum of twenty-year-old contemporary design. "Arnold died in 1971, and, well—it all just *reminds* me."

Martin nodded, to show that he understood. Mrs. Harper said, "*He* didn't like the Boofuls furniture, either. I mean he actually hated it. But his father had bought it, just before the war. His father was setting up house, you see, and he went to an auction and bought it—well, because it was so *cheap*. It was only afterward that somebody told him who it used to belong to. And what's more . . . it used to stand in the *very room* where poor little Boofuls was—you know—done away with. Quite the most awful thing ever. I mean even worse than Charles Manson, because she *chopped* that dear little child into—well, I don't even like to think about it. And nor does anybody else, more's the pity."

"Can we—er—look at it?" asked Martin.

"Well, of course. It's down in the cellar. I mean it hasn't seen the light of day since Arnold's father gave it to us. Arnold didn't even want it but his father insisted. Arnold never had the nerve to stand up against his father. Well, not many people did. He was an absolute tyrant."

Mrs. Harper led the way through to the kitchen. She stood up on tiptoe, revealing so much skinny leg that Martin had to look away, and groped around on the top shelf of the kitchen cupboard to find the key to the cellar.

"I should sell up, you know, and move to San Diego. My sister lives there. This big old house is such a nuisance."

She unlocked the cellar and switched on the light. Martin hesitated for a moment and then followed her down the steep wooden steps. The smell of drains was even stronger down here, and it was mingled with a smell of dried-out lumber and cats.

"You watch your step, now," said Mrs. Harper. "Those last two steps are pretty rotten. We had termites, you know. Arnold thought they were going to eat the whole house right around our ears."

"They didn't touch the furniture?"

"Don't ask me why," said Mrs. Harper, her pink-fingernailed claw illuminated for a moment as she clutched the stair rail. "They ate just about everything else. They even ate the handle of Arnold's shovel, I'll always remember that. The whole darned handle. But they never touched the furniture. Not a nibble. Perhaps even termites have respect for the dead."

"Yes, maybe they do," said Martin, peering into the gloom of the cellar.

Mrs. Harper beckoned him forward. "It's all over here, behind the boiler."

Martin caught his sleeve on an old horse collar which was hooked on a nail at the side of the stairs. It took him a moment to disentangle himself, but when he had, Mrs. Harper had disappeared into the darkness behind the boiler. "Mrs. Harper?"

There was no reply. Martin groped forward a little farther. The boiler was heavy cast iron, one of those old-fashioned types, and almost looked as if it had a grinning face on it, with mica eyes. "Mrs. Harper?"

He came cautiously around the corner of the boiler and there she was. But the back of his scalp shrank in alarm, because she was suspended three feet above the floor, at a frightening diagonal angle, her white bouffant hair gleaming like the huge chrysalis of some gigantic moth.

"Ah!" Martin shouted; but almost at the same time Mrs. Harper turned her head and he realized that he was looking at a reflection of her; and that the real Mrs. Harper was standing beside him quite normally.

"I'm sorry," she said without much sympathy. "Did I startle you?"

"No, I, uh—" Martin gestured toward the mirror that was hanging from the ceiling.

"Well," Mrs. Harper smiled. She rubbed her hands together. "That was Boofuls' mirror. That was the very mirror that watched him die."

"Very nice," said Martin. He was beginning to wonder whether it had been such a good idea coming down here to look at Boofuls' old furniture. Maybe the tedium of retyping his *A-Team* script had something to recommend it. Maybe some memories are better left alone.

"The chairs and the sofa are back here," said Mrs. Harper. She dragged at the corner of a dustcover and revealed the shadowy outlines of an elegant reproduction sofa and two matching chairs. They were gilded, French chateau style, with pale green watered-satin seats—grubby and damp-stained from so many years in Mrs. Harper's cellar. Martin peered at them through the gloom.

"Do you have any more lights down here?" he asked.

"Well, there's a flashlight someplace . . ." Mrs. Harper fussed, making it quite obvious that she didn't want to go looking for it.

"Don't worry," Martin told her. "I can see them pretty good. Is that the liquor cabinet back there?" He pointed toward a huge rococo piece of bowfront furniture with engraved windows, partially concealed by a sheet.

"That's right; and it still has *all* the original decanters, with solid-silver labels. Gin, whiskey, brandy. Not that Boofuls ever *drank*, of course, at his age."

She thought this was quite amusing and let out a high, whinnying snort.

Martin approached the furniture with a mixture of dread and fascination. He ran his hand along the back of the sofa, and thought, *Boofuls actually sat here.* The experience was more disturbing than he had expected. News clippings and photographs were one thing—but they were flat and two-dimensional. Boofuls had never actually touched them. But here was his furniture. Here were his chairs. Here was the mirror that must have hung over his fireplace. Real, touchable objects. To Martin, they were as potent as Hitler's shirts, or Judy Garland's ruby slippers, or Jackie Kennedy's pink pillbox hats. They were proof that a legend had once been real; that Boofuls had actually lived.

He said nothing for a long time, his hands on his hips, breathing the musty sawdust atmosphere of Mrs. Harper's cellar.

"You said that nobody was interested in buying them," he remarked to Mrs. Harper at last.

"I didn't say that nobody was interested in *buying* them," Mrs. Harper retaliated. "I simply said that nobody seemed interested in selling them for me. It's the profit margin, I suppose."

Martin nodded and looked around him. It was the two chairs he coveted the most—those and the mirror. The mirror would look absolutely stunning on his sitting room wall, instead of all those cuttings and photographs and letters—and it would have a far greater emotional effect. Instead of saying, "Oh, yes, here's my collection of publicity pictures of Boofuls," he would be able to announce, "And this—this is the actual mirror which was hanging in Boofuls' sitting room when he was murdered."

Shock! Shudder! Envy!

"Erm . . . how much do you want for this stuff?" Martin asked Mrs. Harper casually. "Chairs, mirror, sofa, liquor cabinet, stools. Supposing I took them all off your hands?"

"Well . . . I wouldn't mind that at all," said Mrs. Harper. She rubbed the back of the gilded sofa and sucked in her false teeth, and her eyelashes fluttered like chloroformed moths.

"How much?" asked Martin, thinking of the $578 sitting in his savings account at Security Pacific. Surely she wouldn't ask more than five hundred bucks for a few worn-out pieces of 1930s furniture. She might even pay him to cart them away.

Mrs. Harper thought for a moment, her hand pressed to her forehead. "I don't know," she said. "I've had so many different valuations. Some very high, some very low. But you're a real Boofuls fan, aren't you? A genuine devotee. And, you know, it seems kind of *mean* to make you pay an extortionate price—especially since you're trying to keep his memory alive."

Martin shrugged, and shuffled his feet. "That's really generous of you. But I wouldn't like you to take a loss."

"Don't you worry about that. As far as I'm concerned, the most important thing is for Boofuls' belongings to have a loving home."

Martin looked up at the mirror. Now that his eyes were becoming more accustomed to the shadows, he could distinguish the details of the gilded frame. It was quite a large mirror—six feet wide and nearly five feet high—which had obviously hung over a fireplace. The sides of the frame were carved as luxuriant tangles of grapevines. At the top, there was a grinning gilded face which looked like Bacchus or Pan. The glass itself was discolored and measled at one corner, but most of it reflected back Martin's face with a clarity that was almost hallucinatory, as if he were actually looking at himself in the flesh, instead of a reflection. No wonder he had been so alarmed to see Mrs. Harper floating in the air.

He reached out to touch the mirror and felt the chilly glass of its surface, untouched by sunlight for nearly twenty years. How does a mirror feel when it has nothing to reflect—nobody to smile at it, nobody to preen their hair in it, no rooms for it to look at, no evanescent pictures for it to paint of passing lives? *"Mirrors are lonely,"* Tennyson once wrote.

"Seven thousand," said Mrs. Harper. "How about that?"

"I beg your pardon?" asked Martin, caught off-balance.

"Seven thousand for everything," Mrs. Harper repeated. "It's the lowest I can go."

Martin rubbed the back of his neck. Seven thousand was out of the question. Even his car wasn't worth seven thousand. "I'm sorry," he said."That's more than I can afford. I'm not Aaron Spelling, I'm afraid."

"I couldn't go any lower," said Mrs. Harper. "It would be worth a whole lot more, even if it *hadn't* belonged to Boofuls."

"Well, that's that, I guess," said Martin in resignation. "Thank you for letting me look at it, anyway. At least it gives me some idea of how Boofuls' room was furnished. That could be quite a help with my screenplay."

"How much *can* you afford?" asked Mrs. Harper.

Martin smiled and shook his head. "Nothing like seven thousand. Nothing like *one* thousand. Five hundred, and that's tops."

Mrs. Harper looked around. "I guess I could let you have the barstools for five hundred."

"You'd be willing to sell pieces separately?"

"Well, I wasn't planning to. But since you're such a devotee."

"Do you think you could sell me the mirror for five hundred? I really covet the mirror."

Mrs. Harper puckered her lips. "I'm not at all sure about that. That's very special, that mirror. French, originally—that's what Arnold's father told me."

"It's very handsome," Martin agreed. "I can just imagine it in my apartment."

"Maybe seven-fifty?" Mrs. Harper suggested. "Could you go to seven-fifty?"

Martin took a deep breath. "I could pay you five hundred now and the rest of it next month." That wouldn't leave him very much for living on, he thought to himself, but if he finished his *A-Team* rewrite tonight and maybe asked Morris to find him a couple of extra scripts to work on—anything, even *Stir Crazy* or *Silver Spoons*.

Mrs. Harper stood in silence for a long while, and then she said, "Very well. Five hundred now and two-fifty by the end of next month. But you make sure you pay. I don't want any trouble. I've got lawyers, you know."

Martin found an old wooden fruit box and dragged it across the cellar floor so that he could stand on it to reach the mirror. The late Arnold Harper had hung it up on two large brass hooks, screwed firmly into the joists of the sitting room floor above them. Martin lifted the mirror gently down, making sure that he didn't knock the gilded frame on the floor. It was desperately heavy, and he was sweating by the time he had managed to ease it down onto the floor. Mrs. Harper watched him, making no attempt to assist him, smiling benignly.

"It's a wonderful thing, isn't it?" she said, peering into it and teasing her bouffant hair. "They sure don't make mirrors like this one anymore."

Martin found that he didn't have the strength to lift the mirror and carry it up the stairs, so he bundled a dustcover underneath one corner of it and dragged it across the floor. Then, panting, step by step, he pulled it up the wooden staircase until he reached the hallway. It took him almost five minutes to maneuver it through the cellar door into the kitchen. Mrs. Harper stood halfway up the stairs watching, still offering no help. Martin almost wished that he hadn't bought the goddamn thing. His arms were trembling from the weight of it. His cheek was smeared with grime and he was out of breath.

"You can bring your car up to the side of the house if

you want to," said Mrs. Harper—and that was the only contribution she made. Martin nodded, leaning against one of the kitchen cupboards.

"You'll take a personal check?" he asked her.

"Oh, sure. Just so long as you're good for it. It's all money, isn't it? That's what Arnold used to say."

After another ten minutes, Martin managed to drag the mirror out of the kitchen door and tilt it into the back seat of his Mustang. Mrs. Harper allowed him to borrow the dustcover to protect it, provided he promised that he would bring it straight back. "I promise," he told her. "I'll bring it straight back."

He drove off slowly down Hillside, and Mrs. Harper stood on her steps and waved his check. Glancing at her in his rearview mirror, he thought that for somebody who had just let him have a valuable antique at a knock-down price, she looked a little too pleased with herself. She had probably asked him for double what the mirror was actually worth.

Still, he was now the owner of the actual mirror that had graced Boofuls' fireplace, and maybe that would bring him luck. He hummed "Flowers From Tuscaloosa" as he slowly drove his huge angular purchase back to Franklin Avenue.

Mr. Capelli was home early, and he helped Martin to carry the mirror upstairs. Mr. Capelli was small and rotund, with a bald head and spectacles that looked as if they had been ground out of two glass bottle-stoppers. "I shouldn't even lift a basket of groceries," he grumbled. "My doctor's going to kill me alive."

"Mr. Capelli, you don't know how much I appreciate this," Martin told him. "This mirror used to belong to

Boofuls. True. It used to hang over his fireplace, in his sitting room in Bel Air."

Mr. Capelli examined the mirror with his mouth turned down at the corners. "This used to belong to Boofuls? This actual mirror?"

"This actual mirror. In fact, when his grandmother chopped him up, this actual mirror was probably reflecting the whole scene."

Mr. Capelli shuddered. "That's bad, you shouldn't keep something like this."

"It's a mirror, Mr. Capelli, that's all."

"Well, that's what you say. But in Sicily, you know what my grandmother always used to do? Whenever somebody died, she went around and smashed every mirror in the house, and this was because every time a person looks in a mirror, the mirror takes a little tiny teentsy bit of their soul. So the only way that their whole soul can go to heaven when they die is for somebody to smash all of their mirrors, and let out that little bit that the mirror took away from them when they were alive."

Martin shoved his hands into the back pockets of his jeans and smiled. "What's that famous Italian sausage?" he asked.

"Mortadella," said Mr. Capelli.

"No, no, the other one. The big, smooth one."

"Baloney."

"That's it!" said Martin. "And I couldn't agree with you more."

"Hey! You don't talk to me that way," snapped Mr. Capelli. "You want me to make you take this mirror back out again?"

"All right, I'm sorry," said Martin, and laid his hand on Mr. Capelli's shoulder. "It's really going to look great. It's going to make this apartment look twice the size."

"Hmh," Mr. Capelli retorted. "Maybe I should charge you twice the rent."

Just then, Mr. Capelli's young grandson, Emilio, came out of Mr. Capelli's apartment to see what all the noise was about. He was five years old, with straight black hair and olive skin and huge eyes like a sentimental painting of a sad puppy. As soon as he saw they were carrying a mirror, he made faces at himself in it.

"That's a great improvement," said Martin as Emilio crossed his eyes and squashed his nose flat with his finger.

"Hey, that's my grandson you're talking about," Mr. Capelli protested. "He's a good-looking boy."

"That's because he doesn't take after his grandfather," Martin said, grinning.

"Treble the rent!" retorted Mr. Capelli.

"Watch yourself, Emilio," Martin warned. "This mirror's real heavy. You don't want to get squished."

"I do too want to get squished," Emilio told him cheekily.

"That can be arranged," said Martin under his breath.

When Mr. Capelli had gone, Martin carefully took down all his Boofuls photographs and cuttings. Then he dragged the mirror noisily up against the wall beside his desk. There were four brass plates at the side of the mirror, two on each side, which had obviously been used to screw the mirror firmly into the chimney breast over Boofuls' fireplace. Martin rooted around in his desk drawer until he found four two-inch screws and half a dozen wall plugs. Jane had taken his electric drill, but the wall was quite soft, and he was able to gouge out four holes in the plaster with his screwdriver.

It took him nearly an hour to fix up the mirror. But when it was screwed firmly into place, he stood back and admired it and didn't regret for one moment that he had spent all of his savings on it, even if Mrs. Harper had probably screwed him for two or three hundred dollars more than it was actually worth. With its gilded frame and its brilliant glass, it gave his apartment a whole new dimension, adding light and space and airiness.

He poured himself a glass of wine. Then he sat down at his desk. Portrait of a successful young screenwriter feeding a sheet of paper into his typewriter. Portrait of a successful young screenwriter knocking next season's *A-Team* into shape.

He worked all afternoon. The sun began to steal away, sliding out of the room inch by inch, lighting the building next door, then shining on nothing but the tallest yuccas in the street outside.

B.A.: I swear—if this fruitcake don't stop—I'm going to take him apart.
Hannibal: Come on now, B.A., we're talking comradeship here. Shoulder to shoulder.

It was well past seven when Martin switched off his typewriter and sat back in his chair. He knew that he was going to have to rewrite the scene in which Hannibal disguises himself as a monk, but apart from that he was just about finished. He was particularly pleased with the moment when Murdock starts juggling pool balls and B.A. joins in the juggling act in spite of himself. He jotted on his notepad, *"Can Mr. T juggle? If not,*

*can he be taught? Are there any brilliant black jugglers?
There must be! But what if there aren't? Can some white
juggler black his hands up and stand right behind him
while he dummies it?"*

He poured himself another glass of wine. Maybe his
luck was going to change, after all. Maybe some of
Boofuls' success would radiate out of his mirror and
bless Martin's work. Martin raised his glass to himself
and said, *"Prost!"*

It was then, in the mirror, that he saw a child's blue
and white ball come bouncing through the open door
behind him, and then roll to a stop in the middle of the
varnished wood floor.

He stared at it in shock, with that same shrinking-
scalp sensation that he had felt this afternoon when he
had seen Mrs. Harper floating in midair. "Emilio?" he
called. "Is that you?"

There was no reply. Martin turned around and
called, "Emilio?" again.

He got up out of his chair, intending to pick the ball
up, but he was only halfway standing when he realized
that it wasn't there anymore.

He frowned, and walked across to the door, and opened
it wider. The passageway was empty; the front door was
locked. "Emilio, what the hell are you playing at?"

He looked in the bedroom. Nobody. He even opened
up the closet doors. Just dirty shirts and shorts, waiting to be washed, and a squash racket that needed re-
stringing. He checked the bathroom, then the kitchen.
Apart from himself, the apartment was deserted.

"Hallucination," he told himself. "Maybe I'm falling
apart."

He returned to the sitting room and picked up his
glass of wine. He froze with the glass almost touching

his lips. *In the mirror, the blue and white ball was still there, lying on the floor where it had first bounced.*

Martin stared at it and then quickly looked back into the real sitting room. No ball. Yet there it was in the mirror, perfectly clear, as plain as milk.

Martin walked carefully across the room. Watching himself in the mirror, he reached down and tried to pick the ball up, but in the real room there was nothing there, and in the mirror room his hand appeared simply to pass right through the ball, as if it had no substance at all.

He scooped at it two or three times and waved his hand from side to side exactly where the ball should have been. Still nothing. But the really odd part about it was that as he watched his hand intently, it seemed as if it were not the ball that was insubstantial, but his own fingers—as if the ball were real and that reflection of himself in the mirror were a ghost.

He went right up close to the mirror and touched its surface. There was nothing unusual about it. It was simply cold glass. But the ball remained there, whether it was a hallucination or a trick of the light, or whatever. He sat in his chair and watched it and it refused to disappear.

After half an hour, he got up and went to the bathroom to shower. The ball was still there when he returned. He finished the wine, watching it all the time. He was going to have a hangover in the morning, but right now he didn't much care.

"What the hell *are* you?" he asked the ball.

He pressed his cheek against the left side of the mirror and tried to peer into his own reflected hallway, to see if it was somehow different. *Looking-Glass House*, he thought to himself, and all those unsettling childhood feelings came back to him. If you could walk through the door in the mirror, would the hallway be the same? Was there another different world in there, not just back to front but disturbingly different?

In his bookshelf, he had a dog-eared copy of *Alice Through the Looking-Glass* which Jane had bought him when they were first dating. He took it out and opened it up and quickly located the half-remembered words.

Alice was looking into the mirror over her sitting room fireplace, wondering about the room that she could see on the other side of the glass.

It's just the same as our drawing-room, only the things go the other way. I can see all of it when I get upon a chair—all but the bit just behind the fire-place. Oh! I do so wish I could see that bit! I want so much to know whether they've a fire in the winter: you never can tell, you know, unless our fire smokes, and then smoke comes up in that room, too—but that may only be pretence, just to make it look as if they had a fire. Well then, the books are something like our books, only the words go the wrong way: I know that, because I've held up one of our books to the glass, and then they hold one up in the other room. But now we come to the passage. You can see just a little peep of the passage in Looking-Glass House, if you leave the door of our drawing-room wide open: and it's very like our passage as far as you can see, only you know it may be quite different on beyond.

Martin closed the book. The ball was still there. He stood looking at it for a long time, not moving. Then he went across to his desk and switched off the light, so that the sitting room was completely dark. He paused, and then he switched it back on again. The ball in the mirror hadn't moved.

"Shit," he said; and for the very first time in his life

he felt that something was happening to him which he couldn't control.

He could have gotten Jane back if he had really wanted to—at least, he believed that he could. He could have been wealthier if he had written all the dumb teleplays that Morris had wanted him to write. But he had been able to make his own decisions about things like that. This ball was something else altogether. A ball that existed only as a reflection in a mirror, and not in reality?

"Shit," he repeated, and switched off the light again and shuffled off to the bedroom. He dropped his red flannel bathrobe and climbed naked onto his futon. He was about to switch off his bedside light when a thought occurred to him. He padded back to the sitting room and closed the door. If there was anything funny about that mirror, he didn't want it coming out and jumping on him in the middle of the night.

Irrational, yes, but he was tired and a little drunk and it was well past midnight.

He dragged the covers well up to his neck, even though he was too hot, and closed his eyes, and tried to sleep.

He was awakened by what sounded like a child laughing. He lifted his head from the pillow and thought, *Goddamned Emilio, why do kids always have to wake up at the crack of dawn?* But then he heard the laughter again, and it didn't sound as if it were coming from downstairs at all. It sounded as if it were coming from his own sitting room.

He sat up straight, holding his breath, listening. There it was again. A small boy, laughing out loud; but with a curious echo to his voice, as if he were laughing in a large empty room. Martin checked his clock radio. It wasn't the crack of dawn at all: it was only 3:17 in the morning.

He switched on his light, wincing at the brightness of it. He found his bathrobe and tugged it on, inside out, so that he had to hold it together instead of tying it. Then he went to the sitting room door and listened.

He listened for almost a minute. Then he asked himself: *What are you afraid of, wimp? It's your own apartment, your own sitting room, and all you can hear is a child.*

He licked his lips, and then he opened the sitting room door. Immediately, he reached out for the light switch and turned on the main light. Immediately, he looked toward the mirror.

There was nobody there, no boy laughing. Only himself, frowsy and pale, in his inside-out bathrobe. Only the desk and the typewriter and the bookshelf and the pictures of Boofuls.

He approached the mirror slowly. One thing was different. One thing that he could never *prove* was different, not even to himself. The blue and white ball had gone.

He looked toward the reflected door, half open, and the peep of the passageway outside. *It's very like our own passage as far as you can see, only you know it may be quite different on beyond.*

How different? thought Martin with a dry mouth. How different? Because if a ball had come bouncing into the reflected room, there must have been *somebody there to throw it; and if it had disappeared, then somebody must have walked into that reflected room when he was asleep and picked it up.*

"Oh, God." He swallowed. "Oh, God, don't let it be Boofuls."

Two

Henry Polowski, the gatekeeper at Metro-Gold-wyn-Mayer, swore that when Boofuls was driven out of the studio that night in August 1939, he pressed his face to the rear window of his limousine and just for one terrible second he looked like a skull. Bone-white, with hollow eye sockets and naked teeth. Henry had shouted out loud.

"You can laugh all you want, but it was a genuine premonition," Henry told the reporters who had been crowded all night around the Hollywood police head-quarters. "I saw it, and if you don't believe it, then that's your problem, not mine."

"Didn't you tell anybody what you saw?" Henry was asked by Lydia Haskins of the *Los Angeles Times*. "If you really saw it, and you really believed it to be a genuine premonition, why didn't you make any attempt to warn somebody?"

"What would *you* have done?" Henry retaliated. "My

32

partner heard me shout and asked me what was
wrong, and I said Boofuls just went by and—I don't
know—he was looking funny. So my partner said,
what kind of funny? Making faces, that kind of funny? I
said no, but I was sure something bad was going to
happen to that boy."

"And that was the only attempt you made to tell
anybody what you thought you saw?" Lydia Haskins
persisted.

"Lady," said Henry, "I didn't *think* I saw it. I saw it."

"How does that make you feel now?" called out Jim
Keller, from the *Hollywood Reporter*. "Does that make
you feel guilty in any way, now that Boofuls is dead?"

"How would *you* feel?" Henry retorted. "I saw that
little boy looking like a skull at 5:27 that evening, and
by 6:30 he was hacked into pieces. I loved that little
boy. We all did. How the hell would *you* feel?"

Jim Keller shrugged. "Pretty damn bad, I guess."

"Well," said Henry, "that's the way I feel. Pretty
damn bad."

Martin pressed his remote control, and the video-
recorded newsreel shrank from his television screen.
He had watched that recording over and over during
his research for *Boofuls!* For some perverse reason, he
had always wanted to believe that Henry Polowski was
telling the truth—even though the gatekeeper had been
fired two weeks later after the *Hollywood Reporter* revealed that he was an alcoholic and had twice been
hospitalized for DTs.

Martin had the discolored press cutting lying on his
desk. " 'I Saw Skull' Gatekeeper Saw Giant Roaches,
Martians." Martin had some sympathy for him. Anybody would, if they had seen in their sitting room mirror the reflection of a blue and white ball for which

there was no corresponding blue and white ball in the material world.

But the ball had vanished, just as Boofuls had vanished. Not just the boy, but his glory, too. Martin thought it was remarkable that so few people could recall the hysterical adulation that used to be showered on the small golden-haired boy called Boofuls. His limousine was often mobbed to a standstill in the middle of the street. Women were caught almost every night trying to break into his mansion in Bel Air to kidnap him. "He *needs* me," they used to plead as they were dragged away across the lawns. "He needs a mother!"

It was true, of course, that Boofuls was an orphan. He had been born Walter Lemuel Crossley in Boise, Idaho, in March 1931, the illegitimate son of Mary Louise Crossley, a nineteen-year-old stenog at Ressequie State Insurance on Fort Street, Boise.

Mary Crossley brought Boofuls up alone for two years, apparently relying on welfare and home typing and occasional *ex gratia* payments from Boofuls' unknown father.

The day before Boofuls' second birthday, however, Mary Crossley took an overdose of aspirin after an argument with one of her boyfriends (not, apparently, Boofuls' father). As far as Martin had been able to make out, it seemed unlikely that she seriously intended to kill herself. She had taken overdoses before. But this time she developed pneumonia after being stomach-pumped, and died four days later. Boofuls was taken into state care for six months, then fostered for a further three months, and eventually sent to live with his recently widowed grandmother, Mrs. Alicia Crossley, ninety miles away in Twin Falls.

In February 1935—for reasons that Martin had never

been able to discover—Mrs. Alicia Crossley took
Boofuls to Los Angeles, California. They lived for a
while at the Palms Boarding House in Venice. Mrs.
Crossley appears to have supported them both by taking a waitressing job and then housecleaning. But in
May of the following year—again for no clear reason—
Boofuls was taken by his grandmother to audition for
Jacob Levitz' new musical, *Whistlin' Dixie*. Almost mi-
raculously, he was selected out of more than six hundred juvenile hopefuls for the part of Tiny Joe. He had
no drama experience, he couldn't tap, his voice was un-
trained. His only assets were his golden curls and his
heart-shaped face and his sweet, endearing lisp.

Jacob Levitz, however, was thrilled with his discov-
ery. He called him "the Boy Shirley Temple." His only
stipulation was that the boy would have to change his
name. "Walter Lemuel Crossley" didn't sound like a
five-year-old child movie star; it sounded more like a
middle-aged insurance agent from Boise.

Metro held a "Name the Child Star" contest in the
newspapers, and the short list of names was sent to
Louis B. Mayer. Mr. Mayer read them, hated them all,
and scribbled in the margin, "B. Awful." This half-
illegible comment was taken by a wholly illiterate
secretary to be Mr. Mayer's own suggestion for little
Walter's new name, and she typed it and sent it to the
publicity office. At least, that was the way that Mr.
Mayer told the story, and Boofuls himself never contradicted him.

Whistlin' Dixie, of course, became one of the most
successful musicals of all time. Boofuls' show-stopping
song "Heartstrings" sold more copies that year than
"All My Eggs in One Basket"; and when he accepted
his Oscar in 1937 for *Captains Courageous*, Spencer

Tracy joked that he had only beaten Boofuls for the award "because they thought it was too heavy for him, and he might drop it."

Boofuls never won an Oscar, although one hit musical followed another—*Dancing on the Clouds, Suwannee Song, Sunshine Serenade*, and *Flowers From Tuscaloosa*. Boofuls appeared on the cover of every major magazine, golden-haired, shining-eyed, from *Screenland* to *McCall's*. It was reported in *Variety* in the spring of 1938 that he was a millionaire six times over. Just before Christmas, 1938, he and his grandmother moved into a huge white mock-Gothic house on Stone Canyon Drive in Bel Air. They engaged sixteen servants, including a butler and a cook; two private tutors; a dance teacher; and a drama coach. They owned seven automobiles, including two white Lincoln limousines, one for each of them. They named the mansion "Espejo."

In June 1939, Boofuls was cast for the leading role of Billy Bright in Jacob Levitz' most ambitious musical to date—a nine-million-dollar production called *Sweet Chariot*. Billy Bright was supposed to be a dead-end kid accidentally shot dead while trying to prevent his father robbing a bank—to become (almost inevitably) a do-gooding angel.

On Friday, August 18, three days after the start of principal photography, Boofuls was driven home in his limousine from M-G-M at 5:27 P.M., according to the log kept by doorman Henry Polowski. He was seen by a group of fans turning into the east gate of Bel Air, and he waved to them and smiled.

His head gardener, Manuel Estovez, saw Boofuls come out onto the loggia at the back of the mansion at approximately 6:12 P.M. He was wearing a yellow short-sleeved shirt and white shorts and white ankle socks. He waved to Mr. Estovez, and Mr. Estovez waved back.

Shortly after 6:21 P.M., the Bel Air police received a garbled telephone call from the Crossley mansion, a woman's voice saying, "He's dead now. I've got him at last. He's dead." A police patrol arrived at the house just before 6:35 P.M. and gained entry to the house through the French windows which overlooked the swimming pool. It appeared that—unusually—all of the indoor servants had been given the day or the after-noon off.

Inside the white-carpeted sitting room, they found what was left of Boofuls—"chopped into spareribs," as one officer put it. Another officer said that he had never seen so much blood in his life. A quick search of the twelve-bedroom house also revealed the body of Mrs. Crossley, hanging by a noose from the wrought-iron chandelier in the main stairwell, half strangulated but still alive. She died twenty minutes later without say-ing anything at all.

The coroner's verdict three weeks later was that Mrs. Alicia Crossley had murdered her grandson, Walter Lemuel Crossley, while suffering from temporary men-tal disorder and had then taken her own life. Boofuls was buried with unusual quietness at Forest Lawn. The horror of what had happened kept many people away—the thought that they were burying nothing more than a box of bits. A plain white Carrera marble headstone was erected, with the simple gold inscrip-tion "BOOFULS, 1931–1939." You can still see it now.

Over the years, nine books had been written about the Boofuls murder, probably the best of which was *Boofuls: The Truth*, by Kenneth Mellon. Martin had read them all; and to put it kindly, some of them were more sensational than others. All of them agreed, however, that Mrs. Crossley's irrational attack on her celebrated young charge could probably be traced back to earlier bouts of depression that she had suffered when she was younger. She had lost a little boy of her own in 1911, and after she had given birth to Mary, Boofuls' mother, she had been warned by her doctor not to get pregnant again.

Three of the books suggested that Mrs. Crossley was taking revenge on Boofuls for her daughter's suicide attempt and subsequent death. Punishing him, as it were, for living a life of wealth and fame when her dear dead daughter had died in poverty, and known none of it.

The author of *Hollywood Hack!* claimed that she had killed Boofuls to get her revenge on his unknown father, but there was no serious evidence to support this theory, and in any case nobody had ever been able to find out who his unknown father was. Some reporters had pointed the finger at Howard Q. Forbes, the vice-president of Ressequie State Insurance, but Howard Q. Forbes had been balding and bespectacled, with a cardiac history, and even if it was not impossible that he was Boofuls' father, it seemed at least unlikely.

There was an unconfirmed report that Mary Crossley had been seen one night on Kootenal Street in Boise in the passenger seat of a large black Cadillac limousine, but the supposed witness had later admitted that he might have been "overtired."

Martin had collected scores of magazine articles, too—even the ridiculous "true life" dramatizations from *Thrilling Detective* and *Sensational Police Stories*. "The tiny body desperately twisted and turned beneath her as she hacked into his snow-white sailor suit with her blood-spattered cleaver." Boofuls hadn't been wearing a sailor suit, of course; and oddly enough, the murder weapon had never been found.

In spite of Boofuls' gruesome and infamous death, however, Martin had always felt that the child had been possessed of some kind of special magic. Some incandescence that was almost unreal. His friend Gerry at the M-G-M library had videotaped all of Boofuls' musicals for him, and he watched them again and again. Every time he saw that curly-headed little boy dancing and singing, he found it harder to believe that a seven-year-old could have such brightness and energy and wit, such absolute perfection of timing.

Every time he looked at Boofuls' movements, listened to his breathing, watched his choreography—and in particular when he looked at his eyes—he felt as if he were watching a grown man masquerading in a child's body.

"He passed me by as close as this, and I wasn't mistook. I saw it clear like daylight. He was white, white like bone, and his eyes were empty, no eyeballs, just like a skull, and naked teeth."

Martin had played the fifty-year-old newsreel over and over. The same blurting sound track, the same flickering of flashbulbs, the same evasive ducking of the head, as if Henry Polowski had been damned by his inattention to play the same scene over and over and over again.

"And what did you do, Mr. Polowski?"

"What would *you* do? You wouldn't believe your eyes. You can laugh all you want, but it was a genuine premonition. I saw it, and if you don't believe it, then that's your problem, not mine."

Martin switched off the video recorder with his remote control. It was almost ten o'clock; and in twenty
minutes he had an appointment with June Lassiter at
20th Century-Fox. He knew June well enough to wave
at her across the crowded bar of the Cock 'n' Bull, and
to be assured of a wave back; but he didn't know how
sympathetic she was going to be to the idea of a big-
budget musical. Especially a big-budget musical about
Boofuls.

Still, he thought, gathering up his screenplay and
sliding it carefully into his Reel Thing tote bag, nobody
ever got anywhere in Hollywood by sitting at home
and wishing.

He took one last look at the mirror before he left. It
reflected nothing but the sitting room and himself and
the morning sunlight. He was beginning to think that
he must have hallucinated that ball. Maybe he would
go talk to his friend Marion Gidley about it. She was
into self-hypnosis and self-induced hallucinations and
all that kind of stuff.

As he closed the door of his apartment behind him,
he came across Emilio playing on the landing with a
Transformer robot. "How're you doing, Emilio?" he
asked him.

Emilio looked up with big Hershey-colored eyes. "Hi,
Martin. Doing good."

"What's that you've got there?"

"Datson 280 sports car, turns into an evil robot,
look."

With a complicated fury of clicking and elbow twisting, Emilio turned the sports car into a robot with a
pin head and spindly legs. Martin hunkered down and
inspected it. "Pretty radical, hunh? I wish my car
would turn into a robot."

"Your car's junk."

"Who said that?"

"My grandpa, he said your car's junk, and he wishes you wouldn't park it right outside the house, people are gonna think it belongs to him."

"My car's better than that hearse that *he* drives."

"My grandpa's car turns into a robot."

"Oh, yeah?"

"It does, too, turn into a robot. He told me."

Martin affectionately scruffed Emilio's hair, which Emilio hated, and got up to leave. He was halfway down the next flight of stairs, however, when he thought of something. "You don't happen to own a ball, do you?" he asked Emilio through the banister rails.

"Grandpa gave me a baseball."

"No, no—I mean one of those bouncing plastic balls, blue and white."

Emilio wrinkled up his nose and shook his head, as if the idea that he would own a bouncing blue and white ball was utterly contemptible. "No way, José."

Martin reached through the banister and tried to scruff his hair again, but Emilio ducked away. "Don't keep *doing* that!" he protested. "What do you think I am, some kind of a gerbil?"

Martin laughed, and went off to keep his appointment at Fox.

June Lassiter was very calm and together and California-friendly; a woman's woman with frizzed-up black hair and pale, immaculate, hypo-allergenic makeup that had been created without causing any pain to animals. She wore a flowing white suit and a scarf around her neck that had been hand-printed on raw silk by

Hopi Indians. She took Martin to the Fox commissary and bought him a huge spinach salad and a carafe of domestic Chablis that was almost too cold to drink.

"You're raising ghosts, that's the trouble," she drawled. Martin had a large mouthful of spinach, and all he could do was look at her thin wrist lying on the table with its faded tan and its huge loose gold bangle, and munch, and nod.

June said, "Boofuls is one of those code words in Hollywood that immediately make people's brains go blank; you know, like Charles Manson."

"People have tackled difficult Hollywood topics before. Look at *Mommie Dearest*."

"Oh, sure," June agreed. "But in *Mommie Dearest*, Joan Crawford eventually redeemed herself, and all the terrible things that she was supposed to have done to her children were rationalized and forgiven. She was a drunken carping bitch but she was a star, and in Hollywood that excuses everything. How can you do that with Boofuls? The boy was chopped up by his crazed grandmother and that was the end of the story. No redemption, no explanation, just an abrupt and brutal ending—even if you *don't* depict it on the screen."

Martin wiped his mouth with his napkin. "So what's the verdict?"

"Well, Martin, I haven't read your screenplay yet and it may be brilliant. I mean I've heard Morris talking about you and he's *very* complimentary about your work. But I have to tell you that Boofuls is the kiss of death. The only person who might conceivably touch it is Ken Russell; and you know what kind of a reputation *he's* got; *enfant terrible*, even at his age. Even if he'd agree to do it, you'd still have the devil's own job raising the money for it."

Martin sat back. "I don't know. It seems like such a natural. The music, the dancing, and if you could find the right kid to play Boofuls . . ."

June shook her head. "My advice to you is to file it and forget it. Maybe one day you'll be wealthy enough and influential enough to develop it yourself."

They spent the rest of their lunch talking gossip: who was making which picture, and who was making whom. When they were leaving, June stood in the empty parking space marked G. Wilder and said, "Get your name painted here first, Martin. Then make your musical."

Martin gave her what he hoped was a laconic wave and walked back to his car, with his screenplay under his arm. As he went, he whistled "Heartstrings."

> You play . . . such sweet music
> How can . . . I resist
> Every song . . . from your heartstrings
> Makes me feel I've . . . just been kissed

But he drove back along Santa Monica Boulevard with the wind whirring in the pages of the screenplay as it lay on the seat beside him, and he felt like tossing it out of the car. He was beginning to believe that Morris was right, that he was carrying this screenplay around like a sackful of stinking meat.

Hollywood's golden boy of he 1930s had died more than one kind of death.

He returned to his apartment shortly before three o'clock. Emilio was playing in the sunshine on the front steps. Emilio had obviously finished his lunch, because his T-shirt was stained with catsup. The steps were proving an almost insurmountable obstacle to a deadpan plastic Rambo; and the afternoon was thick with the sound of machine-gun fire.

"Full-scale war, hey?" asked Martin. Emilio didn't look up. Martin sat down on the steps and watched him for a while. "It beats me, you know, how *Rambo* can gross seventy-five million dollars, with all its shooting and killing and phony philosophy . . . and here, *here*"—slapping his screenplay in the palm of his hand—"is the most entertaining and enchanting musical ever made, and everybody sniffs at me as if I've trodden in something."

Emilio continued his war; this time with heavy shelling, which involved extra saliva.

"You should come up and watch some of my Boofuls movies," Martin told him. "Then you'd believe, you little Philistine."

Emilio shaded his eyes with his grubby hand and looked at him. "Who's Boofuls? Is he a cartoon?"

"Is he a cartoon? My God, doesn't that grandfather of yours teach you anything? Boofuls was a boy, just like you, except that he could sing and dance and make people happy. In other words he didn't sit in the dirt all day with some grotesque reproduction of Sylvester Stallone, pretending to zap Asiatics. Who's Boofuls, for God's sake."

Emilio picked up a green plastic helicopter and waved it around for a while. "That boy in your room can dance," he remarked.

"Well, that's Boofuls," said Martin. "The boy in the poster, just above my bed."

"No," Emilio contradicted, shaking his head. "The boy in your other room. The real boy."

Martin frowned; and then reached out and took hold of Emilio's wrist, so that the helicopter was stopped in midattack. "What real boy? What are you talking about?"

Emilio pouted and wouldn't answer.

"You went into my room?" Martin asked him. "Today, when I was out, you went into my room?"

Emilio refused to do anything but pout.

"Listen, Emilio, if you went into my room I won't be mad at you. Come on, it's your grandfather's house, you can go where you want."

Emilio slowly and sulkily twisted his wrist away.

Martin glanced up toward his sitting room window. It was blank, as usual, with the sky reflecting off the glass.

"You won't talk?" he said to Emilio. "In that case, I'd better go see for myself."

He got up from the steps and bounded quickly upstairs, three steps at a time, until he reached the landing just outside his front door. There was a small plastic name tag on it saying *M. Williams*. Underneath, *J. Berrywell* had been scratched out. Even when they were living together, Jane had insisted on keeping her maiden name.

He hesitated. *A real boy.* For some irrational reason, he felt a prickle of genuine alarm. There were no boys in his apartment, of course, real or unreal. Emilio had simply invented an imaginary playmate. He was just the age for it, after all, and he had no friends of his own age, not on this block. But all the same, Martin found the idea of it unexpectedly unsettling, as if his apartment had been intruded upon by something he didn't understand.

He opened the front door. He hardly ever locked it, because there was nothing worth stealing, except for his typewriter, and he had been hoping for years that somebody would take that, so that he could buy a new one with the insurance money.

The apartment was silent. The midafternoon sunlight fell across the wood-block floor in a dazzling diagonal. From the bedroom, the pale face of Boofuls watched him as he trod softly along the corridor to the sitting room door.

He paused. He called, "Hello?" But there was no reply.

What did you expect? he asked himself. *A whole chorus of Walt Disney ghosts to come charging out of the closets chorusing "Fooled you, Martin!"?*

He eased the sitting room door wide open. Then he peered around it. In the mirror, his own face peered back. There was nobody else in the room. No boy; not even a *sign* of a boy, like an abandoned blue and white ball.

"Kids," he said under his breath, meaning Emilio in particular.

It took him only a couple of moments to look around the rest of the apartment. There were no boys hiding in the closets among his clothes; there were no boys crouching under the bed. But as he went through to the kitchen to find himself a fresh bottle of wine, he was sure for an instant that he could hear somebody giggling.

He hesitated and listened, but there was nothing. He stepped out of the kitchen into the hallway, holding the bottle of wine in his hand, and there was Emilio with his hands in the pockets of his shorts. Martin looked at him without saying anything.

"Can I play with him?" asked Emilio.

"Can you play with whom, Emilio?" Martin replied, deliberately pedantic.

Emilio swung one shoulder toward the sitting room. "The boy, of course."

Martin said, "Emilio, my little lunatic, there is no boy."

"There is, too, a boy."

"Well, that's right, and your grandfather's car turns into a robot."

"I've seen it! He showed me!"

"All right," cooed Martin. "All right, don't lose your cool. Let's just say that I'm one of these real skeptical adults you see on children's television—you know the kind of adult I mean. The kind of adult who can't understand what the hell Flipper is trying to say to him, and takes a swipe at Lassie when she's trying to drag him off to the abandoned mine by the trouser leg."

Emilio didn't understand a word of what Martin was saying; but it made Martin feel better, and it stopped Emilio's fretting.

"If there really is a boy," said Martin gently, "all you have to do is introduce him to me. Let me shake the boy by the hand, and say good afternoon, boy. Then I'll believe you."

"You can't shake his hand," Emilio retorted.

"I know I can't, Emilio, because he's imaginary." He tapped Emilio's forehead with his fingertip quite hard. "He exists only in there."

"No," Emilio protested. "He's real. But you can't shake his hand because he's in the mirror."

Martin straightened himself up. Emilio was looking up at him, his grubby little face serious, his eyes wide, his fists clenched.

"Emilio," he said, "has it occurred to that one-byte brain of yours that the real boy in the mirror might be you? A reflection of you? Or was your face so filthy that

you just didn't recognize yourself? Maybe you thought
it was Paul Robeson."

Emilio was getting cross again. "He's real! He's real!
But he's only in the mirror! I'm in the mirror, and he's
in the mirror. But I'm in the room, and he's not in the
room!"

Martin thought of the blue and white ball, and how
it had come bouncing into the mirror. He thought of
how he had gone back to look at it again and found
that it had vanished. *It's very like our passage as far as
you can see, only you know it may be quite different on
beyond.*

A slow cold feeling crawled down his back, like a
snail making its way down a frozen drainpipe.

"This boy . . . did he look anything like you?" he
asked Emilio.

Emilio wiped his hand over his face as if he were
attempting to erase his own features and come up with
some other face: placid, blank, with eyes like Little Orphan Annie.

"He looked like . . ." and he tried to explain, but he
couldn't, even with mime. "He looked like . . ." and
then he suddenly rushed through to the bedroom and
pointed to the poster of Boofuls pinned to the wall.

"He looked like that?" Martin asked him, with a
deeper feeling of dread.

"He's a real boy," Emilio repeated. "He's a *real* boy!"

Martin laid his hands on Emilio's shoulders and
looked him straight in the eye. "Emilio, he *was* a real
boy, but he's been dead for nearly fifty years."

Emilio frowned.

"I don't know what you saw in that mirror," Martin
told him, "but it wasn't a real boy. It was just your
imagination. Do you understand what I mean? It was

just like ... I don't know, your mind was playing a trick on you."

"I saw him," Emilio whispered. "I *talked* to him."

Martin couldn't think what else to say. He stood up and rubbed his hands on the legs of his pants, the way pitchers do. "I don't know, Emilio, man. It sounds pretty screwy to me."

At that moment there was a cautious knock at the apartment door, and Emilio's grandmother came in. She was carrying a glass oven dish with a checkered cloth draped over the top of it.

Martin had always liked Mrs. Capelli. She was the grandmother that everybody should have had: cheerful, philosophical, always baking. She had white hair braided into elaborate plaits and a face as plain and honest as a breadboard. She wore black; she always wore black. She was mourning for her dead sister. Before that, she had been mourning for her dead brother. When she and Mr. Capelli went out shopping in their long black Lincoln together, they looked as if they were going to a funeral.

"I brought you lasagne," she said.

Martin accepted the dish with a nod of his head. "I'm trying to diet. But thanks."

"Well, you can share it with the boy." Mrs. Capelli glanced around the apartment as if she expected to see someone else.

"The boy?" asked Martin.

"Emilio told me you had a boy staying here. He was playing with him all morning. He's your nephew you spoke to me about?"

Martin exchanged an uncomfortable look with Emilio. If he said that there was no boy, then Emilio would get a hard time for lying. On the other hand—

But, no. He needed Emilio's confidence right now. If there *was* something odd in the mirror, if there *was* some kind of manifestation, then so far young Emilio was the only person who had seen it. Emilio might be the only contact with it, like a medium. After all, he was a boy and Boofuls had been a boy. Maybe there was some kind of left-over vibe in the mirror that Emilio was tuning in to. Or something.

He lifted up the cloth that covered the lasagne and inhaled the aroma of fresh tomatoes and thyme and fresh-grated Parmesan cheese. "Petey will probably eat all of this on his own," he remarked as casually as he could. "Petey's a real pasta maven."

He saw Emilio's eyes widen; as if the Hershey chocolate of his irises had melted into larger pools. But he winked at Emilio behind the upraised cloth, and he could see that Emilio understood.

"He's here now?" asked Mrs. Capelli, beaming. "I love boys! Always rough-and-tumble."

"Well, he—er—he's running an errand for me—down at the supermarket."

"You send a little boy all on his own to the supermarket? Ralph's, you mean?"

"Oh, no, no, just to Hughes, on the corner."

"Still," said Mrs. Capelli disapprovingly. "That's a bad road to cross, Highland Avenue."

"Oh, he's okay, he walks to school in New York City, crosses Fifty-seventh Street every morning, hasn't been squished yet."

Mrs. Capelli's forehead furrowed. "I thought you said he lived in Indianapolis."

"Sure, yes, Indianapolis! But that was a couple of years ago. Now he lives in New York."

Slowly, Mrs. Capelli turned to leave, her eyes still

restlessly looking around the apartment as if she ex-epected "Petey" to come popping out from behind a chair. Martin knew that she kept a constant watch on the landing from her chair in the parlor downstairs, and since she hadn't seen Petey go out, she was ob-viously suspicious that Martin was keeping him hid-den. Maybe he had measles, this Petey, and Martin didn't want her to know, because Emilio may catch them.

"You do me a favor," she said at last as she went out through the door. "You bring your Petey down to see me when he gets back. I give him chocolate cake."

"Sure thing, Mrs. Capelli," Martin told her, and opened the door for her. She eased herself down the stairs, one stair at a time, holding on to the banister. When she reached the door of her apartment, Martin gave her a little finger-wave, and said, "Don't you worry, I'll bring him down. He'll feed your canary for you. If there's anything he likes better than pasta, it's chocolate cake."

Mrs. Capelli paused, and then nodded, and then dis-appeared into her apartment, leaving the door slightly ajar.

Martin came back to Emilio and stood in front of him with his arms folded.

"You believe me," said Emilio. "You believe there's a boy."

"Did I say that?"

"But you said 'Petey.'"

"Emilio, there is no boy. I said that just to get you out of trouble. What do you think your grandmother would have said if I had totally denied it? She would have thought you were some kind of juvenile fruitcake. She would have had you locked up, or worse."

Emilio looked bewildered. "There *is* a boy," he insisted. "Come and see him."

"All right," said Martin, "let's take a look at him; even if we can't shake him by the hand."

Emilio ran into the sitting room and stood right in front of the mirror, impatient to prove that he was right. Martin followed him more slowly, checking the details of the real room against the reflected room. Two realities, side by side, but which one was real?

He checked everything carefully, but there were no obvious discrepancies. The screenplay of *Boofuls!* lay on his desk at corresponding angles in each room; one of his shoes lay tilted over, under the chair. The venetian blinds shivered in the sunlight.

Emilio pressed the palms of his hands against the glass. "Boy!" he called loudly. "Boy, are you there? Come out and play, boy! Come say hello to Martin!"

Martin, in spite of himself, found his attention fixed on the doorway in the mirror. It didn't move; not even a fraction; and no boy appeared.

"Boy!" Emilio demanded. "Come out and play!"

They watched and waited. Nothing happened. No blue and white ball, no laughter, no boy. Martin was seriously beginning to believe that this was all a hallucination.

"Maybe he doesn't feel like playing anymore," Martin suggested.

"He does, too!" Emilio protested. "He said he *always* wants to play. The trouble is, they make him work, even when he's tired, and they always make him wear clothes he doesn't like, and he has to sing when he doesn't want to and dance when he doesn't want to."

"Did he tell you what his name was?" asked Martin.

Emilio said nothing.

"Emilio, listen to me, this is important, did he tell you what his name was? He didn't call himself Boofuls, did he? Or Walter maybe? Or just Walt?"

Emilio shook his head.

"Well, what did he do? Did he play ball? Did he dance? Did he sing?"

Emilio stared at Martin but remained silent.

"Listen," said Martin, turning back toward the mirror, "maybe he doesn't want to play right now. Maybe it's—I don't know, bathtime or something. Even boys who live in mirrors have to take baths, right? Why don't you come back tomorrow and we'll try again?"

Emilio banged both hands on the mirror. "Boy!" he shouted, his voice more high-pitched and panicky. "Boy! Come out and play!"

Martin hunkered down beside him. "I really don't think he wants to come out, Emilio. Come back tomorrow morning, okay, and we'll call him again."

Emilio suddenly turned on him. His voice was a sharp little bark. "You don't *want* me to see him, do you? You don't want me to play with him! You think he belongs to you! It's not your mirror! It's not your mirror! It's *his* mirror! He lives in it! And you can't tell him what to do, so there!"

Martin had never heard Emilio screaming like this before, and he was mildly shocked. He took hold of Emilio's shoulder and said, "Listen . . . this may be a story that you've made up to impress me, and on the other hand it may not. But either way, I'm on your side. If there is a boy in that mirror, I want to find him."

"And let him out?" asked Emilio.

Martin made a face. "I don't know. Maybe there just isn't any way of *getting* him out."

"There's a way," Emilio told him quite firmly.

"Well, how do you know?"

"Because the boy told me, there's a way."

"All right, as long as it doesn't involve breaking the mirror—I just paid seven hundred fifty dollars for that thing."

"We won't break the mirror," Emilio assured him with unsettling maturity.

Martin leaned back against the peach-painted landing wall and looked down at this self-confident little child with his chocolate-brown eyes and his tousled hair and the catsup stains on his T-shirt, and he didn't know whether to feel amused or frightened.

After all, the likelihood was that this was the biggest leg-pull ever. Either that, or Emilio was simply making it all up. After all, there were pictures of Boofuls all over Martin's apartment. If he was going to pretend that he had played with an imaginary boy there, what could be more natural than pretending he looked like him?

He closed the apartment door and walked back into his bedroom. The soulful eyes of little Boofuls stared at him from the *Whistlin' Dixie* poster. He reached up and touched with his fingertips the golden curls, the pale, heart-shaped face.

"You don't scare me, little boy," he said out loud. "You don't scare me at all."

But he gave the poster a quick backward look as he left the room, and went back to work on the *A-Team*.

He awoke abruptly at three o'clock in the morning, his eyes wide, his ears singing with alertness. He hesitated for a moment, then he sat up in his futon so that he could hear better. He was quite sure that he could hear somebody crying, a child.

The sound was muffled by the rattling of the yuccas in the street outside, and by the steady warbling of the wind through the crack at the side of his bedroom window. But it was a child, all right, a boy, keening and crying as if his heart were going to break.

Shivering with apprehension, and with the chill of the night, Martin reached across the floor and dragged his red flannel bathrobe toward him. He wrapped himself up in it and tied the belt tight, and then he climbed out of his futon and tiptoed across the bedroom and opened the door.

The sobbing kept on, high and despairing and strangely echoing. There was no doubt about where it was coming from, though. The sitting room door was half open, and the moonlight was shining hard and detailed on the wood-block floor, and that was where the crying was coming from.

The real boy, thought Martin. *Oh, Jesus, it's the real boy.*

But the real boy, whoever he was—*whatever* he was—would have to be confronted. *Come on, Martin, he's only a kid, right? And if he turns out to be Boofuls, then he's not only a kid but a ghost, too. I mean—how can you possibly be frightened by the prospect of coming face-to-face with a ghost kid?*

He reached out his hand as stiffly as if it were attached to the end of an artificial arm, and pushed the sitting room door open wide. The door gave a low groan as it strained on its hinges. The boy's crying went on, a hair-raising *oh-oh-oh-oh-oh* that aroused in Martin both urgency and terror. Urgency to save the child from whatever it was that was causing him to cry so pitifully. Terror that it might be something so unexpected and so dreadful that he wouldn't be able to do anything at all but freeze.

Shortly after Jane had left him, Martin had dreamed
again and again of being rooted to the spot, unable to
move while people laughed at him, while bristle-haired
monkeys ran away with his furniture, while Jane was
gruesomely raped in front of him by grinning clowns.

The greatest fear of all was the fear of walking into
this sitting room and finding that he couldn't do anything but stand paralyzed and helpless.

He took a steadying breath, then another, and adrenaline surged around his veins like nighttime traffic on
the interstate. Then he took three decisive steps into
the room, and immediately ducked and turned to
face the mirror, with a heavy off-balance interpretation
of the football block that his high school coach had always been trying to teach him, *duck, Williams, weave,
for Christ's sake, you're a quarterback, not a fucking
cheerleader*, and he couldn't help shouting out *ah!* because he came face-to-face in the mirror with his own
terrified wildness—white cheeks, staring eyes, sticking-
up hair, and his bright red bathrobe wrapped around
him like bloodstained bandages.

He paused for a moment while his heaving chest subsided and his pulse gradually slowed, and he caught
his breath.

"Shit," he whispered; because his own appearance
still unnerved him. But cautiously, he took two or
three steps toward the mirror, and then hesitated and
listened. The boy's sobbing continued, although it had
become quieter and more miserable now, an endless
low-key *oh, oh, oh*, that was even more heartrending
than the loud sobs and cries that Martin had heard before.

He reached out and touched the mirror. The glass
was cold and flawless and impenetrable. There was no

question of it melting into a silver mist like Alice's mirror in *Through the Looking-Glass*. He pressed his forehead against it. His gray eyes stared expressionlessly back at him from only an inch away. *God*, he thought, *what can I do?* But the boy continued to weep.

Martin moved to the extreme left side of the mirror, in an effort to see into the corridor. He could make out two or three feet of it, but that was all. He went back to the sitting room door and wedged a folded-up copy of *Variety* underneath it to keep it wide open, but when he returned to the mirror he found that he couldn't see very much more.

Yet it sounded as if the child was crying in his bedroom. Not his real bedroom, but the bedroom in the mirror.

He shivered. The sitting room felt unnaturally cold. And the strained, high, pitiable voice of that crying child was enough to make anyone shiver. He thought, *What the hell am I going to do? How the hell can I stop this sobbing?*

He remembered what Mr. Capelli had told him about his grandmother, how she smashed every mirror in the house when somebody died, because mirrors took a little piece of your soul every time you looked into them. Maybe if he broke this mirror, the real boy's soul would be released, and he wouldn't have to suffer anymore. On the other hand, supposing this mirror was his only contact with the real world, and with anybody who could help him? Supposing he was crying out to be saved? Yet from what, or from whom? And if life in the mirror was that desperate, why hadn't he cried out before, during all those years when the mirror had been hanging up in Mrs. Harper's cellar?

Or maybe he had, and Mrs. Harper had chosen to ignore him.

The weeping went on, *oh-oh-oh-oh-oh!*

Martin slapped the flat of his hand against the mirror. "Listen!" he shouted. "Can you hear me? Whoever's in there—can you hear me?"

He waited, but there was no reply. He felt an extraordinary mixture of rage and helplessness, pinned against this mirror, and because he was hyperventilating, he felt that he was floating, too, like a fly pressed against a window, and for one moment he didn't know whether he was up or down. It was a split-second insight into life without gravity, life without an understanding of glass. A fly can beat against a window until it dies, and never realize that the world outside can easily be reached by flying around a different way.

"Can you hear me?" Martin shouted. "I'm here! I'm right here! I can help you!"

Then suddenly he thought: *What the hell am I doing? If the boy's in my bedroom, I can take the mirror down from the wall and drag it into the bedroom and then I can see him for myself.*

He went to his desk, opened up two or three drawers, and at last found his ratchet screwdriver. Fumbling, overexcited, he took out the screws that held the mirror to the wall, one by one; and then hefted the mirror as gently as he could manage onto the floor. When he had done so, the mocking carving of Pan or Bacchus was grinning directly into his face: ancient carnality staring with gilded eyeballs at modern fright.

Martin lifted his jacket off the back of his chair, folded it up, and wedged it under the bottom of the frame so that it wouldn't be damaged when he dragged it across the floor. Then, a little at a time, he pulled it toward the open door, pausing every now and then to wipe his forehead with the back of his arm and to catch his breath.

"Jesus, why am I doing this?" he asked himself. But the child's weeping went on; and that was why.

He dragged the mirror across the room until it faced the open door which led to the hallway. Then he leaned over the glass and peered inside. The real hallway was empty, and so was the hallway in the mirror. Everything was identical. Identical door, identical carpet, identical wallpaper, brightly illuminated by the light that fell across the corridor from Martin's bedroom.

But the light appeared only in the mirror. When Martin glanced back toward the real corridor, his bedroom was in darkness, just the way he had left it. He had gone looking for the real boy without switching on his bedside lamp. Quite apart from which, the light that shone out of his mirror-bedroom was bright and clinical, like the lights in a hospital or an institution, while his real bedside lamp was muted by an orangey shade.

The boy's whimpering suddenly turned to high-pitched, terrified gasps. Martin rested the huge mirror against the corner of his desk and hurried clumsily toward his bedroom.

He hadn't yet reached the door, however, when the light in the mirror-bedroom was hurriedly switched off, and the child's gasps died away. Martin stood in the doorway for nearly a minute, straining his eyes, straining his ears, but the manifestation had gone. The apartment was silent, the mirror reflected nothing more than the sitting room door and part of the wall and a 1937 poster for *Sunshine Serenade*.

"You're . . . Whistlin' Dixie . . ." whispered the faint-

est of echoes; and it might have been nothing more
than a truck horn blaring, far across the valley, or the
early morning wind blowing under the door.

Martin looked around his bedroom, although he
knew that he wouldn't find anything. The spirit of the
mirror had gradually evaporated with the false dawn.
He went back into the sitting room and looked at it,
gilded and baroque and full of its own secrets.

He could take it back to Mrs. Harper, he supposed;
but she would probably insist that a contract of sale
was a contract of sale, and refuse to return his money.
He could try to sell it to Ramone Perez at the Reel
Thing, but he doubted if Ramone would give him more
than a couple of hundred bucks for it. Or he could take
it down to the city dump and heave it onto the smoldering piles of trash and forget that he had ever seen it.

But, cautiously laying his hand on it, he began to feel
that this mirror and all its mysteries were a burden
which he had been chosen by destiny to accept. Not
great historical destiny; not the kind of destiny which
had steered the lives of Julius Caesar or Alexander the
Great or George Washington; but that quirky, acciden-
tal, walked-through-door-A-instead-of-door-B destiny
that affects the lives of almost all of us. The mirror had
been hanging in Mrs. Harper's cellar waiting for him,
ever since he was small. He had gone to school, played
ball, grown up, started writing teleplays, argued with
Morris Nathan, and all the time the mirror had been
there, waiting for that phone call, waiting for those last
few steps up Mrs. Harper's cracked concrete path.

Grunting with effort, he dragged the mirror back to
the wall where it had hung before, propped it up on his
typewriter case, just as he had before, and screwed it
back into place. Then he tossed his screwdriver back

into his desk drawer and went through to the kitchen.
He opened up the refrigerator, took out a carton of
deeply chilled orange juice, and drank almost half of it
straight from the carton. His palate ached with the
cold, and he stood in the middle of the kitchen for a
while with his hand clamped over his mouth, his eyes
watering.

"You're a martyr," he told himself. "You know
that?"

He went back to the bedroom, loosened the sash of
his bathrobe, and straightened his futon. Above him,
Boofuls smiled up at heaven, with his golden curls and
his wide eyes and his white, heart-shaped face.

"Could be that you've scared me just a *little*," Martin
admitted.

Then he frowned at the poster more closely. He stood
on his futon, and raised his hand, and gently touched
the paper with his fingertips. Beneath Boofuls' eyes it
was dimpled, as if it had been moistened and then left
to dry.

He stared at Boofuls for a very long time. "Could be
that you've scared me a hell of a lot."

Later that morning he drove over to Morris' house with
the rewritten *A-Team* script. It was roastingly hot, and
he walked up Morrie's pathway between the red-
flowering bougainvillea, feeling exhausted and irrita-
ble. Alison was lying on her inflatable sunbed, slowly
rotating on the pool, her nose gleaming with sunscreen
like a white beacon. A stereo tape player on the diving
board played music from *Cats*.

He found Morrie in the white Mexican-tile solarium,
reclining on a huge white ottoman surrounded by
white telephones and stacks of multicolored screen-

plays. Morris was swathed in white toweling, and he was feeding himself with small green grapes.

"Good morning, Morris," he said, dropping the rewrite onto the floor beside him.

"Ah, just the man I was looking for," Morris replied. "Pull up a seat. Pour yourself a glass of Perrier. Do you want a grape?"

Martin noisily dragged over a white-painted cast-iron chair, startling a white crested cockatoo that hung from the solarium ceiling in a white cage that Morris had brought back from Tangiers. The cockatoo screeched while Morris gave Martin one of his long old-fashioned looks and fed his mouth with grapes as if he were loading the chamber of a .38 with bullets.

"Listen, Martin," he said at last, and then paused while the cockatoo let out one more screech. "This Boofuls thing, it's going to do you some damage if you're not careful. Yesterday evening I was having dinner at the Bel Air Hotel and June Lassiter came over and gave me a *very* difficult time about that dreck you tried to sell her. She said she doesn't like to deal with writers direct, and more than that she doesn't like to deal with projects like that. It's a hoodoo, I told you. You're going to embarrass everybody. You've already embarrassed me. What could I say, that I washed my hands of it? But in any case I apologized on your behalf."

Martin snapped, "You had absolutely no right to do that."

"Well, somebody had to." Morris smirked, shifting his weight on the ottoman. "You drag that idea around to one more major studio, my friend, and you will find that the drawbridge of opportunity has lifted and you are standing like a *shlemiel* on the outside. And let me tell you this: I'm not going to be the *nebach* who throws you a rope to get back across the moat."

Martin stood up, noisily scraping his chair back and setting off the crested cockatoo into a frenzy of whooping and screaming. "You've been watching too many old Burt Lancaster movies," he retorted. "And do you think I'd take hold of the rope even if you threw it to me?"

"Calm down, will you?" Morris told him; and then turned around to the cockatoo and bellowed, "Stop that *krechsing*, you dumb bird!"

"Morris," said Martin, "this sounds crazy, but I think I've found him."

"Who? What are you talking about? Shut up, bird! You know what Alison calls that bird? Dreyfuss. She thinks it looks like Richard Dreyfuss."

"Boofuls," Martin told him, his voice unsteady.

"Whunh?" Morris frowned. "Martin, will you make yourself clear? I have sixty screenplays to go through here, sixty. Look at this one, *Scarlett O'Hara, the Early Years*. What's the matter with these people? And you've turned into some kind of *nar* over Boofuls. All I hear from you is Boofuls, Boofuls, Boofuls. I would wish him dead, if he weren't already."

"Well, that's it," Martin interrupted. "I don't think he is. I mean, not properly."

Morris picked another grape and ate it very slowly. "You don't think that Boofuls is properly dead?"

Martin nodded.

Morris heaved himself up into a sitting position. "Martin, if I thought that you could afford it, I'd send you along to Dr. Eisenbaum. What is it, the heat? I'm giving you too many *A-Team* rewrites, what?"

Martin took a deep breath. "I bought a mirror that

used to hang in Boofuls' house. In fact, it was supposed to be hanging over the fireplace the day that his grandmother killed him."

"Go on," said Morris, his voice low with apprehension. Whatever Martin was going to say, Morris definitely wasn't going to like it.

"Well—I've only had it a couple of days—I bought it Wednesday—just after I came out to see you—some woman on Hillside Avenue had it stored in her cellar."

"And?"

"It's pretty difficult to explain, Morris, but I think he's in it."

"In what?" Morris frowned.

"In the mirror," Martin explained. "I think that, somehow, Boofuls is kind of—well, it's real hard to describe it, but he's kind of *stuck*, you know, stuck inside the mirror. Maybe not him, but his spirit, or part of his spirit. Jesus, Morris, he was crying last night, he was crying for almost a half hour! I heard him!"

Morris thought about this for a long time, his hand poised just in front of his open lips. "Boofuls is stuck inside your mirror?"

"I knew it!" said Martin. "I knew you'd think I was crazy! But it's true, Morris. I don't know how it's happened and it's scaring me shitless; but he's there!"

"You've seen him?"

"No, I haven't, but I heard him crying."

"How do you know it's Boofuls if you haven't seen him? How do you know it wasn't some kid crying in the next apartment?"

"Because there are no kids in the next apartment, and because I've watched every single movie that Boofuls ever made, over and over and over. If I don't know Boofuls' voice when I hear it, then nobody does!"

Morris pressed his grape into his mouth, burst it between his bright gold teeth, and flapped his chubby little hand at Martin dismissively, almost effeminately. "Martin, you're letting this whole thing get to you, that's all. It's got to your brain! It happens, I've seen it happen before. Some writer called Jack Posnik wanted to make an epic war picture about the Philippine War, that's another one of those hoodoo subjects. He ended up wearing an army uniform and calling himself Lieutenant Roosevelt."

"Morris," said Martin, "I went back to my room and my poster was wet. My poster of Boofuls had tear stains on it. I swear it!"

Morris looked at him narrowly. "Are you a Catholic?" he asked him, and his tone was unusually fierce. "You know, I've heard of weeping madonnas, stuff like that—"

"Morris, listen to me, for God's sake. Think what kind of a story we've got here! Think what kind of a picture this could make!"

At that moment, Alison came padding into the room on wet bare feet. Today she was wearing a bright yellow bikini that scarcely covered her at all. She was a darker shade of brown than she had been before, apart from that white blob of sunscreen on her nose.

"Martin!" she exclaimed. "I thought it was you!"

"Well, I think I was just leaving," said Martin.

"I guess you were," Morris told him. "But listen—*please*—for your own sake and for mine, too, let this Boofuls business rest for a while. I'll tell you what I'll do. Next week, you and I will fly down to San Diego together, and we'll spend a lazy weekend on my boat, yes? Fishing and eating and drinking wine, and we'll talk this whole thing through, unh? See if we can't come up with something a little more acceptable, yes? Something with a little more taste? And, you know, something you can *sell*, already, without raising everybody's hackles."

Martin looked at Alison, and Alison laid her hand possessively on Morris' shoulder and gave Martin an encouraging smile. Nice girl, he thought, not so much of a *tsatskeh* as he had first thought. She deserved better than Morris and his chauvinistic garbage about jugs.

"My mother used to adore Boofuls," she said by way of being conciliatory.

"Sure," said Martin. Then, to Morris, "Enjoy the rewrite. I may be a *shlemiel* but I can still write first-rate dialogue."

He walked back out into the hot sunshine. This was one of those times when he felt like buying himself a very large bottle of chardonnay and sitting in his room listening to Z.Z. Top records and getting drunk.

On his way home, he felt so hot that he stopped at a 7-Eleven and bought two frozen juice bars, one for himself and one for Emilio. When he arrived home, however, carrying one empty stick and one leaking juice bar, he found Emilio's toy cars lying in the dust beside the front steps, but no sign of Emilio.

"Emilio!" he called around the side of the house. The sticky orange juice was already running down his wrist.

A small boy in a rainbow-striped T-shirt was walking a scruffy ginger mongrel along the sidewalk. "Hey, kid!" Martin called. "How would you like a juice bar? It's a little runny but it won't kill you."

The boy stuck out his tongue and ran away, sneakers

pit-patting on the sidewalk, all the way to the corner of Yucca. Martin shrugged. He guessed it was better that children didn't talk to strange sweating screenwriters with melting juice bars. He dropped the bar into the gutter, and across the street an elderly woman in a cotton hat stared at him as if she had discovered at last the man responsible for polluting the whole of the Southern California environment.

Martin went into the house and climbed the stairs. It smelled of disinfectant and Parmesan cheese, but at least it was cool.

Morris had depressed him this morning. He didn't mind so much that Morris disliked the idea of a Boofuls musical; he was professional enough to accept that some people were going to regurgitate their breakfast at nothing more than the mention of motion pictures that other people swooned over. But he was deeply upset that June Lassiter could have called up Morris behind his back and complained about him. It made him feel like a clumsy amateur, an outsider; as if he hadn't yet been accepted by Hollywood Proper.

He had almost reached the top landing when he heard Emilio laughing. Too bad, he thought philosophically—the juice bar wouldn't have survived the climb from the street in any case. But as he turned the corner of the stairs he saw that his own apartment door was ajar and that the upper landing was illuminated by a triangular section of sunlight.

He approached the apartment door as quietly as he could. He heard Emilio giggling again.

"You can't throw it! You can't throw it!" And then more laughter. Then, "You can't throw it, it won't come through!"

Martin eased open the door and tiptoed as quickly as

he could along the hallway toward the sitting room.
Emilio was scuffling around, his sneakers squeaking on
the wood-block floor, and he was giggling so much that
Martin was worried for a moment that he was choking.

Martin tried to see through the crack in the door-
jamb. He glimpsed Emilio's faded red sneakers, flash-
ing for a moment, and then Emilio's black tousled hair.
But the door wasn't open wide enough for him to be
able to see the mirror on the end wall; and if he had
opened it any farther, he suspected that he would scare
away *who*ever or *what*ever Emilio was playing with.

Emilio laughed. "Stop throwing it!"

But then Martin heard another voice—a voice that
didn't sound like Emilio's at all. A young, clear voice,
echoing slightly as if he were talking in a tunnel or a
high-ceilinged bathroom. *"Get another ball! Get another
ball!"* And then a strange ringing giggle.

Martin felt as if somebody had lifted up his shirt collar at the back and gradually emptied a jug of ice
water down his back.

What had he said to Morris? *If I don't know Boofuls'
voice when I hear it, then nobody does.*

Emilio said, "What? What? Another ball?"

*"We have to have two! If you throw a ball to me, I can
throw a ball back to you!"*

A moment's hesitation. Then Emilio saying, "Okay,
then, wait up," and dodging toward the door on those
squeaking sneakers.

At once, Martin swung the door open wide. It banged
and shuddered against the wall. He lifted Emilio
bodily out of his way and jumped right into the middle
of the room.

He thought he saw a blur that could have been an
arm or could have been a leg. But then again, it could
have been nothing at all.

The mirror was empty, except for himself and the room and the late morning sunlight; and just behind him, a bewildered-looking Emilio.

Martin swung around. "Where is he?" he demanded, his voice cracking.

Emilio shook his head. "I don't know what you mean."

"The boy, the real boy. Where is he?"

"He's—"

"Listen, Emilio, I was standing right behind the door. I *heard* him. I heard him with my own ears."

Two clear tears unexpectedly dropped onto Emilio's cheeks, and rolled down on either side of his mouth, and fell on the floor.

"He said I mustn't tell anybody. He said they punish him if anybody finds out."

Martin got down on one knee and hugged Emilio close. "You listen to me, old buddy, I'm not going to hurt him. I'm his friend, the same way that you are."

"He says he's frightened."

"Well, what does he have to be frightened about? He doesn't have to be frightened of me. I can help him. At least, I *think* I can help him."

Emilio shook his head. "He says he's frightened."

"All right," said Martin, and stood up. He looked toward the mirror and wondered if the real boy was listening to them. "But if that boy really is who I think he is—and if he's gotten himself trapped inside that mirror or something—for whatever reason—and he's frightened—well, I'm sure that I can find some way to help him—because I know more about him than he knows about himself."

Emilio glanced quickly at the mirror, almost furtively, and then asked, "Can I go now?"

Martin grinned and shrugged. "Sure you can go. This isn't the third degree."

Emilio didn't know what he meant but he went, anyway. He was passing the kitchen door, however, when he said, "Are you going to have him through for dinner?"

"*Through?*"

"Well, you know, like through the mirror."

Martin came along the hallway and gave Emilio a pretend Rocky punch. "You're way ahead of yourself, Emilio."

"But he likes lasagne."

"He told you that?"

"He likes Swedish meatballs and he likes lasagne and he likes pecan pie."

"So your grandmother's lasagne won't go to waste?"

"No, sir."

Martin watched Emilio climb back down the stairs. It was extraordinary how easily children accept the strange and the supernatural, he thought. But maybe this mirror wasn't as strange and as supernatural as it appeared to be. He had read in *Popular Radio* that mirrors could sometimes pick up radio signals from powerful transmitters, because of their silver backing, and that their glass could vibrate sufficiently to make people hear disembodied voices. Late one night in 1961, in Pasadena, the wife of a grocery-store manager was lying in bed waiting for her husband to come home when her dressing-table mirror began to pick up a live Frank Sinatra interview from Palm Springs. Her husband, coming home late, heard a man's voice in his wife's bedroom, and shot to kill. He wounded his wife and then turned the gun on himself.

He returned to the sitting room and leaned against

the mirror with his arms upraised and listened and waited for a long time. No boy. Nothing.

"Walter!" he shouted. "Boofuls! Come here, Boofuls, let me take a look at you! I'm your biggest fan, Boofuls! Why'n't you step out and give me that sailor's hornpipe, hunh? Come on, Boofuls, I've devoted three years of my life to writing and rewriting about you. Three years—and three complete transfusions of blood and sweat. The least you can give me is a couple of minutes of hornpipe."

He waited five minutes, ten. Nothing happened. No Boofuls appeared. After a while, Martin turned away from the mirror and looked across at his typewriter. He had some work to do on a *Knight Rider* teleplay. He might just as well sit down and get to it. Trying to get in touch with boys who lived in mirrors wasn't going to pay the rent.

He switched on his tape player and inserted the sound track of *Suwannee Song*. Immediately the flutes thrilled and the drums rattled, and the sitting room was filled with the opening march, when Boofuls was strutting like a drum major in front of a regiment of two hundred black minstrels, as they paraded along the levee.

> *Surrr . . . wannee Song! Suwannee Song!*
> *You can blow your flute and you can bang your drum*
>   *and you can march along!*

Martin sat down at his desk, zipped a fresh sheet of paper into his typewriter, and started work on the latest adventures of David Knight. He wondered mischievously if Kit the talking car could turn out to be gay: if he could come out of the garage, so to speak.

Surr . . . wannee Song! Suwannee Song!
It's the song, it's the song, it's the song of the South!

He didn't know what it was that caught his eye;
what it was that stopped him typing *"What is it,
David? Bad guys?"* and turn around in his chair and
stare intently at the mirror. But the blue and white
ball came rolling out from under the table, halfway
across the room, to settle there, rocking slightly from
side to side before it came completely to rest.

He turned to look at the real room. The ball wasn't
there. He switched off his typewriter and walked up to
the mirror and stared at the blue and white ball for
two or three thoughtful minutes. Then he went back to
his desk and opened up the bottom drawer and took
out a tennis ball that he had used for practice last summer.

"We have to have two!" the boy had called out. *"If
you throw a ball to me, I can throw a ball back to you."*

Martin hesitated for a while, tossing the old gray tennis ball up and down in his hand. Then, without warning, he threw it at the mirror, quite hard, half
expecting to break it, half *hoping* to break it.

There was a sharp smacking sound, and the ball rico-
cheted off the glass and rolled across the floor. It came
to rest only five or six inches away from the toe of his
Nike sneakers.

But it wasn't a dingy gray tennis ball. It was a bright
new blue and white bouncing ball. And when he turned
in shock and looked toward the mirror, he saw his own
tennis ball there, in exactly the corresponding place,
five or six inches away from his toe.

He picked up the blue and white ball. It was quite
hard and smelled strongly of rubber and paint. His

mirror image picked up the tennis ball and sniffed that, too.

"My God," he whispered; and approached the mirror, holding up the blue and white ball until it was touching the mirror's surface. His reflection did the same with the tennis ball, until the two balls apparently touched.

Martin could scarcely believe what he was seeing. He turned the ball this way and that way, but it remained, without argument, a blue and white ball, while the ball in the mirror remained the same balding gray tennis ball that he had been punting around last year.

He tried one more experiment. He stepped back, and wound back his arm, and pitched the blue and white ball straight toward the glass. Again, there was a smacking sound; but this time the blue and white ball came bouncing back into the real room.

Martin picked up the blue and white ball, turned it around in his hand, and then set it down on his desk, next to his bronze paperweight of a *fin de siècle* plume dancer. He sat there and watched it, and then poured himself some wine, and watched it some more.

The sun rotated around the room. Next door, beside the pool, Maria Bocanegra came and went, sunning herself with Sno-Cones to protect her nipples; but Martin didn't bother to get up and look. He couldn't keep his eyes off the blue and white ball.

The day died. He didn't understand it. It was a clear night, the lights were sparkling all the way to Watts.

He slept in his chair. The blue and white ball stayed where it was, unmoving.

Three

He DREAMED that night that he was the smallest of sea creatures, crouched in the tiniest of shells, on a broad moonlit beach.

He could feel the grit. He could taste the salt. He could hear the slow, restless convulsions of the ocean; rocks into stones, stones into pebbles, pebbles into sand, year in and year out, even when there was nobody to listen to it.

He felt the terrible fear of being small and defenseless.

He opened his eyes. He was sweating. It should have been hot, but it was stunningly cold. He shivered. He sat up in bed and his breath smoked. He couldn't decide if he was awake or still asleep—if he was Martin Williams or if he was still a mollusk. He called, "Hello?" even before he was properly awake.

From the sitting room, he could hear whispered

voices: two children sharing secrets. He could see lights flickering, too: cold clinical lights, as if somebody were silently welding.

"Emilio?" he called. Then, louder, "Emilio?"

He drew back his futon and reached for his robe. Quickly he stepped out into the hallway and approached the sitting room door. The light inside the sitting room was spasmodic but intense, and he had to lift his hand to shield his eyes.

He paused outside the door. This time, he didn't feel so much frightened as deeply curious. If he was right, and it *was* Boofuls, or Boofuls' spirit, then what an encounter this was going to be. If he had lived, Boofuls would be coming up to his sixtieth birthday; Martin was only thirty-four.

He pushed open the door. The room was glaring with static and crackling with cold. He turned and saw Emilio in his Care Bears nightshirt, kneeling in front of the mirror, one hand lifted, and facing him—instead of a true reflection—a small white-faced boy with golden curls, dressed in pale-yellow pajamas.

Martin's heart hesitated, bumped, hesitated, the same way it did on Montezuma's Revenge at Knott's Berry Farm. And the same hyped-up, almost hysterical reasoning: *I don't want to do this more than anything else I can think of, but I have to, because it scares me so much I can scarcely think how much it scares me.*

There was no doubt about it at all. The boy in the mirror was Boofuls. Martin stared at him in horrified fascination. He was there, smiling, his eyes much smaller and paler than Martin would have imagined, but then the studio makeup artists had probably darkened his lashes before he appeared in front of the lights. His hair was thinner, too. Gold, yes, bright gold;

and very curly; but thin, the way that little children's hair goes when they're anxious, or allergic, or suffering from sibling rivalry.

Emilio bowed his dark head toward the mirror and Boofuls bowed his head toward Emilio. Their movements were exactly reflected, although it was impossible to tell which of them was initiating the action and which was following; or if somehow they were empathising so intensely that they could both move at once, identical movements.

The scene oddly reminded Martin of one of those Marx Brothers movies in which Harpo appeared behind an empty mirror frame, mimicking the movements of the poor sucker who was trying to adjust his necktie in it.

Emilio whispered, "We could do it now."

And Boofuls nodded, and Emilio nodded.

Emilio stood up, his arms by his sides. The white-faced Boofuls stood up, too, and smiled at him, his arms by his sides.

"One! Two! *Three!*" said Boofuls.

And it was then that Martin understood what they were going to do—the old gray tennis ball flying into the mirror-world and the bright blue and white ball flying out of it—except that he had found it impossible to throw the blue and white ball back.

"Emilio!" he bellowed. *"Emilio, no!"*

Emilio turned, startled. Boofuls turned, too—but here his mirror-mimicking failed him, because he looked straight toward Martin the same way that Emilio did. His tiny eyes flared bright sapphire blue for a moment, welding-torch eyes, and he snatched for Emilio with both arms.

But in that instant Williams, who couldn't duck or

weave, did his high school coach proud—with a sliding tackle that caught little Emilio around the waist and sent him sprawling across the floor.

For one second, Martin felt an extraordinary pull on Emilio, as forceful and demanding as if he were being sucked out of a depressurized airplane; but he grabbed hold of his desk with one hand, slipped, grabbed again, and clung on to Emilio with the other. After a split second of ferocious suction, the force subsided, the flickering lights died away, and the two of them were left lying on the floor, in cold and darkness and silence.

Martin ruffled Emilio's hair. "You okay, old buddy?"

To his surprise, there were tears glistening on Emilio's cheeks.

"Hey, come on, now," he said, sitting up. "What's wrong?"

"I wanted to *go*," Emilio sobbed.

"You wanted to go? Go where?"

"Through the mirror, I wanted to go."

Martin looked at the mirror. Boofuls had vanished. All the glass reflected was themselves and the moonlit room. Somewhere outside, heading south on La Brea, a police siren was whooping. Lonely echoes of urgency and danger.

"Come on," said Martin, taking hold of Emilio's hand and helping him up. "Let's go find ourselves a Coke."

Emilio stood up and looked sadly toward the mirror. "He only wanted to play."

"Is that what he said?"

Emilio nodded. "He said we could play all day, I wouldn't have to go to school. He wants me to meet his friends. He wants me to meet his old man."

"His old man? You mean his father?"

"That's right. He says we could go for rides; swim in the sea; anything."

Martin leaned across his desk and picked up the blue and white ball. "Emilio," he said, "do you know where this came from?"

"Unh-hunh."

"Emilio—it came from in there. It came from the mirror. Take a look in the mirror right now. What am I holding up? A worn-out old tennis ball, right? Yet look at this one. It doesn't make any sense. Like seeing that boy doesn't make any sense. You're not supposed to look into mirrors and see somebody else instead of yourself."

Emilio wiped his tears with his sleeve.

Martin said, "The trouble is, Emilio, I can't get my tennis ball back."

"But this ball's okay," Emilio told him. "Why do you want the other one back?"

Martin tossed the ball up into the air and caught it again. "Emilio, that's not the point. I can't get it back whether I want it or not. Now, supposing *you* went through that mirror. The way I see it, for anything to get through, one *real* thing has to be traded for one *mirror* thing. Can you understand that? It's the same as the boy was telling you yesterday. You can't play ball with just a reflection, it won't go through. You need two balls—one to go in and the other to come out. Just like you need two boys. One to step into the mirror, one to step out."

Emilio scratched his head like one of the Little Rascals. "But if that boy has to come out when I go in, how do we play with each other? He said he was going to show me his lead soldiers."

Martin said, "Listen to me, planet brain. If this blue

and white ball came through the mirror and I can't get
my old ball back, do you have any reason to suppose
that when that boy comes through the mirror, I'm
going to be able to get *you* back?"

Emilio was silent for a moment, pouting. Then he
said, "I don't want to come back. I don't care. Anything's better than Grannie and Gramps. They always
smell like garlic, and there are dust balls under the
bed."

"The same dust balls exist in that mirror," Martin
assured him. "So do the beds they're under. They've
got the same garlic, the same people, the same world.
The only difference is that everything's back to front."

Emilio said wistfully, "I wish I could see it."

"It's not so hot, believe me."

"But it is! Look at that writing!" And he pointed to
the letters ɘbɒnɘɿɘƧ ɘniɥƨnuƧ. "I wonder how you
speak it. It's cool."

"Cool." Martin smiled, shaking his head, and laid an
arm around Emilio's shoulder. "You should've been a
printer, that's what printers have to do, read type back
to front. Come, let's get that Coke."

They went through to the kitchen. Emilio perched on
the stool while Martin opened up two cans of Coke.

Emilio said, "That boy, his name's not really Petey,
is it?"

"No," Martin told him. "That boy's name is
Boofuls."

"You mean like the same kid in the picture in your
bedroom?"

"The very same kid."

Emilio made a loud sucking noise with his drinking
straw. "But that picture comes from the olden days."

"That's right. Nineteen thirty-six, to be precise. And that's more than fifty years ago."

Emilio continued to suck Coke while he thought about that. His face was pale because it was the middle of the night and he should have been asleep, and there were plummy little circles under his eyes.

"How come he's still a kid?" Emilio suddenly wanted to know.

"I don't know," Martin admitted. "He's supposed to be dead. I mean, I don't think he's actually a real kid. That kid you can see in the mirror is more like a ghost."

Emilio thought about that and then said, "Wow. I never met a ghost before."

"Me neither." Martin tugged open a bag of Fritos. "That's why I don't think it's such a good idea your playing with him," said Martin. "*You* don't want to wind up a ghost, too, do you?"

"Would I be invisible? I mean if I was a ghost? Could I walk through walls?"

"I don't know. But from everything I've heard about ghosts, ghosts are not too happy. I mean, Boofuls isn't too happy, is he? Listen—do you want anything to eat? Fritos or something? I've got some what-do-you-call-'ems someplace. Twinkies."

Emilio shook his head. He was too tired, and too fascinated by the otherworldly nature of the friend he had met in Martin's sitting room. Martin could almost see it all churning around in his mind, like five different colors of Play-Doh, *"I've been playing ball with a ghost, I've been talking to a ghost. A ghost! A real live ghost! Not like Casper; not like* Poltergeist, *like me! A ghost kid, just like me!"*

Martin said, "It's possible, Emilio—it's just possible—that playing with Boofuls might not be safe. Do you understand that? I mean, Boofuls doesn't mean you any harm. Leastways, I don't think he does. But this is all pretty weird stuff, right? And until we can find out what's happening, why he's here, what he wants—well, I think it's better if you don't come up here."

Emilio looked completely put out. "Doesn't Boofuls like me?"

"Sure he likes you, Emilio. He probably thinks you're his best pal ever. But just at this moment you two guys have got something to work out between you. Like, he lives on one side of a mirror, and you live on the other. And the way I see it, either you're here and he's there, or he's here and you're there. And that's a little too weird for anybody to handle."

Emilio yawned. "All right," he surrendered.

Just then, Mr. Capelli came stomping into the kitchen, wrapped up in a gleaming striped satin bathrobe in chrome yellow and royal purple. Underneath it, Martin glimpsed gray woolen ankle socks.

"Emilio!" he exclaimed. "I've been searching for you everywhere! I walked all the way down to Highland!"

"You've been walking the streets in *that* robe and they didn't arrest you?" asked Martin with pretended astonishment.

Mr. Capelli tugged his bathrobe tighter. "Mrs. Capelli gave me this robe for Christmas."

"Don't tell me, tell the judge. Thank your lucky stars they don't send people to death row for premeditated bad taste."

"And what do *you* call taste, *anh*? Your wreck of a car, parked outside my house?"

Martin lifted Emilio off his stool and gave him a

good-night kiss on the top of the head. Funny how kids' hair always smells the same: fresh, alive, pungent with youth, chestnuts and hot pajamas and summer days.

"Here," he said, "you'd better take this young somnambulist back to his bed."

Mr. Capelli took hold of Emilio and clasped him in his arms. "You're a crazy person, you know that, just like your mamma."

Martin said quietly, as Mr. Capelli carried Emilio toward the door, "Listen, Mr. Capelli . . ." but he realized when Mr. Capelli turned around that there were tears in his eyes, one of those sudden unexpected pangs of grief for his dead daughter; one of those moments of weakness that hit the bereaved when they're least expecting it.

Emilio's mother, Mr. Capelli's daughter, had died three years ago. Her husband, Stanley, had walked out on her. (Mrs. Capelli had told Martin all about this, like a soap opera, complete with actions: you should have seen the fights, you should have heard the cursing, how two people could *hate* each other so much, you'd've never believed it.)

Sad, disoriented, feeling that she had somehow fallen from grace, Emilio's mother had overdosed one Sunday morning on Italian wine and Valium. She had been found dead in her apartment white as Ophelia, her arms outspread, her hair outspread, almost beautiful, but smelling like hell itself, and the whole apartment thunderous with blowflies.

Stanley had gone to Saskatchewan to chop timber. Mr. and Mrs. Capelli had been given custody of Emilio. Garlic, dust balls, and all.

Mr. Capelli said, "It's all right, Martin, he has to get back to bed."

"Mr. Capelli, I have to talk to you," Martin insisted. "Could you come right back?"

"Talk?" Mr. Capelli demanded.

"About Emilio, please.. Can you spare me five minutes?"

"It's gone three o'clock."

"Sure, yes, I know, but please. I don't know whether it's going to keep until tomorrow."

He tore off a piece of kitchen towel and handed it to Mr. Capelli, and Mr. Capelli wiped his eyes. It was an act of acceptance, an act of reconciliation.

"Okay," Mr. Capelli promised. "But five minutes, no more."

Martin looked at Emilio resting against his grandfather's shoulder and Emilio was already asleep.

Mr. Capelli came up ten minutes later and rapped at the door.

"Hey, come on in," Martin told him.

Mr. Capelli stood in the hallway in his yellow and purple bathrobe, looking tired and embarrassed. "I'm sorry," he said, "I shouldn't've sounded off. It just gets to me sometimes, you know what I mean, Andrea and all."

Martin slapped his arm. "I know. I'm sorry, too. You know what scriptwriters are. Smart-asses, all of us. It's the way we make our living."

Mr. Capelli nodded, oblivious to Martin's irony. "She was so beautiful, Andrea; and Emilio looks just the same way; nothing of Stanley; that jerk; Stanley had eyes that were too close together, you know? But Emilio is Andrea. Beautiful, Italian, what can I say?"

Martin suggested, "How about some coffee?"

Mr. Capelli said, "No—no thank you. I don't sleep good already. Just talk."

"Okay," said Martin, taking a deep breath. "This isn't easy, okay? Try to bear with me. But even if it doesn't sound logical, try to accept that I wouldn't be telling you if I weren't worried about Emilio."

"Why are you worried about Emilio?" Mr. Capelli demanded. "Why should *you* worry about Emilio?"

"Listen, Mr. Capelli, Emilio is your grandson, but Emilio is also my friend. Well, I hope he is. I don't think it matters very much how *old* anybody is, do you? I mean the difference between your age and my age is a lot more than the difference between my age and Emilio's age. So you can't say that he and I don't have any right to be buddies, can you?"

"No, I didn't say that," replied Mr. Capelli stiffly, his hands resting on his knees.

"All right, then," said Martin. "What I'm saying is in Emilio's best interest, believe me. If Emilio comes up to my apartment anymore—well, I don't want him here anymore."

Mr. Capelli leaned forward, his hands still clutching his knees. "You're not saying . . . what, you're gay?"

"Oh, shit, Mr. Capelli!" Martin shouted at him, slapping at the hallway wall. "I'm not talking about me! Gay! What the hell is the matter with you? It's that mirror you helped me to carry upstairs."

"The mirror, hah? Boofuls' mirror? What did I tell you, you shouldn't give it houseroom."

"Maybe you were right," Martin admitted. "I don't know what it is, but there's something wrong with it," Martin told him. "It's hard to say what. But it's not your usual kind of everyday mirror."

"It's a trick mirror," said Mr. Capelli, trying to

lighten up this dire and ominous conversation before
Martin started talking about death and hackings and
all the other gory topics of conversation that (along
with *saraghine alla brace*) invariably gave him nightmares and agonies of indigestion. "You look in the mirror and what do you see? You don't got clothes on."

"No, Mr. Capelli, it's nothing like that. I mean, it's a
kind of a trick mirror, but it doesn't make your clothes
disappear or anything like that. It's—well, when you
look at it, you don't always see what's really there."

Mr. Capelli said nothing; but waited for Martin to
explain; his eyes blinking from time to time like a pel-
ican at San Diego Zoo.

"The thing is," said Martin, "if Emilio plays with it,
he might start to see things—*people*, maybe, who don't
really exist. And—well—if he sees things—people—
stuff that doesn't exist—it could be kind of—"

He paused. Mr. Capelli was staring at him in that
same pelicanlike way, as if he believed that he had
completely flipped.

Martin added, "Dangerous," and then gave Mr. Capelli an idiotic grin.

Mr. Capelli tugged at the bulb of his fleshy nose and
thought for a while. Then he said, "Martin, I like you.
You've got a choice. Either that mirror goes, or you go,
whichever."

"You're throwing me *out*?" asked Martin in surprise.

"Of course not. Just the mirror."

"Mr. Capelli, I'm not at all sure I can do that."

"Why not? Are you crazy? One minute you're saying
it's dangerous; you see things in it that aren't there;
you're worried about Emilio; the next minute you're
saying you can't do that; well, you *can* do that, it's
easy, just do it. Am I asking too much?"

Martin laid his hand on Mr. Capelli's shoulder. Mr. Capelli peered at it from very close up. "There's nothing fundamentally wrong with the mirror, Mr. Capelli," said Martin, and Mr. Capelli echoed, "Fundamentally."

"All I'm saying is, it has this vibe. I don't know, you can call it what you like. It's like a visual echo. An echo you can see."

"An echo you can see?" Mr. Capelli repeated, and Martin could see that he was vexed and tired, and that he didn't even *want* to understand. Mr. Capelli's answer to everything that he didn't like, or wasn't sure of, was to turn his back on it.

"All right," said Martin. "Boofuls has come alive. Don't ask me how. He's in the mirror, and Emilio has been playing with him, and Emilio has come within an inch of getting inside the mirror, too."

Mr. Capelli stood up. He glanced quickly at Martin, almost casually, then nodded. "Mumh-humh," he said, and nodded again. Martin watched him with increasing tension.

"Good night, Martin," said Mr. Capelli at length, and turned to leave.

"That's it? Good night?"

"All right, a *very* good night. What more do you want?"

"I just want you to promise me that you won't let Emilio come up here for a while. I mean, tell him he mustn't. This whole apartment is strictly no go."

Mr. Capelli said, "In the morning, Martin, you make up your mind. That mirror goes, or you go. The first thing I told you when you brought that mirror back here, what did I say? No good is going to come out of it. That was the first thing I said. And now what's happened? No good has come out of it."

"Mr. Capelli, it could very well be that there's a real boy trapped in that mirror."

"That's right, and it could very well be that some clever people can train a pig to fly straight into a bacon slicer, and another pig to drive the bacon down to Safeway."

"Mr. Capelli—"

"No!" replied Mr. Capelli. "That mirror goes by tomorrow night, otherwise you go. Now, it's late, I don't want to talk about it no more."

He left, closing the apartment door sharply behind him.

Martin remained in the kitchen, feeling drained and somehow diminished, as if his dream of being a mollusk had shrunk his consciousness down to a microscopic speck. Tired, probably, and anxious, and unsettled by what had happened in the mirror.

He went back to bed and fell asleep almost straightaway. He had no dreams that he could remember, although he was aware of blundering through darkness and wondering if it would ever be light, ever again.

It was nearly eight o'clock, however, when he thought he heard a child's voice, close to his ear, whisper, *"Pickle-nearest-the-wind."*

He sat up. He looked around the room, which was quite bright now. Everything looked normal, although he had the oddest feeling that the drapes and the furniture had jumped back into place when he opened his eyes, as if the whole room had been misbehaving itself, right up until the moment when he had woken up.

The drapes stirred a little, as if a child were hiding behind them, but then Martin realized that it was only the morning breeze.

Pickle-nearest-the-wind. What the hell did that mean?

But all the same, he went through to the sitting room, and found a scrap of typing paper on his desk, and wrote it down in green felt-tip pen. The phrase had a peculiar quality about it that reminded him of something, although he couldn't think what. Some childhood storybook, with drawings of clouds and chimney pots and faraway hills.

He glanced toward the mirror. The grinning gold face of Pan presided over a scene that appeared to be a scrupulous representation of the real room. Only the blue and white ball on his desk remained uncompromisingly different from the gray tennis ball on his reflected desk.

Still holding the scrap of paper in his hand, he walked right up to the mirror and stared at his own face. He looked quite well and quite calm, although he didn't feel it. He wondered if there really *was* a world beyond the door, a different world, a world where Boofuls had survived after death, a Lewis Carroll world where clocks smiled and chess pieces talked and flowers quarreled, and you had to walk backward to go forward.

> *'Twas brillig, and the slithy toves*
> *Did gyre and gimble in the wabe . . .*

He remembered with a smile the words of "Jabberwocky," the mirror-writing nonsense poem in *Alice Through the Looking-Glass;* and how it had always amused him as a small boy to hold the book up to the mirror and read the words the right way around.

It had always seemed so magical that the lettering obediently reversed itself and gave up its secret, every time.

He held up the piece of paper on which he had written "Pickle-nearest-the-wind." Perhaps the words meant something if they were reversed: after all, everything *else* that had been happening to him seemed to have some connection with this damned mirror.

But to his slowly growing astonishment, the words weren't reversed at all. In the mirror, in his own handwriting, the words clearly said, "Pickle-nearest-the-wind," the right way around.

He stared at the real piece of paper, his hand trembling. "Pickle-nearest-the-wind," the right way around. The words refused to be reversed by the mirror. He crumpled the paper up, and then uncrumpled it and held it up again. No difference. For some reason beyond all imagination, those words that had been whispered to him in the early hours of the morning completely denied the laws of optical physics.

He stood still for a while, looking at himself in the mirror, wondering what to do. *My God*, he thought, *what kind of a game is going on here?*

He left the sitting room, step by step, backward, keeping his eyes on the mirror all the time. He shut the door behind him, and locked it, and took out the key. Then he went back to his bedroom, stripped off his bathrobe, and dressed.

Ramone was having breakfast when Martin arrived at the Reel Thing; his custom-made sneakers, purple and white and natural suede, perched on the counter like exhibits unto themselves. He was dark, shock-headed, with multiple-jointed arms and legs, and one of those ugly spread-nosed Latino faces that you couldn't help liking. His breakfast was a giant chili dog, with everything on it, and a bottle of lime-flavored Perrier.

"Hey, Martin!" he cried, waving one of his spidery arms.

Martin came over and leaned tightly against the counter, close to the cash register.

"Allure, Ramone," he greeted him. Saying "allure" instead of "hello" had been kind of a private joke between them ever since they had gone downtown together one evening to watch a Brazilian art movie, in which everybody had said "allure."

"*Allure, Juanita.*"

"*Allure, Gaspar.*"

Ramone said, "That ginger-headed girl was in here, yessday afternoon, asking about you."

"Yeah?" said Martin. "That ginger-headed girl" was a student from his Monday evening tele-writing class, Norma, who had considered his *A-Team* rewrites "miraculous"; and had wanted to take him to bed to "you know, transfuse the talent."

The Reel Thing was more than a store: it was a shrine. Anything and everything that was important to movie buffs was assembled here. Shirley Temple dolls in sailor suits and cowboy outfits and Scottish plaids. Buck Rogers disintegrator guns and rocket ships. Tom Mix pocket knives and six-shooters. And box after box after box of signed studio glossies—Joan Crawford and Adolphe Menjou and Robert Redford and Dorothy Dell.

The whole store smelled of forty-year-old movie programs and dust and old clothes and stale cigarette smoke from a thousand long-forgotten parties. But anybody who cared for movies could spend hours in here, touching with reverence the gowns of Garbo; or the white Stetsons of William Boyd; or the short-sleeved shirts of Mickey Rooney. The artifacts were nothing at all. It was what they conjured up that made them valuable.

Martin picked up a yellowed copy of *Silver Screen* with the enticing headline "What It Takes to Be a 1939 Girl."

"Did you look at the stuff?" Ramone asked him, scooping up chili and pickle with his fingers.

Martin dropped the magazine back into its rack. "Oh, yes, I looked at the stuff, all right."

"No good?" asked Ramone.

"Depends what you mean by no good."

Ramone's tabby cat, Lugosi, was resting on a stack of *Screenlands*, his paws tucked in, his eyes slitted against the sunlight that came in through the window. Martin stroked him under his chin, but Lugosi opened his eyes and stared back at him in irritation, his vexation emphasized by the way one pointed tooth was caught on his lip. Lugosi was definitely a one-man cat.

Ramone said, with his mouth full, "It was genuine Boofuls stuff, I saw the paperwork. It was auctioned by M-G-M along with a whole lot of Shirley Temple properties."

"I bought the mirror," said Martin. Then, "Listen, Ramone, can you get some time off? I have to talk this over with *some*body."

Ramone wiped his hands on a paper napkin, rolled it up, and tossed it with perfect accuracy into a basket. "I was going out to Westwood, anyway. Kelly can take care of the store. Kelly! *Dónde está usted?*"

A small girl with owlish designer spectacles and a long blond braid down the middle of her back came into the store from the back. She wore a loose white T-shirt with the slogan "Of All the T-shirts in All the World, I Had to Pick This One."

"*Hasta luego*, Kelly," said Ramone, picking up his car keys. "I'm going down to Westwood with Fartin' Martin here to look at that stuff in Westwood."

"'Kay," said Kelly in a nasal Valley accent, and began to shuffle movie programs. Ramone whistled to his cat Lugosi, and Lugosi jumped down straightaway and followed them out of the store.

The "stuff in Westwood" proved to be disappointing. Two crushed and faded cocktail gowns that were supposed to have belonged to Marilyn Monroe. The nervy middle-aged woman who was selling them chain-smoked and paced up and down. "They have stains on them," she said at last, as if this were the selling point that was going to make all the difference.

"Stains?" asked Ramone, holding one of the gowns up.

"For goodness' sake, you know, *stains*," the woman snapped back. "Robert Kennedy."

Martin, who was sitting back on the lounger watching Ramone at work, shook his head in disbelief. He couldn't conceive of anything more tasteless than trying to sell Marilyn Monroe's cocktail gowns with Robert Kennedy's stains on them.

Ramone dropped the gowns back onto the chair. "I'm sorry, I can't offer you anything for these. There's no authentication, nothing. They're different sizes, too. They could have belonged to two different people, neither one of whom was Marilyn."

"You're doubting my word?" the woman said stiffly.

"That's not what I'm saying. All I'm saying is, thanks—but no thanks."

They took a walk along the beach. There was a strong ocean breeze blowing, and it ruffled their clothes. Lugosi followed them at a haughty distance, occasionally lifting his head to sniff the wind.

"I never knew cats liked the seashore," Martin remarked.

"Oh, Lugosi loves it. All that fish, all those birds. He'd go swimming if he could find a costume the right size."

Ramone took out a cheroot and lit it with a Zippo emblazoned with the name *Indiana Jones*, his hands cupped over the flame.

"How about that woman with the Marilyn Monroe dresses," said Martin. "Wasn't she something?"

"If they were genuine, I would have given her a hundred fifty apiece," Ramone told him.

"How do you know they weren't?"

Ramone shook his head. "You get an eye for it; a touch for it. Marilyn never would've worn anything that looked like that. A *shmatteh*, that's what the Jewish people call dresses like that. And besides, there are no pictures of Marilyn wearing them, either of them, and if she *ever* wore two tight low-cut gowns like that, don't you think that somebody would've taken pictures? She was a chubby broad, to say the least."

When he saw Martin looking at him in surprise, he grinned and said, "It's true! I can remember every Marilyn Monroe picture ever, in my head. And James Dean. And Jayne Mansfield. *And* what they were wearing."

Martin said, "I want you to come take a look at this boy in the mirror. I want you to tell me that it's Boofuls."

Ramone blew out smoke. "Pretty far-out shit, hunh?"

"You don't have to believe me until you see it for yourself."

"I believe you!" Ramone replied, spreading his arms.

"Why shouldn't I believe you? I come from a very superstitious family."

"I just don't know what to do," said Martin. "I mean, supposing it really is him? Supposing there's some way of getting him out of there?"

"Like the tennis ball, you mean? Well, I don't know. It's pretty far-out shit. But whatever happened, if you did it, if you got him out, you'd be sitting on some kind of a gold mine, hunh? You're the guy who wants to make a Boofuls musical, and what do you got? You got the actual Boofuls. And all this stuff about him being chopped up, well, they're going to have to forget that, aren't they, if he's all in one piece?"

"I guess so," Martin agreed, a little unhappily. "It was just the way that he tried to grab Emilio and pull him into the mirror—well, that scared me. It's possible that nothing would have happened . . . I mean, maybe this particular mirror has some kind of weird scientific property which allows objects to pass right through it. Maybe Emilio could have gone to play in mirrorland and come back whenever he felt like it."

"Do you *really* think that's possible?" asked Ramone.

Martin shook his head. "If the same thing happens to Emilio that happened to that ball . . . well, maybe he could get inside the mirror, but I'm not at all sure we'd ever get him out again."

Ramone tossed away his cheroot and stood for a moment with his hands tucked into the pockets of his jeans, staring out at the ocean. "You know I come down here every time I feel that life is terrible, that people are mean and small and bitter, that human ambition is just a crock of shit."

He paused, watching the gray water glittering in the sunshine. "And you know something?" he said. "Look-

ing out at all that infinity, looking out at all that water,
all that distance, that does nothing for me, whatsoever.
So the sea is big, so what, that doesn't make life any
better."

They drove back along Sunset in Ramone's patched-
up Camaro, with Lugosi sitting primly in the back seat.
Together, they sang two or three verses of "Whistlin'
Dixie"; and then fell silent.

"That's it, then," said Martin, unlocking the sitting
room door and ushering Ramone inside.

Ramone gave a soft whistle and padded toward the
mirror on squeaking sneakers, holding Lugosi in his
arms so that the cat's body hung down. "That's some
piece of glass. Nice frame, too. Who's the dude in the
middle?"

"Pan, I think. Or Bacchus. One of those woodsy Ro-
man gods."

"He's a dead ringer for Charlton Heston, if you ask
me. Do you think Charlton Heston ever posed for mirrors? You know, before he became famous?"

Ramone tentatively touched the mirror's surface,
then stepped back. "It's something, isn't it? What did
she ask you for it?"

"Five hundred," Martin lied.

"Well," said Ramone, "I think she took you. I
wouldn't have paid more than two-fifty, two seventy-
five. But it's a piece of glass, isn't it?"

"There's the ball," said Martin, and pointed out the
blue and white ball on the desk. Ramone glanced at it,
then glanced at the tennis ball in the mirror.

"Now, that is what I call *extraño*," said Ramone. He
peered at the blue and white ball carefully, and then he
said, "Is it okay if I pick it up?"

"Sure. I've picked it up. It doesn't feel any different from any other kind of ball."

Ramone threw the ball in the air and caught it, watching himself in the mirror with delight. "How *about* that!" he said, laughing. "In here I'm throwing a blue ball; in there I'm throwing a totally different ball."

"Try throwing it at the mirror," Martin suggested, walking across to the windowsill to get the bottle of wine. "That's it, directly at the mirror."

"Heyy . . ." said Ramone. "I just thought of something. If this ball here isn't the same as the ball in the mirror, maybe that guy in the mirror who looks like me—well, maybe he isn't me. Maybe he's somebody who *looks* like me, okay, but isn't."

Martin poured them each a glass of chardonnay. "Why don't you ask him?" he suggested.

"Hee! Hee!" Ramone laughed; and then called to his reflection in the mirror, "Hey, buddy, are you me, or are you just somebody pretending to be me? Because, let's be truthful here, you've got your right arm on your left side and your left arm on your right side, and I sure don't. Why don't you take down your pants and let's see that skull-and-crossbones tattoo, which side of your ass it's on?"

"You didn't tell me you had a skull-and-crossbones tattoo on your ass," said Martin.

Ramone looked embarrassed. "I don't either. I was joking, all right? But you say one word!"

"Anyway," said Martin, "try throwing the ball at the mirror. Not too hard. You don't want to break it."

Winding his arm back, Ramone said, "This is it! This is Rip Collins, just about to make the pitch of his whole career!"

"Just not too hard, okay?" Martin told him.

Ramone threw, and the ball smacked against the mirror. Lugosi the cat immediately jumped for it, dancing toward his own reflection. The blue and white ball bounced off the glass and rolled back into the room, but to Martin's horror, *Lugosi dived halfway into the mirror's surface, right up to his middle, as if he had dived into water.*

It looked as if Lugosi had turned into an extraordinary headless beast with a tail at each end, and two pairs of hind legs that clawed and scratched and struggled against each other to get free.

"Get him out!" yelled Ramone, his voice white with terror. "Martin—for God's sake—get him out!"

Martin scrambled down onto the floor and caught hold of Lugosi's narrow body. He could feel the cat's rib cage through his fur, feel his heart racing. Lugosi's hind legs lashed out wildly, and his claws scratched Martin all the way down the inside of his arm.

Ramone did what he could to keep Lugosi's legs from pedaling, while Martin tried to drag him out. But Martin could feel that same irresistible force that he had felt when he tackled Emilio: that same relentless sucking.

"Martin! Help him!" Ramone shouted. "Holy shit, Martin—he's being pulled in!"

The force was too strong, too demanding. The cat's body was dragged through Martin's hands, inch by inch, even though he clung on so tightly that he was pulling out clumps of tabby fur. His body, his hind legs, his shuddering outstretched paws, all of them vanished one by one. His reflection shrank, too—until at the very end there was nothing but a single dark furry caterpillar that appeared to be waving in midair, and that was the tip of his tail.

Then there was nothing at all, he was gone, and the surface of the mirror was flawless and bright.

Ramone was sweating. "If I hadn't of seen that—if I hadn't of seen that, right there in front of me, with my own eyes! *Madre mia!*"

Martin stood up. His face in the mirror was gray, the color of newspaper. "Ramone . . . I don't know what to say. I had no idea it was going to do that."

"But it *pulled* him! It pulled him in!"

Ramone touched the surface of the mirror quickly, as if he were touching a hot plate to make sure that it was switched on.

"Ramone—," warned Martin, "Christalmighty man, be careful. Supposing *you* got sucked in?"

Ramone's fright was fragmenting into grief and anger. "Man—that's my *cat*! That's my fucking cat! Six years I've had that cat! I didn't love and feed and take care of that cat just to have some stupid mirror take him away! Some stupid *mirror*!"

Martin came over and gently gripped Ramone by the shoulders. "Ramone—I'm sorry! If I'd have guessed what was going to happen—"

"Martin, am I blaming you?" Ramone fumed. "I'm not blaming you, okay? It wasn't your fault! But I want my cat back! He went in the mirror, where is he?"

"Ramone, I really don't know. He's gone, I don't know how and I don't know where."

Ramone stood up, his eyes staring. "Well, there's got to be one way to find out, and that's to break this goddamned stupid mirror to pieces!"

"No!" shouted Martin. "Ramone—listen—there's a boy in that mirror. For all we know, he's managed to stay alive some way—you know, by hiding in the mirror, or something. Listen, I don't understand any of it. But until I do—please, Ramone, don't touch that mirror. You don't know what the hell might happen—how many people might die."

Ramone bit his lip for a moment, and took three angry paces away from the mirror, and then three angry paces back again. "Thass bullshit! Thass bullshit, Martin, and you know it! What do you care, how many people might die! What the hell just happened to Lugosi? Thass my *cat*!"

Martin didn't know what to say. Both of them were still shocked by Lugosi's hair-raising disappearance—into where? into what? It didn't make any sense. It wasn't even as if a mirrorland cat had jumped out to replace him, the way that Boofuls' blue and white ball had come bouncing out to replace Martin's tennis ball.

Martin had thought that he had discovered the mirror's logic; that an object could only pass through to the mirror-world if another object was sent back in return. But Lugosi had been sucked into the surface of the mirror and vanished utterly. And—judging from the way in which his hindquarters had struggled and his heart had been beating—it had been an agonizing and terrifying experience.

Ramone touched the surface of the mirror again; quickly, nervously, jerking his hand back.

"It can suck in a ball, it can suck in a cat. Do you really think it can suck in a man?"

"Ramone," said Martin, "that's an experiment I don't even want to think about trying."

"We-e-ell, maybe; maybe not. But that's my cat in

there. I mean he's *in* there some way. And all I want to do is get him out."

"Wait," Martin told him. "I have an idea. Maybe I can get Boofuls to tell us."

"Oh, man, Boofuls? You're cracked. Boofuls is dead, Boofuls is hamburger."

"Yes, well, perhaps he is," Martin replied, trying not to sound too frosty about it. "But his soul or his spirit or something of what he was is still here—still inside this mirror."

"Oh, yeah? Where? I don't see any Boofuls. All I see is me and you and some stupid ball that's blue here and gray there, and that doesn't prove anything, and most of all it doesn't get Lugosi back."

"Will you be patient?" Martin shouted at him.

"I don't want to be patient!" Ramone retorted. "I didn't even want to come here in the first place!"

"Then go!" yelled Martin.

Ramone tugged open the door. He hesitated for a moment, but then he lowered his head, and turned away, and said, "Shit, man," and left. Martin stood in the sitting room, still breathless, still trembling, and heard Ramone take the stairs three and four at a time.

Then he went to the bathroom and stood over the basin for a long time, listening to his stomach growling. He didn't actually vomit, but he felt as though the inside of his mouth and throat were lined with grease.

Mr. Capelli came up to his apartment at half past six that evening. Martin was typing away furiously at an episode of *As the World Turns*. Mr. Capelli knocked on the sitting room door and then stepped in. He was wearing a dark three-piece suit, very formal, and some strong lavender-smelling cologne. He tugged at his cuffs, and cleared his throat, and nodded toward the mirror.

"You don't get rid of it?" he asked.

Martin stopped typing and turned around in his revolving chair. "I'm sorry. Somebody's coming to pick it up first thing tomorrow morning. That was the earliest I could manage."

Mr. Capelli approached the mirror and straightened his black spotted necktie. Then, with the flat of his hand, he smoothed the hair on the back of his head.

"Going out tonight?" asked Martin, watching him, hoping he wouldn't step too close to the mirror.

Mr. Capelli leaned forward and bared his teeth at his reflection. "Twenty-one thousand dollars' worth of dental work," he declared. "Twenty-one thousand dollars! And what do you get? Teeth is all you get."

Martin said, "Thanks for keeping Emilio away."

Mr. Capelli turned around. "Well, it wasn't easy. He said he wanted to play with your nephew."

"Mr. Capelli—"

"Don't say nothing," said Mr. Capelli, raising one hand. "Whatever it is, I don't want to hear it."

"Mr. Capelli, I tried to explain to you yesterday—my nephew isn't here at all. The boy that Emilio was playing with was Boofuls."

"Sure," said Mr. Capelli.

"Boofuls appeared in the mirror and Emilio saw him. He was as clear as you are. I saw him myself, with my own eyes."

"Sure," said Mr. Capelli.

"You don't believe me," said Martin. "You don't believe me for one moment."

"Sure I believe you," Mr. Capelli told him, his mouth taut. "When I was a boy, my mother and father told me all kinds of stories about ghosts and monsters and things that stared at you out of mirrors. My father used to tell me one story, how he went past his parlor one night, and take a quick look at the mirror, and sitting at the dining table was six people dressed in black, with black veils over their heads, sitting silent, but only in the mirror."

Martin looked back at Mr. Capelli but didn't know what to say.

"I believe you," said Mr. Capelli. "I believe you, but I don't want to hear nothing about it. I don't want to hear nothing about no other worlds, no mirror-people. Life is hard enough in this world, praise God."

He turned vehemently back to the mirror. "Every mirror is evil. Mirrors are for nothing but vanity, for look at your own face, and not the face of other people. This mirror has special evil. Tomorrow morning, you get rid of it. Otherwise, I'm sorry, you have to go."

Martin nodded. "All right, Mr. Capelli. The guy's coming around at eleven."

Actually, Martin had made no arrangements yet for getting rid of the mirror. He was simply stalling for time. If Boofuls was really inside it; and if Ramone's cat was inside it, too, he wanted to keep hold of it and make sure that it was safe. He had called Ramone to ask him if he would store the mirror at the Reel Thing for a while, but Ramone had still been out, and Kelly had told him that she didn't have the "athaw'ty" to say yes.

Mr. Capelli laid his hand on Martin's shoulder. "You get rid of that mirror, understand, but you make sure you don't break it, not in this house, anyway. Breaking a mirror like that, who knows what you're going to let out."

"Sure thing, Mr. Capelli," said Martin. "And—you know—have a good time."

Mr. Capelli looked down at his suit. Then he stared at Martin as if he had said something utterly insane. "A good time? We're going to have dinner with my wife's sister."

Four

An old college pal from Wisconsin called him just before seven: Dick Rasmussen, who used to date Jane's younger sister, Rita.

Dick had come to Los Angeles on business, selling luggage, and he insisted they meet for a drink and maybe dinner?

"Dick, I'm real busy. I'm working on *As the World Turns.*"

"You mean somebody actually sits down and *writes* that shit? I thought the actors made it up as they went along."

Reluctantly, Martin agreed to meet Dick at eight o'clock at the Polo Lounge. "I have to tell you, though, Dick, the only people who go to the Polo Lounge these days are tourists."

"Martin, I'm under orders from the commandant. If I get back home and Nancy finds out I didn't go to the Polo Lounge, believe me, she's going to have my balls."

"You married *Nancy*?"

"Not Nancy Untermeyer. Oh, no, no such luck. Nancy Brogan. You remember Nancy Brogan? Little blond girl, used to go around with that pig-faced fat girl, Phyllis whatever-her-name-was. Yeah, we got spliced! Two kids, now, boy and a girl. No—not Nancy Untermeyer, very regretfully. Do you remember the way Nancy Untermeyer used to play the cello in the school orchestra? Whee-oo. She used to look like she was screwing it."

Reluctantly, Martin dressed in a clean blue shirt and put on his best and only white suit, and rubbed a scuff off his white Gucci sneakers with spit and a Kleenex. He made sure he locked the sitting room door before he left. He didn't want Emilio wandering up here while he was out. On the way out he passed a pink ten-speed bicycle parked against the hall stand: it belonged to Emilio's baby-sitter, Wanda.

His evening with Dick was just as bad as he had imagined it was going to be. Dick was energetic and loud and endlessly excited about Hollywood. He wore a small brown toupee to conceal his thinning crown and a red-and-green-plaid sports coat that might just as well have had "Hayseed" embroidered on the back. Whenever anybody came into the Polo Lounge, he nudged Martin conspicuously and asked, "Is that somebody? That isn't Katharine Ross, is it?"

Dick drank piña coladas with paper parasols in them and ate the orange slices with noisy relish. "This is the land of the orange, right? That isn't Warren Beatty, is it? I mean, you must know all of these people personally, right?"

"Well, I get to know one or two of them."

Dick slapped him on the thigh. "George Peppard! I'll bet you know George Peppard!"

An elegantly dressed woman at the next table turned around and gave them a cold, patronizing look. Martin flashed her his Quick Boyish Smile, but she didn't smile back. He felt more like an outsider than ever. He finished up his white-wine spritzer and listened to Dick jabbering and wondered glumly if Rubishness was contagious.

Dick insisted they go for dinner at the Brown Derby. The restaurant was almost empty, apart from a couple from Oregon who had come to Hollywood for a second honeymoon. "*We're* not on our second honeymoon, as you might have guessed," Dick told the wine waiter, and slapped the table and laughed until he was red in the face.

It was midnight before Martin dropped Dick back at the Hyatt on Sunset. Dick wanted to have another drink, but Martin stayed in the car with the engine running. "Dick—I have to work. This may be magic land to you, but to me it's the salt mines. So do me a favor, will you, have a safe journey home, and give Nancy a kiss for me, and good night."

"I loved you, you know," Dick told him, leaning over the side of the Mustang with his eyes boiled and his toupee crooked. He breathed wine and rum straight into Martin's face. "I loved you like a fucking brother."

"Good night, Dick," Martin told him, and clasped his hand for the tenth time, and at last managed to drive away.

"Fartin' Martin!" Dick shouted out as he teetered on the sidewalk outside the hotel. "That's what they always called you! Heeyoo! Far-Tin Mar-Tin!"

"Dick the Prick," Martin replied under his breath as

the traffic signals at Sierra Bonita intersection turned green, and he turned left on squealing tires toward Franklin Avenue.

When he let himself back into the house, Wanda's bicycle was still parked in the hallway, and he tripped over it in the darkness, catching his shin on the pedal. "Goddamn it!" he hissed at it, and would have kicked it if the landing light hadn't been suddenly switched on, and Wanda hadn't appeared.

"Martin?" she called. "Is that you?"

Martin climbed the stairs. "It is I, fair Wanda, and the pedal of your bicycle has just added injury to the most insulting evening of my entire adult life."

Wanda was a short blond girl of seventeen. She was still plump with puppy fat, but her face was pretty, like a little painted *matrioshka* doll, with rosy cheeks and China-blue eyes. She was wearing a pink jogging suit with a printed picture of Bruce Springsteen on the front, and pink sneakers. Oddly, she was carrying a saucer half filled with milk.

"Where are you going with that?" Martin asked her.

"Your cat was crying; I thought it might be hungry."

Martin glanced up toward the door of his apartment. "My cat?" he said in a hollow voice.

"It's been crying for hours; ever since you left, almost."

Martin took a breath. Thank God for that, Lugosi must have reappeared. At least Ramone and he could be friends again. "Come on," he told Wanda, and took the saucer from her, and led the way upstairs. "You couldn't have gotten in, anyway, the door's locked."

"I don't mind cat-sitting as well as baby-sitting," Wanda told him. "I love cats."

Martin unlocked the apartment door. "This cat doesn't belong to me. It just decided to pay me a visit this afternoon, and not to leave." He switched on the light in the hallway. "It's called Lugosi—you know, after Bela Lugosi, who played Dracula. Believe me, it's well named."

He opened the sitting room door. "Lugosi! Your uncle Martin's home!"

He reached around to switch on the light, but the bulb popped instantly, and the room remained dark. "Damn it," said Martin. "That's about the fifth bulb in five weeks. They don't make anything the way they used to. Hold on, I'll switch on the desk lamp."

He crossed the room; and his dark reflection crossed the room toward him. "Mr. and Mrs. Capelli are late," he remarked to Wanda as he reached over to find the desk-lamp switch.

"It's an anniversary or something," Wanda told him. "They said they wouldn't get back until one o'clock."

"You're not going to cycle home at one o'clock?" Martin asked her.

He tried the desk lamp, but that didn't work, either. "Would you believe it? This one's gone, too. Wanda—"

He was about to ask her to go to the kitchen and bring him two new light bulbs when he heard a low, guttural, hissing sound. He froze, still holding the saucer of milk.

"Lugosi?" he called.

"Was that him?" asked Wanda, peering into the shadowy room. "He sure sounded weird."

Martin paused for a moment, listening. Then he heard the scratching of claws on the wood-block floor, and that same hissing sound.

"Lugosi, it's only me. It's your uncle Martin. Come

on, chum. Wanda's brought you some milk; some luvvy-wuvvy nonradioactive low-fat enriched-calcium milk."

There was a very long silence. Wanda said, "What's his name? Lugosi?"

"That's right. Why don't you try calling him?"

"Okay," said Wanda. "Lugosi! Lugosi! Here, pussy-pussy-pussy! Come on, Lugosi!"

Martin set the saucer of milk down on the desk. There was something about Lugosi's utter silence that he didn't like. He strained his eyes to see through the shadows—looking for anything, a paw, a tail, a reflection of yellow feline eye. Maybe the cat's experience in the mirror had traumatized it; maybe it was hurt. He looked and he listened, but for one suspended heartbeat after another the room was silent, except for the muffled growling and grinding of greater Los Angeles, outside the window in the California night.

"Here, Lugosi!" called Wanda. "Here, pussy-pussy!"

It was then that Martin heard the faint *thump-thump-thump* of a furry tail on the floor, and the low death-rattle sound of a cat purring.

"Sounds like he's under the desk someplace," he told Wanda, and hunkered down to take a look.

Thump, thump, thump. Prrrrrr-prrrrrr-prrrrrr.

"Lugosi?" he asked, and his voice was clogged with phlegm.

Two eyes opened in the darkness. Two eyes that burned incandescent blue, like the flames of welding torches.

"Lugosi?" asked Martin, although this time it was scarcely a question at all.

Something hard and vicious came flying out from under the desk and landed directly in his face, knocking him backwards onto the floor. He was so surprised that he didn't even shout out, but Wanda did—a startled wail, and then a piercing scream.

He felt claws tearing at his neck; claws tearing at his cheeks. His mouth was gagged with soft, fetid fur.

Panicking, he seized the cat's body in both hands and tried to drag it away from his face, but its claws were hooked into his ears and his scalp, and he couldn't get it free.

"Aaahh!" he heard himself shouting. "Wanda, help me! Wanda!"

Wanda came blustering into the room and slapped at the cat, but didn't know what else to do. Martin rolled over and over on the floor, tipping over his chair with his pedaling legs, colliding against his desk; but the cat clung viciously to his head, lacerating his face with claws that felt like whips made out of razor wire.

My eyes! thought Martin in terror. *It's trying to claw out my eyes!*

He managed to force his left hand underneath the cat's scrabbling body and cover his face. He could taste blood and choking fur. With his right hand, he groped for his desk, missed it, then found it, and dragged open the bottom drawer with a crash. His hand plunged into it, searching for anything—a knife, a hammer, a pair of pliers.

His fingers closed around the handle of a large screwdriver—the same one he had used to fix the mirror to the sitting room wall. Grunting, struggling, he raised the screwdriver and jabbed it into the cat's body: once, twice, three times—blunt-edged metal into soft, thrashing fur. The third time, the cat spat like a serpent and tore at him wildly, and so he stabbed it again. It uttered a long, harsh scream that was like nothing that Martin had ever heard in his life before.

The cat sprang off him, careened sideways against the wall, then flew at Wanda, tearing at her legs. Wanda screamed and fell. The cat instantly leaped onto her face and ripped at one side of it with an audible crackle of skin and muscle.

But Martin was up on his feet now. Coughing, stumbling, he seized hold of the cat by the scruff of its neck, and lifted it up, and held it high, even though it was flailing and writhing like a maggot on a fishhook, and scrabbling furiously at his hand with its hind legs.

Martin rammed the cat's head against the wall, burying his thumb into its neck so that it cackled for air. Its eyes bulged—those flaring blue eyes—and it stretched its mouth open so wide in strangulated hatred that it dislocated its jaw.

Wanda cried out, *"No!"* but Martin drew back his arm and then crunched the screwdriver straight through the cat's chest and pinned it to the wall.

He stepped back, staggered back. The cat didn't scream. It twisted and struggled and swung from side to side, staring at him, staring at him, as if it didn't mind dying, impaled on this screwdriver, provided it was sure that Martin would soon die, too.

Wanda began to sob hysterically. Martin said, "Come on, come on, it's all over now. The cat went crazy, that's all. It just went crazy."

He led her toward the door, back to the Capellis' apartment. He shielded her face as they passed the cat. It was still alive, bubbling blood from its stretched-open mouth, still staring, still trying to swing itself free.

They opened the door. Wanda leaned against the wall, white and shivering, her forehead and her upper lip beaded with perspiration, her hand pressed against her lacerated cheek. "I'm sorry," she said, "I have to be sick," and she went off to the bathroom. Martin stood light-headed in the hallway, swaying from side to side, and heard her regurgitate the chicken-and-stuffing frozen dinner that the Capellis had left her.

Emilio had heard the screaming and the banging around upstairs, and he was sitting up in his bed wide awake. "Boy," he said, impressed, when Martin came into his bedroom and switched on the light. "What happened to *you*?"

"I had a fight," Martin told him. "Listen—you'd better get back to sleep. Your grandparents will be home soon."

"Who did you fight with?" Emilio wanted to know. "Was it a ninja? Boy, I'll bet you got those cuts from a ninja throwing-star."

"It was a cat, as a matter of fact," Martin told him. He sat down on the end of Emilio's bed and dabbed at his face with his handkerchief. He was amazed by the amount of deep red blood that spattered all over it. "Am I hurt that bad?" he asked Emilio, and stood up to look in his He-Man mirror.

His face was appalling; like a newsreel photograph of somebody who had just been blown up by a terrorist bomb. His eyes were puffy, his cheeks were swollen, his whole face was crisscrossed with deep scratches. His ears were torn, and his left earlobe was almost hanging off, and dangled when he moved his head.

"You'd better get to the hospital," said Emilio sensibly.

Martin saw this grotesque, bloodied face nod back at him. "Yes," he said. "A-one idea." He couldn't understand why it didn't hurt more than it did, or why he was able to walk around and talk so sensibly when he looked so terrible.

Wanda came into the room, still white, pressing a bloodstained pad of toilet tissue to her lacerated cheek. "Oh, my God," she said, and her eyes were filled with tears. "I never knew a cat to do anything like that."

Martin dabbed at his face with his handkerchief. "I'm going down to the hospital, okay? I don't want to wind up like Van Gogh, with only one ear. Wanda— will you be all right?"

"I guess so," she said. "I'll call up my pop and tell him what's happened."

Martin lifted the tissue away from her face and examined her scratches. They were deep, but quite clean, and he hoped for everybody's sake that they wouldn't scar. He didn't relish the idea of being sued by Wanda's parents.

"Come on, you'll be okay," he told her, although he could feel her trembling through her jogging suit; that unstoppable shaking of the shocked, and the truly afraid.

He left the Capellis' apartment and went upstairs to get his car keys. When he reached the landing, he hesitated. Supposing the cat had worked itself free? Supposing he opened the front door and it came flying out at him, just as ferociously as it had before? He wiped his lips with the back of his hand, smearing his knuckles with blood and saliva. Then he cautiously reached out his hand and eased the door open.

The cat was hanging exactly where he had impaled it, its tail and its hind legs dangling, its front paws cocked, its flat anvil-shaped head lolling to one side. Dark rivulets of blood ran down the wall beneath it.

Martin tiptoed along the hallway until he was almost opposite it. Its eyes were closed, its mouth was silently snarling open. It didn't look at all like Lugosi.

It was a big brindled tom, with a heavy shaggy body and vicious claws. It stank of cat's urine and some other unutterable sourness that Martin couldn't even begin to recognize.

"You miserable sonofabitch," he told it between puffed-up lips. The cat had even managed to scratch his tongue.

He went into the sitting room. He tried the light switch again, and this time, unaccountably, it worked. He found his car keys gleaming under the desk. He made a point of not looking in the mirror. If everything in the mirror was the same as it was in here, then that was fine. If it wasn't, then he didn't want to know. Not now, not just yet. His ear was beginning to throb and his face felt as if it were already swollen up to three times its normal size.

He went back into the hallway. He wondered what he ought to do with the cat's body. He couldn't just leave it hanging there, but now that the adrenaline had all drained out of him, he found the thought of touching it almost too repulsive to think about.

But supposing Mr. Capelli came looking for him, when he was down at the hospital, and found it? There wouldn't be any question about it then. Immediate eviction—futon, desk, and typewriter straight out onto the street, no argument, so sue me.

In the kitchen drawer, Martin found a large green trash bag. He went back out to the hallway, rolled up the trash bag like a giant condom, and arranged it under the place where the cat was hanging. His idea was to yank out the screwdriver, whereupon the cat's body would drop neatly into the trash bag. He could then unroll the trash bag, twist-tie the top, and heave it out of his car on some dark and lonely stretch of the freeway.

He stood in front of the cat's body for a long time before he could summon up the courage to take hold of the screwdriver handle. *What's the matter with you, wimp? It's only a cat, and a dead cat at that.*

What's the matter? I'm scared shitless, that's what's the matter. I mean—where did it come from, this cat? The windows were locked, the door was locked, nobody else had a key. Where the hell did it come from, except out of the mirror?

Mr. Capelli's right. That mirror's driving you bananas. Get rid of it, before something comes shimmering out of it that gets rid of you.

He grasped the screwdriver handle tightly and tugged. Nothing happened. The blade was jammed too tight. *God almighty,* he thought, *I must have had the strength of ten men to dig this into the wall. But look at me now. Hundred-and-sixty-pound weakling.*

He placed the flat of his left hand firmly against the plaster, readjusted his grip on the screwdriver handle with his right hand, and tugged again.

The result was instantaneous. The cat's eyes flared open, and it screamed at him. He screamed, too, just as loudly.

The cat dropped. Martin fell backward, jarring his back against the handle of his bedroom door. But as quickly as he could, he bundled the green plastic around the writhing animal and twisted the top of the bag tight.

"Oh, God, please make it die," he gibbered. "Oh God oh God, please make it die."

But the cat twisted and turned and ripped furiously and noisily at the plastic with its claws, screaming all the time with a cry like a tortured baby.

Martin picked up the screwdriver, but dropped it again. It rolled across the floor, out of his reach. The cat savaged a long rent in the plastic. He saw its hate-filled face, with its mouth still stretched wide. He saw its eyes burning.

Crying out with effort, he lifted up the bag and twisted it tighter to keep the cat imprisoned inside it. Then he swung it around his head, once, twice, like a hammer thrower, and smashed it as hard as he could against the wall—and then smashed it again, and again, and again.

When the animal seemed to have stopped struggling, he dropped the bag onto the floor, scooped up his screwdriver, and crunched the blade into the cat's body over and over again, so many times that he completely lost count. Then he knelt back on his heels, gasping for breath.

"Oh, shit," he panted. "Oh, shit."

He dragged the bag toward the front door. It seemed impossibly heavy, just for a cat. But just as he was about to open up the door and heave the bag out, he heard voices. Italian voices, amplified with wine and indignation. The Capellis had arrived home.

"What's that? A cat? He doesn't have no cat! He's not allowed no cat! Terms of the lease! You need a doctor, you know that? Look, you're bleeding! What's your father going to say? Where's Martin? What do you mean, he's worse? What could be worse?"

Martin hesitated: then, with a rustling plasticky noise, he dragged the bag through to the kitchen, leaving calligraphic tracks of blood across the tiles. He took the lid off the big gray plastic trash bin and dropped the cat's body inside. He mopped up the floor with his squeegee mop. He felt like a murderer as he squeezed blood-streaked water into the sink. God, he thought, what was it like when you hacked up a human being? How did you ever get rid of the blood? The blood swirled around the sink like the shower stall in *Psycho*.

Mr. Capelli appeared at the door, flushed, sweating, smelling of brandy. "Martin?" he shouted; then, when Martin turned around, "My God! Look at you? What are you doing? My God!"

Martin leaned against the wall and gave Mr. Capelli a twist of his mouth that was intended to be a smile. "I'm okay, Mr. Capelli, I'm fine. I was just looking for my car keys—you know, to drive myself down to the hospital."

Mr. Capelli frowned at him and then held out his hands. Martin reached out to take hold of them, but somehow they weren't really there, and everything was black, and none of this really mattered, anyway.

He fell flat on his face on the kitchen floor, and he was lucky not to break his nose. Mr. Capelli dithered for a moment and then called down the stairs, "Wanda! Call for an ambulance! Tell them *pronto!*"

He woke up and the first thing that he could hear was clicking. *Clickety-click; clickety-clack;* pause; *clickety-click; clickety-clack*. He lifted his head, and there was Ramone, sitting cross-legged on one of those uncomfortable hospital chairs, furiously working at a Rubik's Magic. The blinds were closed, so that the room was very dim, although he could hear traffic and noise and all the sounds of a busy day. There were flowers everywhere, roses and orchids and huge apricot-colored daisies; and a blowfly was tapping against the window. He tried to speak, but his mouth felt as if it were fifty times the normal size, and he couldn't remember what you had to do to form words.

"Mamown . . ." he blurred. "Mamown . . ."

Ramone turned his head and peered at him. "Hey, man! You're still alive and kicking!" He put down his Rubik's Magic and came across to the bed. His black face loomed over Martin like a bulging-eyed fish looking out of an aquarium. "We all thought you was definitely ready for the coma room—you know, where you don't never wake up, so they cut your legs off and donate them to some rich South American rumba dancer with leg cancer."

"Can you see my legs dancing the rumba?" croaked Martin.

Ramone took hold of his hand and squeezed it. "Guess not, brother, but good to see you're alive. How do you feel?"

Martin tried to lift his head, but his scalp felt as if it had been sewn to the pillow. "Sore," he said. Then, "Jesus."

"Hey—Mr. Caparooparelli told me all about that *cat,*" said Ramone. "That was weird, man, that was definitely far out."

Martin asked. "Could you pour me some water? I can hardly swallow."

Ramone noisily poured him a large glass of Perrier. "It's not surprising you feel like that. It's the anesthetic, always makes you feel like shit. Remember when I totaled that Thunderbird? I was under for four hours, came out feeling like shit."

Martin drank, and then said, "How long was I . . . ?"

"Two and a half hours, man. They gave you thirty-eight stitches."

"Jesus," said Martin. He felt sore and swollen and inflated. He knew that he ought to be worried, too, and working on something or other—some TV script—but he was too drowsy to remember what it was.

"Mr. Caparoopadoopa got rid of the cat," said Ramone. "Dropped it in the trash outside the super-market. Let's just hope the good old Humane Society doesn't hunt him down."

"The cat . . . came through the mirror . . ." said Martin in a blurred voice. "Must have. *Must* have. No other way. Doors locked, windows locked."

"You truly think it came out of the *mirror*?" Ramone asked him. He added, in the Mr. T accent that both he and Martin could mimic, "Now, you listen here, suckah, I've had enough of this jibbah-jabbuh."

"But it's just like I said before," Martin insisted. "One for one. Tit for tat, cat for cat. Balance. Lugosi went into the mirror, and sooner or later some other poor cat had to come out."

"But that kitty cat wasn't anything *like* Lugosi."

"Doesn't matter," Martin told him. "The tennis ball and the rubber ball—they were just as—what do you call it? They were just as dissimilar."

"Dissimilar, right," agreed Ramone, "dis-simil-ah," and nodded; but then said, "What happens now? I mean you killed that cat, right? Does that mean Lugosi was killed in the mirrorland, or what? Is he still alive, or dead, or what?"

"That's just the question I've been asking," said Martin. "Not just about Lugosi, but Boofuls, too."

Ramone picked up his Rubik's Magic and flicked it a few times. "Oh, well, Boofuls, yeah. I haven't had the pleasure yet. If it *is* a pleasure."

Martin drank a little more water. Then he managed to lift himself up onto his elbows. "What time is it?"

"Three o'clock in the afternoon."

"I have to get out of here."

Ramone pushed him back onto the pillow. "You sure as hell don't. You have to stay here one more night, *compadre,* for observation. That's what they said. It's a good thing you got medical insurance."

"But the mirror."

"What about the jive mirror?"

"Mr. Capelli said he wanted it out. And not only that, he wanted it out by tonight. Supposing he does something lunatic, like smash it up or throw it on the dump? What's going to happen to Lugosi then? Or Boofuls, come to that?"

Ramone said, "You don't have to worry yourself about that, man. I already took care of that. I told Mr. Capacloopi that I was going to take the mirror off of your hands. I'm supposed to collect it later this afternoon and store it down at the Reel Thing."

"Will you do that?" asked Martin with relief.

"Sure I'll do it. That's unless some cat-out-of-hell comes jumping out of it and tries the same kind of number on *me* that it did on *you.*"

Martin reached out his hand. "You're a pal, Perez."

"Well, you're all heart, Mart."

Martin lay back and thought for a while, and then he said, "Do you know something? What we need is a medium."

"A medium what?" asked Ramone.

"I mean a medium medium. A clairvoyant. Somebody who can get in contact with the spirits."

"Are you pulling my leg?"

"No," Martin told him, "I'm serious. It seems to me that this mirror is acting like some kind of a *gateway,* do you know what I mean, between the real world and the spirit world. You can't tell me that Boofuls isn't a spirit, can you? And these mediums—they should be used to handling this kind of thing, shouldn't they? Like when they talk to the spirits, they create their own way through to the other side, right? I would have thought that any medium worth his money would jump at the chance of talking to the spirits the same way that Emilio talks to Boofuls. I mean to see the spirit as clearly as your hand in front of your face, that's something else."

"Seeing your favorite cat being swallowed up is something else, too," Ramone complained. "*And* seeing your main man looking like he's just come out of the ring with Ivan Drago. '*You will lose,*'" he said, imitating the Russian boxer in *Rocky IV*.

"Do you know anybody who's into that kind of thing?" said Martin.

Ramone shook his head. "Not me. But I know somebody who might know. One of my customers is Elmore Sweet—you know, the pianist. Liberace without the restraint. His mother died about two or three years ago, but every time he comes in he tells me that he's been rapping with Momsy about this or that. I used to think he'd lost his marbles at first, but then Dorothy Dunkley told me that he *gets in touch*, you know, with séances and everything."

"Good," said Martin. "So why don't you call him and ask him the name of his medium."

"I'll try."

There was a longer pause. Ramone checked his Spiro Agnew wristwatch. "Guess it's time I went back to the store. Kelly's okay, but she can be kind of remote. Also, she doesn't believe in responsibility. It's something to do with this sect she's gotten into. The Maharishi Nerdbrain or something."

"Take care," said Martin. "And thanks for looking after the mirror for me."

"It's not for you, my friend. It's for Lugosi. Wherever the poor bastard may be."

Martin spent a bad night at the hospital. The nurse had given him a sedative to help him sleep, and for three or four hours he slept as heavily as a lumberjack: but all the time his mind was alive with the most vivid and terrifying nightmares. He saw Boofuls—or something he thought was Boofuls—right at the very end of a long tunnel of mirrors. Just an arm, just a leg, just a fleeting glimpse; and then an echo of laughter that sounded melodious at first, and then rang as harshly as a butcher's knife on a butcher's steel.

"*Pickle-nearest-the-wind*," somebody whispered, so close and so distinct that he opened his eyes and looked around the room. "*Pickle-nearest-the-wind*."

Then he was running across a wide, well-mowed lawn, trying to catch up with a scampering boy dressed in lemon yellow. The day was bright. The boy was laughing. But then the boy disappeared behind a long row of cypress bushes; and a cloud dragged its gray skirts over the sun; and the laughter stopped.

Martin walked along the row of cypress bushes, slowly at first. "Boofuls?" he called. "Boofuls?"

He started to jog, and then to run. "Boofuls, where are you? Boofuls!"

"*Pickle-nearest-the-wind*," somebody whispered, and then again, faster, like a train gathering momentum. "*Pickle-nearest-the-wind*."

He ran even harder. He was terrified now. Something burst out of the cypress bushes right behind him and came running after him, just as fast, faster. He turned wild-eyed to see what it was, and it was a small boy, dressed in lemon yellow, but his face was the gilded face of Pan, snarling at him.

He stumbled, fell, rolled over; and then he woke up in bed sweating and clutching the bed rails. The nightmare garden faded; the cypresses were folded up like dark green tents and hurried away; the gilded face gleamed with momentary wickedness and then vanished.

He switched on his bedside light. Outside his door, two nurses and an orderly were loudly discussing next week's Hospital Hootenanny. Sirens wailed down by the casualty department as the victims of the night's violence were hurried in. Tragedy didn't sleep; anger didn't sleep; junkies and hookers didn't sleep; and neither did knives.

He called for the nurse. Nurse Newton opened his door; a huge black woman with an irrepressible smile who reassured him more than all the other nurses put together. "What is it now, Mr. Willy-ams?"

"Do you think you could bring me a bottle of red wine? It's the only thing that gets me to sleep."

"Red wine, Mr. Willy-ams? That's against regulations. And besides, you're up to your ears in sedatives."

"Nurse, I need some sleep."

Nurse Newton came over, took his temperature, and felt his pulse. "You're cold," she remarked, frowning. "How come you're so cold?"

"Nightmares," he said.

"Nightmares? Now, why should a big grown-up man like you have nightmares?"

Martin said, "God knows. I don't."

"Well, what are they about, these nightmares?"

"You're going to think I'm bananas."

Nurse Newton leaned over him and examined the dressings on his ear. "I'm a nurse, Mr. Willy-ams. I'm paid to take care of people, not to make judgments about their mental health. Mind you, I might think differently about you in my spare time."

Martin winced as she turned his head to one side. "Did you ever hear about a little boy called Boofuls?" he asked her. "He was a child star, back in the thirties."

Nurse Newton stared at him in surprise. "Why, what makes you ask that?"

"I just wanted to know, that's all."

"Well, of *course* I heard about Boofuls. Everybody knows about Boofuls here at the Sisters of Mercy."

Martin tried to sit up, but Nurse Newton pushed him back down again. "You stay put. You're not well enough yet to start hopping around."

"But what's so special about the Sisters of Mercy? How come everybody *here* knows about Boofuls?"

Nurse Newton took out his thermometer and frowned at it. "There's a kind of a spooky story about him, that's why. They brought his grandmother here, the evening she killed him."

"That's right. I mean—*I* know that, because I've been making a special study of Boofuls. But how come *you* know that, too?"

Nurse Newton smiled. "It's because of the spooky story, that's why. They tell it to all the nurses and the interns. Usually at the Christmas party, you know, at midnight, when it's all dark and there's just candles."

Martin said, "I thought I knew everything about Boofuls that it was possible to know. But I never heard any stories connected with the Sisters of Mercy."

Nurse Newton lifted her head and half closed her eyes, and said, "What was that song? *'Surrr . . . wannee Song! Suwannee Song! You can* blow *your flute and you can* bang *your drum and you can* march *along!'* That always used to make me cry when I was a child."

Martin nodded. "He was amazing, that little boy."

"But spooky," Nurse Newton added, lifting one finger.

"Can you tell me about it?" Martin asked her.

She winked. "You've been having nightmares about him. Do you think I should?"

"Nurse—listen—I'm the world's expert on Boofuls. If there's something about Boofuls that I don't know—!"

Nurse Newton shook the mercury back down her thermometer with three decisive flicks of her wrist. "Well . . ." she confessed, "don't tell any of the hospital administrators that I told you this. I might get myself into big trouble. The board don't want the paying patients getting hysterical; and, believe me, if you told this story to some of the banana trucks on this floor, they would. Get hysterical, I mean."

She jotted a note on Martin's chart and then sniffed and shook her head. "Besides," she said, "you shouldn't speak ill of the dead, that's what my mamma always used to tell me. Someone who's dead can't defend theirselves."

"Supposing I take you to dinner," Martin coaxed her.

Nurse Newton whacked the side of her thigh in hilarity. "*You*—take *me* for dinner! With all those bandages on your face? Talk about the Invisible Man meets Winifred Atwell! Besides, I'd *eat* you for dinner!"

"Supposing I arrange for you to meet Mr. T, in person," said Martin much more subtly. "I write for the *A-Team*. You could meet him in person. I don't know— lunch, dinner. Maybe a little dancing later."

Nurse Newton stared at him narrowly. "You could do that?"

"Of course I could do that! I've known him for years.

Mr. T and I, we're like this!" and he held up two inter-twined fingers.

"You're not fooling?"

"Cross my heart and hope to die."

"You shouldn't say that. Nobody should hope to die. But could you do that? Me and Mr. T?"

Martin nodded. "You and Mr. T. Just say the word."

Nurse Newton glanced over her shoulder, almost as if she expected the hospital governors to be standing right behind her. "Well," she said quietly, "I wasn't even born when this happened, don't you forget, so no smart remarks."

"It was 1939," said Martin. "August 1939."

Nurse Newton nodded. "Some of the older staff can still remember it. Dr. Rice remembers it, he was an intern in those days; and Sister Boniface remembers it, too. Like I say, they used to tell us all about it at the Christmas party. I guess it was just a ghost story. But they used to sound so serious, you couldn't help believing it, you know? And they made us all promise not to say nothing to nobody, never. Maybe they were worried about libel or something."

Martin said, "I don't think you have to worry about libel. You can't libel the dead, and Boofuls has been dead for a very long time."

The nurse shrugged. "Hmh, that didn't seem to make too much difference. His being dead, I mean."

"What do you mean by that?" asked Martin.

"Oh, come on, now," said Nurse Newton. "It's nothing but a story, really. Every hospital has its spooky stories. There's a lot of stress in hospitals. Lot of *death*, too."

"Story or not, I'd like to hear it."

Nurse Newton went over to the door, listened for a

moment, and then closed it tight. She came tippy-toe-ing back over to the bed. "It was just after Boofuls was found dead," she whispered. "The police had cut his grandmother down—you know she tried to hang her-self?—and brought her here. They thought she was dead, and Dr. Rice said they should have let her die, because her neck was broken, and her throat was so bruised and swollen that she could barely speak. But she was still alive; and I guess they thought they might have a million-in-one chance of saving her."

She hesitated and smiled. "Boofuls, of course—they took him straight to the mortuary. There was nothing else that anybody could do. Can you imagine trying to sew him all back together? Dr. Rice said he was chopped up into two hundred and eleven separate pieces. The coroner had to count them all; and there were still bits of him they couldn't even find. Dr. Rice said that it was a joke for months in the hospital com-missary—anytime somebody found a bone in their pork chop, they'd pick it up on the end of their fork and say, "Hello, piece number two hundred and twelve! Well, you know what doctors are. Doctors have the sickest sense of humor of anybody."

"Boofuls' grandmother didn't say anything before she died?" asked Martin. "I mean—the police say that she didn't, but maybe one of the nurses heard her."

Nurse Newton shook her head. "She died pretty soon after they brought her into the hospital; that's what Sister Boniface said, and she was sitting beside her when she died. I don't think she said anything at all, except that she called out a couple of times for Boofuls."

"So what's this spooky story?" asked Martin.

"Listen, mister—three nurses and two doctors all

saw Boofuls walking around the hospital that night, calling for his grandma. *'Grandma! Grandma! Where are you?'"*

"What do you mean—*after* he was supposed to be dead? After he was chopped up into two hundred eleven pieces?"

Nurse Newton nodded. "That's what's so spooky. Isn't that spooky?"

Martin considered it. "Yes," he said. "That's spooky. But didn't any of them report it? Didn't they tell the newspapers, or the police, or the hospital authorities?"

"Would you?" asked Nurse Newton.

Martin patted his bandages. "No," he admitted. "I guess not."

Nurse Newton leaned forward and plumped up Martin's pillows. "Of course, what was spookiest of all was that every time one of the nurses or the doctors caught sight of him, they'd go after him—you know, imagining that he was a real boy—but every time they got to where he was at, they realized that he wasn't there at all. What they could see was just a reflection in one of the mirrors at the end of the corridors."

This time, Martin sat bolt upright. "They saw Boofuls in the *mirrors?*"

"Hey, now, calm down," Nurse Newton urged him. "You don't want to go getting yourself so waxed up. You'll split your stitches."

"They saw Boofuls in the mirrors—nowhere else?"

"Well, that's right, that's what Dr. Rice says; and he was one of the doctors who saw it. But you're not supposed to know about this. It's just one of those little bits of hospital history, you know? Like, Ripley's Believe It or Not."

Martin swung his legs out of bed. "I have to talk to this Dr. Rice. Can you find him for me?"

"Come on, honky, this is the middle of the night. Dr. Rice is at home, getting his ugly-sleep. And you need yours, too. Now, you just get yourself back in that bed before I do you a physical injury they'll *never* be able to stitch together."

Martin's heart was racing. "Listen," he said, "I'll get back into bed on one condition—that as soon as Dr. Rice gets here in the morning, he comes in to see me. Now, is that a promise?"

"Mr. Willy-ams, I can't promise anything like that."

"Then so help me God, I'll scream. I'll scream so loud that the whole goddamned hospital will wake up."

"My goodness, Felicity-Ann!" said Nurse Newton. "Aren't you the fierce person? But all right, I'll go right down to Dr. Rice's office now, and I'll leave him a message. He doesn't come in till eleven o'clock, he only does consultancy these days. But I'll do my best to get him up here right away."

"Nurse Newton, you're an angel."

Nurse Newton forced him back onto the pillow. "I am not an angel, Mr. Willy-ams. I am a *nurse*."

Martin dozed for the rest of the night. His nightmares rushed through his head like a carousel that had broken away from its moorings; dark and urgent, wild and clamorous, the carnival rides of the mind.

He dreamed that he was running down a long sliding corridor; and at the very end of that corridor stood Boofuls, smiling and innocent. As he approached, however, Boofuls' head began to revolve on his neck, slowly at first, with a low grating noise, then faster and faster, until it began to spray out blood. A fine drizzle of gore.

Martin shouted out, and woke up; or thought he had woken up. He sat up in bed, listening. He could hear someone whispering outside the door of his hospital room. *"Pickle-di-pickle-di-pickle-di-pickle."*

He stayed where he was, listening, sweating. Then he climbed out of bed and glided toward the door with his hand outstretched. *"Pickle-nearest-the-wind,"* giggled the voice outside in the corridor.

Slowly, fearfully, he turned the handle and opened the door. There was nobody there: only the black, echoing corridor, only the distant whooping of sirens. Tragedy never sleeps, knives never sleep. *"Martin,"* whispered the tiny wee voice. *"Come on, Martin, don't be afraid. Why are you afraid, Martin?"*

He stepped out into the corridor. At the very far end, he saw Boofuls. Small and smiling, sweet as candy, sugar-dandy, but in some peculiar way more dwarflike and crunched up than he had appeared in the mirror in Martin's sitting room. Boofuls looked white: so white that his face could have been poured out of alabaster.

"Are you afraid, Martin?" he whispered. His voice and his lips didn't seem to synchronize, like a badly dubbed film. He stretched out his arms, a young messiah. *"You don't have to be afraid of anything."*

It was then that Martin realized that Boofuls wasn't standing on the floor at all, but was suspended halfway between the floor and the ceiling. Martin's hair prickled in fear, but something compelled him to start running toward Boofuls, to catch him, to prove at last that he was nothing more than a memory.

Boofuls laughed as Martin waded toward him through the treacle of his nightmare. A sweet, high laugh that echoed and reechoed until it sounded like thousands of pairs of clashing scissors. Martin reached the end of the corridor at last, and reached out to Boofuls to snatch him down from his invisible crucifix.

But—with a cold and bruising collision—he came up against a sheet of frigid plate glass. Boofuls laughed at him. He was nothing more than an image in a mirror— a reflection of a boy who was long dead.

Martin struck out wildly, shouting and kicking and thrashing his arms. "Boofuls! Boofuls! For God's sake, Boofuls!"

Dr. Ewart Rice poured himself another cup of lemon tea. The late morning sunshine played softly through the rising steam and across the olive-green leather of his desk. There was such quiet in his office, and such tranquillity in his manner, that Martin felt almost as if he had found a sanctuary, and this was its priest.

"You're sure you won't have another cup?" Dr. Rice asked him. He was a thin, drawn man, with a beak of a nose and furiously tangled white eyebrows. He wore a brown tweed suit, and a very clean soft shirt in tatter-sall check. There was the faintest lilt of Scottishness in his accent; a great precision in the way he pronounced his words.

"We tell the story for amusement, of course," he explained, tapping his spoon on the side of his teacup. "But I suppose, in a way, we also tell it as a ritual of faith. Because it *did* happen, you know. We *did* see Boofuls, all five of us. We all decided that it would be worse than useless to tell the newspapers or the police. At the very least, we would have been laughed at. At the very worst, we might have ruined our careers. But it was real enough, don't you know, the first and last time that any of us had seen what you might describe as a ghost, and that was why we embroidered it into a hospital legend."

He smiled. "I suppose you could say that by keeping

the story alive, we were exorcising the ghost. An annual ritual of bell, book, and candle. Or, at the very least, a way of reassuring ourselves that we hadn't all gone mad."

"You're not mad," Martin told him.

Dr. Rice sipped his tea and then set his cup down. "You seem very certain about that."

Martin nodded. "I am. Because *I'm* not mad, and I've seen Boofuls, too."

"*You've* seen him?" Dr. Rice asked with care. "I suppose by that you mean recently?"

Martin said, "I've been a Boofuls fan ever since I was young. I'm a screenwriter now; I write for movies and television. I've written a musical based on his life—not that I've managed to sell it yet. In Hollywood, the name of Boofuls seems to carry a built-in smell of its own. The smell of failure, if you know what I mean."

Dr. Rice said, "Aye," and sipped more tea.

"This week, I bought the mirror that used to hang over Boofuls' fireplace," Martin explained. "Ever since then, I've had nothing but trouble."

"And you say you've *seen* him?"

"In the mirror, yes. And that's why I wanted to talk to you."

Dr. Rice said, "Yes, I can see why. It's all very disturbing. As a rule, I am not a believer in mysterious occurrences. I am a gynecologist; and once you have seen the mystery of human creation repeated over and over again in front of your eyes, then I am afraid that, by comparison, other mysteries tend to dwindle into insignificance."

"I don't think there's anything insignificant about this mystery," Martin told him, and explained about the two mismatched balls; and how Emilio had tried

to step into the mirror; and what had happened to
Lugosi.

"I'm in the hospital because of that mirror," said
Martin. "I've had thirty-eight stitches, and I could have
been killed. That's not insignificant to me."

Dr. Rice was silent for a long time, his soft, withered
hands lying in his lap like fallen chestnut leaves. When
he spoke, his voice was quiet and controlled, but that
made his account of what had happened on the night
that Mrs. Alicia Crossley was brought in to the Sisters
of Mercy sound even more frightening.

"There was, of course, enormous excitement. The
press were everywhere. The lobby was filled with reporters and photographers and cameramen from the
movie newsreels. I arrived at seven o'clock for my
night duty, and I had to struggle to get into the building."

He paused, and then he said, "Mrs. Crossley died
around eight o'clock, I think. After that, there were a
few hours of comparative quiet, because the press had
all rushed off to file their stories for the morning edi-
tions. I was on the gynecological floor, that's floor five.
There were two babies being delivered that night, so I
was constantly to-ing and fro-ing between the two delivery rooms."

"Is that when you saw Boofuls?" asked Martin.

Dr. Rice said, "Yes. It was a quarter of ten. I was
walking along the corridor between what they used to
call Delivery Room B and the main stairs when I saw a
small boy standing at the end of the corridor, looking
lost. I called out to him, but he didn't seem to hear me.
He was crying, and saying 'Grandma, where's
grandma?' over and over.

"I went right up to him. I was as close to him as you

and I are sitting now. Closer, maybe. I put my hand out, I could see what was right in front of my eyes, but somehow my brain wouldn't believe it. I put my hand out to touch him even though he was standing not outside but *inside* the mirror. The mirror was like a glass door, no more; or a window. It was completely impossible; it couldn't happen. It flew right in the face of everything I'd ever understood about science, about the world, about what can exist and what can't exist. And, believe me, this couldn't exist, but there it was, right in front of my eyes.

"The boy had stopped crying, and he had covered his face with his hands, and was playing peek-a-boo through his fingers. I shouted at him, 'Can you hear me?' two or three times, and then at last he took his hands away from his face. I wish he hadn't."

Martin sat back, waiting for Dr. Rice to finish, knowing that it took extra courage for him to explain what he had seen.

"His face looked normal at first. A little pale, maybe, but in those days a lot of children used to suffer from anemia. But then suddenly something red and thin started to dangle from his nostril, then another, then another, until they were dropping out onto the floor. He opened his mouth and stuck out his tongue, and his whole tongue was wriggling with them. Meat worms, the kind that eat corpses. They were pouring out of him everywhere. I expect you can understand that I dropped my clipboard and my smart new stethoscope and ran outside. I was in a terrible state."

"Do you think it was some kind of hallucination?" asked Martin. "After all, everybody knew that Boofuls was dead; there was mass hysteria; and you were right there in the thick of it."

Dr. Rice smiled ruefully. "Don't you think I've asked myself that same question a thousand times? Was it a hallucination? Was it a dream? Was it tiredness? But no, my friend, I'm afraid not. I saw Boofuls quite clearly. I was in perfectly sound health, well rested, no hangovers. I couldn't afford to drink in those days! The only conceivable explanation as far as I'm concerned was that he was really there. Or, at least, that his *spirit* was really there."

"Do you believe in spirits?" asked Martin.

"Do you?" Dr. Rice retaliated.

"I don't *dis*believe in them, let's put it that way. Especially now that I've seen Boofuls."

Dr. Rice said, "Altogether, five of us saw him. Well— I believe six, but one of the nurses refused to admit that she'd seen anything out of the ordinary. All five of us had similar experiences—that is, we all saw Boofuls weeping in a mirror—all at approximately the same time, about a quarter of ten, but what makes the whole affair so fascinating is that we were all on different floors, and two out of the five who saw him I didn't even know."

Martin cautiously touched his bandaged chin. "So there could have been no—what would you call it?— group hysteria, something like that? I mean you didn't get together and discuss the Boofuls murder to the point where you all temporarily flipped?"

Dr. Rice shook his head. "There was no 'flipping' that night, I can assure you. I had to drink three large Scotches one after the other, just to reassure myself that I wasn't completely losing my reason."

"The other doctors and nurses—are they still here?"

"Only Sister Boniface. The rest, I regret, have passed

on. Cirrhosis, cancer, auto accident; a fair cross section of modern fatalities."

"Can I speak to Sister Boniface?"

"You may, if you wish; but her sighting was extremely brief. She had been sitting with Mrs. Crossley before she died; and after her death she stayed to do the usual tidying up. She was covering Mrs. Crossley's face with a sheet when she thought she heard a noise, just above her head. She looked up, and there was Boofuls—well, *lying,* as it were, on the ceiling. She screamed, and the police guard came in, and Boofuls vanished."

Dr. Rice picked up a gold mechanical pencil from his desk and began to turn it end over end. "It disturbed her deeply, seeing Boofuls like that. Who would ever believe that she had seen a dead boy smiling at her from the ceiling? She went quite to pieces. Well—it was only our annual storytelling rituals that helped her to keep her feelings in perspective. She's a poor soul, Sister Boniface, and no mistake."

Martin looked at Dr. Rice narrowly. "What do *you* think of all this?" he asked him bluntly. "I mean, is it bullshit, or are we all going crazy, or what?"

Dr. Rice gave him a tight smile. "I saw what I saw, Mr. Williams. You saw what you saw. To each, his own experience. Let us simply say that no one can take that experience away from us, no matter how unhinged they think we might be."

He raised his head and looked at Martin benignly. "Either we were all witnesses to an extraordinary manifestation—the power of love, perhaps, to extend beyond the moment of death—or else we are all quite mad."

Martin sniffed, and found it painful. "Welcome to the nuthouse, in other words."

*   *   *

Sister Boniface was taking her lunch in the hospital
gardens when they found her. She was sitting in the
shade of an Engelmann oak, eating a vege-burger out
of a polystyrene box. She was so thin that she was almost transparent; with rimless spectacles; and a face
that looked like Woody Allen if he had been seventy
years old, and a nun. She blinked as Martin and Dr.
Rice approached, and closed her lunch box, as if she
had been caught doing something indiscreet.

"Hello, Sister," said Dr. Rice. "This is Martin Williams. Martin, this is Sister Boniface. Martin writes for
television, Sister."

"Yes?" Sister Boniface smiled. "How do you do, Mr.
Williams? You're not writing one of those hospital series, are you? *St. Elsewhere?* Something like that?"

Martin shook his head. "You watch all of those
things? Do you know something, I can never imagine
nuns watching television."

"We tend not to *collectively,*" said Sister Boniface.
"The wimples get in the way."

"Humorist, too," Dr. Rice muttered out of the side of
his mouth. "You know what I mean?"

Sister Boniface said, with some precision, "You came
about Boofuls."

Martin glanced at Dr. Rice. "How did you know
about that?"

"Well, Mr. Williams, all hospitals have their grapevines. I understand you had nightmares last night;
Nurse Newton told me. Naturally, I asked her whether
you were suffering from any particular anxieties—and,
well, Nurse Newton is an excellent nurse, but not dis-
creet."

Martin was sweating. The midday sun was hot; and
the salt from his perspiration irritated his stitches.

"I understand that you saw Boofuls in his grand-mother's room, the night she died."

Sister Boniface nodded, her starched wimple waving up and down like a snow-white sea gull. "That is correct."

"He was floating on the ceiling, right?"

"That is quite correct. He was floating on the ceiling."

Her voice was so equable that when she looked up at Martin and her eyes were filled with tears, he was taken by surprise. She put aside her vege-burger and reached out her hand and clutched the sleeve of his shirt. "Oh, Mr. Williams, that poor child! It still haunts me now!"

Dr. Rice said, "Mr. Williams has seen Boofuls, too, Sister Boniface, just this week."

"Then you *believe*?" asked Sister Boniface, her eyes widening.

"Well, of course I believe," said Martin. "I saw—"

Sister Boniface awkwardly climbed onto her knees on the Pebble Paving. "Mr. Williams, all these years, it's been such a trial! Whether to believe in it or not! A miracle, a vision, right in front of my eyes!"

Martin knelt down beside her and gently helped her up onto her feet again. Underneath her voluminous white robes, she felt as skeletal as a bird. "Sister Boniface, I'm not at all sure that it's a miracle. I don't know what it is. I'm trying to find out. But I'm not at all sure that it's—well, I'm not at all sure that it comes from God."

Sister Boniface reached out her long-fingered hand and gently touched Martin's cheek. "You are a good man," she said. "I can feel it in you. But it had to be a miracle. What else? He was floating on the ceiling, smiling at me. As clear as daylight."

"He didn't speak?" asked Martin.

"No, nothing," said Sister Boniface. "He was there for a second, then he was gone."

"You screamed?"

"Of course I screamed! I was very frightened."

"Well, sure, of course you were. What with Mrs. Crossley's body and everything."

Sister Boniface sat up straight. "I am not frightened by death, Mr. Williams. I am frightened only by the face of pure goodness; and by the face of pure evil."

"How long did you stay with Mrs. Crossley that evening?" Martin wanted to know.

Sister Boniface shrugged. "They asked me to come into the room to help with the last rites. Mrs. Crossley was a Catholic, you know. Afterward . . . well, I just stayed where I was, helping, until it was time for them to take her away."

Martin slowly massaged the back of his neck. This was getting him nowhere at all. He had learned that Boofuls had appeared as a mirror-ghost on the night he was murdered; but he had learned nothing at all about why he had been killed; and how he had gotten into the mirror-world, or why he should have decided to reappear now.

"You've been very helpful," he told Sister Boniface. "I'm sorry if I brought it all back to you."

Sister Boniface smiled distantly. "You haven't brought it back to me, Mr. Williams. I never forget it. I never stop thinking about it. Was I visited by God, do you think, or by the devil? I fear that I shall never know. Not in this life, anyway."

Martin hesitated for a moment, and then bent his head forward and kissed her hand. Her skin was dry and soft, like very fine tissue paper.

"There is one thing," she said.

Martin looked up. Sister Boniface's eyes were unfocused, as if she were trying to distance herself from what she was going to say next.

"What is it?" he asked her.

"I was the only member of the hospital staff who stayed with Mrs. Crossley from the moment she was brought into the hospital to the moment she died."

"And?"

"She didn't speak," said Sister Boniface. "But she did regain consciousness for a very short time. She lay there, staring at the ceiling, gasping for breath. Then, when she and I were alone together for a short while, she beckoned me closer. She pointed toward her bracelet, which they had taken off when they first tried to resuscitate her, but which was still lying on the table beside the bed. It was a charm bracelet, with little gold figures of cats and moons and stars on it. But there was a key attached to it, too; quite an ordinary key. She gestured that I should take the key off the bracelet, and when I had done so, she pressed it into my hand, and closed my fingers over it."

Sister Boniface reached under the folds of her habit and took out a small leather change purse. She opened it up, and reached inside, and produced a small steel key. "This is the very key, Mr. Williams."

"I see . . . what does it unlock?"

"I have absolutely no idea. Mrs. Crossley did nothing more than press it on me, insisting that I keep it. Her throat was almost completely closed, poor thing, and she could scarcely catch her breath, let alone speak. But it seemed as if the key were terribly important, because she kept staring at me and trying to nod, and catching at my sleeve."

Martin said, "May I?" and took the key out of Sister

Boniface's hand. It was small and plain, with the number 531 punched on it. He turned it over. The manufacturer's name, Woods Key, was embossed on it, but that was all. There was no clue where it might have come from, or what door it might have fitted.

"Whatever secret this key was guarding, it probably vanished years ago," said Dr. Rice.

Martin said, "It looks like a suitcase key. No—maybe it's a little too big for that. A locker room key, what do you think? Or the key to a cash box?"

"Could be anything," said Dr. Rice. "Sister Boniface showed it to us before, and we tried it on every locker and cupboard we could find. We thought we might discover a hidden fortune, I suppose. Pretty fruitless exercise. All it proved was that it didn't fit any of the lockers in the hospital. I think Dr. Weddell took it down to the bus depot one afternoon and tried locker number 531 there, but that was no use. It didn't fit the lockers at any of the local airports, either."

"Well, it's probably a bank key or a hotel safe-deposit key," said Martin. "In which case we have about as much chance of finding it as a—" He was about to say "cat in hell," but he suddenly thought of that stinking brindled tomcat snatching at his eyes, and he left his sentence unfinished. Despite the midday heat, he shivered, and felt uncomfortably cold.

Sister Boniface said, "Mr. Williams, why don't you keep that key? Perhaps you can find the lock it fits. You are the one who is closest to Boofuls now. Perhaps Boofuls himself will tell you."

Dr. Rice laid a hand on Martin's shoulder. "Go on, take it," he said. "It'll make her feel happy."

"Sure," Martin agreed, and slipped the key into his pocket.

They walked back across the hospital courtyard. Martin turned around, shielding his eyes against the sunlight. Sister Boniface had returned to her vege-burger and was placidly munching it.

"She's tormented, you see," said Dr. Rice. "She can't decide if she's been blessed with a vision of heaven or cursed with a glimpse of hell."

Martin took out the key. He felt, oddly, that he had always been meant to have it; in the same way that he had been meant to buy the mirror. He also felt that— one day soon—he was going to discover what lock it fitted, what secret it hid. The trouble was, he wasn't at all sure that he wanted to know.

Five

HE DROVE BACK to his apartment late that afternoon to find a rusty blue and white pickup parked outside and Ramone arguing with Mr. Capelli in the front yard.

"Hey, what's going on?" he asked, slamming his car door and crossing the sidewalk.

Mr. Capelli immediately looked around. "They let you out of the hospital? Look at you! You look like the curse of the mummy's tomb!"

"Thanks, Mr. Capelli, I feel better already. What's wrong here? Didn't Ramone pick up the mirror?"

"He says he can't," Mr. Capelli interjected before Ramone could open his mouth. "He says it's too heavy, he can't lift it, and *I* can't help him, my doctor will do worse to me than that cat did to you."

Ramone lit a cheroot and inhaled the smoke up his nostrils. "This guy thinks I'm Arnold Schwarzeneggs-benedict or something."

"Oh, come on, Ramone," said Martin. "The mirror's

heavy but it's not *that* heavy. I moved it myself the other evening."

"Well, maybe you did, but you must of been taking some kind of evening classes in You Too Can Have a Body Like Mine. *I* can't shift it, and that's all there is to it, and if you want to call me Mr. Weak'n'weedy, well, there's nothing I can do about it, because, man, that mirror will not *move*."

Mr. Capelli tugged and twisted at the crocodile on his Lacoste T-shirt. It was a nervous habit, that was all. When he wasn't wearing a Lacoste T-shirt, he twisted his back hair around his finger. "This fellow, he doesn't even try! You and me, Martin, didn't we carry that mirror inside the house, just you and me, and God knows what kind of a physical shape *I'm* in! I surprise myself I'm not dead!"

"Plenty of people your age are," Ramone retorted. "And some of them *ain't*, and should be."

"Come on, let's take a look," said Martin. "Ramone and I can probably manage it between us."

"Thinks I'm Arnold Schwarzenfriedeggs," Ramone grumbled as he followed Martin and Mr. Capelli upstairs.

They reached Martin's apartment. The door was open, and they could hear singing. High, piping singing—Emilio. Martin stopped and listened, and felt a sudden surge of fear. "I thought I told you not to let Emilio up here, for Christ's sake!" he barked at Mr. Capelli, and he bounded up the last flight of steps three and four at a time.

"*Sur . . . wannee Song! Suwannee Song!*" Emilio was singing.

Martin burst into the room. The door shuddered. Emilio was marching up and down in front of the mirror, his head held high, his elbows swinging, his knees prancing like a young circus horse.

"You can blow your flute and you can bang your drum and you can march along!"

Martin turned toward the mirror. For one fraction of a fraction of a fraction of an instant, he thought he glimpsed Boofuls, prancing up and down the mirrored sitting room. But then all he could see was Emilio's own reflection, brown eyes bright, dark hair shining.

"Sur . . . wannee Song! Suwannee Song!"

"Emilio?" said Martin.

Emilio stopped marching and turned around. "Hey, look at you!" he gasped. "You look just like the mummy!"

"Thank you," said Martin. "But didn't I tell you not to come up here anymore?"

"He wanted to play, that's all," Emilio protested.

"Hey, now—*who* wanted to play?" Mr. Capelli demanded. "There's nobody here, just you and us."

"Well, Mickey Mouse, of course," Emilio replied, wrinkling up his nose in sarcasm. Without hesitation, Mr. Capelli pushed his way past Martin and slapped Emilio hard across the side of the head.

"You don't talk like that to your elder-better! You dare! You want to grow up to be a deadbeat?"

"The way he's going, I think he's probably going to grow up to be President," remarked Ramone laconically.

"That's what I mean!" Mr. Capelli retorted.

Emilio's eyes were wet with tears. He rubbed his head and said, "I'm sorry, Grandpa. But he was here. That boy, Boofuls. He learned me that song."

Mr. Capelli clutched Emilio close and affectionately scruffed his hair. "Eh . . . I'm sorry, too. It's my fault.

Martin told me not to let you come up here. Eh, no crying, unh? I'm just your silly old grandpa."

But Emilio struggled free from his grandpa's embrace and turned toward the mirror. "He's gone," he said sadly. "You frightened him away."

Mr. Capelli chuckled and shook his head. "Some imagination, hunh?" But he looked toward Martin, and Martin could see the anxiety in his eyes. Mr. Capelli believed in things that lived in mirrors; and Mr. Capelli was afraid of them.

"Now, then, let's get this mirror out of here, hey?" Mr. Capelli suggested. "You can take one end, Ramone; and you can take the other end, Martin; and lift; and then I can direct you down the stairs."

Ramone said, "I've got a better idea. You carry it downstairs on your own and we'll just sit here and watch you."

Nonetheless, Ramone and Martin bent down on each side of the mirror and prepared to lift it up. Ramone had already taken out the screws and laid a blanket on the floor to protect the gilt frame, and so all they had to do was pick up the mirror and carry it down to the street.

"When I say three!" announced Mr. Capelli.

He counted three, and they lifted. Or they tried to lift. But they couldn't budge the mirror even half an inch off the floor. It felt as if it had been nailed down.

"Come on, Ramone, let's try it again," said Martin; and they grunted and heaved; but still the mirror refused to move.

Martin propped his elbow against the mirror and puffed out his cheeks in exhaustion. "I don't understand this. I mean, this is ridiculous. If Mr. Capelli and I could carry it up three flights of stairs and screw it up on the wall, then you'd think that you and I could lift it between us—I mean, easily."

"You're out of shape, that's all," said Mr. Capelli.

"Who's out of shape?" Ramone demanded. "I play two hours of squash every afternoon, and I don't even get out of breath!"

"Sure, but what do you have to lift in squash? Just that little racket. That doesn't weigh nothing at all."

Ramone lifted up his arms in resignation, then dropped them again, like one of the crows in *Dumbo* flapping its wings. "*Me duele!* What can you do with a man who thinks like this?"

"Come on, Ramone, let's give it another try," Martin suggested.

"You don't get that mirror out of here, I'm going to call professional removers, and charge you what it costs, *and* throw you out, too!" Mr. Capelli yelled at him.

"Come on, Ramone," Martin urged him. "He's getting into one of his Don Corleone moods."

"Schwarzeneggburger," Ramone growled under his breath.

They took hold of the mirror. Mr. Capelli chanted, "One-a, two-a, three-a—"

Without a word, both Martin and Ramone released their grip, and stood up, and stepped away. They looked into each other's eyes; and each of them knew that the other had shared his experience.

When they had tried to lift the mirror, a strong dark wave had gone through each of their minds, black and inhuman but undeniably alive, like centipede legs rippling, or the cilia of some soulless sea creature, cold, pressurized, an intelligence without emotion and without remorse and with no interest in anything at all but its own supremacy and its own survival.

For the first time, Martin felt that he had touched the very core of the mirror's existence, and it was more pitiless than anything he could have imagined.

Martin and Ramone stood facing each other, as stunned and subdued as if they had experienced an unexpected electric shock. But there was no question in either of their minds what that wave of feeling had been intended to tell them. They had been categorically ordered by whatever lived in the mirror to leave it where it was.

Mr. Capelli was not so insensitive that he couldn't appreciate that something had gone badly wrong—that some feeling of hostility had suddenly caused them to back away.

"What is it?" he demanded. "Martin—what is it?"

"I don't know," Martin told him. "I'm sorry, Mr. Capelli, I don't know. But I'm not touching that mirror again, not just now."

"Well, what?" Mr. Capelli shouted. "What do you mean, you're not touching it again? Why? What's the reason? Why don't you touch it again?"

Ramone said plainly, "This mirror, Mr. Caparooparelli—this mirror wants to stay right here. This mirror does not plan to be moved. Not that we *can* move it. I mean, we're too weak, right? We can only lift squash rackets, and suchlike. We can only lift stuff that is seriously deficient in avoirdupois."

Mr. Capelli stood rigid, his hands by his sides, the blood draining from his face so that he looked quite waxy, and his head too big for his body.

"All right," he said. "You brought this mirror here, what are you going to do?"

"I don't know," Martin confessed. "If I *could* get rid of it, right now I believe that I would. Boofuls or not."

"Boofuls," said Mr. Capelli, keeping his false teeth clenched close together. "That's the problem, right? Boofuls. That woman, she killed that little boy, she chopped him into millions of pieces—"

"Two hundred eleven, I'm reliably informed," put in Martin, but he wasn't joking.

Mr. Capelli spat out of the side of his mouth. "How many exactly, who cares? But his spirit is here! His ghost! You found him a home, and now he doesn't want to go! And so what do I have? I have a house that's haunted, that's what! A haunted house with a ghost!"

"Maybe we should go get ourselves a priest," Ramone suggested.

"I thought you were looking for a medium," Martin reminded him.

"A priest, yes!" Mr. Capelli enthused. "A priest!"

"We could get both," said Ramone. "A priest *and* a medium."

"Oh, God, this is ridiculous," Martin told him. "I don't know what to do. Maybe the best thing we can do is do nothing. Just wait it out, see what the mirror wants."

It was then that—without warning—the blue and white ball dropped off Martin's desk and bounced onto the wood-block floor—once, twice, three times. Then it rolled toward the mirror, almost as if the floor were tilting, like the deck of a ship. At the same time, the dirty gray tennis ball dropped off the desk in the mirror and came rolling to meet it.

"Something's happening, man," warned Ramone. "Something's happening. I can feel it."

None of them knew what to do. But they could all feel the air in the sitting room *warping* almost; like ripples of heat rising from a hot blacktop; or the distortion of a highly polished sheet of thin steel. Their voices sounded strange, too—muffled and indistinct.

"It's *pulling*," said Martin. "Can you feel that? It's pulling things toward it."

They didn't notice Emilio at first. He had been standing two or three feet behind his grandfather, staring at the mirror wide-eyed. Gradually, however, he began to move forward, his arms by his sides; and as he passed them by he started to laugh, an extraordinary high-pitched laugh just like Boofuls.

At once, Martin turned around. "Emilio?" he said. Then, *"Emilio!"*

"Holy God!" Mr. Capelli cried out.

Emilio was sliding toward the mirror without even moving his feet. He was being drawn toward it as if it were an irresistible magnet.

"Emilio!" Mr. Capelli shouted, and tried to snatch him.

Emilio threw both his arms wide and tossed back his head, and his laugh was loud and metallic like garden shears. In the mirror, his reflection slid toward him just as irresistibly, but there was something in his reflected face that didn't match his real face. Something different, something whiter, something smaller-eyed, piggy, untrustworthy, something that jumped and smirked like a face from a long-forgotten movie.

"Ramone!" Martin yelled; and Ramone dodged, and feinted, and caught hold of Emilio's arm at the very moment that Emilio collided with the surface of the mirror. Emilio screamed: a hideous piercing scream that went through Martin's head like a chisel. He

thrashed and clawed and kicked at Ramone, and it took all of Ramone's strength to hold him.

"*Bastard!*" Emilio screamed. "*Bastard!*"

"Emilio, what are you doing! Emilio!" Mr. Capelli quivered and tried to snatch Emilio's flailing arm. But Emilio screamed "*Bastard!*" at him, too, and kicked him first in the stomach and then between the legs. Mr. Capelli coughed, gasped, and dropped to the floor.

"*Bastard! Bastard! Bastard!*" Emilio screeched. He threw himself from side to side like a wild animal, hair flying, spit spraying.

Ramone shouted hoarsely, "Martin! I can't hold him! Martin!"

For one desperate moment it looked as if the mirror was going to drag both Emilio and Ramone into its brilliant shining surface. But then Martin grabbed hold of Ramone's collar and deliberately fell backward, using his whole weight to pull them over. The three of them collapsed against the desk and tumbled onto the floor next to Mr. Capelli. Emilio knocked his head against the corner of the desk: Martin heard it crack. Then Emilio lay still with his face against the floorboards, suddenly white, his eyes still open but flickering with concussion, and just as suddenly as it had begun, the magnetism from the mirror died away.

"*Madre mia,*" said Ramone, heaving himself up onto his feet, his sneakers squeaking on the boards.

Martin grasped Emilio's T-shirt and dragged him toward him. "*Out*, Ramone. We have to get him out."

Mr. Capelli was up on his knees now, coughing and coughing as if he were going to choke. Martin laid a hand on his shoulder and said, "Mr. Capelli? You all right, Mr. Capelli? I have to get Emilio out of here."

Mr. Capelli coughed and nodded and coughed some more.

Ramone helped Martin to pick Emilio up and carry him through the hallway and down to the Capellis' apartment. Emilio wasn't badly hurt. There was a swelling red bruise on the left side of his forehead, and his eyes wandered sightlessly, but he was beginning to regain consciousness.

"Boofuls," he murmured. "Where's Boofuls?"

"No more Boofuls," Martin told him. "Boofuls is gone for good."

"Or just about to, if I have anything to do with it," growled Ramone.

Mrs. Capelli came flapping out of her parlor. "What now? All this noise! Did somebody fall over? Where is Constantine? Emilio! What's happened? Look at his head! Nothing but noise and trouble this past week! Oh, what a bruise! You men, you're like children! Nothing but thumping! Can't you do anything quietly? Now he's hurt! My poor Emilio! Come on now, bring him in here!"

"He'll be okay," Martin told her. "Just knocked his head on the side of the desk, that's all."

"My poor boy! You men are all the same!"

Once they had left Emilio with his grandmother, Martin and Ramone went back upstairs to see what they could do to help Mr. Capelli. He had managed to pull himself upright, but he looked gray in the face, and he had to lean against the wall to help himself along.

"Come on, Mr. Capelli, let's get you downstairs," Martin told him.

Mr. Capelli coughed and sniffed. "That mirror—that mirror has the devil in it! What did I say, no good would come out of it! You get rid of that mirror, you get rid of it right now! Right now! No argument!"

"You may want that mirror out of your house, but I'm not at all sure that mirror wants to *go*," said Ramone.

Mr. Capelli clung heavily on Martin's arm. "That mirror goes, right now! I don't care how! You get rid of it! You smash it into small pieces, if that's what it takes!"

"Breaking a mirror, that's serious bad luck," Ramone cautioned him as they helped him to shuffle down the stairs, one stair at a time.

"A kick in the nuts from my five-year-old grandson, that's *good* luck?" hissed Mr. Capelli.

"All right, Mr. Capelli, we'll do what we can," Martin soothed him. "Let's just get you downstairs."

Ramone peered at Martin and said pessimistically, "Your bandages are all bloody. Looks like you burst some stitches."

"That's all I need," said Martin, wincing with effort as the taut bulk of Mr. Capelli's belly forced him against the banister.

Mrs. Capelli came out again and fussed over her husband just as much as she had fussed over Emilio. "This house is a madhouse! Never again! Tenants, always the same!"

"It's all right, Mrs. Capelli," said Martin, "everything's under control."

"Under control!" Mr. Capelli burst out. "My grandson goes crazy! That's under control? Look at you! Blood, bandages! Everybody hurt!"

Martin tried to give Mrs. Capelli a reassuring smile and backed off onto the landing. Ramone followed him.

"The old man's right," said Ramone as they climbed back up again to Martin's apartment. "That mirror has to go. Somebody's going to get hurt, or worse, and I sure don't like to imagine what that 'worse' might be. Come on, Martin, we almost lost that boy, same way we lost Lugosi."

"But if we break the mirror, you're going to lose any chance you ever had of getting Lugosi back," said Martin. He was frightened by the mirror; but he was still reluctant to get rid of it until he knew more about Boofuls, and why he was trapped, and why Boofuls' dying grandmother had given Sister Boniface that key.

But Ramone shook his head. "Lugosi is probably dead, anyway. Think about it, man. I've accepted it already. I was hoping he had a chance, you know, but the more I think about it . . . Man, he disappeared into *glass*, didn't he? Solid glass. You don't think he lived through that? I sure as hell don't. I'm going to light a candle for him, that's all, and say a little prayer. I don't think there's very much else I can do."

Martin said, "I'm sorry, Ramone."

"Ah, forget it," said Ramone dismissively.

They walked back into the sitting room; and their mirror reflections walked back into the sitting room, too. They stood staring at themselves for a very long time.

"He was right, you know," Ramone remarked.

"Who was?"

"Mr. Caparooparelli. You heard what he said. That mirror's bad news."

Martin said, "Boofuls is still inside it."

"And that's your reason for not getting rid of it? Some kid who's been dead for fifty years is lurking around—where? Behind it? Inside it? Mirrors are flat. Mirrors don't have no insides."

"But your cat's inside it."

Ramone was angry. "*My* cat is *my* business, okay? And nothing lives *inside* a mirror, right? A mirror is glass, and silver, and that's it. Reflections, nothing else. Optical illusions; no depth; nothing you can walk into. I mean—what's behind that mirror? Nothing! A solid wall, nothing! There's no Boofuls living there, man. There's nothing at all!"

Martin said, "Look."

His voice was so cold, so prickly with alarm, that Ramone looked around without saying a word. There, in the mirror, sitting on Martin's reflected desk, was the blue and white ball. And there, on the floor, in both the mirror-room and the real room, was the dingy gray tennis ball.

But on Martin's desk in the real room, what looked liked a new ball had appeared. A furry, bristling, gray and black ball. A living ball, with eyes that blinked. A ball which soundlessly opened and closed its mouth. A ball which wasn't a ball at all, but Lugosi's detached head— still panting for breath, but without a body, without ears, a grotesque living plaything.

Ramone approached the head in terror and disgust. Its yellow eyes were dimmed with a film of mucus, but they managed to follow him as he came nearer.

"What the hell is it?" whispered Ramone. The furry ball stretched open its mouth and silently cried.

"What the hell is it?" Ramone screamed out loud, almost hysterical.

Martin didn't know what to say. His stomach tightened, and he suddenly broke out into the cold sweat of rising nausea.

Ramone reached out for the ball-head with fingers that shook uncontrollably. The head opened its mouth, biting or crying, and Ramone instantly snatched his fingers away.

"Oh, God, I can't touch it," he quaked. "Oh, God, forgive me, Martin, I just can't touch it."

Martin swallowed bile and approached the desk as near as he dared. The head opened its mouth yet again, and its eyes stared at him in agonized desperation.

"I don't know what to *do*!" shouted Ramone, hoarse with panic. "He's hurting, Martin! I don't know what to do!"

Martin said, "Go out of the room."

"What?"

"You heard me—go out of the room."

Ramone stared at him. "What you going to do?"

"Just go!" Martin shouted.

Still shaking, Ramone retreated from the sitting room. Martin heard his sneakers squeaking along the hallway toward the kitchen, heard the kitchen door slide shut.

With a bitter-tasting mouth, Martin edged up to the desk and took hold of his typewriter. It was a heavy Olivetti electric. His father had given it to him when he sold his first teleplay: it was reconditioned, from the typing pool at the Security Pacific Bank. It hadn't ever worked too well: it kept skipping *j*'s and *m*'s. But all that Martin cared about right now was that it was the heaviest liftable object in the room.

He tugged out the electric cable, rolled out the page of screenplay he had been working on. The cat's head opened its mouth in another hideous yawn, its eyes trying to focus on him as he circled around the back of the desk and picked the typewriter up in both hands. He licked his lips. His heart was thumping like a skin drum. His blood rushed through his head and almost deafened him.

"Oh, God," he whispered, and lifted the typewriter up above his head. If he caught Lugosi's head with one of the corners, he should be able to shatter his skull in one blow. It was crucial, however, that he didn't lose his nerve and pull the typewriter back at the very last moment.

Give yourself a count of three, he told himself. *Then do it.*

The typewriter was so heavy that his arms were beginning to tremble. *Do it!* he ordered himself. *One, two, three, and do it!*

At that second, though, the cat's head seemed to rear up from the desk and swivel around. Martin almost dropped the typewriter, then cradled it in his arms, staring at the head in paralyzed horror.

It rose higher and higher, on a furry neck that seemed to pour right out of the surface of the desk like a snake, yard after yard of it, until it looped and coiled down the side of the drawers and onto the floor. It was more like a python than a cat, and its sleek strange head remained lifted up in front of him on its endless ribboning neck, staring at him with agony and venomous hostility.

There was a moment when Martin believed he was really going mad—when he could hardly grasp that he was standing here at all, clutching his typewriter, with his cat-apparition swaying in front of him, and still pouring out of his desk.

He was breathing through his mouth in harsh, staccato gasps, as if he had been running. *Ha—ha—ha—ha!*

Then the cat started to lean toward him, its teeth bared, and he knew that it was no joke, no dream, no optical illusion. He heaved the typewriter—but it missed and bounded noisily across the floor. Then he threw his jelly jar of pencils and ballpoints, and that caught Lugosi on the side of the neck; but all the cat did was to sway back and hiss at him in fury.

"Ramone!" he yelled. But whatever Ramone was doing, he didn't hear. He was probably standing in the kitchen with his fingers jammed into his ears, so that he wouldn't have to listen to Martin crushing Lugosi's head.

Martin edged around his desk and the cat-snake began to flow around it after him, its head still balanced five or six feet in the air, at eye level, fixing him with its unblinking yellow stare. He hesitated, and the cat-snake hesitated. There was no sound in the room but his own tightened breathing and the whispering of the cat-snake's fur across the boarded floor, like a woman trailing a long mink scarf.

"Ramone," Martin repeated, but so quietly that Ramone couldn't possibly have heard him.

He cautiously reached forward, keeping his eyes on the cat-snake all the time, until his fingers touched the brass handle of his top drawer. The handle rattled, and the cat-snake flared its mouth open, its teeth dripping strings of glistening saliva, and its body began to slide toward him across the floor.

Now or never, he told himself. He yanked open the drawer, scattering the contents everywhere—pencils, erasers, rubber bands, paper clips, typewriter ribbons, book matches, correction fluid, and, most important of all, correction-fluid thinner.

The small plastic bottle of thinner rolled across the room and under his sofa. Martin glanced quickly at the cat-snake and then scrambled for it. The bottle had rolled almost out of reach, right under the back of the sofa next to the woven basket which contained his yucca pot.

He lay flat on his stomach and stretched his arm under the sofa. His fingertips touched the very edge of the bottle. It rolled a half inch farther away. Straining his arm even more, his shoulder pressing painfully against the underside of the sofa's frame, he just managed to reach the bottle and delicately take hold of the cap between two fingertips, so that he could tease it nearer.

"Come on, suckah," he said under his breath.

He had just managed to flick it into the palm of his hand when he felt something indescribable slide around his right thigh. He screamed out loud and rolled over, and there was Lugosi, the cat who had metamorphosed into a snake, winding itself around his leg and forcing its sleek reptilian head under his left arm and around the back of his neck.

Martin scrabbled behind him and snatched at the cat-snake's fur. Underneath the softness, there was a hard muscular hosepipe of a body. Martin managed to get a grip on it, grunting with effort, and then he rolled over twice on the floor, like a child turning somersaults at nursery school, so that the cat-snake unwound from his back.

"Ramone!" Martin shouted. *"Ramone, for God's sake!"*

He managed to catch the cat-snake just below the jaw and clench it tight. It spat and fumed at him and twisted its head from one side to the other. It was unbelievably strong; and the tighter he gripped it, the stronger it seemed to grow—until he was using every ounce of strength just to keep its spitting jaws away from his face.

He rolled over again, and again, and this time he managed to wedge up his knee and pin the cat-snake against the floor. It thrashed and whipped and writhed, fifteen or sixteen feet of it. In seconds, it

would thrash its way free, and then God only knew
what it was going to do.

With his teeth, Martin unscrewed the cap of the thinner fluid, and then held Lugosi's head flat against the
floor while he squirted almost the whole contents
straight into the cat-snake's eyes and mouth and all
over its head, until its furry scalp was furrowed with
pungent liquid.

The cat-snake twisted and turned in agony; and for
the first time uttered more than a hiss: a low, guttural
kkhakk-khhakk-khakkkk witch prickled the hair at the
back of Martin's neck. He dropped the bottle of thinner
and grasped the cat-snake's neck in both hands,
squeezing and squeezing as tightly as he could.

The sitting room door opened: Ramone walked in.
He was obviously expecting to see Martin clearing up
the remains of Lugosi's smashed head. Instead, he was
confronted with a flailing snake out of a nightmare.

"Lighter!" Martin shouted. *"Lighter—before it dries!"*

Ramone was open-mouthed. "Wha—*dries*? What
dries? What are you talking about? What, man? What
the hell is that? Oh, Christ!"

"Your lighter!" Martin repeated, practically shrieking
at him now. *"Set light to its head! I've just sprayed it
with thinner!"*

Ramone, stunned, fumbled in his shirt pocket for his
Zippo. He thumbed it clumsily, but it flared up, and he
held it out to Martin at arm's length.

"Light it!" Martin shouted. *"Light it, for pete's sake!"*

With jiggling, juggling hands, Ramone touched the
flaming Zippo to the top of Lugosi's head. Immediately, the cat-snake's fur burst into flame, and its
yellow eyes bulged with pain. A terrible convulsion
went right through its body, a convulsion that Martin

felt right down to his stomach: a shudder of fear and
suffering and self-disgust. But all he could do was hold
on tight, while the cat-snake wagged its fiery head
from side to side. He knew for a certainty that if he
released his grip, it would still go after him, and it
would probably burn *him* to death, too.

The sitting room began to fill with the suffocating
smell of burned fur and burned flesh. As Martin held
the cat-snake up in front of him, like a torchbearer, the
creature's head blazed and crackled, fur and skin and
muscle. It was still staring at him as its yellow eyes
milked over, its optic fluid cooked. Its mouth was still
gasping that *khakkk-khakkk-khhakkk!* as fire began to
lick out of its throat and between its needle-sharp
teeth, and the skin of its tongue frizzled and charred.

At last, it died, and Martin was left gripping a snake
with a smoking head, its jawbones showing yellowish-
brown through its incinerated cheeks, its mouth
stretched wide in a hideous snarl.

Martin dropped it, and the head broke off and lay
smoldering in a corner. The rest of the body shrank
and dwindled and thickened, and even while Martin
and Ramone watched it, it took on the shape of a normal tabby cat.

"Lugosi," Ramone whispered. "I just killed Lugosi. I
wanted to save him, man, and I *killed* him."

Martin walked stiffly to the window and opened it,
so that some of the sour-smelling smoke could eddy out
of the room. He retched once, then again, then pressed
his fist against his mouth and managed to steady himself.

"That wasn't Lugosi," he managed to say with a dry
mouth.

"You think I don't know my own cat?" Ramone protested. "Look at him!"

Martin took a deep breath. Below the window, next door, Maria Bocanegra was strutting out on a date with her bodybuilder boyfriend. Tight white skirt, dagger-sharp white stiletto heels that made her totter along with her hips swaying from side to side, tight white T-shirt through which her nubby Sno-Cone-protected nipples were startlingly obvious, even to those who didn't particularly want to see them.

God, thought Martin, *normality*.

They heard loud footsteps clattering up the stairs. An imperious banging on the apartment door. "More noise!" shouted Mrs. Capelli. "What's that noise? And smoke? Is something burning? No fires allowed!"

"It's okay, Mrs. Capelli, no problem. Just a cigarette butt, dropped on the couch."

Martin sat unsteadily down at his desk, and dry-washed his face with his hands.

Ramone kept shaking his head and saying, "I *killed* him, man! You told me to do it, and I did! I can't believe it! I *killed* him!"

"No," said Martin. "You didn't kill him. It wasn't your fault. But we've learned something—or at least, I think we have."

"What? What? What have we learned?" grieved Ramone, his face wet with tears.

"Well, for beginners, we learned that if something comes out of that mirror, something else has to go in. And vice versa, get it? Kind of a trade. I mean it may be weird but it has a certain kind of logic to it, like Isaac Newton saying that for every action there has to be an equal and opposite reaction."

"All right," said Ramone suspiciously, keeping his eyes averted from Lugosi's body.

"There's something else, too," said Martin. "The way it looks now—what happened to Lugosi—whatever happens inside that mirror, it *changes* things. Look—it changed Lugosi into God knows what. A snake? A cat? Some kind of mirage? I don't know what it was, but it damn near killed me. So—can you imagine what would have happened if Emilio had gotten sucked in? What would have happened to him? A boy-snake? It doesn't even bear thinking about."

Ramone said nothing, but jammed his hands into the pockets of his jeans, and flared his nostrils, and paced up and down with his sneakers ferociously squeaking.

"I'd better get a trash bag," said Martin.

"An eye for an eye," Ramone remarked with vehemence. "We kill the mirror-cat; the mirror kills my cat. But whatever it is, that's only some jive mirror, that's all. Nothing else. It's a piece of glass."

Martin didn't say anything. He knew that Ramone had experienced just as acutely as he had the wave of darkness that had flowed out of the mirror. He knew that Ramone wouldn't attempt to move it or break it, no matter how bitter he felt about what had happened to Lugosi.

He also knew that, however much Ramone dismissed the mirror as "a piece of glass," it was time for them to seek the help of people who knew about such things. A priest or a spiritualist. Someone who could tell them exactly what kind of a souvenir Martin had bought for himself; and what influences were at work behind its shining surface; whether they were holy or whether they were evil; and what they could do to protect themselves against it.

He opened the door, and the smoke from Lugosi's charred head swirled and eddied in the draft.

Homer Theobald arrived that Sunday morning in a
bright yellow Volkswagen Rabbit and parked it right
in Mr. Capelli's driveway. Mr. and Mrs. Capelli had
taken Emilio to church—to pray for his immortal soul,
and to keep him away from the mirror while Homer
Theobald came to see it.

Martin let Homer in. Homer Theobald was plump
and hairless like Uncle Fester in the *Addams Family*,
with horn-rimmed spectacles and a splashy red and
green Waikiki shirt. He smiled like a visiting doctor
and held out his plump, damp hand.

"Mr. Williams? I'm Homer Theobald. Your friend
Ramone Perez called me?"

"That's right, come on in. Ramone isn't here yet, but
you can take a look at the mirror if you want to."

"Well, yes," Homer Theobald beamed. "He told me it
was something to do with a mirror. That's not unusual,
you know? Mirrors reflect the soul, don't they, as well
as the face?"

Martin led the way upstairs. Homer Theobald sniffed
and said, "Italian?"

"I'm sorry?"

"I was just wondering if you were Italian."

"Oh, no. But my landlord is. First-generation."

Homer Theobald giggled. "I didn't divine that by
psychic means, I'm afraid. It's just that I have a keen
nose for aromas. I can smell bolognese sauce simmer-
ing."

"Mrs. Capelli's a wonderful cook," Martin told him.
"Maybe we can settle your fee in pizzas."

"Well," giggled Homer Theobald, "I'm not so sure
about that. Did Ramone tell you that I do for Elmore
Sweet? Well, and lots of other stars besides. Jocelyn

Grice, Nahum Ferris, the Polo Sisters. We all like to keep in touch with our loved ones, don't we, the rich and the poor, the famous and the faces in the crowd?"

Martin stopped on the landing and Homer Theobald almost collided with him.

"You can really do that?" Martin asked. "I mean— you can *really* get in touch?"

Homer Theobald's smile lost something of its scout-master brightness. "I hope you're not questioning my psychic credentials, Mr. Williams. I'm known through-out Southern California as the Maestro of Mediums. I once talked to Will Rogers."

Martin said, "I'm sorry. I didn't mean to suggest—"

"No, no, not at all," said Homer Theobald, patting Martin's arm and immediately regaining his cheer-fulness. "Most people are skeptical at first, even though they want to believe. It's only natural. But once they realize that they can speak to their lost loved ones as easily as making a long-distance telephone call—well, that skepticism just *melts* away!"

Martin opened the door of his apartment and let Homer Theobald in.

"You don't mind if I just stand here a moment and *take in* the atmosphere?" asked Homer Theobald.

Martin shrugged. "Go ahead. This is all new to me. I never came across anything psychic in my life. Not un-til this, anyway."

Homer Theobald suddenly looked at him more acutely. "Those cuts—" he said, indicating the ban-dages around Martin's neck and the dressings on his cheeks and ears. "If you don't mind my asking you a personal question—did you sustain those cuts in an auto accident, or are they anything to do with this mir-ror business?"

"I don't think you'd believe me if I told you."

"Mr. Williams," said Homer Theobald, suddenly
testy, "you may think that I do nothing more for my
considerable income than kid movie stars that I'm
talking to their dead relatives. I told you, most people
think that at first. But the fact remains that I have a
gift of sensitivity that extends beyond the normal
range of human faculties."

He reached out and he gently drew his fingertip
along the stitches in Martin's chin. "These injuries
have some connection with the mirror, am I right? I
sense that you're frightened. I sense that you feel out of
your depth. You don't know how to handle what's happening to you. You don't know whether to laugh or
scream. Well, that's right. The beyond is always alarm-
ing. In the beyond, the same physical rules don't apply.
Objects fly; people change shape. I don't often tell my
clients that. They wouldn't understand, most of them,
if I told them that their beloved parents are appearing
to me in the shape of intelligent turtles, or that their
heads have been stretched until they're nine feet high.
But, you know, it stands to reason, in a way. Why
should the world beyond obey any of the laws of our
own world? It would be more bizarre if it *did*."

Martin nodded, and quoted, "*It may be quite different
on beyond.*"

Homer Theobald frowned. "I beg your pardon?"

"I was quoting. From *Alice Through the Looking-
Glass.*"

"Yes, well," said Homer Theobald. "There was always more to *that* book than meets the eye. The Vic-
torians had a *very* finely developed sense of death and
the world beyond."

He lifted his head, and looked around the hallway,

and listened. Then, without hesitation, he crossed to the wall where Martin had impaled the brindled tom-cat, and touched it. At least, he was about to touch it, but he suddenly drew his hand back.

"Anything wrong?" asked Martin.

Homer Theobald turned to stare at him. "Something *very* unpleasant has happened here."

Martin nodded.

"Do you want to tell me about it?" asked Homer Theobald.

"Why don't we take a look at the mirror first?" Martin suggested. "Then I can tell you the whole story from the beginning."

"I just want to know one thing," said Homer Theobald. "Is there something in this mirror that isn't reflected in the outside world?"

"Yes," said Martin.

"Is it a person? If it is, say yes, but don't tell me what his or her name is. I have to keep my mind clear, you see. Thinking of somebody's name is an immediate invitation for them to get inside my mind."

"It's a person," said Martin.

"Is it somebody you knew?"

"Somebody I know of; but not somebody I knew. He died a long time before I was born."

"I see," said Homer Theobald. He took out a clean handkerchief, unfolded it, and patted the perspiration from his bald head. "So it's a man."

"A boy, as matter of fact."

"So he died an unnatural death?"

"Extremely unnatural, yes. He was murdered."

Homer Theobald closed his eyes and thought for a while. Then he said, "Cats."

"Yes," Martin agreed.

Without opening his eyes, Homer Theobald stretched out both arms and felt cautiously at the air all around him. "There was a cat. There was more than one cat. But the first cat came to the back door and wouldn't go away. It sat there and sat there and the boy used to feed it. There was an argument. No, you can't feed the cat. The cat is unhealthy, you only have to smell it, it stinks. But I love it. Nobody can love a cat like that. I want it in the house. Certainly not, you can't have a filthy animal like that in this beautiful house, we'll all get fleas."

Homer Theobald stopped talking as abruptly as he had started. He opened his eyes and he looked at Martin with the same kind of expression as an auto mechanic when he's about to tell you that your whole transmission's shot.

"I'm still in the hallway, right? I haven't even *seen* this mirror yet. It's in there, right, in that room, against the wall?"

"Yes," said Martin.

Homer Theobald rubbed his forehead. "I don't know what I'm going to be able to do for you here, Mr. Williams. I truly don't. This isn't anything like I'm used to dealing with. It's spirits, yes. It's something trying to get in touch with us from beyond the moment of death. But if I can pick it up as clearly as this from the *hallway* . . ."

"What are you saying?" Martin asked him. "You can't do anything about it, or what? All I want to do is get rid of it!"

"Mr. Williams," Homer Theobald appealed to him, "what I'm trying to tell you is that I'm too frightened."

Martin licked his scabby, split lips. "You mean you won't even take a look at it?"

"No, sir."

"Do you have any idea who it is? Whose spirit it is?"

"I have a pretty fair idea. Come on, Mr. Williams, I've been living and working in Hollywood all my life. I know what goes on."

"And what's *that* supposed to mean?"

Homer Theobald took a deep breath. "Mr. Williams, you bought yourself a whole load of trouble when you bought this mirror. You didn't do it on purpose, of course not. Most people could have bought it and hung it on their wall and never noticed a thing. But you yourself have latent psychic powers. Nothing amazing. Compared with mine, they're about as strong as a kid's flashlight compared with a klieg light. But you're intensely interested in the spirit which possesses this mirror—I say 'possesses' for want of any better word. And your intense interest, coupled with your psychic powers, low-voltage as they are—well, they've obviously been enough to stir this spirit out of his stasis. It's not sleep, spirits don't sleep in the normal sense."

Martin said, "Why don't you take a look at it? I mean, just take a *look*!"

"No-o-o, sir," said Homer Theobald. He was adamant.

"You're just going to turn around and walk out?" Martin demanded. "You're going to leave me here, not just me, but the people downstairs, everybody who comes into contact with this thing—you're just going to leave us to be terrorized by this spirit for the rest of our lives? There's a kid threatened here, too. A boy of five. What do you want me to tell him?"

"Do you seriously think that I don't *want* to help?" Homer Theobald shouted back. "Do you think I'd turn my back on you if there was anything else that I could do?"

"Well, that's what it looks like," Martin challenged him.

"Listen, my friend," said Homer Theobald, stubbing his finger against Martin's chest. "I'm not a medium or a spiritualist or a psychic. I'm a sensitive. That means my *mind* is sensitive. What you have in this apartment is a raging beast, my friend. It's already tried to claw you to pieces, but only your face. If *I* go in there, it's going to claw my *mind* to pieces. I'm sorry, I understand your problem, but I don't wish to spend the rest of my life with the IQ of a head of broccoli."

"All right," said Martin, "if that's the way you feel."

"I'm *sorry*," Homer Theobald repeated. He took a menthol cough drop out of the pocket of his shirt, unwrapped it, and popped it into his mouth. "Talking to somebody's dead husband is one thing. Raging beasts from beyond is quite another. I'm not putting you on, Mr. Williams, it's a raging beast. So what you're asking me to consider here is the same as putting my head into the mouth of a hungry lion which has a special taste for heads."

"Can't we just talk about it?" asked Martin. "I mean, you keep telling me this is a raging beast—what kind of raging beast? And all this stuff about the cats?"

Homer Theobald hesitated, noisily sucking his candy. "All right," he agreed at last. "But not here. There's just too much vibration here." He lifted his fingers to his temples and winced. "You can't believe it. The *voices*."

"You can actually hear voices in here?"

Homer Theobald shrugged. "Let's say that 'hear' isn't quite the right way of describing it. But, essentially, yes. I can hear voices."

"The boy's voice?"

"Sure. And a woman's voice, too. An elderly woman. And somebody else."

"Somebody else? Who? Is it a man or a woman?"

Homer Theobald grimaced. "I don't know. It's hard to tell. It's kind of harsh, and shrill, and metallic; but it sounds like it's closed up somewhere, do you understand what I'm saying? As if it's muffled. Somebody talking in another room, or maybe inside a box."

"Can you make out what it's saying?"

"I'm not too sure that I want to."

"Could you please try?" Martin begged him.

Homer Theobald reluctantly took off his spectacles and closed his eyes. "I'm warning you, though, your little-boy spirit may get itself real worked up and excited by this."

"Please," said Martin.

"It's the way this kid keeps carrying on about the cat. The cat is real important to him for some reason. But I've never had a pet before. You had those terrapins, what was wrong with those terrapins. You can't cuddle a terrapin, they're not the same and besides they all got away. Oh sure, they got away, they were crawling all over the kitchen, cook was standing on a stool. But I love Pickle, I love him."

Martin grabbed hold of Homer Theobald's furry bare forearm. "Mr. Theobald!"

Homer Theobald blinked open his eyes. "What's the matter? What's wrong?"

"*Pickle*, that's what you said."

Homer Theobald nodded. "That's right. The cat's name was Pickle."

"None of the books ever mentioned him."

"None of what books?"

"The books about—"

"Ah-ah!" Homer Theobald interrupted. "Don't you mention his name! I've got a pretty good idea of who he is, but I don't want to start speaking any names in my mind, you understand? No mental pictures. The mind is a mirror, too, Mr. Williams."

"You'd better call me Martin if we're going to get *this* damned frightened together."

"Well, I'm Homer, but most of my friends call me Theo. You know, on account of the hair loss. Theo Bald."

Martin said, "I'm sorry I interrupted you. It was just that the name Pickle came as a shock. Do you think you can pick up any more?"

"I don't know," said Theo, but he was plainly not happy.

"Just the voice—you know, the shrill voice. The voice you said sounded like it was shut up in a box."

"Well . . . okay. But I may get nothing. And I'm sure not staying around if it begins to wake up to the fact that I'm here, and that I'm listening in."

"All right, I understand."

Theo closed his eyes. "The boy's still talking. He's a real chatterbox, that boy. When he was alive, he was real popular, real sweet. But there was something which he always kept hidden. Some important part of his personality which he never showed to anybody. He's still keeping it hidden, even now, and that's very strange indeed, because once people are dead they don't keep their personalities hidden anymore. They let themselves go. That's why they take on all kinds of weird shapes. They begin to *look* like they actually should. They drop the sheep's clothing, if you understand what I mean, and show you the wolf. Or vice versa, of course."

He "listened" harder. Clear buttons of perspiration popped up on his freckled scalp and on his upper lip. He began to mutter and mumble, a higgledy-piggledy rush of conversation, pleading, argument.

"I can't, Grannie, I told you I can't. You have to. You have to give thanks. I don't want to, I can't. Well, what do you think everybody's going to say about you if you don't go."

Theo lifted one plump hand, his eyes still tightly shut. He was indicating to Martin that he was picking up the other voice, the shrill voice. "Don't you go, she can't tell you what to do, don't you go, Pickle will fix her if she argues, don't you go, don't you go.

"I'm not going. You can't make me. Pickle will fix you if you make me. That cat, how dare you talk to me like that. That cat is going to go out and that's all there is to it. You're a hateful child. You're a disgrace to your poor mother. And you're *damned* for saying that, you're *damned*."

While Theo was hurriedly muttering all of this argument between Boofuls and his grandmother, the latch of the sitting room door, without warning, released itself, and the door swung slowly open. Because his eyes were closed, and because he was concentrating on the voices in his head, Theo didn't realize that a sharp geometric pattern of light was gradually illuminating him brighter and brighter.

"Theo—" Martin warned him, his heart racing. "The door."

Theo opened his eyes and stared at the door in alarm. "Did you open it?" he asked Martin.

Martin shook his head.

"Did you touch it at all?"

"I didn't go anywhere near it."

Theo wiped his mouth with the back of his hand. "I
have to tell you, Martin, I don't know what's going on
here, and I don't particularly *want* to know. I'll talk,
yes, I'll tell you whatever I can. But I'm not staying
here any longer, and I sure as hell am not going anywhere near that mirror of yours."

"All right," said Martin. "Agreed. Let's go down to
Butterfield's, I'll buy you a drink. You look like you
could use it."

Theo replaced his spectacles. As he did so, the sitting
room door slammed so thunderously loudly that one of
the panels was cracked.

"God, what was that?" Martin asked him.

Theo smiled grimly. "That was your mirror, saying
good riddance."

Martin left a note on the door for Ramone, telling him
that they had gone to Butterfield's. They drove there in
Theo's Rabbit. Theo steered like a taxi driver, grinding
the gears with every change, sweating, swearing under
his breath, challenging every other car he encountered
on the Strip, whether they were Porsches or Rolls-
Royces or Eldorados.

"I don't believe in being protean," he remarked as he
parked halfway up the curb outside Butterfield's.
"Sometimes it's refreshing to do something really
badly."

Butterfield's was on the south side of Sunset, with
steps leading down through frondy palms and flowering shrubs to the table areas, where lean brown people
in designer khaki sat under green and white umbrellas
and talked about movies and other people's diets and
themselves, but mostly themselves. There was plenty
of fresh fruit and yogurt and Perrier water in evidence.

Of all people, Morris Nathan was there, his wide back-side bulging out on either side of a small white cast-iron chair. Alison was leaning against his shoulder, her face shaded by a dipping white hat, her eyes concealed by Mulberry sunglasses, her darkly suntanned breasts bulging out of a small white Fiorucci sun top. The Nabobs of Bulge, thought Martin.

"Martin!" called Morris, waving one fat arm. "Join us!"

But Martin's need to talk to Theo was urgent: and, besides, Martin was sitting with Ahab Greene, an independent producer with wavy blond hair and protuberant eyes and white cowboy boots who always reeked of Armani after-shave, and Martin couldn't sit next to Ahab Greene for more than six and a half minutes without starting a blistering argument.

"Thanks!" he called back. "But—you know—business!"

Morris peered suspiciously at Theo, wondering if he was another agent, but Alison whispered something in his ear and he was obviously reassured. Alison wasn't particularly bright, but she was one of those well-connected Hollywood girls who knew every modish astrologer and every up-to-the minute masseuse and every fashionable beautician; she had once been a manicurist, and she had probably come across Homer Theobald more than once. After all, Hollywood husbands were always dying, and Hollywood wives were always feeling a need to get in touch, if only to reassure their loved ones that their money was being well spent.

A pretty, disinterested waitress found them a table, and Martin ordered champagne. "Champagne?" queried Theo, although he was obviously used to champagne.

"I feel like it," said Martin. "What the hell."

Theo leaned his elbow on the table. "Let me tell you something, Martin. When people die their spirits move on. There's no question about that. Like I said, the place they move on to—the beyond, if you want to call it that—it's totally different from the world we know here. It doesn't abide by the same rules. Morally, physiologically, or scientifically. I don't know. It's very hard to describe. You can't think of it in normal terms—left, right, top, bottom. But it's there. It's where people go when they die."

Martin looked away for a while. In spite of everything that had happened in the past few days, he still found it difficult to believe in Theo's beyond. He still found it difficult to believe in Theo.

When he spoke, it was almost a complaint—an aggrieved and baffled student asking his lecturer to explain some inconceivable theory about space and time. "But how can this place—how can this world beyond—how can it appear in a mirror? And not just appear, but send things jumping out? I mean, I haven't told you the half of it. I saw a child's ball in that mirror that wasn't there at all. And Ramone's cat was sucked right into it—literally sucked into the glass. And then there was Pickle, the cat who came out of the mirror—at least I believe that was Pickle—he came out of that mirror and I can prove it, because the door was locked and the windows were locked and there was no way that cat could have gotten into my sitting room. And he almost killed me—well, look at me. And then Ramone's cat came back out of the mirror and he was like some kind of snake, like a python, you know, or a boa constrictor, and we had to burn him to death, I mean literally burn him. And that's why we called you. But of course you can't help. Or won't."

The girl poured out their champagne. It wasn't very good quality, but it was cold and fizzy, and that was all Martin wanted. "Okay," he told her, and she went prancing off.

Theo sipped his champagne and then said heavily, "That happened, all of that stuff?"

Martin said, "You don't believe me, do you?"

"Oh, I believe you," said Theo. "Martin—let me tell you this—mirrors are no joke. Mirrors never *have* been a joke, particularly for us sensitives. A mirror is, what? People think of them like pictures on the wall; but they're into pictures, they're more like cameras. Think about it. You look at your mirror with more *intensity* than anything else you look at in your whole life. People don't even look at their husbands and wives with the same intensity they do their mirror."

"I don't understand," Martin admitted; and he really didn't.

"Listen," said Theo, "you've heard of rooms that somehow retain the feelings of stressful or tragic events that happened in them, long after those events are over? Sometimes it happens not just to rooms, but to whole houses, like Amityville. Oh, they turned that into a series of horror flicks, but the house was truly afflicted, as many houses are. Some people can sense it the moment they walk into a place, some people can't. Some people have an ear for music, others don't. Being sensitive to the world beyond isn't something you can study in night class."

"What are you trying to say?" asked Martin. "You're trying to tell me this mirror has kind of *remembered* what happened to Boofuls?"

Theo winced. "I did ask you not to mention his name."

"I'm sorry. But you must have guessed."

"Oh, certainly. Who else could it have been? So you bought a mirror that belonged to Boofuls, did you, and you hung it on your wall? In psychic terms, that's a little like buying Adolf Eichmann's toothbrush and using it. Do you know where the mirror used to hang? What I'm trying to say is—is there any chance that it might have been a witness to what happened to him—that the mirror might have seen Boofuls die?"

Martin said, "It was hanging over the fireplace in the main living room. That was where Boofuls was killed."

Theo took a deep breath and sharply drummed his fingers on the table. "That accounts for it. That's why you're having all this trouble. The mirror *remembers* Boofuls being killed. Now all of those feelings, all of that fear, all of that pain, all of that hatred, it's all coming back to you. It's like a delayed reflection, that's all. But it can seem real. It can take on real shape, and it can do real damage. That cat Pickles—for some reason it was obviously important to Boofuls. Boofuls loved it but his grandmother didn't want him to keep it. So the situation about the cat was all part of the stress."

Martin set down his glass. "I don't know. It seems to me that there's more to this than just reflections. People must have murdered other people in front of mirrors before. I mean, almost every house has a mirror someplace. But you don't hear about cats and monsters and God knows what jumping out of mirrors all the time, do you?"

Theo said, "You asked me for an explanation. I gave it to you."

"But what about the third voice you heard? That voice that was supposed to sound like somebody in a box or something?"

Theo was beginning to sweat. "Don't you think it's hot out here? Maybe we should go inside."

Martin reached into his shirt pocket and produced the key that Sister Boniface had given him. "When you said box, I thought about this key, because this key was given to one of the nurses at the Sisters of Mercy Hospital by Mrs. Crossley, Boofuls' grandmother, the night she killed him. And what I was wondering was—"

Theo stared at the key with bulging eyes. The sun reflected from it and played a bright key pattern on his forehead.

"My God, put that away," whispered Theo.

"But Theo—what I want to know is—since you're sensitive—maybe you could hold this key and tell me—"

"Put it away!" Theo ordered him, his voice so hoarse and penetrating that several people looked around.

"Theo . . . the nurse told me that Mrs. Crossley couldn't speak, but the nurse was absolutely convinced that this key was very important. If you could just touch it, hold it, see if it gives off any kind of vibrations. It could be the key to the whole darn thing."

"Put—that—key—" Theo began; but then abruptly his nose fountained blood, all over his Waikiki shirt, all over his twill pants, spattering the tablecloth and turning his champagne cloudy pink. A girl at the next table screamed. Martin dropped the key and reached out for Theo at once.

"Theo! What's the matter? Theo!"

"Lung!" gasped Theo; and then vomited up a basinful of startlingly red blood that splashed all over Martin and all over the flagstones and dripped from the white-painted chair like glutinous paint.

"Ambulance!" Martin shouted. "Somebody call an ambulance, for Christ's sake!"

Theo lurched sideways in his chair. Martin tried to keep him upright, but he was enormously heavy and off-balance and slimy with blood. At last, with the help of one of the waiters, Martin managed to lower him gently onto the ground.

"Is he dying, or what?" the waiter asked him, his eyes wide open with fright.

"Martin—are you okay?" shouted Morris. "They've just called for the paramedics."

Alison gave him an anxious little wave, too. Martin waved back to tell them they were doing all they could. Theo was lying with his face against the paving stones, a bubble of blood between his lips, his eyes filmy.

"*Key* . . ." he whispered. He lifted his right hand and took hold of Martin's wrist, drawing him closer. "*Key* . . ."

"What about it?" asked Martin. "Listen, just rest. They've sent for an ambulance."

"Key . . . acts like . . . lightning conductor . . ."

"What? What do you mean?"

"Mirror . . . doesn't want me to pry . . . punctured my lung. Located us . . . you got it? . . . moment you said . . , Boofuls."

Martin said, "I'm sorry, Theo. I didn't have any idea."

"Well . . . not your fault," Theo grunted. "I should have said no . . . right from the very beginning . . . moment I felt that coldness . . . moment I felt that *black*."

"I felt that, too," Martin told him.

Theo coughed a gout of blood. In the distance, they could hear the ambulance siren whooping. "Come on, Theo," said Martin. "You're going to make it . . . the paramedics are almost here."

"Where's that . . . key?" asked Theo.

"I don't know. I guess I dropped it."

"Find it . . . give it to me. Come on, quickly."

"Theo—if it's that dangerous—"

Theo lifted his head. His mouth was so bloodstained he looked as if he had been cramming raspberries into it all morning. Sticky, red, peculiarly childish.

"If you don't give me that key, I'm never going to speak to you again."

The threat was so absurd that Martin realized Theo was serious. He dabbled around in the spreading lake of blood, and there by the leg of Theo's dark-stained pants was the key. Theo reached out for it, and Martin pressed it reluctantly into his hand.

The ambulance had parked on Sunset, outside the entrance to Butterfield's; and the paramedics were already hurrying down the steps. Theo closed his eyes and for a moment Martin, kneeling in his rapidly cooling blood, was sure that he was dead. The paramedics came up to him and lifted the table aside and said, "Okay, sir, give us some space, will you?"

Theo lifted one bloody arm. "Martin . . ." he mouthed. "Martin . . ."

Martin tried to get close to him, but one of the paramedics backhanded him away. "Come on, friend, this man needs space."

"Martin!" Theo choked. "Martin!"

Martin pleaded with the paramedic, "I have to get close. Listen, I have to hear what he's got to say."

"You want to kill him, or what?" the paramedic demanded. "This man has a punctured lung. Now, do us all a favor, and take a powder—and that's being polite."

They were testing Theo's vital signs and unwrapping an oxygen mask. But before they could press the mask over Theo's face, he propped himself up on one elbow and bubbled, "Martin! Martin, listen to me! The Hollywood Divine! The Hollywood Divine!"

"What?" asked Martin, baffled.

"Used to go there . . . when I was a boy . . . father took me . . . cocktail lounge . . . Here! take the key! The Hollywood Divine! Leopard-skin banquettes . . . gold-tinted mirrors . . . Here! Martin! The key!"

Theo waved the key; and impatiently, one of the paramedics passed it back to Martin. "Guy's out of his tree," the paramedic remarked, covering Theo's face with the oxygen mask.

Martin waited while the paramedics sent back Theo's vital signs to the hospital. Then he asked, "Where are you going to take him?"

"Sisters of Mercy, that's the nearest."

"All right," said Martin, "I'll follow you."

"No tailgating, that's all," the paramedic told him as he rolled Theo's bloody body onto a stretcher.

"In a Rabbit?" said Martin bitterly.

Six

THEO DIED at 3:46 that afternoon. Martin was sitting in the reception area when Sister Michael came rustling up in her white habit and white wimple to tell him that all their efforts to save him had been to no avail.

"Was he a close friend of yours, Mr. Williams?" Sister Michael asked him, with a face like the Angel of Solicitude carved in wax.

Martin said, "No, I met him for the first time today."

"We did everything possible. But his lungs collapsed. You can talk to the doctors later, if you wish."

Ramone appeared, wearing a black T-shirt and black jeans and looking unhappy. "I called his house. Some boy answered. His boyfriend, I guess. Said he thought there was a sister in Indiana, anyway he's going to check through his address book and call her."

"At least he's at peace now, in the Kingdom of Heaven," said Sister Michael.

"What?" asked Ramone. Then, "Sure—oh, yes." He

183

glanced at Martin and made a face. Martin had already told him about Theo's description of the world beyond, with its talking turtles and its people with stretched-out heads.

Sister Michael laid a cool pale hand on Martin's shoulder. "If there's anything else that I can do, please don't hesitate to call me. When somebody passes on, we do recognize the need to comfort those who are left behind."

"Yes, thank you," said Martin.

Ramone sat down on one of the gray fabric couches and tightly crossed his arms. Up above his head, a painting of a gentle-faced Madonna smiled down at him, with an expression that forgave all human weakness. "What do we do now?" Ramone wanted to know. "If Homer Theobald couldn't help us—if *he* wound up getting wasted—then what hope do the rest of us have?" He leaned forward and asked, "You really think it was the *mirror* that wasted him? All that way away?"

Martin shrugged. "He seemed to think so. I showed him that key and he went white. I mean he was *gibbering*. I wish to God I hadn't now. He might still be alive."

Ramone took out a cheroot, but the nun at the nurses' station silently pointed to the sign which said *No fumadores.*

"How did she know I speak Spanish?" Ramone whispered, replacing the cheroot in its carton.

"She must've guessed. Or maybe she read *¡Viva Las Patillas!* on the back of your T-shirt."

Ramone said, "Let's take a look at that key."

Martin handed it to him. While he had been waiting to hear if Theo would survive, he had taken it to the hospital washroom and carefully rinsed Theo's blood off it. Ramone turned it over and over and then handed it back. "It's just a plain ordinary key."

"Well, maybe it is and maybe it isn't. I think we should go to the Hollywood Divine and find out, don't you? There's nothing to keep us here."

"I don't even know if the Hollywood Divine is still standing," said Ramone. "They demolished most of that block last year."

"All we can do is take a look."

Sister Michael intercepted them again as they walked toward the elevators. "Mr. Williams! Mr. Perez! Did you want to *view* Mr. Theobald before you left?"

Martin looked at Ramone, and Ramone bulged his eyes in an expression which unequivocally meant "no way."

"Thanks," said Martin. "But I think I'd just like to remember him the way he was."

"How was that?" asked Ramone as they went down in the elevator to the hospital lobby.

"Alive," Martin replied.

The Hollywood Divine Hotel had been erected in 1927 by Daniel T. Rolls, the wealthy second son of the Rolls hotel family of Pasadena. It stood two blocks north of the celebrated intersection of Hollywood and Vine, a fanciful creation in the neoclassical picture-palace style that had been popularized by Eve Leo.

In its heyday, the Hollywood Divine had been cele-brated for its eccentric and arty clientele—the West Coast equivalent of the Algonquin in New York. But with the squalid death of its founder in 1938 (cocaine, bourbon, inhalation of vomit), it had quickly lost its cachet. Now it stood shabby and seedy and ready for

demolition, its pale pink stone corroded by vehicle
fumes, its marquee half collapsed, its marble steps
stained with urine and measled with chewing gum.

"I could of sworn they knocked this place down already," Ramone remarked as they parked outside in
Martin's Mustang.

They were immediately approached by a thin-faced
kid with a crimson punk hairstyle. "Hey, friend, take
care of your car?"

Martin reached into his shirt pocket and gave the kid
two dollars. "There's another three where that came
from if the stereo stays where it is."

"You got it," the kid told him.

Three young hookers were standing outside the
hotel, two black and one white, in skintight satin min-
iskirts and halter tops. They were all pretty: one of
them was almost beautiful. She winked at Martin as he
went up the steps and he couldn't help smiling back.

"Made yourself a friend?" asked Ramone.

They pushed their way through the bronze and glass
doors of the Hollywood Divine and into the gloomy
lobby. The carpet was rancid; so filthy and stained that
it was impossible to tell what color it had originally
been. There was a suffocating smell of marijuana and
body odor and disinfectant. Six or seven scarecrows
were sitting on the ripped-open leopard-skin seats
where John Barrymore and Bette Davis had once sat,
sharing bottles of muscatel from brown paper bags and
sniffing in chorus.

The great chandelier hung from the lobby ceiling like
the desiccated corpse of a giant spider, still dangling in
its web.

Martin and Ramone approached the desk. The desk
clerk was surprisingly young and clean: a young man

in a shocking-pink shirt with blond crew-cut hair. It was only when he laid his thin arms on the marble counter that Martin saw the needle tracks.

"You people checking in?" he asked them. His eyes were as pale and as expressionless as two stones you find on the beach.

Martin shook his head. "I was wondering if you still had safe-deposit boxes here."

"Safe-deposit boxes?" The young man blinked.

"Yes, you know. Somewhere your guests can keep their valuables."

"What, are you kidding? If any of our guests happen to have any valuables, they keep them on their persons. Besides, they don't usually stay for longer than a half hour."

"But are the original boxes still here—the boxes that were put in when the hotel was built?"

"I don't think so," the young man told him. "Pretty much everything has gone. Somebody walked out with a goddamned bathtub last week. Can you imagine that? Nobody knows how he got it through the door."

Martin gave a tight grimace and looked around him. One of the scarecrows was waving his arms and singing. "*Sur . . . wannee song! Suwannee song! You c'n blow your flute 'n' you c'n bang y'r drum 'n' you c'n—*"

"Will you shut up?" one of his companions screeched at him. "Will you shut up?"

Martin stared at the old scarecrow for a while. Then he turned back to the desk clerk and said, "Who's that?"

"Who's what?" The young man may have looked quite presentable, but his brain was somewhere in another galaxy.

"That old bum singing. The one singing 'Suwannee Song.'"

The young man focused his eyes across the lobby. "Oh, that's Fido. Well, everybody calls him Fido. He's been hanging out for just about a hundred years. I think he used to work here or something. He's always telling stories about how he walked in on Bill Haines, and Bill Haines was wearing nothing but a brassiere and a garter belt and a picture hat."

Martin left the desk and walked across to the group of scarecrows. Fido was sitting right in the middle of them, on one of the leopard-skin banquettes. His face was puffy and flowered with gin blossoms. He wore a fifties-style suit with wide flappy lapels. It had once been fawn, but now it was greasy gray. Martin couldn't approach too close. The collective stench of these down-and-outs was overwhelming.

"Fido?" he asked.

Fido looked up at him blearily. "That's me, your honor."

"They tell me you used to work here," said Martin.

There was a chorus of groans and raspberries from Fido's companions. "Don't ask him!" one of them begged in a voice reedy with phlegm. "Do us a favor, will you, friend? Don't ask him!"

"Was the gemmun addressing *you*?" Fido demanded with all the indignation of an Oliver Hardy.

"He worked here, he worked here, now go!" the other scarecrow appealed.

Martin said to Fido, "Maybe we can talk in private? I wouldn't like to antagonize your friends."

"Friends? Call this riffraff friends? These just happen to be items of flotsam who have eddied their way into the same backwater."

"Oh, can it, Fido," groaned another scarecrow. "You make my ears want to scream."

Fido teetered his way out of the assembly of winos around the banquette and accompanied Martin and Ramone to the far side of the lobby, beside the gilded fountain that had long ago dried up, and whose shell-shaped bowl was now crammed with cigarette butts and empty bottles and used needles.

Ramone wrinkled up his nose as Fido lurched a little too close to him. "You won't get arrested for taking a shower, did you know that?"

Martin said, "Ssh," and waved Ramone to keep quiet. He didn't want to upset Fido before he'd had the chance to talk to him.

"Is it true you worked here?" he asked.

"What's it worth?" Fido wanted to know.

Martin held up a ten-dollar bill. Fido sniffed, and took it, and snapped it between his fingers to make sure that it was genuine. "All right, then," he said. "I worked here."

"Were you here in 1939?"

Fido nodded, his white prickly chin making a crackling sound against the collar of his grubby shirt. "Sure, 1939. I was promoted to bell captain that year. March 1939."

"Did you ever see Boofuls here?"

"Boofuls?" said Fido suspiciously. "Why'd you ask that?"

"I'm just interested, that's all. I'm writing a book about his life."

"Well," sniffed Fido, "he didn't have too much of a life, did he? But he sure had a memorable death."

"Did you see him?"

"Of course I saw him. He was here all the time, him

and that Redd woman. Every month; and all kinds of others, too. Famous actors, you'd know them all. Famous directors, too."

Martin frowned. "You mean Boofuls used to meet a whole lot of other actors and directors here, every month?"

"That's right. It was a joke. Nobody was supposed to know. Big secret, don't tell the press, that kind of thing. And to tell you the truth, I don't think the press ever did find out. But we knew, all of the staff. You couldn't help recognizing somebody like Clark Gable, now, could you? And there was George Cukor and Lionel Atwill and dozens of others. All the big names from 1939, they came here. Maybe not every month, but pretty well."

Ramone warned, "You'd better not be putting us on, Mr. Fido."

"Why should I put you on?" Fido challenged him. "It's true, it happened. Every month, here at the Hollywood Divine, in the Leicester Suite."

"And Boofuls was *always* here?" Martin asked him.

Fido nodded. "They wouldn't start without Boofuls."

"Wouldn't start what?" said Ramone.

Fido puffed out his blotchy cheeks. "Don't ask me, how should I know? It was all supposed to be secret, right? We laid them on a spread before they started—chicken, lobster, stuff like that—and then we had to lock the doors and leave them to it—whatever it was they were doing. But believe me, they were all famous. You'd have known them all. Errol Flynn, he used to come. Joan Crawford. Wilfred Buckland, the art director. Fifty or sixty of them, every month, sometimes more."

Martin said, "You're *sure* about this?"

"Sure I'm sure. I was the bell captain."

"Well, how long did these get-togethers go on for?"

"Two, three in the morning, sometimes longer."

"And Boofuls stayed there all that time?"

"I used to see him leaving, four o'clock in the morning sometimes. That Redd woman used to cover him up with a cloak and a hood, but you couldn't mistake him."

Martin said, "He was only eight years old, what was he doing staying up all night?"

Fido coughed and then noisily cleared his throat. "*I* don't know what the hell he was doing, staying up all night. We used to listen at the door sometimes, but we could never hear nothing. Sometimes music. But they used to have girls in as well. Not exactly hookers but what you might call starlets."

Martin looked at Ramone, but all Ramone could do was shake his head. "Don't ask me, man, I never heard of anything like this. Either this guy's shooting us a line, or else his brain's gone, or else we just came across the biggest Hollywood mystery that ever was."

"Listen," Martin told Fido, "when you were working here, where did they keep the safe-deposit boxes? Can you remember that?"

"Certainly I can remember," said Fido. "What's it worth?"

Reluctantly, Martin handed Fido another ten-dollar bill. He snapped it, the same way he had snapped the first one. Then he sniffed and said, "They used to keep the safe-deposit boxes in back of the manager's office, through the archway behind the desk. But if you're looking for them, I can save you some trouble, because they ain't there now. Round about 1951, when the Hollywood Divine really started losing money, there was some kind of plan to refurbish it, you know, and they shifted a whole lot of stuff down to the basement. The only trouble was, the plan fell through, lack of money, zoning problems, something like that, and everything that was shifted down to the basement just stayed there."

"So that's where the safe-deposit boxes are now?"

"You've got it, your honor. Not to mention two thousand square feet of moldy carpet, and enough velvet drapes to make Little Lord Fauntleroy pants for every down-and-out in Greater L.A."

Ramone gave a sharp, unamused laugh. Fido shrugged and gave a goofy grin, baring abscessed gums and brown, tartar-clogged teeth.

"One more thing . . ." put in Martin. "Who's this Redd woman you keep talking about? I thought that Boofuls was looked after by his grandmother."

Fido said, "I never knew too much about her. But she was the one who booked the suite, that's how we got to know her name. R–E–D–D, Redd, that was it, but it could have been a what's-it's-name, you know, pursue-dough-name."

"Do you have any idea what her relationship to Boofuls was?"

Fido shook his head. "No idea. She just rushed him in before it began and rushed him out again when it was over."

"Did you get to see her face? What she looked like?"

"Well . . . briefly. It's a long time ago now. But she was pale, you know what I mean, the sort of pale that looks like somebody's been ill, or shut up for a long time without going out in the sunshine. Pretty, in a way, but kind of *sharp* pretty. Sharp nose, sharp chin, sharp eyes. Classy, too. Definitely classy. But sharp."

"What did she used to wear?"

"Always the same, black evening cloak, red dress underneath. Never saw what style it was. She was in and out of here so darned quick."

Martin was mystified by all this. He had never heard of any other woman escorting Boofuls besides his grandmother; and he had certainly never heard of monthly get-togethers of movie stars at the Hollywood Divine Hotel, with Boofuls apparently presiding.

"I hope for your sake this is on the level," he told Fido.

Fido saluted with a hand that was gray with grease. "You never came across a servant so true, your honor."

For twenty more dollars, the vacant-eyed desk clerk took Martin and Ramone up to what had once been the Leicester Suite. They climbed the wide marble stairs to the mezzanine floor and crossed an echoing landing that smelled of Sterno. The desk clerk led them up to two wide carved doors—some of their panels broken now and nailed up with sheets of ply—and unlocked them with keys from a huge jangling ring.

"We have to keep this place locked, every junkie in town was using it as a shooting gallery. We used to drag out two or three stiffs every single morning, OD'd on crack."

Inside, by the light of half a dozen bare bulbs, they cautiously explored a hotel suite that must once have been magnificent. Because it was on the mezzanine floor, its rooms were half as high again as any other rooms in the hotel. It walls gleamed with gold and silver wallpaper, and there were gilded Renaissance moldings on its murky ceilings and around the doors.

The desk clerk led them through an inner lobby, and

then through more double doors to a cavernous room that must have been the lounge. There was a grand gilded fireplace and a gilded chandelier, but all the furniture and the carpets had been taken out. The floor was littered with old yellowed newspapers and rat droppings; and in the far corner there stood, unaccountably, a green and white garden swing-seat.

Their footsteps scuffed and echoed. Ramone, with his hands in his pockets, said, "You can't believe that Clark Gable was ever here, can you?"

"What was he *doing* here, that's what I want to know," said Martin. "What was Boofuls doing here?"

"Orgies, maybe?" suggested Ramone. He walked around the swing-seat and then pushed it. It creaked backward and forward, backward and forward, *squueeaakkk-squikkkk, squeeeaakk-squikkkk.*

Martin said, "A small boy holding orgies? It doesn't make sense."

"Well, don't ask me, man," said Ramone. He sniffed. "This place gives me the heebie-jeebies."

The desk clerk asked, "You done now? There's nothing else to see."

"Yes," said Martin, "I guess we're done. Can you take us down to the cellars?"

They left the Leicester Suite and the double doors were locked behind them. The desk clerk took them downstairs to the lobby and then along a narrow corridor to the kitchens and the service areas. The kitchens were filthy: strewn with rubbish and deserted. The grease-encrusted oven doors hung open. It was difficult for Martin to believe that the Hollywood Divine's celebrated *homard orientale* had once been prepared here, as well as the famous fiery pudding of red cherries and Grand Marnier created especially for Gloria Swanson.

The desk clerk unlocked the cellar doors. "There's a light switch down on the left. You can look all you want; I have to get back to the desk. Just tell me when you're through."

Together, Martin and Ramone groped their way down the first flight of wide concrete steps. Martin found the light switch and flicked it; a row of fluorescent tubes illuminated a wide vaulted cellar stacked to the ceiling with chairs, tables, folding beds, mattresses, chalkboards, lampshades, statuettes, signs saying Exit and No Smoking, boxes, crates, and rolled-up carpets.

Martin began carefully to climb through this collected detritus of the Hollywood Divine's history, his arms stretched out to keep his balance. He trod on a cardboard box full of brass lamp sockets, and they showered onto the floor like Aladdin's treasure.

"Any sign of those safe-deposit boxes?" Ramone asked him.

"I don't know. There's a whole lot of stuff covered by sheets, right at the back. I'm going to take a look now."

Martin clambered across stacks of rollaway beds to reach the far side of the cellar, where it was darker and the air was suffocatingly still. Something tall and angular was concealed by a stained gray sheet; something as tall as a man with one arm outstretched. Martin tugged at the sheet, but it was caught.

"What's that?" called Ramone, clambering after him across the beds. He pushed one foot through the springs of a rollaway bed, and there was a loud *gddoinngg* noise, followed by a sharp exclamation of "Goddamn it!"

Martin pulled at the sheet again, and this time it tore wide open. He shouted out in fright, and trod backward, and almost lost his balance. Out of the ripped sheet a shining black face was staring at him, a face with white eyes and reddened lips.

Ramone came forward and tore off the rest of the sheet. "Heyy . . ." He grinned. "Not bad. She shouldn't've scared you."

It was a 1930s statue of an African dancer, probably made out of plaster. She was wearing ostrich feathers in her hair and a grass skirt and carrying a zebra-skin shield. "Very bodacious ta-tas," Ramone remarked, peering inside the sheet.

They climbed farther along the length of the wall, and, at last, jammed into one of the corners, they came across the safe-deposit boxes. There were four banks of them, lying on their backs on the floor, and almost completely buried under dozens of folding wooden chairs.

"At least nobody could stroll out with *these*," said Ramone.

It took them more than ten minutes simply to move all the chairs off the top of the safe-deposit boxes. Martin rubbed dust and grime from the topmost bank of boxes. 1–100. That meant that they would have to lift the entire bank of boxes out of the way in order to get to number 531 somewhere underneath.

They each took hold of one end of the boxes and tried to lift them up. They were impossibly heavy. "We're going to rupture ourselves, shifting these," said Martin. "Maybe we'd better slide them instead."

Grunting, cursing, they managed to slide the top bank of boxes off to one side; then tilt it so that it dropped upright onto the floor.

"What do you bet the numbers we want are right at the bottom of the stack?" said Ramone.

He peered at the labels of the next bank of safe-deposit boxes and then rubbed one or two of them with the heel of his hand. "Numbers 500 through 600, thank the Lord."

Martin climbed up onto the boxes and ran his fingers down the labels until he found 531.

"I'll give you a thousand to one the key don't fit," said Ramone. "Nobody with *your* luck is going to find the right box first time."

"Theo said the Hollywood Divine," Martin told him. "And, believe me, Theo was really psychic. Well, sensitive, that's what he said."

"I guess anybody would be sensitive working for Elmore Sweet," Ramone commented.

Martin took out the key that Sister Boniface had given him and fitted it into the lock of the safe-deposit box. As he did so, he was certain that he heard somebody whistling, somewhere upstairs in the derelict hotel. He hesitated, and listened, and then he heard it again. It was an odd little melody from *Sunshine Serenade*. Boofuls sang it at the very end of the movie, when he believed (mistakenly, of course) that he had lost his mother.

> *Apples are sweeter than lemons*
> *Lemons are sweeter than limes*
> *But there's nothing so sweet as the mem'ry of you*
> *And the sadness of happier times*

The song was unusual because it had been written by George Garratt rather than Boofuls' regular team of writers; and because—after Garratt had argued with L. B. Mayer over "artistic differences"—the whole sequence had been cut out of the prints that had been sent out on general release. Martin knew the song because it was still included in the video of *Sunshine Ser-*

enade that his friend Gerry had sent him from the M-G-M archives, but who else would have known it?

Fido, possibly, if he had ever heard Boofuls singing it. Or George Garratt, except that in 1958 George Garratt had washed down two bottles of chloral hydrate pills with a fifth of Polish vodka and been found to be DOA at Laurel Canyon Hospital. Or—if his image in Martin's mirror had been more than just an image, and if there was any truth at all in what Nurse Newton had said about him—Boofuls himself.

"That didn't seem to make too much difference—him being dead."

Ramone said, "What's wrong, man? You look like you seen a ghost."

Martin strained his ears, but the whistling had died away, faint and echoing, somewhere upstairs in the gloomy corridors of the Hollywood Divine Hotel.

"Did you hear something?" he asked Ramone.

Ramone shook his head.

"I don't know . . . I thought I heard somebody whistling."

Ramone sniffed. "Probably the wind, *mi amigo*. Or the plumbing."

All the same, Martin was sure that he had heard that plaintive, unremembered song. "The Sadness of Happier Times," words and music by George Garratt, vocal rendition by Walter Lemuel Crossley, known all over the world as Boofuls.

Martin tried to turn the key in the lock of the safe-deposit box. It was stiff and rusted, but he gradually managed to budge it. "There! It's the right key, I'm sure of it! It's just so darn hard to turn it!"

"Just don't break it, that's all," Ramone cautioned him, "otherwise you're never going to get this suckah open."

The levers grated together; and then quite suddenly the key turned all the way around, and Martin was able to lift open the door. The door of the safe-deposit box was quite small—only nine inches by four—but the inside was nearly two feet deep. Now that it was resting on its back, Martin would have to put his hand inside it like a lucky dip. He peered into it cautiously. Ever since that brindled cat Pickle had come flying out at him from the darkness underneath his desk, he had felt cautious about sticking his head in where it wasn't wanted, and also where it *was* wanted.

Ramone tried to look inside, too, and they bumped heads.

"Looks like it's empty," said Ramone; not without relief.

"Well, I won't be able to tell until I put my hand in," Martin replied.

"You're going to put your hand in? Supposing there's something *in* there?"

Martin lifted his head and looked at him. "Something *in* there? Something like what?"

"Well, I don't know, man, supposing it's a trap. Supposing that nun that gave you the key wasn't a real nun, supposing she was just another one of these hallucinations—well, it *could* have happened, you can't deny it *could* have happened—and supposing she knows there's some kind of booby trap inside here, just waiting for somebody like you to stick his hot little hand right into it. I mean, supposing it's something as bad as that cat? I mean, do you *like* your hand, or what?"

"Ramone—" Martin interrupted him. "The likelihood of there being *any*thing inside this box is pretty damn remote, wouldn't you say? Quite apart from the high probability that whatever was in here was probably collected by its rightful owner fifty years ago, the hotel management wouldn't have simply dragged these boxes down here and dumped them without going through them first. People used to keep money and diamonds and passports in these boxes, my friend. I can't believe that anything like *that* would have gotten left behind, can you?"

Ramone said, "Money and diamonds and passports don't bite your fingers off. I'm talking about that supernatural stuff."

Martin hesitated for a moment. He didn't like to admit it, but it had occurred to him, too, that something vicious from the world beyond might be nestling in the bottom of this safe-deposit box; or even something vicious from the here and now. Hadn't he read that scorpions can survive for fifty years without food or water?

At length, however, he carefully dipped his bare hand into the darkness of the open box, feeling all around the sides as he did so. Bare metal, nothing so far. He ventured further. All the time, Ramone was watching him intently, chewing at his lip. "You feel anything, man? Is there anything there?"

Martin was about to take his hand out when his fingertips skimmed something that felt like soft tissue paper. "Hold on," he said. "There's something here."

He patted the bottom of the safe-deposit box and felt a package of some sort, in very fine crinkled paper.

"It's not a booby trap, is it?" Ramone asked him.

"No, no. I don't think so. It's a package. I can't work out what's in it. Something hard, by the feel of it; no—more than one, maybe three or four. They're hard and they're curved. There's something *crunchy*, too. Maybe it's straw, or wood shavings. Hold on—if I can squeeze my other hand in, I can lift it out."

With intense concentration, Martin pushed his other hand into the safe-deposit box until he could take hold of the package on both sides. It was very loosely wrapped together, and he was worried that if he lifted it up with one hand, the contents—whatever they were—would tumble out.

"Steady, man," said Ramone as he slowly raised the package out of the safe-deposit box and laid it carefully down.

Martin reached back inside the box, but there was nothing else there. "This is it," he said. "The sole contents."

The package was a loose assembly of thin black tissue paper, tied with a thin greasy braid of something that could have been human hair. Where the hair was knotted, it was sealed with black wax, on which somebody had imprinted the crest from a signet ring or a brass seal. Martin gently shook the package, and inside he could feel a number of heavy curved objects, about four or five inches long, and a wad of crisp padding.

"Let's take it under the light and open it up," Martin suggested.

Ramone's eyes widened. "Supposing the mirror doesn't want us to? Supposing it tries to fix *us* the way it fixed Homer Theobald? You want to die with your lungs coming out of your mouth, because sure as hell I don't."

"I always thought you were the great *Huevo Duro*," Martin teased him.

"*Huevo Duro*," Ramone repeated with contempt. It was Spanish for hard-cooked egg.

Martin gently carried the package over to one of the scores of tables that had been stored in the Hollywood Divine's cellar. He cleared off the dust and the rat droppings, and then he laid the package down. "Do

you have a knife?" he asked Ramone. Without saying a
word, Ramone unenthusiastically produced a switch-
blade and flicked it open.

"*Huevo Duro*," he muttered.

Handling the knife with extreme care, Martin sawed
through the braided hair which seemed to be all that
was keeping this messily tied package together. Then
he folded back each leaf of the black tissue paper until
he revealed what was inside. As soon as the package
was open, Ramone crossed himself and whispered,
"*Madre mia.*"

Lying on the black paper were four claws—thick and
horny and black. They were like no other claws that
Martin had seen before. They weren't lion claws, because lion claws are narrow and hooked at the end.
They weren't eagle talons—they were far too large.
Martin reached out and picked one up between finger
and thumb, and asked, "What in hell kind of a creature
did these come from?"

"Believe me, I'm sure glad the rest of it ain't here,"
Ramone told him. "Come on, man, that stuff is bad
news. I mean really bad news."

Martin laid down the claw and picked up the wad of
padding. It was black and shiny, not unlike horsehair.
In fact it *was* hair of some kind, and it was attached to
a small soft leathery patch that looked like a torn piece
of dried-up scalp. It felt extremely old, almost mum-
mified, and it felt extremely nasty.

"What do you think it could be?" Martin asked.

"Well, I don't know," said Ramone, "but I *hate* it."
He peered at it more closely, and then he said, "You
know what it reminds me of? It reminds me of voodoo.
You know, witch doctors, that kind of thing. And those
disgusting African statues all covered in skin and bits

of fabric and you don't know for sure where any of it's *been*, you know?"

Martin juggled the heavy claws in the palm of his hand. "I don't know. What on earth was Boofuls' grandmother doing with the key to *this* stuff?"

"Maybe she wasn't," Ramone suggested. "It's been fifty years, right? Maybe this stuff belongs to somebody else altogether."

"You don't think that, do you?" Martin replied. "Not after what's been happening with the mirror? This all ties up somehow."

Ramone peeled back the tissue paper a little farther. "Hey, look—you missed something."

In one corner of the package, there was a small screwed-up piece of black tissue. Martin opened it up and found another key, identical to the key with which he had opened the safe-deposit box. He held it up and examined it closely.

"I wonder what *this* opens?" he asked.

He turned it over. There was the same manufacturer's name on it, Woods, and it looked as if it probably opened another of the boxes. But this time there was no number on it.

"If we had all night, we could try opening every box here," Ramone suggested.

But at that moment, the desk clerk reappeared, wending his way through the furniture. "I got to lock up now. Did you find what you were looking for?"

"More or less," said Martin.

The desk clerk frowned at the black-tissue package. "That's not dope or anything?"

Martin shook his head. "Sorry to disappoint you. This is just relics; and not particularly valuable relics

at that. You know what I mean, sentimental value
only."

The desk clerk sniffed dryly; the thumping sniff of
the habitual cokehead. "Sure, sentimental value only.
Now I got to lock up."

Dr. Ewart Rice stood in his dressing room in his undershirt and his formal black pants, his suspenders hanging down like a recently released catapult. He was
shaving, and humming to himself. The early evening
sun shone warmly through the white percale blind that
he had drawn down over the window, and reflected in
the hot water in the washbasin, so that a spindly light-
fairy danced on the wall in front of him.

He and Mrs. Rice had been invited to dinner that
evening by one of his pleasantest friends, Bill Asscher,
the movie producer. The Asschers' dinners could always be counted on for superb food, hilarious conversation, pretty girls, and generous martinis. Mrs. Rice
always said that he made a fool of himself when he
went to the Asschers' dinners, but Dr. Rice always replied that if a man couldn't make a fool of himself by
the time he was sixty years old, then he was a fool.

He rinsed his razor in the washbasin and reached for
his hand towel. From the bedroom next door, he heard
Mrs. Rice calling, "Aren't you ready yet, Ewart? If we
have to go, we might as well go on time. Then we can
leave on time!"

"Won't be a moment!" Dr. Rice called back.

He examined himself closely in the mirror. He never
let it show, not to other people, but he was really quite
vain. He liked to look absolutely immaculate: immaculately groomed, immaculately shaved. As far as he
was concerned, the thought of going out in public with

sleep in the corner of his eye or hair growing out of his
nostrils was anathema.

He turned his face from one side to the other. Sixty,
but still handsome in a Celtic way. Perhaps that left-
hand sideburn could do with a trim. He couldn't stand
the thought of a pretty girl sitting next to him at dinner and covertly glancing at his left-hand sideburn and
thinking, *What raggedy sideburns this old coot has.* Dr.
Rice's vanity was vanity of top Wesselton quality, in
that he could imagine himself inside the minds of
everybody he met, and of course in his imagination
they were all thinking about *him* and nothing else.

Dr. Rice opened the drawer next to the washbasin
and took out his sharp hairdressing scissors—professional scissors, not on sale to the public. He leaned toward the mirror again, holding up the scissors in his
right hand, tugging the skin of his cheek with the fingertips of the left hand, taking a last appraising look.

He blinked. His eyes seemed to blur. He blinked
again, but his face in the mirror was still blurry. He
wiped the glass with a dry facecloth, thinking it must
have steamed up, but his face remained just as indistinct.

"Agnes!" he called, thinking that the maid had tried
to clean his mirror with wax polish. "Agnes, this mirror, I can't see a thing!"

"I'm just putting on my eyelashes," Mrs. Rice replied.

Dr. Rice looked back at the mirror; and then he shivered, the way people do in a sudden icy draft. *Staring
at him out of the reflected bathroom was not his own
face, but the face of a child, a blond-haired, bland-faced
child, with pinprick eyes and an expression of bright
childish malice.*

Almost paralyzed with fright, Dr. Rice widened his eyes and tried to outstare the image in the mirror. If he stared at it hard enough, it would go away. Ghosts and spirits can never stand up to scrutiny in broad daylight.

But outside the window, the evening sun began to die, and the dressing room suddenly grew darker, as if it were a cage that had been draped in black baize. And the pale child's face remained, staring back at Dr. Rice fierce and unabashed, almost gleeful.

"Pickle-nearest-the-wind," the child mouthed. *"Pickle-nearest-the-wind."*

"Go away," said Dr. Rice in a hoarse whisper. "Go away, do you hear me? Go away!"

"Did you say something, dear?" his wife called out.

"Go away, go away, go away," Dr. Rice intoned.

"You told tales," the child replied. *"Tell-tale-tit, your tongue shall be split, and every cat and dog in town shall have a little bit."*

"Go away," Dr. Rice begged him.

But now the child's eyes opened wider, and his smile grew broader and merrier, and Dr. Rice found himself raising his right hand up to the side of his face, his right hand in which he was holding his sharp professional scissors.

"No," he pleaded.

The child smiled. *"Tell-tale-tit."*

"I didn't mean to tell. He asked me. I didn't think I was doing anything wrong."

"You told, you told, you told."

"I didn't mean to!" Dr. Rice wept. "Please, my God, I didn't mean to. He *asked* me about you, that's all. I didn't think you were still—"

"You didn't think I was still alive? You didn't think I

was still here? Then you are foolish, aren't you? Just as foolish as your wife says you are. Because I have been here since time began and I shall always be here, long after *you* are ashes!"

Mrs. Rice said, "Ewart? Is anything wrong? You really do sound most peculiar."

But Dr. Rice, when he opened his mouth, found that he was unable to speak. His throat felt as if it were being gripped in a steel claw; he couldn't do anything but gag for air. His left hand scrabbled against the counter beside the washbasin, knocking over his Gucci razor stand and his bottles of after-shave and his porcelain dish of Chanel soap. His right hand turned toward his face, his thumb and fingers slowly and inexorably prized apart by some uncontrollable tightening of his muscles, so that the pointed blades of the scissors opened, too.

As he gargled for air, his mouth stretched open and his tongue protruded, mauve from lack of oxygen, fat with effort, glistening and wagging.

"Tell-tale-tit, your tongue shall be split, and every cat and dog in town shall have a little bit!"

Dr. Rice cut into his own tongue with the hairdressing scissors. There was a terrible crunch of flesh that he could feel right down to the roots of his tongue, right down to the pit of his stomach. His throat muscles contracted in an attempt to scream, but the grip on his neck remained, and there was nothing he could do but choke and struggle.

Blood gushed down the front of his undershirt as if he were pulling on a bright red sweater, and splattered into his shaving water. But the child in the mirror hadn't finished with him yet. His trembling hand opened up the blades of the scissors again, and enclosed his tongue from the side this time, so close to his lips that he cut his mouth as well. He could feel the sharpness of the scissors on the top and the bottom of his tongue, and his eyes bulged in hysterical terror.

If I've split my tongue, that can be sewn up and healed. But oh, God, if I cut it right off—

The boy's face was sparkling with delight. "You told, you told, you *told!*"

"*Gggnnggghh,*" pleaded Dr. Rice.

"You told, and you shouldn't, and now you have to pay!"

Dr. Rice's right hand went into a taut slow-motion convulsion and closed the grips of the scissors. He cut right through to the first split, and half of his tongue dropped into his washbasin. Then, shuddering all over, he raised his left hand and gripped the remaining half of his tongue by its tip, and scissored that off, too.

Then he stood in front of the mirror, staring at it in shock, his lips closed, but a thin, dark, glutinous cascade of blood poured down his chin. Everything was bloody: his face and his hair and his clothes and his dressing room. He looked like a circus clown who had gone berserk with his pot of scarlet makeup.

Mrs. Rice came into the dressing room, her hair stiffly lacquered, buttoning up the cuff of her shiny blue evening dress as she came. "Ewart, what on *earth* are you playing at? We've only got fifteen minutes before we—"

Her husband stared at her pitifully out of a mask of blood. She stood with her hand over her mouth, staring back at him, and she didn't know what to do.

The man came flip-flapping on monkish leather sandals along the sidewalk, his spectacles reflecting the streetlights, his pipe clenched comfortably between his teeth. His Standard poodle trotted beside him on a long leash.

"Just as far as the bushes at the end of the development," he informed his poodle. "Then you can do your ah-ahs and we can turn around and head for home."

He passed the front of the Rice house. "That poor Dr. Rice. God alone knows what happened to *him*. Taken away like that, in an ambulance. God alone knows."

It was then that the poodle stopped and stiffened and started to growl, way down deep in its throat.

"What's the matter, Redford? What is it, boy?"

The poodle continued to growl. The Rices' neighbor peered through the shadows at the side of the Rice residence; and there was a window open and a white blind flapping.

The neighbor hesitated. He wasn't too keen to go and investigate, since he knew that Dr. Rice was still in the hospital and Mrs. Rice was with him, and that the house was empty. There had been three armed burglaries already that month in the Hollywood Reservoir district; and in one of them, a friend of his had been shot in the shoulder. All the same, he waited, frowning, to see if there was any sign of a burglar in the house, and he slipped his poodle off the leash.

"Heel, Redford."

There was a lengthy pause. All the man could hear were the endless orchestrations of the cicadas and the distant muttering of traffic on the freeways. The poodle whined and snuffled.

Suddenly, the white blind at the side of the house snapped up, with a heart-stopping clatter, and a large dark shape bounded out of the window and ran across the lawn.

The poodle rushed silently after it and caught up with it just behind a large flowering shrub. The neighbor ran forward, then abruptly stopped and told himself "Whoa!" when he heard the ferocity of the snarling in the shadows. He reached into his coat pocket and took out his flashlight, and cautiously probed the darkness with its thin beam.

He didn't understand what he saw; but it still made his stomach feel as if it were gradually filling up with ice water. A hefty brindled tomcat was crouched in the bush, savagely gnawing at a piece of blue-gray meat. His own poodle was standing beside the cat, and he was chewing something, too. A shredded piece of it was hanging from one side of his jaw.

"Redford!" the neighbor screamed at his dog. And then, to the cat, he screamed, "Shoo! Get the hell out of it! Shoo!"

The cat stayed where it was, staring at him with eyes that gleamed frighteningly blue in the light of his flashlight. The poodle, too, refused to come to heel.

"Redford, you son of a bitch!" the neighbor screeched, and lifted the leash to smack his poodle across the nose.

But the cat spat at him so evilly, and Redford growled with such mutinous ferocity, that the man backed away, and shrugged, and said, "Okay, forget it. Forget it. You want to squat in a bush and eat squirrels, see if I care. Just don't expect any Gravy Train tomorrow, that's all."

Detective Ernest Oeste of the Hollywood police was sent back to the Rice residence at eleven-thirty that evening in order to retrieve two pieces of Dr. Rice's tongue which had been overlooked by paramedics when they first answered his wife's emergency call.

There was no question of the pieces being sewn back into place. The damage to Dr. Rice's tongue was far too extensive. But they were needed as evidence that Dr. Rice had (almost unbelievably) inflicted his injuries upon himself.

"He loved to talk, why should he do such a thing?" Mrs. Rice had wept.

Detective Oeste had to report after a lengthy search that Dr. Rice's tongue had apparently been taken and eaten by a rat or a cat.

Detective Oeste's immediate superior, Sergeant Frederick Quinn, sat for a very long time in front of his report sheet before typing, *"Cat got his tongue."* Almost immediately, he deleted it, and typed, *"Evidence removed by predatory animals."*

"Can you believe this case?" he asked the world.

Seven

MARTIN RETURNED to Franklin Avenue that Sunday night exhausted; and a little drunk, too. Ramone had taken him to his favorite restaurant and bar, Una Porción, on Santa Monica, three blocks west of the Palm. They had drunk three bottles of López de Heredia and eaten countless *tapas*—cheese, squid, spicy sausage, sardines, meatballs.

Ramone had said, as they drove home along Santa Monica with the warm gasoline-fumy breeze blowing in their faces, "Sometimes you have to make a deliberate effort to forget things, you know that? Otherwise you'd end up crazy. I forgot Lugosi already. He never happened. He was nothing but a figment of my imagination. When you forget, there's no pain. And who needs pain?"

"I'm trying to forget that my stomach is having a protest march," Martin replied.

"What's the matter, you don't like Spanish food?"

212

"Each individual piece is okay, but somehow they don't seem to cohabit in my stomach very well. I can hear the sausages arguing with the squid. What are *you* doing here, eight-legs, this stomach isn't big enough for the two of us."

Ramone had slapped him on the shoulder. "Heyy, come on, you're going to be all right. What you need is a nice big glass of Fundador."

"Ramone," Martin had insisted, "I'm going to take you home."

He had dropped Ramone off; gripped his hand for a second as a thank-you; and then headed back toward his apartment. He parked awkwardly, his rear wheels well away from the curb, but he decided that whatever was good enough for Hunter was good enough for him. He switched off the car stereo, cutting off Simply Red in midfalsetto, and vaulted out of the car without opening the door.

He had only just pushed his key into the lock, however, when the landing lights were switched on, and by the time he had stepped into the hall, Mr. Capelli appeared at the head of the stairs, in his lurid gold bathrobe and his monogrammed slippers. "Martin? Martin? Is that you? I've been calling all over!"

"Oh, hello, Mr. Capelli. How are you doing? Did you have to wear that robe? I'm feeling a little nauseous."

"Is Emilio with you?" Mr. Capelli demanded, ignoring his gibe.

"Emilio? Of course not. I've been out with Ramone."

Mr. Capelli came halfway down the stairs, and then stopped, holding the railing, looking gray-faced and serious. "Emilio is gone, Martin. Disappeared."

"What do you mean, gone?" asked Martin, trying to

keep a steady eye on Mr. Capelli in spite of three bottles of Spanish rosé. Then, "*Gone?* Gone where?"

"How should I know? One minute he was playing on the stairs with his toy cars; then his grandmother called him in for his bath; and he was gone."

"He didn't go upstairs, did he? He didn't go up to my apartment?"

"How should I know? I don't know where he went!"

Martin clasped Mr. Capelli's shoulder and gave him a reassuring squeeze. "Don't worry, Mr. Capelli, we'll find him. Everything's going to be fine."

"But where is he? He never wandered off before."

"Listen, really, he's going to be fine."

"We called the police," said Mr. Capelli. "We called the police straightaway."

"And what did they say?"

"Well, they said they were going to put out a bulletin, what else could they do? But still no word."

Martin said, "Please—if you hear anything—don't forget to tell me, okay?"

"I tell you, I tell you." Mr. Capelli was deeply distressed. First to lose his daughter; then to lose his daughter's only child.

Martin climbed the stairs to his apartment. He had locked the door before he went out, but Mr. Capelli had a drawerful of spare keys, and it was quite possible that Emilio had found one and let himself in. He prayed not. But he had a terrible feeling that the playmate in the mirror had proved irresistible and that Emilio had come upstairs to see him. He opened the door and went inside. He listened. No voices, no singing. Silence. He waited for a little while, and then he walked along the hallway and opened the sitting room door.

The room was empty. Only the sofa, only the desk, only the mirror, with its chilly, uncompromising surface. Martin stepped slowly in, his shoes sounding loudly on the bare boards, his heart silently racing. *Pickle-di-pickle-di-pickle-di-pickle.*

He approached the mirror, reached out his hand, and touched it. It was cold, unyielding.

"Emilio?" he called quietly.

There was no reply. Only the sound of nighttime traffic on Highland; only the drone of an airplane headed toward Burbank. Only the wind, tapping at the venetian blinds like Blind Pew groping his way toward the Admiral Benbow.

"Emilio?"

Again, no answer. Martin stood for a long time in front of the mirror, quivering, cold, wondering what the hell he was going to do. Because what *could* he do if Emilio had actually disappeared into the mirror, looking for Boofuls? How could he find him? How could he get him out? And what, finally, could he tell Mr. and Mrs. Capelli? That his obsession with Boofuls had lost them their only grandchild? How could he possibly compensate them for that?

He felt a chill in his body that was worse than the chill of death. It was the chill of total helplessness; of total loss.

Mr. Capelli came into the room and stood staring at him.

"You called out Emilio," he said.

"I, uh—"

"You called out Emilio. Why did you do that?"

"Mr. Capelli, I have to be honest."

"Honest, yes," said Mr. Capelli. "Be honest. Be honest and tell me what you really think, that your mirror has taken Emilio. Your mirror has taken my grand-son!"

Martin rubbed his aching head. "Mr. Capelli, I have no way of telling. You saw what happened before—you saw the way he was almost sucked into it. Well, I locked the door when I left the apartment this morn-ing, but it's possible, isn't it, that Emilio might have found one of your spare keys? And if he did that . . ."

He paused. He didn't really know what to say.

Mr. Capelli shuffled forward in his slippers and peered into the mirror. All he could see, however, was his own gray face and Martin's empty sitting-room.

"If the mirror has taken him," he said in a thick voice, without looking around, "what can we do? How can we get him back?"

"I have no idea," Martin admitted.

Mr. Capelli kept on staring at his own reflection. "There isn't anybody who knows about these things? You talked about finding a priest. Maybe a priest would know. My own priest, Father Lucas."

Martin swallowed. "I had somebody here this morn-ing . . . a kind of a medium called Homer Theobald. I'm afraid he wouldn't go near it."

"He wouldn't go near this mirror? Did he say why not?"

"Well, he said it was—powerful, dangerous, I don't know."

"And he wouldn't help?"

Martin shook his head.

"Maybe I can talk to him," said Mr. Capelli. "Maybe I can persuade him."

"I don't think so, Mr. Capelli. Homer Theobald died this afternoon. He had some kind of hemorrhage. I don't know whether it had anything to do with the mirror, but believe me, it seems like the mirror doesn't like to be crossed."

Mr. Capelli said, "I'm going to call Father Lucas."

"All right," Martin agreed. "I guess anything's better than sitting on our hands."

Mr. Capelli went downstairs. Martin waited for a while, watching the mirror in the hope that Emilio might reappear; then he went through to the bathroom and took a hot shower. By the time Mr. Capelli came back he had sobered up, and coffee was perking in the kitchen.

"Did you talk to the priest?" Martin asked him.

"I talked to his housekeeper. She says he's at the hospital, somebody's dying, he has to give them the last rites. He's going to call me when he returns home."

Martin poured out coffee. "In that case, there isn't anything else we can do, is there? Just sit tight and hope that Emilio *hasn't* gone into the mirror; and that the cops find him."

Mr. Capelli went through to the sitting room, and Martin followed him.

"I never dreamed such a terrible thing could happen," said Mr. Capelli. He approached the mirror and touched its surface with both hands. "I never dreamed."

He turned around and there were tears streaming down his cheeks. "You don't know what Emilio means to me, Martin. You just don't know. He's all I have left, all I have left. And now I can't find him, I feel like I've lost my own soul."

Martin hugged Mr. Capelli close and patted his back to soothe him. "Come on, Mr. Capelli, everything's going to work out. We'll find Emilio, I promise you."

Mr. Capelli looked up. "How can you make such a promise?"

"Because I'm not going to rest until we get him back. I'm going to try everything. Police, priests, mediums, everything. And I'm going to find out all about this mirror, why it's got this power, what the hell it wants."

"Well, you're a good boy, Martin," said Mr. Capelli with a sniff. "I just wish you never bring this terrible mirror home with you. I could cut off my own hands for helping you to carry it."

When Mr. Capelli had gone back downstairs, Martin went into the kitchen and drank two strong cups of black coffee, one after the other. Then he returned to the sitting room and pushed the sofa around so that it faced the mirror. He was determined he was going to keep a vigil here, in case Emilio reappeared.

He switched out the lights and made himself comfortable on the sofa under an Indian blanket that Jane had bought when she went to Phoenix that time. The only reason she hadn't taken it with her was that Martin had kept it in the trunk of his car and she hadn't found it.

He took off his wristwatch and propped it on the arm of the sofa so that he could see it easily. It was a few minutes after midnight, Monday morning already. He yawned, stifled it, and then yawned again. He shouldn't find it difficult to stay awake all night. After all, his mind was racing and he was up to his ears in caffeine; and if he *did* start feeling at all sleepy, he had a few bennies in the bottom drawer of his desk.

He stared at himself in the mirror. A pale-faced man sitting on a sofa in a moonlit room. It looked rather like one of those surrealistic paintings by Magritte. He

remembered seeing one Magritte painting in which a
man is looking into a mirror, and all he can see is the
back of his own head.

Mirrors, he thought, have always been mysterious.
But he was going to unravel the particular mystery of
this mirror even if it killed him.

He didn't realize that he was gradually falling asleep;
that his head was drooping to one side, that his fingers
were slowly opening like the petals of a water lily.

He jerked, and his eyes fluttered open for a moment,
but then he dropped even more deeply into sleep than
he had been before. His breathing became thick and
harsh, the breathing of a man who has drunk too much
wine. His wristwatch ticked softly beside him: one
o'clock, one-thirty. Outside, the street was deserted,
the night was silent.

He dreamed that he was traveling through the night on
a bus, mile after mile, hour after hour, and that he was
the sole passenger. He knew that the bus was traveling
in the wrong direction, and that it would take him
days to get back to where he really wanted to go. He
tried to stand up, to talk to the driver, but the bus was
swaying so much that he kept overbalancing back into
his seat.

He shouted out. His voice sounded small and con-
gested, but he was sure the driver could hear him. The
driver, however, refused to turn around, refused to answer.

They drove farther and farther into the darkness.
"Where are we going?" he kept shouting. "Where are
we going?"

At last the driver turned around. To Martin's terror,

his face was the gilded face of Pan. He grinned wolf-
ishly and stared at Martin with gilded eyeballs.

"*Pickle-nearest-the-wind,*" somebody said, with cold
breath, close to Martin's ear.

He whispered and groaned and shifted in his sleep, but
he didn't wake up. His wristwatch showed that it was
two o'clock.

In the mirror, the sitting room door opened a little
way, although the real sitting room door didn't move
at all. A cold stripe of moonlight fell across the floor,
and in that moonlight was a small shadow, the shadow
of a boy.

The shadow remained still, unmoving, for almost a
minute; but you could have told by the faintest trembling of the door that the boy was holding the handle,
and listening, and waiting.

At last the boy came into the reflected room. He was
about eight years old, with curly blond hair and a pale
face with tiny pinpricked eyes. He was wearing a
lemon-yellow shirt and a pair of lemon-yellow shorts,
and white ankle socks and sandals.

The moonlight caught his curls so that they gleamed
like white flames. His expression was extraordinary:
elated, fierce, like a child who has become so overexcited that he begins to hyperventilate.

He stood motionless for a moment; and then he
smiled even more widely and began to walk toward the
mirror. He didn't hesitate for a second, but stepped
straight through it, so that he was standing in the
moonlight in the real room. Behind him, the surface of
the mirror warped and rippled for a moment, as if it
were a pool of mercury.

The boy approached the man sleeping on the sofa.

He watched the man for a very long time. The man's
watch softly chirruped away the minutes. The man
snuffled and groaned and said something indistinct.
The boy smiled to himself; and then reached out and
took hold of the man's open hand.

Martin, in his sleep, felt the small cold hand slide into
his.

"Emilio?" he asked. His mouth felt dry, and he
opened and closed it two or three times to try to
moisten his tongue. His eyes flickered, then opened.

The boy grinned. "Hello, Martin."

Martin opened his eyes wide and stared. The shock of
waking up and finding that Boofuls was actually holding his hand was so violent and numbing that he
couldn't do anything at all, he couldn't move, couldn't
speak.

"Did I frighten you?" asked Boofuls. His voice was
clear and reedy, with the precise enunciation of prewar
years. "I didn't mean to frighten you. You knew I was
coming, didn't you? You did *know*."

Martin's hand shrank out of Boofuls' grasp. He began
to shudder and to draw his legs up on the sofa. For one
instant, his mind was right on the very edge of complete madness; right on the brink of giving up any kind
of responsibility whatsoever. But the boy was so calm
and smiling, so utterly real, that the madness shrank
away, like a shadow disappearing under a door, and
Martin found himself sitting on his sofa face-to-face
with a real boy who had been horribly and publicly
killed nearly fifty years ago.

"I *have* frightened you, haven't I?" said Boofuls.

Martin gradually eased his feet back onto the floor.
He didn't take his eyes off Boofuls even for a moment.

He was frightened that, if he glanced away, Boofuls would disappear. He was just as frightened that he would still be here.

"You mustn't be frightened, really," said Boofuls. "I'm only a boy, after all."

"You're a *dead* boy," Martin whispered.

Boofuls laughed. "Do I *look* dead? Do I *feel* dead? Here—take my hand and tell me that I'm dead."

Martin hesitated, but Boofuls took his hand and pressed it against his chest. Martin could feel the steady beating of his heart; the rising and falling of his lungs.

"Well, okay, you're not dead," he said. "You ought to be dead, but you're not."

"You don't *want* me to be dead, do you?" asked Boofuls. "Not like *she* did. And she wasn't the only one, either. Lots of people wanted me dead. But I'm here, I'm me. That's enough, isn't it? And you *like* me, don't you? I know you do!"

"I liked your pictures," said Martin, although it seemed like a pretty vapid thing to say, under the circumstances. But then—looking over Boofuls' shoulder, back toward the mirror—he said, "Where's Emilio? Did Emilio go into the mirror?"

"Emilio?" Boofuls replied quite tartly. "I don't know anybody called Emilio."

"The boy you were playing with. The little Italian boy."

"Oh, *him*," said Boofuls. "He's all right."

"Is he *in* there?" Martin demanded, pointing toward the mirror. "That's what I want to know."

Boofuls said, "You mustn't shout at me, you know. If anybody shouts at me, I have one of my fits."

"I know about your fits. I know pretty well everything about you." Martin stood up, circling around Boofuls and then approaching the mirror. "But you listen to me, I know something about this mirror, too. It has its own particular properties. It tries to suck things in; it *can* suck things in if it's allowed to. But for everything that goes in, something else has to come out. A ball for a ball, a cat for a cat, and now what? *You're* here—and the only way you could have gotten out is if somebody similar went into the mirror to take your place. I think that somebody similar was Emilio."

Boofuls listened to this, and then smirked, and then burst out laughing, a brassy little childish laugh.

"Did I say something funny?" Martin asked him savagely. And all the time he was thinking: *What am I doing? I'm actually talking to Boofuls, the real Boofuls, the real genuine murdered boy from all those years ago.* The shadow of madness still quivered behind the door.

"He *wanted* to play," said Boofuls. "I didn't *make* him. He came because he wanted to. I didn't make him, I promise."

"So where is he now, exactly?"

"I don't know. He's probably playing somewhere. There are lots of children to play with. Well, some of them want to play, anyway."

"It's nearly three o'clock in the morning."

"Well," said Boofuls, "it's *different* in there."

"Is he safe?" Martin demanded. "If I were to go into that mirror, too, could I find him and bring him back?"

Boofuls frowned and looked away.

"I asked you a question," Martin shouted at him.

Boofuls' lower lip stuck out, and his eyes suddenly filled up with tears. "I didn't—I didn't mean to do anything wrong—I thought—it would be all right. He wanted to play—he said that he *wanted* to play—and it was all right—his grandfather said it was all right."

Martin hunkered down beside this strange curly-headed boy in his lemon-yellow clothes and laid a hand on his shoulder. "Emilio told you that? Emilio said that he had permission from his grandfather?"

Boofuls nodded tearfully and wiped his eyes with the back of his hand. "I didn't mean to do anything wrong."

Martin held Boofuls close. He felt cold, under his thin summer clothing, but apart from that he felt just like any other child. His tears fell on Martin's shoulder.

At last, Martin sat down on the sofa and took hold of Boofuls' hands and looked him straight in the face. "Walter," he said, "I have to ask you some serious questions."

"You mustn't call me Walter. Nobody's allowed to call me Walter."

"That's your name, though, isn't it?"

"That was *his* name."

"Your father's name, you mean?"

Boofuls nodded. "I'm not allowed to talk about my father."

"Do you know who he was? Did you ever meet him?"

"I'm not allowed to talk about my father."

"But, Boofuls, listen, those people who didn't allow you to talk about your father, they're all dead now; and they've been dead for a very long time. It doesn't matter anymore. What we have to do now is find out how *you* managed to stay alive in that mirror and how we're going to get Emilio back and what we're going to do about you."

"You can't get Emilio back."

Martin felt a small sick feeling in the bottom of his stomach; and it wasn't only caused by last night's Spanish wine. When he thought about Lugosi's grisly transmogrification into a cat-snake, the prospects of getting Emilio back from beyond the mirror seemed desperately remote. Or even if they *could* get him back, it seemed highly unlikely that he would be the same normal five-year-old boy that he had been before.

It seemed to Martin that the mirror changed the shapes of living creatures so that they took on the physical appearance of what they really were. Lugosi, like most cats, had been sinuous and coldhearted and carnivorously minded. That was why he had taken on the shape of a snake.

Maybe he was wrong, but Martin strongly suspected that the world beyond the mirror was just like the world of the dead, the way that Theo had described it to him. Maybe it was the very same world. Maybe the mirror was a window that looked into heaven; or purgatory; or straight into hell.

The strongest piece of evidence was Boofuls, the living, breathing, long-dead Boofuls.

Martin said, a little unsteadily, "Okay . . . let's take this one step at a time. First of all, what's beyond that mirror?"

Boofuls turned to the mirror and frowned. "Hollywood," he said.

"But not *this* Hollywood?"

"No," Boofuls agreed. "Hollywood the other way around."

"Let me ask you this: where do you live in Hollywood?"

"Sixteen sixty-five Stone Canyon Drive, Bel Air. The house is called Espejo."

"Is your grandmother still alive?"

Boofuls shook his head. "She hung herself."

"But she didn't hang herself until she'd killed *you*. So how come you're still alive and she's not?"

"Because I didn't want her to be."

"But that's not up to you, is it? Deciding whether people live or die?"

Boofuls said nothing in reply to that question, but stared at Martin intently with those piggy little eyes. Martin could see now just what the M-G-M makeup department had done to give him that wide, dreaming look. Boofuls was pretty, in a way, but if Martin had been Jacob Levitz, he certainly wouldn't have looked at him twice when he auditioned for *Whistlin' Dixie*.

Perhaps Boofuls had been fresher looking in 1935, thought Martin, with a sudden dash of black humor. After all, in those days, he hadn't been dead for fifty years.

Martin slowly rubbed the palms of his hands together. "Okay," he said, "if your grandmother's dead, who takes care of you?"

"Miss Redd takes care of me. Miss Redd always took care of me."

Martin sat back. "I never heard of Miss Redd."

Boofuls shrugged, as if to say that wasn't *his* fault.

"Would you like some orange juice?" Martin asked him. "Anything to eat?"

Boofuls brightened up. "Do you have Ralston's?"

Martin said, "I'm sorry. How about Count Chokula?"

Boofuls looked disappointed. "I'm collecting Ralston box tops, for the Tom Mix Straight-Shooters ring."

"The Tom Mix Straight-Shooters ring? That's a radio premium, isn't it? Or *wasn't* it? They haven't given away stuff like that on the radio since—"

He stared at Boofuls in horrified fascination. He suddenly realized that he wasn't simply talking to a living ghost, he was talking to a ghost who still lived in 1939.

Boofuls sat at the kitchen table with a large bowl of Count Chokula and a glass of milk. Martin had made himself another cup of strong coffee. It was four o'clock in the morning, and his head felt as if it were slowly being closed in a car door. Outside the kitchen window, the sky was gradually beginning to lighten; false dawn, the hour of false promises.

Martin sat opposite Boofuls, straddling one of the kitchen chairs. He had tried to discover what kind of life Boofuls lived in "Hollywood the Other Way Around." He found it almost impossible to imagine an entire city in complete reverse. Yet of course he glimpsed it every day of the week, every hour of the day. Hollywood the Other Way Around appeared in store windows, barbershop mirrors, polished automobiles, shiny cutlery—everywhere and anywhere he came across a reflecting surface.

It was the idea of walking around *inside* those reflecting surfaces that he found so difficult to grasp. But Boofuls, with his mouth full of chocolate cereal, said, "Why? You do it all the time. You can see yourself there."

"Well, sure," said Martin, "but that's not actually *me*, is it, that's Me the Other Way Around. A left-handed me, a me who parts his hair on the opposite side, a me with a mole on my right cheek instead of my left."

Boofuls smiled at him. Martin wasn't too keen on his smiles. They had a sly coldness to them that he couldn't quite pin down. Boofuls said, "That you in the mirror is more like you than you are."

"And what's that supposed to mean?"

"Look in any mirror, Martin, and you'll see the truth."

It wasn't only Boofuls' smile that Martin found disturbing. It was the way he talked. Sometimes he was quite childish, only using eight-year-old words and eight-year-old ideas. But occasionally the mask of childhood would slip slightly, and he would say something that was too calculating and too philosophical for a boy of his supposed age. Although, what *was* his age? He was ageless; he was dead. He was nothing more than a glamorous memory that had stepped out of a mirror.

"Tell me something else," said Martin after a while. "If I lay a mirror flat on the ground and look down into it, the world looks upside down, as well as the other way around. Everybody's clinging onto the ground by the soles of their feet. How do you guys cope with that?"

Boofuls finished his milk and wiped his mouth with his hand. "It's different, that's all."

"I'll say," Martin remarked.

Boofuls propped his chin on his hands and stared at Martin with supreme confidence. "The thing is, Martin, she didn't kill the real me. That's why she hanged herself. When she was doing it, she suddenly realized that she wasn't killing the real me."

Martin thought about that. Then he said, "All right, if she didn't kill the real you, which one of you was the real you? The Boofuls in this Hollywood or the Boofuls in Hollywood the Other Way Around?"

Boofuls smiled. "Which one of you is the real you,

Martin? If I were to kill *this* you, who would be left? What would be left?"

"I really don't know, to tell you the truth," Martin admitted.

"Well, you'd know if it happened. You'd *know*."

"All right," Martin agreed, "she didn't murder the real you. But what happened then, after the you who *wasn't* you got himself chopped up into two hundred eleven pieces?"

"There was nothing I could do but go away," said Boofuls. "Everybody thought I was dead. They closed down *Sweet Chariot* and everybody was paid off. Have you seen any rushes from *Sweet Chariot*?"

Martin shook his head. "I've seen everything else you've done. I've even seen your screen tests for *Flowers From Tuscaloosa*. They were pretty dire, weren't they?"

"I had the grippe. I still got the part."

"Well, sure you did. There was nobody else." There was only one Boofuls. Well—*is* only one Boofuls."

The hot coffee had steamed up Martin's glasses. He took them off and polished them with the pulled-out tail of his shirt. Boofuls watched him for a little while and then said, "We could finish that picture, couldn't we?"

Martin peered at him. He was shortsighted, and without his glasses Boofuls' face appeared white and fuzzy, with dark circles around his eyes. Almost—for a moment—like a skull.

"What do you mean we could finish the picture?"

"Well, imagine it," said Boofuls, licking his lips with the tip of his tongue. "Screenwriter discovers boy who can sing and dance and act just like Boofuls, *just* like

Boofuls, and plans to finish Boofuls' last unfinished picture."

"But I *don't* plan to finish Boofuls' last unfinished picture. I plan to present a musical of my own called *Boofuls!*"

Boofuls was silent for a long time. He traced a pattern on the Formica tabletop with his finger. At last he said, "I want to finish *Sweet Chariot*."

"Well . . . it's a possibility, I suppose," said Martin. "But it's going to be pretty difficult finding backing. I had enough grief trying to sell my own musical. And the whole idea of *Sweet Chariot* is pretty much out of date these days. A boy turning into an angel? Everybody's done it—Warren Beatty, Michael Landon . . . all that *Heaven Can Wait* stuff. George Burns even played God."

"George Burns is still alive?" asked Boofuls in surprise.

"Well," said Martin, "some people like to think so."

"I want to finish *Sweet Chariot*," Boofuls repeated. His eyes widened in sudden ferocity. "It's *important*!"

"Come on, you're talking about a twenty-five-million-dollar production here. I don't think many producers are going to risk that kind of money on a remake of a 1939 musical."

"But it's a Boofuls musical," Boofuls insisted.

"Ho, ho, ho, don't tell me that," replied Martin. "In this town, there are half a dozen names that stink, and as far as I can make out, Boofuls is the Least Desirable Aroma of the Year."

Boofuls slowly shook his head. His eyes had a tiny, faraway look, as if he were peering down the wrong end of a telescope. "You're wrong, Martin. Things are going to change. Boofuls is going to be famous again. Boofuls is going to be loved!"

Martin stood up and collected Boofuls' bowl and glass. "All I can say to that is, convince me."

"I will. I promise."

"Meanwhile," said Martin, "I have something a whole lot more serious to talk about. I want to get Emilio back."

"I told you. You *can't* get him back."

"Does that mean *ever*?"

Boofuls was silent. Martin leaned forward across the table and snapped, "Does that mean *ever*? Or what?"

"There is a way," said Boofuls.

"Oh, really? And what way is that?"

Boofuls glanced up, and smiled, and looked away again. "We could make a deal. If you help me to finish *Sweet Chariot*, if you take care of me, then when it's finished, you can get Emilio back."

"Why not before?" Martin demanded.

"Because I won't," said Boofuls.

"What the hell do you mean you won't?"

"I won't, that's all. I can, but I won't. That's the deal."

Martin banged the kitchen table with his fist. "Listen to me, you beady-eyed sprout! There's an old couple downstairs and Emilio is all they've got in the whole entire world! Either you get Emilio back or you don't get squat from me, *comprende*?"

"I won't," Boofuls repeated.

"What do you want me to do?" Martin challenged him. "Put you over my knee and spank you?"

"You mustn't shout at me," Boofuls replied. "If you shout at me, it brings on my fits."

"I want Emilio back," Martin told him in a soft, low, threatening voice.

"I want to finish *Sweet Chariot*."

Martin tried to stare Boofuls out; but there was

something about the little boy's eyes that made him feel unnerved; almost vertiginous; as if he were about to fall into a cold and echoing elevator shaft forever.

He backed away. Boofuls didn't take his eyes away from him once.

"I don't lift one finger until I get Emilio back," Martin told him, but much less convincingly than before.

"But—if you *do* get Emilio back—how will I be sure that you will still help me to make *Sweet Chariot*?" Boofuls asked him.

"You don't know. You'll have to trust me."

"I don't trust anybody."

Martin finished his cup of coffee. "Maybe it's time you started."

At seven-thirty that morning, Martin tugged up the venetian blinds and greeted the bright California sunshine. Boofuls was sitting at the desk, solemnly doodling with Martin's black Conté pen: clouds and faces and disembodied smiles.

Martin turned around and looked at him. He was a real boy, right enough, flesh and blood, freckles and buck teeth. His legs were lightly tanned, and there was a grazing of white skin on his knee where he must have fallen. Martin crossed the sitting room and watched him drawing for a while, and Boofuls even *smelled* like a boy—biscuity and hot. Without even thinking about it, Martin ruffled his curls.

Boofuls immediately knocked his hand away. "Don't do that. Nobody's allowed to do that."

"All right, I'm sorry." Martin smiled. "I guess I wasn't treating you quite like a big movie star."

"I am a big movie star," Boofuls said petulantly.

"You *were* a big movie star," Martin reminded him.

Boofuls didn't bother to reply to that; but by the look on his face Martin could tell just how contemptuous he felt about it. Martin knew plenty of grown-up movie stars, and their total egotism never came as any surprise. It was as much a part of the job they did as a steady hand is to a carpenter. But it was a shock to meet such consummate vanity in a child of eight— even a child of eight who had walked into his life in wildly unnatural circumstances. Somehow Martin had always liked to believe that prepubescent children had a natural cynicism, a gift for self-squelching, which made such vanity impossible.

Not this kid, however. As far as Martin could tell, Boofuls had no interest in anybody but himself. Martin could already begin to understand why he had won such rapid and rapturous success—what star quality it was that Jacob Levitz had seen in him that first day he had auditioned for *Whistlin' Dixie*. A good movie star is interested in nothing but what other people think about him; and a brilliant movie star is *obsessed* by what other people think about him.

Martin said, "We're going to have to think about what we're going to do with you. You can't suddenly appear out of nowhere at all and expect to continue living your life as if nothing had happened. If you're going to stay this side of the mirror, you're going to need education, social security . . . And how are you going to get those? Your birth certificate shows you were born in 1931 and yet you're only eight years old."

Boofuls stared at him. "All I want is new clothes. Then we can start making the picture."

"What's so important about this damned picture?"

But Boofuls wouldn't answer. He sat on Martin's

chair swinging his legs and doodling: clouds as high as clifftops and strange seductive smiles.

Just then, there was a knock at Martin's apartment door. Boofuls glanced up, and there was a look of cold curiosity in his eyes, but Martin said, "Stay here, okay? I don't want anybody finding out that you're here yet." He went to answer the door. It was Mr. Capelli, in a blue Jack Nicklaus T-shirt and blue-and-white-checkered seersucker golfing pants. He had dark damson-colored circles under his eyes, and he was a little out of breath from climbing the stairs.

"Hey, Martin, I didn't wake you?"

"No, I was up already. Come on in."

"I called the police about ten minutes ago," said Mr. Capelli. "They told me no news."

Martin closed the door. "How's Mrs. Capelli taking it?"

"Terrible, how do you think? I had to give her Tranxene last night."

"You want some coffee?" Martin asked him.

"Sure, why not?"

"Have you eaten anything? I've got a couple of raspberry Danishes in the freezer."

Mr. Capelli gave him an odd look. "Is something wrong?"

"Wrong?" said Martin in feigned surprise. "What do you mean wrong?"

"You're fussing," said Mr. Capelli. "I don't know, you're all *flibberty.*"

Martin shrugged. "I'm a little tired, that's all. I didn't sleep too good, worrying about Emilio."

He ushered Mr. Capelli into the kitchen, glancing quickly toward the sitting room to make sure that Boofuls hadn't decided to make an appearance. Mr. Ca-

pelli said, "I called Father Lucas, too. He's coming
around at nine o'clock."

Martin spooned Folger's Mountain Blend into the
percolator. "Oh, yes, Father Lucas. I'd forgotten about
him."

"I don't know how serious he took it," Mr. Capelli
replied, dragging out one of Martin's kitchen stools and
perching his wide backside on it. "When I told him we
were having trouble with a mirror, you know, the way
it nearly sucked in Emilio and all that stuff—well, he
sounded a little distracted. You know what I mean by
distracted? Like he was thinking about his breakfast
instead, or maybe what he was going to preach in
church next week."

"Sure," said Martin. "I know what you mean by distracted."

"He's a good priest, though," Mr. Capelli remarked.
"Kind of old-fashioned, you know, traditional. But I
like him. He baptized Emilio; he buried my daughter."

The water in the percolator began to jump and pop.
Martin took down two ceramic mugs and set them on
the table. As he did so, Boofuls appeared in the open
doorway, behind Mr. Capelli's back. The look on his
face was unreadable. Martin couldn't tell if he was angry or bored or amused. His eyes flared in tiny
pinpricks of blue light, as if they could cut through
steel.

"Some of these young priests, they seem to take a
pleasure in challenging the old ways. You know what I
mean by challenging? They say, why shouldn't a priest
marry? Why shouldn't people use a contraceptive?
What's so special about the Latin mass?"

Mr. Capelli looked up at Martin's face.

"Hey," he said. "What's wrong? You look like you

just remembered it was your mother's birthday yesterday."

Slowly, frowning, Mr. Capelli twisted around on his
stool so that he was facing the door. He saw Boofuls
standing there, silent and small, with that eerie expression on his face that wasn't smiling and wasn't scowl-
ing and wasn't anything at all but *triumph*, sheer, cold
triumph.

Mr. Capelli was silent for one long second, and then
he shouted out *"Yah!"* in terror, and jumped off from
his stool, which toppled noisily over backward onto the
kitchen floor. He stood with his back pressed against
the cupboards, both hands raised, too shocked and
frightened even to cross himself. When he managed to
shout out a few desperate guttural words, his Italian
accent was so dense that Martin could scarcely understand what he was saying.

"Whosa dis? Whosa dis boy? Donta tellmi. Martin
donta tellmi!"

Boofuls remained silent: still triumphant, but placid.
Mr. Capelli edged away from him, right around to the
far side of the kitchen, and stood staring at him in horror.

Martin said, "It's Boofuls. He came out of the mirror."

"He came out of the mirror, he tells me. Holy God
and All His Angels. Ho Lee *God*!"

Martin laid a hand on Mr. Capelli's shoulder. "I was
hoping he wouldn't come in. I didn't want to frighten
you."

"He didn't want to frighten me!" Mr. Capelli repeated.

Boofuls came gliding forward into the kitchen. He
held out his hand. "You mustn't be frightened," he told

Mr. Capelli. "There's nothing to be frightened of at all."

Mr. Capelli crossed himself five times in succession, his hand flurrying wildly. "You're a dead person! You stay back!"

Boofuls smiled gently. "Do I *look* dead?" he asked.

Mr. Capelli was shaking. "Don't you touch me, you stay back. You're a dead person."

But Martin came forward and laid his hand on Mr. Capelli's shoulder and said, "Mr. Capelli, he *should* be dead, by rights. But he isn't. You can see that he isn't. And I don't think that he's going to do anything to hurt us."

"Nothing to hurt us, eh? So where's Emilio? Emilio went into the mirror, and this boy came out, is that it?"

Martin was about to explain that, yes, there was a chance that Emilio might have gone into the mirror, but that Boofuls was certainly going to help to get him back. But Boofuls forestalled him by saying in that piping voice of his, "You're quite right, sir. Emilio is in the mirror. He went to play with some of my chums."

This was more than Mr. Capelli could take. His face turned ashy blue, and Martin had to drag over a chair for him so that he could sit down. He sat with his hand pressed over his heart, breathing deeply. Boofuls stood beside him, still smiling.

"Emilio's quite *safe*, sir," he told Mr. Capelli.

"Safe?" said Mr. Capelli harshly, in between breaths. "Who cares about safe? I want him back."

"I'll get him back," said Boofuls.

"Well, then, go on then, what are you waiting for?" Mr. Capelli demanded.

But Boofuls shook his pretty little head. "All in good time, sir. All in good time."

Mr. Capelli reared up; and Martin had to grab hold of his shoulders to make him sit down again. "What's this, 'all in good time'? You go in there, and you go get my grandson for me, and if he isn't here in five minutes, *five* minutes, I'm going to give you the hiding of your life whether you're a dead person or not, do you got me?"

Boofuls stared at Mr. Capelli in surprise, and then lowered his head and covered his face with his hands.

Mr. Capelli said with less confidence. "What're you doing? You go get Emilio, do you hear me?"

Boofuls' face remained concealed. Martin stepped toward him, but he sidestepped away, without lowering his hands. For a moment, Martin had the disturbing feeling that if he tried to prize Boofuls' hands away, he would uncover not the pretty pale features of Boofuls, but the gilded sardonic face of Pan. He hesitated, glanced back at Mr. Capelli, then shrugged. He didn't know what he ought to do.

It was then that Mr. Capelli saw the tears that were squeezing out between Boofuls' fingers. The boy's shoulders were trembling; and it was clear that he was deeply upset. Mr. Capelli frowned and reached one hand forward.

"Listen, young man . . ."

"It's Boofuls, Mr. Capelli," said Martin. "It really is. And that's what he likes to be called."

Mr. Capelli cleared his throat. "Well, here, listen, Boofuls. I'm sorry. I didn't mean to yell like that. But the truth is, I'm real worried about Emilio. I don't like that mirror at all, and I don't want him wandering around in there, it's not healthy, do you know what I mean by healthy?"

Boofuls' hands remained closed over his face. Mr. Capelli looked anxious now and shifted his chair a little closer. Boofuls, in response, stepped back another pace.

"Listen to me," said Mr. Capelli, "I'm a grandfather. I love children. I don't know where you've come from, I don't know how you can be dead but still walking around and talking, but I'm willing to accept that maybe I don't understand absolutely everything in this universe. I don't understand accumulated earnings tax, does that make me a bad person? But I love Emilio. Emilio is all I've got. And even if he's safe wherever he is, I need to have him back."

Boofuls at last lowered his hands. His face was stained with tears. He looked utterly bereft and miserable.

"Oh, Mr. Capelli," he said, "I'm so unhappy."

"Hey, come on," said Mr. Capelli, and held out his arms. Boofuls hesitated for a moment and then came up to Mr. Capelli and hugged him as if he were his own grandfather.

"Do you know something, you're right," said Mr. Capelli, beginning to smile. "You don't look dead at all. You sure don't *feel* dead. I don't know how it happened, but you're a live boy!"

Martin watched all this with caution. There was no doubt at all that Boofuls was a most appealing child, yet he couldn't rid himself of that feeling he always had when he watched a Boofuls musical: that here was a grown-up man, a cunning grown-up man, masquerading as a small boy. Boofuls was just a little too clever; just a little too calculating. Seeing him win over Mr. Capelli was almost like watching a skillfully written scene in a movie, specifically aimed at tugging at the audience's heartstrings.

"Oh, aunt," Freddie Bartholomew had wept in *David*

Copperfield, "I'm so unhappy." And Boofuls had used the same line in exactly the same way. A last desperate tug at a grandfather's heartstrings. *David Copperfield* had been released in 1935, so Boofuls could easily have seen it.

"Mr. Capelli—" warned Martin.

But Mr. Capelli said, "Shush now, Martin. I'm a grandfather. Besides, what have we got here? A famous movie star."

"Mr. Capelli—" Martin repeated, but there was little that he could do. Boofuls shot him a quick hostile look that Mr. Capelli didn't see: a look which meant *you stay out of this, or you'll never see Emilio again.*

"Emilio's safe, sir," he told Mr. Capelli, wiping his tears with the back of his hand. "There are plenty of people who are going to take care of him. But the moment Emilio comes back, then I have to go back into the mirror, I *have* to."

"But inside the mirror," said Mr. Capelli, "that's where you really live, right? You don't truly *belong* in this world anymore."

Boofuls swallowed miserably, and tears began to fill up his eyes again. "I don't *live* there, sir, nobody *lives* there. It's a kind of a place where you go if you can't get to heaven."

"Purgatory," put in Martin.

"Well, some people call it that," said Boofuls. "But you *can* get to heaven if you fulfill your life's work, the work that God intended you to do."

"And making *Sweet Chariot*, that was the work that God intended *you* to do?"

Boofuls nodded. "If I can make that picture, then I can rest."

"What's this *Sweet Chariot*?" Mr. Capelli wanted to know.

Martin said nothing for a moment, watching Boofuls. Then he poured out coffee, and passed a cup to Mr. Capelli, and explained, "It was Boofuls' last picture, wasn't it, Boofuls, before his grandmother murdered him. Or *thought* she'd murdered him. It was about a street urchin who becomes an angel, and who flies around doing good deeds in order to meet with the Almighty's approval. A musical; something of a tearjerker, believe me."

Boofuls clung to Mr. Capelli's neck. "I never finished the picture, I never managed to finish it, and if I don't finish the picture I'm going to have to say in the mirror forever and ever, and never get out."

Martin sipped his coffee. "You see what he's asking, Mr. Capelli? He's asking if you'll allow Emilio to stay in the mirror so that he can make his picture and fulfill his life's destiny and go to meet his Maker."

Boofuls sobbed, "I know it's an awful lot to ask you, sir. I know it is. And I know how much Emilio means to you. But please, I beg of you. Otherwise I can never sleep for all eternity. And I'm so tired, sir. So terribly, *terribly* tired."

Tears welled up in Mr. Capelli's eyes, too, and he patted Boofuls' narrow back. "I don't know what to say," he replied thickly. "I don't know what to say. How can a man and a grandfather turn away somebody like this, some little boy who needs his help?"

"Mr. Capelli," said Martin, "doesn't Emilio have any kind of say in this?"

"Well, sure he does," agreed Mr. Capelli. "But if Boofuls is telling us the truth, then Emilio *wanted* to go play in the mirror. He *wanted* to."

"Couldn't we ask Emilio for ourselves?" Martin suggested.

"Can we do that?" Mr. Capelli asked Boofuls.

Boofuls nodded. "We can ask him, yes. But you mustn't try to get him out of the mirror. Until I'm ready, it could be very dangerous. He could die."

"Let's just go see him, shall we?" said Martin.

They went through to the sitting room. The sunlight was very bright in here, and Mr. Capelli shielded his eyes with his hand. The mirror seemed larger than it had before: larger and clearer. Anybody who hadn't known that there was a mirror there might have been forgiven for thinking that it was nothing more than a gilded archway through to another identical room.

As they approached the mirror, Martin saw with a prickle of surprise that he and Mr. Capelli were accompanied not by a reflection of Boofuls, but by a reflection of Emilio. The two boys stood in perfectly matching positions, and if one of them nodded his head, then the other one nodded, too.

"Emilio . . ." whispered Mr. Capelli. Then, rushing up to the mirror, *"Emilio!"*

But of course all that Mr. Capelli managed to do was to press himself against his own reflection. Emilio stood *behind* Mr. Capelli's reflection, just as Boofuls was standing behind him in the real room. Mr. Capelli hesitated and then stepped back again, so that he could see Emilio more clearly.

"Emilio?" asked Martin. "Are you okay?"

Emilio was wearing a *Star Trek* T-shirt and red shorts and scruffy red and white trainers. He looked a little pale and tired, but otherwise well. The lick of black hair which usually fell across the left side of his forehead fell across the right side instead, and his wristwatch was on his right wrist. His face had an oddly asymmetrical appearance, simply because Martin was used to seeing it the other way around.

Emilio called, "I'm fine, I'm okay. I'm having fun."

"Who's taking care of you?" Mr. Capelli asked him.

Emilio held hands with the reflected Mr. Capelli, and Boofuls held hands with the real Mr. Capelli. Both of them smiled.

"*You're* looking after me, of course," said Emilio.

"Me?" asked Mr. Capelli, mystified.

"You and Granma. You're in here, too. So's Martin; so's everybody. It's just like home."

Mr. Capelli pressed the heel of his hand against his forehead. He couldn't understand this at all. "All I want to know is, are you okay? Me and Granma, we're taking care of you okay? Feeding you good? Nobody's hurting you, nothing like that? Nobody's telling you that you *have* to stay there?"

"Granpa, I like it here. I'm happy."

Mr. Capelli looked toward Martin for support; but Martin was too busy examining their reflections in the mirror for something which gave him a clue to how this apparent hallucination actually worked. Yet there seemed to be nothing, no tricks at all. He was seeing a blond-haired motion-picture star of the late 1930s whose reflection in the mirror was a dark-haired Italian boy of the late 1980s, and that was all there was to it.

"Emilio," Martin said, "if I told you that you could come back over here, right now, right this second, what would you say to me?"

"I like it here," Emilio repeated. "I'm happy."

But there was an edginess in Emilio's voice that made Martin feel that he wasn't telling the whole truth.

"Emilio," he asked, "what's it *like* in there? Is it really like home? Boofuls said it was different."

"Well, sure, it's *different*," said Emilio. He wasn't smiling at all.

"Listen, I have a suggestion," said Martin to Boofuls. Boofuls wasn't smiling, either. "Why don't you get back into the mirror while I start putting your movie package together? It's going to take months before anybody's going to tell us yes or no; and months more to rewrite and cast the picture; and even more months before they can get around to set building and costumes. We'll be lucky to have this production finished in eighteen months, two years. And Emilio can't stay behind that mirror for two years."

Boofuls' eyes tightened and darkened. "I was trapped in the mirror for fifty years, Martin. Fifty! If I don't get out now, I'm never going to get out, ever."

"But you can't possibly expect Emilio to stay in that mirror-world until he's seven!"

"The picture won't take two years to make," said Boofuls.

"Oh, yes, and how can you be so sure about that?"

"I'm sure, that's all. Once it starts production, it'll be easy. None of the sets were destroyed; none of the costumes were spoiled."

"How do you know that?"

"I *know*, that's all. They're all at a warehouse in Long Beach."

"Well, well," Martin replied, trying not to sound too bitter about it, "we're all ready to roll, then. We've got the star, we've got the screenplay, we've got the costumes, we've got the sets. All we seem to have forgotten is that minor detail called finance. Twenty-five million dollars for a full-scale musical, and that's the bottom line."

Boofuls didn't respond to Martin's sarcasm, but smiled and said, "We'll see."

Mr. Capelli, confused, called out to Emilio. "Emilio, hey, I love you?"

"I know, Granpa," said Emilio. "But Boofuls can't rest if I come back now."

"Emilio, listen—"

"You must help him," little Emilio insisted in a tone far graver than any that Martin had heard him adopt before.

"Martin," begged Mr. Capelli, "what can I do?"

"Quite seriously, Mr. Capelli," said Martin, "if I were you I'd *demand*—"

But Mr. Capelli's dilemma was settled for him; because at that moment a cat's tail swished black and gingery from behind the door in the reflected sitting room, and Emilio immediately darted after it, out of the door, and disappeared. Martin turned around. Boofuls had run out of the room, too. They heard him giggling in the kitchen, as if he were playing with a pet.

"*What* can we believe?" asked Mr. Capelli, stretching his arms out wide. Martin could see that he was very close to collapse; and the shock of this morning's events was beginning to make *him* feel swimmy and light-headed, too. Too much caffeine, not enough sleep, not enough to eat.

Martin said, "I don't know, Mr. Capelli. I really don't know. Maybe your Father Lucas will tell us what to believe."

Sister Boniface was kneeling at early prayer in the chapel of Our Lady of Mercy Hospital; her head bowed; her eyes tightly closed; her mind very close to God.

The chapel was modern and very simple. Plain oak pews, plain oak floor, an altar of polished gray marble.

Its richest feature was its stained-glass window, depicting the Madonna holding the·naked Christ-child, with rays of multicolored light transporting her up to the clouds. Sister Boniface adored this window. The light strained through it differently at different times of the day. Sometimes it looked peaceful and slightly melancholy: at other times, when the sun shone fully, it blazed with holy glory.

Today Sister Boniface was praying in particular for the soul of Homer Theobald. She had learned through the hospital grapevine that he had died; and she had learned from Sister Michael that Martin and Ramone had been with him. However, she had been afraid to call Martin to confirm her deepest anxiety—that the key which she had given him had attracted the attention of a vengeful Satan. She was mortified that she believed in evil spirits; and she was wracked with guilt for having given Martin the key.

When she met him last week, it had seemed to Sister Boniface that Martin could well be the messenger for whom she had been waiting for fifty years: the man who would settle her torment once and for all, and give her peace. She had sensed an aura of honesty about him; an aura of blessed destiny. But now she was beginning to suspect that Satan might have been deceiving her, and that all he had wanted to do was to relieve her of the key which she guarded for so long.

She had no idea what the key unlocked, but she knew that it was more terrible than anybody could imagine.

She prayed for her fellow sisters, she prayed for the hospital, she prayed for a small boy in St. Francis of Assisi ward who was dying of AIDS from a contaminated blood transfusion. She prayed for peace and fulfillment, and that Homer Theobald had found his place in the Kingdom of Heaven.

She was finishing her prayers when a voice whispered, *"Sister Boniface."*

She looked up; looked around. There was nobody there. The chapel was deserted.

"Sister Boniface."

She listened. At last, she stood up, brushing down her white habit, and said in a quavering voice, "Who's there? Is anybody there?"

"Sister Boniface, you betrayed me," the voice said.

"I betrayed no one," said Sister Boniface. "I have always kept my word and my sacred trust."

"You gave away the key, Sister Boniface."

Sister Boniface stepped out into the aisle and walked toward the altar, looking from left to right for any sign of the whisperer hiding behind the pews or the pillars.

"You betrayed me, Sister Boniface, now you will have to be punished."

Sister Boniface stopped in front of the altar. On her right, beside one of the smooth Italian-marble pillars, scores of votive candles burned brightly and were reflected in her eyes. The dear Madonna smiled down at her from the stained-glass window. She knew that nothing terrible could happen to her in the sight of the dear Madonna.

"Nobody can betray me and go unpunished," the voice said, just as close to her ear as it had been before. *"Warm hands, warm, the men have gone to plough; if you want to warm your hands, warm your hands now."*

Sister Boniface said, "Who are you? *What* are you? What do you want?"

"She gave you the key to keep," whispered the voice. *"She gave you the key to keep. Not to lose, not to give*

away. To keep forever, and to take with you to your grave."

Sister Boniface whirled around, but there was nobody behind her, nobody anywhere to be seen. Her mouth felt suddenly parched, and she started to tremble. "O Holy Mother, protect me," she prayed. But she was beginning to feel that prayer alone was not going to be enough. "In the name of the Father, and of the Son, and of the Holy Spirit . . ."

"Warm hands, warm," murmured the voice. *"The men have gone to plough. If you want to warm your hands, warm your hands now."*

It was then that she caught sight of his face; and she screamed out loud. Her scream echoed in the chapel, but there was nobody there to hear her.

He was smiling at her from the small mirror just above the banks of votive candles—childish, white-faced. The same boy who had floated over his grandmother's bed all those years ago. The same boy whose unearthly appearance had tormented Sister Boniface for the rest of her life.

"Ah," whispered Boofuls, *"you've seen me."*

Sister Boniface walked toward the mirror, her left foot dragging slightly, her habit rustling on the marble floor. Boofuls watched her approach and his eyes were tiny piercing lights.

"I never betrayed you," said Sister Boniface, her voice shaking.

"You were supposed to take that key to your grave, you miserable old witch," Boofuls spat back at her. *"When you gave that key away, you gave away part of my secret. You should have known better than that, witch, even you."*

Then, in a slow, measured rhythm, he sang, *"Warm hands, warm; the men have gone to plough; if you want to warm your hands, warm your hands now."*

Sister Boniface shuddered. "You are Satan," she declared. "I know you now! You are Satan!"

Boofuls laughed. He laughed and laughed. He laughed so much that—for one peculiar second—his face in the mirror almost seemed to turn itself inside out, and reveal something dark and gristly and insect-like. Sister Boniface cried out *"Satan!"* and reached up over the banks of votive candles to take the mirror down.

It was then that she felt every muscle in her body lock tight. She was paralyzed, with her arms held over the candles. She tried to move, tried to cry out, but her nervous system simply refused to obey her.

Satan, she thought wildly. Satan!

There were more than seventy candles burning just below her outstretched hands. What at first had felt like a wave of warmth now began to feel like a furnace. The boy's face in the mirror watched her in delight as Sister Boniface gradually began to realize what was going to happen to her.

O Mother of God, protect me, the pain! thought Sister Boniface. But she was completely powerless to move her hands away from the heat of the candles, or to scream out for help. She had never known anything so agonizing. Her hands began to redden, and she began to smell a strong aroma of scorched meat. Each finger-nail felt as if it were white-hot.

Please, she begged Boofuls inside her mind. *Please release me, please! I'll get back the key, I promise you! I'll take it to the grave with me, just as you ask!*

But all Boofuls did was to chant, *"Warm hands, warm, the men have gone to plough; if you want to warm your hands, warm your hands now!"*

Slowly, inch by inch, Sister Boniface found that she was lowering her hands toward the candle flames. The heat was so intense that she could scarcely feel it. The skin on the palms of her hands blackened and shriveled, and strips of it dropped off and fell onto the candleholders, where it hung, smoking. The sleeves of her habit began to smolder; and as her hands came lower and lower, they burst into flame, so that her bare wrists were licked by the fire as well.

Tears poured from Sister Boniface's eyes and down her wrinkled cheeks. The agony was thunderous. She wanted to do nothing but die, even though her paralysis made it impossible for her to turn and see the face of the dear Madonna.

The flesh of her hands was actually alight now, and it burned with a sputtering sizzle. Gradually the layers of skin were burned through, and the flesh charred, and the bones were exposed, her own fingerbones bared in front of her eyes.

"Warm hands, warm, the men have gone to plough!"

It was just when the agony reached its greatest that Boofuls released Sister Boniface from her paralysis. She didn't realize what had happened at first; but then she let out a scream of sheer tormented pain that pierced the chapel from end to end.

She lurched back, away from the candles, holding her blazing arms out in front of her like a sleepwalker. *The holy water*, she thought in desperation, *I can douse my hands in the holy water.*

She began to make her way step by step along the aisle. Her hands were nothing but blackened stumps now, and her sleeves were leaping with orange flame. Her wimple, incendiary with starch, suddenly flared up like a crown of fire and set light to her short-cropped hair underneath.

By the time she had managed to make her way halfway down the aisle, her habit was ablaze from hem to shoulder. She was a shuffling mass of fire, her head alight, her eyes wide with shock and terror, no longer able to scream or even to whimper.

She knew that she would never be able to reach the holy water. She twisted, collapsed, then fell onto her side. She could hear the fire roaring in her ears. She could see the flames dancing past her eyes.

In a last agonized effort, she managed to lift her head, just long enough to glimpse the stained-glass window behind the pews. The dear Madonna still smiled at her, as she had always done. Sister Boniface tried to say something, the smallest of prayers, but her habit had burned through to her underclothing now, and the skin of her legs was alight, and she died before she could whisper even one word.

Although he was patrolling the second floor, one of the hospital security officers had heard Sister Boniface screaming, and had gone to investigate. He had thought at first that it was one of the cleaners laughing or larking about. He opened a dozen office doors before he eventually reached the chapel.

"Jesus," he said when he opened the doors.

The chapel was dense with smoke. In the middle of the center aisle, a blackened figure was huddled on the floor, a few last flames still flickering on its chest. The security officer felt his throat tighten with nausea, and he didn't know whether he ought to go into the chapel or not. There was no chance at all that the figure on the floor was still alive.

Eventually, he took a deep breath, masked his nose and mouth with his padded-up handkerchief, and cautiously stepped inside. He made his way up the aisle until he reached Sister Boniface's body. Then he just stood and stared at it in horror.

Her head had been burned so fiercely that most of her skull had collapsed into ashes. Her ribs curved up from an indistinguishable heap of burned cloth and carbonized flesh; her pelvis lay like an unwanted wash-basin.

The only way in which the security officer could tell at once that it was Sister Boniface was her crucifix, a large bronze cross, mottled with heat, from which the figure of Christ had melted into small distorted blobs of silver.

He thought he heard a rustling noise in the chapel, like somebody moving about on tiptoe, but when he peered through the smoke he saw nobody at all.

He unhitched his walkie-talkie from his belt, switched it on, and said, "Douglas? This is Andrej. Listen, you'd better get down to the chapel. Sister Boniface has had some kind of an accident. No, burned. I don't know, maybe she got too close to the candles. No, dead. No, *dead*. Are you kidding? She hasn't even got a mouth left to *give* the kiss of life to."

He clipped the walkie-talkie back on his belt and then stood staring at the ashes of the woman who had made the mistake of giving away Boofuls' key.

Eight

FATHER LUCAS HAD SPRAINED his ankle that weekend playing baseball with the boys of St. Ignatius' Little League team. He came heavily up the stairs to Martin's apartment, rocking himself between the banister rails, and grunting noisily. Mr. Capelli came up behind him, trying to make himself useful, but proving to be more of an irritation than a help.

"It's all right, Mr. Capelli," Father Lucas insisted. "I've worked out my own rhythm. Don't upset it, or you'll have me falling down the stairs backward."

"Watch for this corner," fussed Mr. Capelli. "Sometimes I trip here myself, and how long have I lived here?"

Upstairs in the sitting room Boofuls sat placidly watching *Sesame Street.* Martin stood by the window, watching Maria Bocanegra sunning herself before going off to work. She must have fallen asleep, because one of the Sno-Cones had been blown off by the morning breeze, and one nipple was bared. It looked like a soft, wrinkled prune, thought Martin. The kind you could gently sink your teeth into.

From time to time, he glanced at Boofuls. As soon as Father Lucas had visited, he was going to take Boofuls out to Sears and buy him some new clothes. T-shirts, sneakers, so that at least he *looked* like a kid from the 1980s. He thought it was extraordinary that he had come to accept Boofuls' presence so easily. Yet if somebody's actually *there*, he thought, talking and walking and living and breathing, what else can you do? It doesn't matter if they came out of a mirror or down from the moon.

Father Lucas knocked at Martin's front door. "Hello there! Mr. Williams!" Martin lowered the venetian blind and came away from the window. "This'll be the priest," he told Boofuls. He had already told him that Father Lucas was coming to visit, but Boofuls had appeared to be completely uninterested. He didn't seem to be any more interested now.

Without waiting to be shown in, Father Lucas appeared at the sitting room door. He was a barrel-chested man with a leonine head that seemed to be far too big for the rest of his body. His silver hair was combed straight back from his forehead. He wore heavy horn-rimmed glasses that reminded Martin of a pair of 1950s television sets, side by side, each showing a test transmission of a single gray eye.

Father Lucas swung himself into the room and grasped Martin's hand. "Mr. Capelli tells me you've been having some trouble, Mr. Williams." He looked around, and then he said, "You won't mind if I have a seat? I was trying to show my Little Leaguers how to throw a forkball, and I got rather carried away."

He limped across to the sofa where Boofuls was sitting watching *Sesame Street.* "Hello, young fellow!" he said, beaming and ruffling Boofuls' hair. "You don't mind if I park myself next to you, do you?"

Without even looking at him, Boofuls said, "Yes, I *do* mind. And don't scruff up my hair again. You're not allowed to."

Father Lucas stared at Boofuls in bewilderment. He had always liked to think that he was "pretty darn good" with children, especially young boys.

Mr. Capelli snapped, "Hey! You! Kid! You're talking to a priest here! You're talking to a holy father!"

Boofuls reluctantly took his eyes away from Kermit the Frog and looked Father Lucas up and down.

"I'm Father Lucas," said Father Lucas. "And you are—?"

For one moment—so quickly that it was like a rubber glove being rolled inside out and then the right way around again—an expression rippled through Boofuls' face which made Martin shiver. He had seen hostility in children's faces before; but nothing like the concentrated venom which disfigured Boofuls. He scarcely looked like a child at all: more like an evil-tempered dwarf.

But then the hostility vanished, and Boofuls was smiling and pretty once more—so angelic, in fact, that Father Lucas smiled back at him with pleasure, and said, "Well, now, aren't *you* the uppity one?"

All the same, he backed off, and sat down at Martin's desk, and nodded and smiled at Boofuls almost as if he were afraid of him.

"It's the mirror," said Mr. Capelli, his eyes glancing from Boofuls to Father Lucas and back again.

"I'm sorry? The mirror?" asked Father Lucas. He

turned around in his chair and looked at himself in the mirror on the far wall. "Oh, yes. The mirror. Well, it's very handsome, isn't it?"

"It took my grandson," said Mr. Capelli.

"It—?" asked Father Lucas, lifting his spectacles, not at all sure what Mr. Capelli meant.

"It took my grandson, took him away. He's in there now."

Father Lucas looked at Martin for some reassurance that Mr. Capelli was quite all right and not suffering from some temporary brainstorm. The heat, you know. Maybe the male menopause. Men of this particular age sometimes acted a little feverish. But Martin gave him a nod to assure him that it was true.

"We didn't expect for one minute that you were going to find this easy to believe," he told Father Lucas. "But this definitely isn't your ordinary common or garden mirror. It's like a way through to another world."

"Another world?" said Father Lucas, looking even more unsettled.

"It's still Hollywood in there," Martin told him. "But it's Hollywood the other way around. And the reflections that appear in that mirror aren't always the same as the real people and objects that are standing in front of it. Did you ever read *Alice Through the Looking-Glass*?"

"Yes, of course," said Father Lucas, still baffled.

"Then that'll give you some idea of what's happening here. You remember in *Alice* how the looking-glass world was completely different once Alice was out of sight of the mirror. I think this mirror's similar. Once you walk through that sitting room door in there, the whole world's turned on its head."

Without looking at Boofuls, Martin said, "I know for a fact that people can survive after death, inside that mirror."

"You know that for a *fact*?" queried Father Lucas.

Martin nodded.

There was a lengthy and embarrassing silence. Boofuls continued to watch *Sesame Street* with no obvious concern at Father Lucas' presence. Father Lucas sat on his chair with his double chins squashed up by his dog collar, his eyes fixed on the floor, his forehead furrowed like a Shar-Pei, trying to think of an appropriate response. He had known Mr. Capelli for years and years, and he had never known him to be anything but sincere. Pompous, occasionally irascible; but never foolish or dishonest.

Father Lucas had never met Martin before, but Martin certainly didn't *look* wild or eccentric; or like a malicious practical joker.

"You'll have to forgive me," he said. "I'm not at all sure that I understand what you're asking; and even if I *could* understand what you're asking, I'm not at all sure why you're asking *me*."

He stood up and walked toward the mirror. "You're trying to tell me that people can walk in and out of this mirror?"

Martin said, "Sometimes. Not always."

Father Lucas knocked on the glass with his knuckle. "Seems pretty solid to me. What's behind it?"

"An outside wall. Back of the house."

Father Lucas breathed on the mirror's surface and wiped it with his cuff. "And you say that if you *can* get into the mirror . . . then beyond that sitting room door, things are very different from the real world?"

Mr. Capelli put in, "We saw a ball, yes? A child's

ball. In here it was blue and white, in there it was a tennis ball."

He swallowed hard, and then he added, "I saw Emilio in there, my own flesh and blood; but here it was—" He lifted one arm toward Boofuls, then dropped it against his side. "In here it was this boy."

"*This* boy?" queried Father Lucas, inclining his head toward Boofuls.

Uneasy, Mr. Capelli wiped his sweating palms on the sides of his pants. Father Lucas walked back toward Boofuls and hunkered down beside him, inspecting him through his television-set spectacles as if he were a doctor and Boofuls had been brought to him with suspected mumps. Boofuls completely ignored him and carried on watching television.

Father Lucas held out his hand, but Boofuls, without looking at him, moved his own hand away.

"What's your name, son?" Father Lucas asked him in a gentle voice.

Boofuls' eyes remained fixed on Grover. "My name is Lejeune," he said.

"Lejeune? Is that French?"

Boofuls shook his head. Father Lucas waited for him to say something else, but when he didn't, he rose to his feet and said, "He's a relative of yours?"

"He's my—" Martin began; but Mr. Capelli immediately interrupted.

"He's a friend of Emilio's; a good, good friend. Best buddies. His parents had to go away for a week or two. So—well—he's staying with us. With me and Mrs. Capelli."

Boofuls didn't make any attempt to deny this fiction; but kept on smiling.

"Well . . ." said Father Lucas. "I'm not too sure what it is you want me to do."

Mr. Capelli grasped his arm and spoke to him racetrack-confidential. "I want you to tell me if that mirror is a good mirror or an evil mirror. I want you to tell me what you feel when you touch it. Also, I was hoping that maybe you could think of some way to get Emilio out. Some *holy* way, do you understand what I mean by holy? Just so that nobody gets hurt. You see Lejeune here, well, I wouldn't want *him* to get hurt, for instance."

"Why should there by any danger of him getting hurt?" asked Father Lucas.

"Father," Mr. Capelli replied, "I just don't know. But maybe prayer can help. You know—maybe you can ask God."

Father Lucas tried to look benign. "God isn't exactly an agony uncle on some local radio station, somebody you can call up just whenever you feel like it."

"I know that. He's better. Look at His ratings. God has better ratings than anybody you can think of, on any station."

"Mr. Capelli," said Father Lucas, "let's just take this one step at a time. You're asking me to tell you whether the mirror is good or evil. Well, let's find out. There's a little test we can do. I suppose you could call it a litmus test for blasphemy."

"Litmus?" frowned Mr. Capelli, as Father Lucas took a small phial of silver and dark blue glass out of his coat pocket.

"Didn't you do any science at school?" Martin asked him. "Litmus is a powder that turns red in acid and blue in alkali. They make it out of moss."

"And this is litmus?" Mr. Capelli asked, pointing to Father Lucas' phial.

Father Lucas smiled and shook his head. "Not quite, Mr. Capelli. But it has a similar effect. It is water from

the Holy Shrine at Lourdes, mixed with salt from the
Sea of Galilee. It is said that if it touches any evil or
desecrated object or person, it will burn them, like
acid."

Boofuls looked across in interest when Father Lucas
said this; but after a while he returned to the television. *Little House on the Prairie* seemed to entertain
him more than foolish priests who sprained their ankles playing baseball.

Father Lucas unscrewed the cap of the phial and
lifted it up in front of the mirror. "In the name of the
Father, the Son, and the Holy Ghost," he intoned, and
cast drops of holy water at the surface of the mirror in
the sign of the cross.

To his astonishment, the holy water *flew right
through the surface of the mirror and splattered onto the
floor in the reflected sitting room.*

Father Lucas stared at the image in the mirror, then
touched the glass of the mirror itself, then stepped
back to stare at the real floor.

"My God," he whispered. "It's *there*, in the mirror,
but it's not *here*." He licked his lips anxiously. "It went
right through. How could that happen? It's solid
glass."

Martin said, "Now you know why we called you."

Father Lucas waited for a moment, plainly unsure
what he was going to do next. "There could be some
scientific explanation," he suggested. "I always look for
the scientific explanation before I start imagining that
I'm face-to-face with something demonic. Well, it's
only right. Science in itself is a wonder of the Lord;
and if a phenomenon eventually turns out to *defy* science, well, then, it's all the more wonderful for that."

"So what are you going to do?" asked Mr. Capelli.

"All you lost in there was some holy water. I lost my grandson."

"Well," said Father Lucas. "This isn't really my bag, so to speak. I'm not an exorcist; and I'm not too sure than an exorcist is what you need. You may be better off with a physicist."

Boofuls laughed out loud, but it wasn't at all clear whether he was laughing at the television or at Father Lucas. Mr. Capelli gave him a stern look, and he said, "I'm sorry."

Stiffly, Father Lucas got down on his hands and knees and patted the floorboards where (in the mirror) they were wet. Martin had done the same thing when Boofuls' ball first bounced into the reflected room; and with an equal lack of success.

"I can see myself touching it," he said, "and yet my hands aren't wet. It's quite astonishing."

He held out his hand to Martin to help him back up again; but just as he did so, something came flying *out* of the mirror in exactly the same parabola as the holy water had flown *in*. It splattered onto Father Lucas' forehead and down the side of his cheek.

He cried out "Ah!" in surprise, and lifted his fingers to his face. He had been hit by several white glutinous droplets, which dripped onto the floor, and hung from his fingers in thin sticky strings.

"Here," said Mr. Capelli, taking out a large clean handkerchief and unfolding it. "Here, Father, wipe yourself with this."

"What in God's name is it?" Father Lucas asked in disgust. He lifted his fingers to his nose and sniffed. Then he sniffed again. Then—his horror so strong that he almost panicked—he snatched the handkerchief from Mr. Capelli's hand and wiped and wiped his face until it was bright scarlet all down one side.

"Semen!" He quivered. "Semen!"

Mr. Capelli crossed himself, and then crossed himself again. Martin helped Father Lucas to climb to his feet. Once he had steadied himself, Father Lucas stared at the mirror in anger and frustration. "This is the work of the devil, you must have realized from the very start."

"But what can you do?" Mr. Capelli begged him. "The work of the devil is something that priests are trained to handle, eh? So you can do something for us?"

Father Lucas was about to say something when he turned unexpectedly and looked at Boofuls. Boofuls was staring at him with one of his triumphant, expressionless faces.

For a moment, their eyes engaged in a silent, careful game of question and answer. Then Father Lucas walked over to him and said, "What do *you* know about this mirror?"

Mr. Capelli caught hold of Father Lucas' arm. "Listen, Father, he doesn't know nothing at all. He's only been in town since yesterday."

Father Lucas continued to stare at Boofuls in the way that a confident man stares at a dog which has a reputation for being vicious and mad. "Lejeune," he said. "That's your name, is it? Lejeune."

Boofuls smiled fleetingly and said nothing, but he didn't take his eyes away from Father Lucas, not once. Martin didn't like the look of that smile at all. It made him shudder, as if somebody were stepping on his grave.

*   *   *

They went downstairs to Mr. Capelli's apartment, leaving Boofuls on his own. "Come in and have coffee," Mrs. Capelli begged Father Lucas. "I have some beautiful polenta."

Martin said, "Go ahead, Father, please. There's something I want to show you."

"All right, all right," Father Lucas agreed. He took out his handkerchief and gave his reddened cheek yet another rub. "But I can only stay for a quarter of an hour."

"It won't take any longer," Martin assured him.

While Mr. and Mrs. Capelli took Father Lucas through to their parlor, Martin ran downstairs and out into the street. He unlocked the trunk of his Mustang and carefully lifted out the black-tissue package that he and Ramone had discovered at the Hollywood Divine. Then he returned to the house with it and carried it upstairs.

Mrs. Capelli was setting the table with plates and cups. She looked fretful and unsettled, and her braided hair was coming loose on one side. Father Lucas was talking to Mr. Capelli about the mirror. They obviously hadn't told Mrs. Capelli that it had ejaculated in Father Lucas' face. But Father Lucas looked extremely worried.

"You always associate this kind of demonic event with the Middle Ages," he was saying, "but the truth is that the devil never rests, any more than the Lord Almighty."

"Amen, amen," put in Mrs. Capelli, clattering coffee spoons.

Martin came in and laid the black-tissue package on the lace tablecloth. Father Lucas shifted his chair around to examine it. "What's this?" he wanted to know. "Is it anything to do with the mirror?"

"I think so, but I don't know what. Let me tell you something, Father, before you open it. A man was killed yesterday, helping me to find this stuff. Whether it was an accident or not, I can't say. He might just have hemorrhaged. But I don't really think so."

Mrs. Capelli crossed herself. "Holy Mother of God, what is it?"

Father Lucas untied the braided hair and teased open the tissue paper. He lifted one sheet up, and the black claws tumbled out onto the table with a rattling sound.

"God protect us," Mr. Capelli said hoarsely.

"Where did you get these?" Father Lucas asked, picking one of the claws up and turning it over.

Martin said, "Just at the moment, I don't want to tell you. Well, I want to tell you, but I can't. It's all to do with protecting Emilio. But they *do* seem to have some connection with the mirror. A very strong connection."

Father Lucas wrinkled up his nose as he took out the piece of dried scalp. Then he found the key.

"Do you have any idea what this opens?"

"A safe-deposit box, I think, in the same place where we found all of this stuff. But there are dozens of them, and we don't know the number."

"What was the number of the box you found these in?"

Martin dug into the pocket of his jeans and took out the key that Sister Boniface had given him. "Here it is, 531."

Father Lucas examined it carefully. "Well . . ." he said. "I know only a little about occult numerology, but I know enough to recognize the Number of the Beast when I see it."

"The Number of the Beast?"

"Satan's number, 666. Don't you remember that film *The Omen*? They made great play of it in that."

"Oh, yes . . ." said Martin. "Wasn't it tattooed on Damien's scalp or something? I mean, is that real? Is that really the number of the devil?"

Father Lucas looked almost embarrassed. "The story was fiction, of course, but the number was real. As far as I know it came from biblical times. But, you know, it used to be disguised by Satanists . . . split into quarters or tenths or halves or whatever. This is one of the things they taught us at Bible college. You see—what is the *reverse* of 531?"

Martin said without hesitation, "135."

"Quite right . . . but if you add them together? 135 and 531?"

Martin said nothing. Mrs. Capelli stood in the doorway with a dangerously tilting plate of polenta with pine nuts and stared at Father Lucas openmouthed, even though she didn't have the slightest idea what was going on.

Father Lucas gestured toward the claws. "It would appear to me that what you have come across here is *half* of the artifacts used in the satanic Sabbat. It doesn't take a genius to guess that the other half can be found in locker number 135."

Martin slowly sat down. He picked up one of the claws and held it up to the light. It was jet black, opaque, and extraordinarily heavy. "So what are these things? What are they used for?"

Father Lucas said, "I'm not an exorcist."

"But?" asked Martin, catching the implication in his voice that he probably knew more.

"Well," said Father Lucas, "they used to tell us at St. Patrick's that there were relics of Satan, just as there were relics of the True Cross, and the Holy Shroud, and the crown of thorns."

"And that's what you think these are? Relics of Satan?"

"Well, now, who can tell? It could all be nonsense."

"But it isn't nonsense, is it?" said Martin. "You saw that mirror for yourself. You threw the holy water and it went right through. You know that something evil is going down here, just as well as we do."

Father Lucas sat and stared for a long time at the scattered claws. Then he said, "They taught us at St. Patrick's that the beast had been beaten, years ago, and that his body had been torn to pieces and scattered to the ends of the earth."

"And?" asked Mr. Capelli impatiently.

"And that's all," said Father Lucas. "Except that what you have here—these claws, this skin, this hair—they are all pieces of the beast. And whoever left them in that locker was obviously determined to bring them back together again—all the pieces, no matter where they were scattered—and re-create the creature that the Bible calls Satan. The *true* Satan, the very core of all evil—in the flesh."

Martin rearranged the claws by nudging them with the tips of his fingers; but he didn't feel like holding them as tightly as he had before. Satan may be an old-fashioned concept, but it was still frightening.

Father Lucas asked, "You really can't tell me where you found these, or where the remaining pieces might be?"

Martin thought about it for a while, but then he shook his head. He wanted to know more about Boofuls' monthly meetings at the Hollywood Divine before he let Father Lucas get involved. He wanted to know more about Boofuls himself. He had a feeling that if Father Lucas realized who Boofuls was, he would be back at the house within the hour with a busload of exorcists; and that their chances of getting Emilio back whole and undistorted would be put at serious risk.

What would be worse, the slightest hint of an exorcism would bring out the newspaper reporters and the television cameras, and Boofuls' appearance would be turned into a three-ring media circus.

Maybe there was another reason why Martin didn't want to divulge everything to Father Lucas just yet, a selfish reason. Maybe he wanted to see through this proposed remake of *Sweet Chariot*. If it could ever be filmed, it would be the sensation of all time—the only motion picture to star a reincarnated murder victim—and Martin would have his name on it. There would be no stopping his career after that. He would become a movie legend. Notorious, perhaps, but never forgotten.

Father Lucas cut himself a slice of polenta and ate it thoughtfully. Martin found it rather dry, with too many pine nuts in it. At length, wiping his hands on one of Mrs. Capelli's best white embroidered napkins, Father Lucas said, "That boy upstairs; your grandson's friend, Lejeune. Does he have anything to do with this in any way?"

"What makes you say that?" asked Martin before Mr. Capelli could answer.

"He has a *presence* about him, that's all. I can't quite put my finger on it. Perhaps it's nothing more than a freshness of youth."

"He's a very bright young boy," said Martin.

Father Lucas looked at him challengingly for a moment; and Martin looked back at him and steadily held his eye but gave nothing away.

"You're asking me to help you, yet you won't tell me the whole story," Father Lucas told him. He turned around to Mr. Capelli. "Isn't that so, Mr. Capelli?"

Mr. Capelli looked embarrassed. But Martin said, "Father—let's just say that we're hedging our bets a little. We're not quite sure what we're up against yet; and it could be dangerous if we go storming in with bells, books, and candles, trying to exorcise something that may not even *need* exorcising; or may not even *respond* to being exorcised."

He paused for a moment, and then he said, "We're not trying to be obstructive, Father. It's just that we're very worried about Emilio. One wrong step and we may never see him again; not whole, anyway; and not the way he was before. We need your help very badly. If there's anything you can find out about mirrors and worlds beyond mirrors—well, we're looking for anything, anything at all. But Emilio is at serious risk; and if we lose him forever simply because we weren't careful enough . . . well, I don't think *our* souls are going to rest, either."

Father Lucas frowned. "What do you mean by that? Your souls aren't going to rest, *either*? Who else has a soul that isn't at rest?"

Martin was almost tempted to tell him; but then he shook his head and said, "Please, Father. Let's just take one step at a time."

Father Lucas stood up and brushed crumbs from his coat. "I really have to go now," he said. "But—all right—I'll accept your word that you can't tell me everything about the mirror. After all, Emilio's safety should be our first concern."

He reached across the table and picked up the black-tissue package. "Let me take these, however. I have a friend at St. Patrick's who may be able to throw some light on these, and may even be able to tell us what the *other* safe-deposit box contains, before we risk opening it."

Martin took hold of Father Lucas' hand and grasped it firmly. "Thank you for having faith in all this," he told him.

Father Lucas gave him a wry smile. "I am regularly required to believe in the impossible, Mr. Williams. It's not so hard for me to believe in the outrageous."

Out on the landing, Father Lucas said good-bye to Mr. and Mrs. Capelli and thanked Mrs. Capelli for her coffee and her cake. He was just about to go down the stairs when Boofuls appeared at the doorway of Martin's apartment. He stood there silently, staring down at Father Lucas with undisguised contempt.

"Good-bye, Lejeune," Father Lucas called out, trying to be cheerful.

"Good-bye, Father," Boofuls replied.

There was a moment of awkward silence. "Well, then," said Father Lucas, "I must be off."

"Father Lucas!" said Boofuls in a clear voice.

"What is it, my boy?"

Boofuls smiled at him. Then he said, "Take care of your teeth, Father Lucas."

Father Lucas laughed. "Don't you worry, my boy. I brush them three times a day!"

Boofuls laughed, too; and then turned and disappeared back into Martin's apartment.

Martin looked serious. "Take care of your teeth?" he said. "What on earth did he mean by that?"

Father Lucas grasped Martin's arm. "You just take care of yourself, Mr. Williams. I'll call you if I find out anything about these relics. You work at home, don't you?"

Martin nodded. He stood at the head of the stairs watching Father Lucas go.

"I don't like this," said Mr. Capelli, rubbing his chin. "I don't like this at all."

Martin clapped him on the shoulder, and then slowly went back upstairs to see what Boofuls was doing.

Nine

THE FOLLOWING MORNING WAS DULL and humid; one of those overcast Hollywood days when all the buildings look tawdry and unreal, like a low-budget movie set. They drove up to Morris Nathan's house shortly after eleven o'clock. Morris had told Martin on the phone that he was too busy that morning to see anybody, but Martin had persisted. In the end, Morris had agreed to wedge him in between Joe Willmore and Henry Winkler. "But four minutes only—*four*—no more."

Because the day was so gray, there was nobody in the pool. Alison's inflatable sunbed circled around on its own, speckled with flies. Martin could see Alison herself in the sun-room, wearing a white silk caftan. Her manicurist was sitting at her feet like a religious supplicant, painting her toenails the color of 1956 Cadillacs. Alison waved as Martin and Boofuls walked across the patio to the front door.

Inside, Morris was saying good-bye to Joe Willmore.

There was a strong smell of cigar smoke around. "Come on in, Martin," said Morris as Joe Willmore nodded to Martin, winked at Boofuls, and left. Martin followed Morris into his huge oak-paneled office with its sage-green shag-pile carpet and its framed photographs of Morris arm in arm with everybody who was anybody, from Frank Sinatra to Ronald Reagan.

"It's one of those days, you know?" said Morris. "That *fonfer* David Santini has been arguing about the percentages on *Robot Killer III;* and don't ask me what Fox is trying to pull over *Headhunters*."

"What *is* Fox trying to pull over *Headhunters*?" Martin inquired.

"I said don't ask," said Morris. "Believe me, if I told you, you wouldn't want to know."

Martin laid a hand on Boofuls' shoulder. Boofuls had stayed quiet all this time, looking around. Today, he looked very much like any other small boy: Martin had taken him out yesterday afternoon and bought him shirts and T-shirts, shorts and jeans. He had stuck his hair down with gel, too, so that he didn't look quite so girly and ringleted.

Boofuls was still pale; and there was still something about him that wasn't quite ordinary; but at least he wasn't quite so obviously quaint.

"This is Lejeune," said Martin. To avoid complications, they had decided to stick to the name that Boofuls had given to Father Lucas.

"Oh, yeah?" said Morris, leafing through a red-jacketed screenplay on his desk. "Pleased to meet you, Lejeune. Don't tell me you're unlucky enough to have this *letz* for an uncle?"

"We're not related," Martin explained. "Lejeune here is my choice to play Boofuls."

Morris slowly raised his eyes and stared first at Boofuls and then at Martin.

"Martin," he said, "I can spare you four minutes to talk about anything except Boofuls."

"Will you listen for just *one* minute?" said Martin. "I've decided to shelve my original idea. Instead, I want to put together a remake of Boofuls' last movie—the movie he never finished."

Morris lowered his eyes toward the screenplay again. "Martin," he said with exaggerated patience, "how long are you going to keep on *mutshing* me about Boofuls? Can't you take some advice? It's a loser. It's a dead duck. It's deader than a dead duck."

But now Boofuls took one step forward and said in a high-pitched voice, "No, sir. It's not dead at all."

Morris looked at Martin in displeased surprise. "Who's the *mazik*?" he wanted to know. *Mazik* was Yiddish for a mischievous little devil. It was less insulting than *mamzer*, the way Morris said it, but not very much less insulting.

Boofuls lisped, "The picture was called *Sweet Chariot*. Maybe you don't remember it."

"Remember it?" Morris protested. "Of course I remember it. And if I hadn't of remembered it, this uncle of yours would have reminded me, in any case, as if he wouldn't."

"He's not my uncle," Boofuls corrected him. "He's my script editor, that's all."

Morris couldn't believe this. "*He* is *your* script editor?"

Boofuls nodded. "We're going to make this picture, Mr. Nathan, and you're going to help us."

"Martin, is this some kind of a practical joke?" Morris demanded. "I'm a busy man, can you come to terms with that? I just can't stand here listening to all of this—"

He stopped in midsentence, with his mouth open. Because—without any further hesitation, and with stunning grace—Boofuls lifted both his arms, and began to dance slowly around Morris Nathan's office. His head was held high, his eyes were penetratingly bright, his arms and legs flowed through one complicated dance movement after another. Martin stepped back so that Boofuls could twirl past him, his toes scarcely touching the carpet as he went. He seemed to be unaffected by gravity—light and soundless, keeping perfectly in time with some unheard music. One-two-*three*-four, one-two-*three*-four, around and around and around.

Morris stared in fascination as Boofuls completed his dance, and bowed, and paused; and then clasped his hands together and stared up at the ceiling with an expression of pathos.

"I never saw *anybody*—" he began, but Martin shushed him, because Boofuls had started to sing. Martin had never heard this song before, although he had read the score. It came about halfway through *Sweet Chariot*, when the dead-end kid rises from his body as an angel.

Boofuls' voice was clear and sweet and penetrating. It sounded inhuman, as if it had come from the silvery throat of some long-forgotten musical instrument, rather than a child's larynx. It was so moving that Martin couldn't believe what he was hearing—and nor could Morris, from the expression on his face. There were tears in his eyes, and Martin had never ever seen tears in Morris Nathan's eyes before, and (except for his mother, when he was a tiny baby) neither had anybody else.

Like the dew, rising
To kiss the morning sun
I'm rising, I'm rising
To kiss the ones I love

Like the light, dancing
Where the river waters run
I'm dancing, I'm dancing
To that joyful place above

Boofuls finished the song and then stood with his head bowed and his eyes closed. There had been no music; no accompaniment; and yet Martin was almost sure that he had heard a sweeping orchestra; and that when Boofuls had finished singing, a single melancholy violin had laid his last note to rest. As for Morris, he dragged out a handkerchief and blew his nose loudly and looked toward Martin and lifted one hand as if to say, *Amazing, I take it all back, whatever I said about Boofuls, whatever I said about anything.*

Boofuls opened his eyes and smiled a sly little smile that only Martin saw.

"Well?" said Martin. "What do you think?"

"I think I should shoot myself," Morris told him, shaking his head in admiration. "Then I should talk to June Lassiter."

"You really like it?"

Morris came around his desk beaming. He laid his arm around Martin's shoulders and gave him an affectionate squeeze. "Let me tell you something, Martin, there's a world of difference between concept and product. If you're talking *concept,* the idea of reviving Boofuls totally stunk. I told you it stunk, didn't I, how many times?"

He stretched over to ruffle Boofuls' hair, although Boofuls stepped back so that he was out of reach.

"What you have here, Martin, this is different, this is *product*. This is something that a studio can understand in terms of box office. What did you say your name was, kid?"

"My name is Lejeune," said Boofuls.

"Well, we're going to have to think about *that*." Morris grinned. "Don't want you sounding too Frenchified, do we? Perhaps we can call you Boofuls II. Martin— you fix yourself a drink. How about you, Lejeune? What about a Seven-Up? Let me call Alison; she can take care of Lejeune for a while so that you and I can talk a little business."

"I'd rather stay here and listen," said Boofuls.

"Well, you don't want to do that," Morris told him. "This is grown-up talk; very boring. Alison will show you the peacocks. We have five now, did you know that, Martin? They make incredible watchdogs. Anyone comes within five hundred feet of the house, they scream out like somebody strangling your grandmother."

Boofuls suddenly looked white. "I want to go," he said.

"We won't be long," said Morris, parking half of his enormous bottom on the side of his desk and punching out the sun-room telephone number. "We just have to talk about how we're going to lick this whole thing into some kind of shape."

"*I want to go*," Boofuls insisted.

"Sure," said Morris, "sure. Just as soon as we've sorted things out. Oh—Alison? How are you doing, sweetie-pie? Would you mind coming into the den for a moment? Well, I've got a cute young friend here I'd like you to meet. All right, then, okay. Bysie-bye."

The phone rang again. Morris picked it up. "Hello?

Oh, Henry, how are you? Where are you calling from? You're kidding! Well—if it's unavoidable. What time can you get here? Okay, all right, that's fine. I can see you at two-thirty. Fine."

"That was Henry Winkler," he told Martin as he put down the phone. "He's been held up at ABC. Now, how about that drink? I could use one myself. Lejeune, my friend, the lovely Mrs. Nathan is going to show you around the yard while Martin and I have a little pow-wow, all right?"

"I'm going," said Boofuls, his lips blue with rage; and he turned around and stalked out of Morris' study and slammed the door behind him.

"Morris," Martin appealed, "just give me a moment, will you?"

He went after Boofuls and saw him marching past the swimming pool, his chin lowered, his arms swinging angrily.

"Boofuls!" he called out. "Just hold up a minute, will you?"

At that moment, however, Alison came out of the sun-room and began to walk toward the swimming pool in the opposite direction. When she saw Boofuls she waved and smiled and quickened her pace. Her white silk caftan floated in the gray daylight like a Pacific roller photographed in slow motion. She had almost reached Boofuls, however, when she covered her face with both hands, so that only her eyes were visible; and for no apparent reason at all she let him pass straight by, and disappear down the steps toward the front gate.

Martin hurried across the flagstones and took hold of Alison's hand. "Alison? Are you okay?"

Alison nodded. She was shuddering. "I think I'm

going to have to sit down," she said. Martin brought
over a cast-iron garden chair, and she sat on it unsteadily and hung her head between her knees, breathing deeply.

"Who was *that*?" she managed to ask Martin at last.

"You mean that boy? He's a child actor I discovered.
You know, singer and dancer. I brought him along to
meet Morris because he's really got something special."

Alison was still quaking. "Is he sick?" she wanted to
know.

Martin couldn't help letting out a grunt of amusement. "Not so far as I know."

Alison sat up straight, and clung on to Martin's
sleeve. "If he's not sick—why does he look so white?
He looks so sick, like he's dead already."

Martin said, "What do you mean by that?" He
glanced up. Morris was walking toward them now, his
white sandals flapping loudly on the flagstones. "What
do you mean, he looks like he's dead already?"

"His face . . . oh, God, Martin—it was just like a
skull."

Martin found Boofuls sitting in the passenger seat of
his Mustang, throwing stones at lizards, and usually
missing. Martin climbed in behind the steering wheel
and sat there saying nothing for two or three minutes,
drumming his fingers on top of the dash.

At last, Boofuls said, "I'm sorry, Martin. I didn't
mean to spoil things. I haven't lost my temper like that
in a long time."

"You could have screwed things up permanently,"
said Martin. He took off his glasses and breathed on
the lenses, buffing them up with his handkerchief. "If

Morris Nathan can't or won't fix anything for you, then
you might just as well pack your suitcase and go back
to wherever you came from."

"Back through the mirror, you mean?" asked
Boofuls. He hesitated for a while, and then he said,
"No, never. I'm never going back through there."

"I'm talking in terms of making this movie," Martin
told him.

"The movie has to be made," Boofuls insisted, not
for the first time that day.

"The movie *will* be made," Martin assured him. "And
when you've done that, you can do whatever the hell
you like, just so long as we get Emilio back. But right
now, be nice to Morris, because if Morris starts to think
that you're unreliable or flaky, then this picture will
take us *years* to get together—even if we can manage to
get it together at all."

Just then, Alison appeared at the gate. Boofuls
moved his head to one side so that he could look at her.
Alison said, "Morris says he's sorry and do you want to
come back in and talk turkey?"

Martin couldn't take his eyes off Boofuls' expression.
It was both adult and lecherous. It was more like the
gilded face of Pan than ever—hairy, wily, foxy-eyed.
Alison was standing in the gateway with one hand
raised against the gate. The faintest wash of late morning sunlight shone through the sheer white fabric of
her caftan, and she was obviously nude underneath.
She peered at Boofuls a little shortsightedly, and
brushed the breeze-blown hair away from her face.

Boofuls climbed out of the car and walked ahead of
them back to the house. Alison stayed close to Martin;
and when Boofuls turned around from time to time to

make sure that they were following, she hesitated, as if she were frightened of him.

"Was it *that* scary, what you saw?" asked Martin.

Alison nodded. "He looked like a Halloween mask, you know? Just for a second. Then he looked normal."

"Well, I don't know," said Martin, trying to be reassuring. "He's a pretty funny sort of a kid."

"Is he your nephew or something? You don't have children, do you?"

Martin shook his head. "He's what you might call my protégé."

Alison stopped and took hold of Martin's forearm. "I don't want you to think I'm stupid or anything, I'm not exactly Miss IQ of America but I'm not stupid. All my life I've been able to see things that other people can't see. Even when I was little. I mean nothing important but kind of *auras*. Like when somebody's happy they shine; or when somebody's sad or sick or something bad's going to happen to them, there's this kind of dark smudge over their face, so that I can hardly see what they look like."

Boofuls had reached the doorway. He turned around and waited for them. Martin lifted a hand and waved to him, to show him that they were coming.

Martin asked Alison, "Seeing Lejeune's face like a skull . . . do you think that was the same kind of thing?"

Alison nodded. "My aunt always said that I was— what do you call it?—*psychic*. She used to say that *every*body's psychic, just a little bit. You know when you get feelings that something's going to go wrong, you shouldn't get on that particular airplane, or you shouldn't cross the street. She said that was all part of being psychic. But some people can see much more than others. Some people can see things that haven't even happened yet: like when other people are going to die."

She paused and glanced toward Boofuls. "I don't mean to be rude or anything, but Lejeune gives me the *weirdest* sensations. I look at him, and I feel like I'm going down in an express elevator."

Martin took hold of her arm and led her toward the house. "Can you do me a favor?" he asked her. "Can you keep these feelings to yourself, just for now?"

"Is there something *wrong*?" Alison asked him.

"I don't know. Right now, it's too difficult to explain; and even if I *did* explain it, I don't really think that it would help. But trust me."

Alison hesitated for a moment, looking at Martin carefully as if she wanted to make quite sure that he wasn't lying. "All right," she said at last. "But he's not sick, is he, Lejeune? He's not going to die? It wasn't just his face that upset me. There was a kind of a *smell* about him, like something gone bad, and a *noise*, like hundreds of flies buzzing."

"Are you coming, Martin?" called Boofuls impatiently.

"Sure, I'm coming. Let's go see what we can do to get this motion picture on the road."

Martin led the way into the house. Alison stayed where she was, on the patio, her caftan ruffled in the breeze. Just as he stepped into the house, Boofuls turned around and stuck out his tongue at her in a lascivious licking gesture.

Alison stayed where she was, shocked and frightened. Boofuls had licked at her so quickly that it was impossible for her to tell for sure, but she could have sworn that his tongue was long and narrow and gray, the color of a snail's foot, and cloven at the end, like a snake's.

In spite of his disturbing precociousness, Boofuls ate and drank and slept like a normal boy. Martin gave him supper at eight o'clock, ravioli out of a can, and tucked him up on the sofa in the sitting room. He insisted on sleeping in the sitting room so that he could lie awake and watch the surface of the mirror. Martin didn't even like to look at the mirror now: all he could think about was Emilio, trapped in some unimaginable world where everything was back to front.

"You see," said Boofuls as Martin went to turn off the light. "I told you that it wouldn't be difficult, finding somebody to remake *Sweet Chariot.*"

"We're seeing June Lassiter tomorrow," Martin told him. "I think you're going to find her a whole lot tougher to win over than Morris Nathan."

Boofuls smiled to himself. Martin switched off the light and stood in the doorway for a moment. He found it particularly disturbing the way Boofuls' eyes glittered blue in the darkness. It was the blue of decaying mackerel; the blue of cutting torches. He said, "Good night, Boofuls," and closed the door. He thought that he had probably never been so consistently frightened in the whole of his life, not just for himself, but for Emilio, too.

He went through to the kitchen, opened up the refrigerator, and helped himself to a red apple and a can of Coors Lite. Then he sat down at the kitchen table, where he had set up his typewriter, and began to peck out a few lines of corrected dialogue for *Sweet Chariot.* Boofuls had wanted him to update some of the story line, "so that it isn't old-fashioned, and so that people really believe it."

He had asked Boofuls yet again why he wanted so badly to make this film; but Boofuls had ignored his question and given him a brassy laugh.

He typed for almost an hour, gradually changing a bunch of 1930s kids from the Lower East Side into a gang of 1980s Hollywood Boulevard scuzzballs. The changes came surprisingly easily, and Martin began to feel quite proud of himself. "Once a pro, always a pro," he remarked, zipping out another piece of paper.

It was then that the phone rang. He scraped back his chair and picked up the receiver. A familiar voice said softly, "Mr. Williams? Is that you? I haven't caught you at an inconvenient moment?"

"Father Lucas? Is that you?"

"The very same, Mr. Williams. Can I safely speak?"

"I'm not sure what you mean."

"Is the boy there, that's what I mean."

"No, no. He's asleep in the other room."

"Very well, then, good enough. I have some news for you. I went to see my old friend Father Quinlan at St. Patrick's this afternoon, and I took the relics with me. I also told him about the mirror."

"And?"

"He wants to see you. He says it's desperately urgent. He says that something terrible is about to happen and that he must speak to you at once."

Martin checked his watch. It was twenty after nine. "Do you mean *now*? He wants to see me *now*?"

"He says there's no time to waste. Please, Mr. Williams. It's very urgent indeed."

Martin wearily rubbed his eyes. "All right, tell me how to get there. Hang on—let me get my pencil. Okay, left off Alden Drive, just past Mt. Sinai. All right . . . give me fifteen minutes at least. I have to make sure that Mrs. Capelli can keep an eye on the boy."

He folded the sheet of paper with Father Quinlan's address, tucked it into the pocket of his jeans, and then went through the hallway to the sitting room. The door was slightly ajar. Martin listened, and all he could hear was steady childish breathing. The little *mazik* was asleep.

Martin closed his apartment door quietly, then crept downstairs and knocked at Mrs. Capelli's door. Mrs. Capelli crossed herself when she saw who it was.

"Mrs. Capelli, can you keep an eye on the boy for me . . . just for an hour or two?"

"Hmh! I should keep a watch on the devil's own? The one who stole my Emilio?"

"Mrs. Capelli, please. The chances are that he's completely innocent."

Mrs. Capelli pointed fiercely upstairs. "If that child is innocent, then God has abandoned this world altogether!"

Eventually, however, Mrs. Capelli agreed to keep an ear open for Boofuls, no more. "If he cries, he cries. I don't like that child. I don't trust him." Martin gave her two quick kisses, one on each cheek, and galloped downstairs. He U-turned his Mustang on Franklin Avenue and headed westward. He didn't want to waste any more time. Father Lucas had sounded as if he expected the Apocalypse at any moment, or worse.

St. Patrick's Theological College was one of those extraordinary 1930s structures that give Hollywood the appearance of being somewhere you remembered from a dream. It had been designed in the style of an English Tudor mansion, with latticed windows and red-brick battlements. It was easy to imagine Errol Flynn in doublet and pantaloons, rapier-fighting up and down the staircases.

Martin parked at the side, where Father Lucas had instructed him, and went up to the illuminated porch marked History Dept./Maintenance. He rang the doorbell and waited. A distant electrical storm flickered like snakes' tongues over the Hollywood Reservoir.

A young priest with a gray tweed sports coat and a shaven head answered the door. "Yes?"

"I've come to see Father Quinlan. He said it was urgent."

"Urgent?" the young priest asked. Nothing *urgent* ever happened at St. Patrick's Theological College. The faculty had been discussing the implications of verses 20 and 21 of the first chapter of St. Peter's second letter for the past seventeen years, "no prophecy was ever made by an act of human will," and were still no nearer to an agreement on what they meant.

Martin followed the young priest along a narrow corridor with paneled walls and a highly waxed floor. At the very end of the corridor was a table with a flower arrangement on it; and above the flower arrangement, a painting of St. Peter with a radiant gilded halo. Martin's shoes squeaked busily on the floor.

The young priest knocked at the second-to-last door. Martin didn't hear anybody inviting him to come in, but the young priest opened it and admitted Martin to a large untidy study, with leather sofas, side tables stacked with books, and a desk crowded with files and Bibles and framed photographs and dirty coffee cups.

Father Lucas was sitting next to the fireplace, although there was nothing in the hearth but an arrangement of dried flowers. Beside him stood a thin tall priest with a pinched face and long white hair and dark expressive eyes. He came forward to greet Martin with all the easy, stylized movements of a ballet dancer.

"I appreciate your promptness, Mr. Williams," he said, smiling. "I am Father Quinlan, the head of historical studies here at St. Patrick's."

The young priest had been standing in the doorway, obviously hoping to pick up some gist of what they were going to discuss; but Father Quinlan, still smiling, waved him away. "Do sit down," he said to Martin. "Perhaps you'd care for a glass of wine."

"Don't mind if I do, thanks," Martin told him, and sat down on one of the leather sofas. The seat cushion let out a loud exhalation of dusty air. Martin gave Father Lucas an embarrassed smirk. On the low coffee table between them, the black-tissue package had been opened out and the horny claws neatly laid out in a line. The fragment of hair had been laid to one side, along with the key.

Father Quinlan went to his bureau and stood with his back to Martin, carefully pouring out a glass of red wine from a Baccarat decanter.

"Mr. Williams," he said, "it seems that you have managed to open up what you might call a Pandora's box."

"You said it was urgent," Martin commented.

Father Quinlan came over and handed him his glass. The wine smelled strong and aromatic. "'Urgent' was actually an understatement." He smiled. "Actually, it's critical."

He watched as Martin sipped the wine and then beamed. "Stag's Leap, 1976. I thought you'd enjoy it."

"Tell me what's critical," said Martin. He wasn't a wine connoisseur. As far as he was concerned, wine in itself was nothing important. It was the occasion on which you drank it, and whom you drank it with—that was what made an average wine into a memorable wine. Tonight he felt sour and edgy and any wine would have tasted the same.

Father Quinlan sat down at the opposite end of the sofa and elegantly crossed his legs. "Father Lucas came to me yesterday and told me how worried he was. He described his experience with the mirror. Quite frightening, yes? to say the least. And he told me that both you and Mr. Capelli appeared to be extremely anxious about what had happened to Mr. Capelli's grandson."

"If you want to talk about understatements," Martin remarked, "'extremely anxious' is an understatement. Emilio disappeared into that mirror and we still haven't been able to get him out again."

Father Quinlan nodded, to show that he understood, or—even if he didn't understand—that he was willing to help. "Let's talk about mirrors first," he suggested. "Mirrors in general, and then *your* particular mirror."

Martin glanced toward Father Lucas; but Father Lucas took off his magnifying spectacles and nodded reassuringly. "All right," said Martin, "let's talk about mirrors in general."

"There's an old Yiddish story about mirrors," said Father Quinlan. "A rich man tells his rabbi that he sees no point in giving charity to the poor. So the rabbi takes him to the window and tells him to look out over the marketplace, and then says, 'What do you see?' The rich man says, 'People, of course.' So then the rabbi holds up a mirror in front of him and says, 'What do you see now?' and he says 'Myself.' Well, the rabbi smiles and says, 'Window and mirror, two pieces of glass, that's all. But it's extraordinary how a little silver makes it impossible for a man to see anything through that glass but himself.'"

Father Quinlan sipped his wine, obviously conscious
that he may have sounded too simplistic and patronizing; a fault with most priests, even when they mean it
kindly. But then he said, "Mirrors capture the soul, Mr.
Williams. Not metaphorically, but literally. They
really do. They capture living pieces of our lives and
our characters whenever we pass in front of them.
Sometimes, in moments of terrible stress, they can
take almost all of us."

Martin deliberately said nothing but waited for Father Quinlan to continue.

Father Quinlan looked at Martin keenly, as if he were
challenging him to not to believe in what he was saying. "A mirror is like a living camera, Mr. Williams.
It's no coincidence that silver forms the backing for
mirrors; and that silver salts are the light-sensitive medium which makes photography possible. Neither is it
a coincidence that silver bullets kill those unfortunate
afflicted people who are popularly known as
werewolves. Like a mirror, like a photograph, a silver
bullet instantaneously absorbs the wolf-image which
has overwhelmed the human-image."

"Werewolves?" asked Martin cautiously. He didn't
want to hurt Father Quinlan's feelings, but really—

Father Quinlan said, "I'm afraid I'm getting ahead of
myself, Mr. Williams. You can mock me if you like. But
the historical records concerning the appearance of
werewolves are quite clear. And so are the records concerning the extraordinary properties of mirrors."

He paused, and sipped his wine, and watched Martin
closely. Then he said, "Your mirror—do you know anything at all about it?"

Martin shrugged. "I'm not sure that it's a good idea
to tell you."

"Where did you get it?"

"I bought it from a woman up on Hillrise Avenue, near the Reservoir."

"And was she the original owner?"

Martin shook his head.

Father Quinlan waited for a moment in the hope that Martin was going to tell him who the original owner was, but when Martin stayed silent, he said, "Let me give you some background, Martin. Then perhaps you and I can come to some arrangement and do what we can to deal with this situation."

"I'm listening," Martin told him.

"These claws," said Father Quinlan, picking up one of the black hooked nails that was laid out on the table. "These are the claws of Satan himself, do you understand what I'm saying? The *real* claws of Satan himself, in the dragon manifestation that was clearly predicted in the Book of Revelation."

He went across to his desk and picked up one of his Bibles. "Here it is. *'And I saw another beast coming up out of the earth; and he spoke as a dragon. And there was given to him to give breath to the image of the beast, that the image of the beast might even speak and cause as many who do not worship the image of the beast to be killed.'*"

Father Quinlan was silent for a moment, and then he read, *"'Let him who has understanding calculate the number of the beast; and his number is six hundred and sixty-six.'"*

He closed the Bible. "The legend, Mr. Williams, is that Satan was cast out of heaven by the angel Michael, and fell, and was shattered, so that the pieces of his body were strewn all over the earth. A claw here, a horn there, a hoof beyond the horizon.

"But the legend also says that—seconds before he struck the earth—his image was momentarily reflected in a river, and that the image in the river became the spirit of Satan, although he had no body in the real material world. His *real* body was spread around everywhere . . . rather like the body of somebody who has died in an air disaster, except that Satan had fallen not from 23,000 feet, but from the vaults of heaven itself.

"For thousands of years, Satan was trapped inside the reflected world. Behind glass, behind mirrors, in rivers and lakes. He was able to *influence* the events of the real world. He was able to enter it, in a limited way, by possessing the souls of children and gullible people who were prepared to give him admission. But he was never able to escape. To escape, he required his material body to be reassembled. He needed somebody else to put back together again the jigsaw of his shattered body. Hence these claws, Mr. Williams; hence this scalp. Whoever used to own these was undoubtedly the agent of Satan—trying to reincarnate the devil himself in the modern world. In the second deposit box, you will probably find more pieces; and you may even find another key, which will lead you on to yet more pieces."

Martin said, "Satan. I can't believe it. You mean the real genuine Satan?"

Father Quinlan nodded. "The real genuine Satan, from the Bible."

"But if he ever gets back together again, what will he do?"

Father Quinlan gave a tight smile. "He has only one purpose in life, and that is to tear apart whatever God has created. That means us. He wants to bring the world to a spectacular and grisly end."

Martin was silent for a moment. Then he said, "Two weeks ago, I wouldn't have believed any of this stuff. I wouldn't have wasted my time."

"But now?"

"Well—maybe it's a little different. I've seen enough to understand that what you're trying to say is true. Well, *partly* true; or *mostly* true. These bits of Satan, these claws and stuff—they were used by devil worshipers in Hollywood in the late 1930s. They used to meet once a month at the Hollywood Divine, and hold a what-d'you-call-it, don't tell me, Sabbath."

Father Quinlan smiled in admiration. "You know about the Hollywood Divine?"

Martin said, "Yes. That's where we found these relics."

"Well," said Father Quinlan, "I congratulate you. I've been looking for them for years. It never occurred to me that they might still be there."

"In the basement," Martin told him, "in the safe-deposit boxes."

Father Quinlan was silent for a moment; then he said, "As far as I can discover, it all started in the winter of 1935. There were so many stars in Hollywood who felt insecure. The studio system was tyrannical. One minute you were adored; the next minute you were sliding into oblivion. It was all alcohol and drugs and fast cars and promiscuity. You see those actors smiling and waving: my God, they lived on the very edge of their nerves. If there was any group of people who were ready for the promises of Satan, it was them."

"What happened?" asked Martin.

Father Quinlan tapped the side of his nose with his finger. "Father Lucas may have Coke-bottle eyeglasses,

my friend, but he isn't blind and he isn't stupid. He
saw all those pictures of Boofuls on your wall; and he
found out that you've been trying to sell a musical of
Boofuls for the past six months."

"Oh, he did, did he?" said Martin.

"You're offended?" asked Father Quinlan.

"I don't know, a little."

"How can you be offended? Don't you realize how
serious this is? Don't you realize how *dangerous* it is?
Oh, we're talking about Satan, are we? What a laugh!
But my God, my friend, we're talking about the very
antithesis of peace and happiness; we're talking about
plague and war and famine and destruction. My dear
Mr. Williams, we're talking about the world torn from
pole to pole!"

He stopped for a moment, breathing deeply, and
then he said, "And *why* do we face such an appalling
Apocalypse? Let me tell you why, Mr. Williams. Because of the vanity of a handful of poor insecure actors
who lived in Hollywood in the 1930s. Those glamorous
people of the silver screen, Joan Crawford, Errol Flynn,
John Barrymore, those people we used to idolize! They
weren't glamorous at all, they were obsessed with the
fear of failure. They were little and frightened, and terrified of the adoration that was showered on them. So
they sought encouragement. They sought reassurance.
And when one small boy came among them and said
that they could be successful and happy forever, how
do you think they reacted?"

Martin said nothing, but finished his wine and set
down his empty glass next to the black-tissue package.

Father Quinlan said, "I've been through St. Patrick's
files for the late 1930s. You wouldn't believe it, but we
were given anonymous tip-offs year after year that

somebody, somewhere in L.A., was holding Black Sabbaths on a monumental scale. Phone calls, scrawled letters; one or two photographs. The Hollywood Divine was mentioned several times. But almost all of those tip-offs were ignored—even though one of the letters specifically warned that *'they have the relics.'"*

"But what were these actors actually trying to do?" asked Martin.

Father Quinlan ran his hand through his wild white hair. "They were trying to do nothing more than bring back Satan. The real, reincarnated Satan, in the flesh. It was a pretty straightforward arrangement. In return for bringing him back, Satan would give them youth and glamor and eternal popularity."

Martin said nothing, but lowered his head in silent acknowledgment. He had seen too much in the past few days to be a disbeliever.

Father Quinlan said more quietly, "It all started, somehow, with Boofuls. I had my suspicions, from the moment I started researching. I found a letter written by Bill Tilden . . . well, you know what *he* was like, Stumpy Tilden. Tennis coaching for pretty young boys, that kind of thing. In 1936, he wrote a letter to a close friend, and said that he had met an exquisite child who had offered him hope and happiness, "unimaginable" hope and happiness. The boy's name was Walter Crossley, a.k.a. Boofuls. But Bill Tilden wasn't the only one. Everybody in Hollywood, whether they were homosexual or not, was entranced by Boofuls: his sweetness, his apparent purity, and the feeling that, when they were around him, he made them feel confident and happy and capable of everlasting success."

Father Quinlan said more seriously, "He was nothing more and nothing less than a child possessed by Satan.

That's my opinion, anyway. I was never able to confirm it. How can you confirm such a thing? I could never discover who his father was, and I could never discover the identity of the woman who always used to accompany him to the Hollywood Divine."

"Miss Redd?" put in Martin.

Father Quinlan nodded. "That's right, the mysterious Miss Redd. I've never been able to find any pictures of her or press references or anything at all. But several anonymous letters that were sent to the church in 1938 mention Miss Redd." He reached over and poured Martin some more wine. "However," he said, "let's get back to your mirror."

"Boofuls' mirror," Martin admitted.

Father Quinlan smiled. "I thought so. Well—Father Lucas thought so."

"He was quite right," said Martin. He turned to Father Lucas and gave him a nod of admiration. Father Lucas, in return, lifted up his glass of wine.

Father Quinlan said, "This isn't easy to piece together. Some of the faculty here think that I'm obsessive about it. But the Revelation contains some remarkably clear facts and figures, apart from scores of extraordinary implications. Miss Redd, for example. In the Revelation, Satan appears as a *red* dragon. Perhaps it means nothing at all. Perhaps I'm being paranoid. Oh, yes, priests can be paranoid. But we have one more important authority to turn to; and I'm rather proud of this."

He walked across the room to a large oak cabinet, carved with bunches of grapes. He took a small key out of his vest pocket and opened it. Inside, there were rows of small shelves. Father Quinlan drew out a small package of papers, closed the door, locked it, and returned to the sofa.

"This," he said, "is an unpublished commentary on *Unusual Properties of Looking-Glasses*, by Charles Lutwidge Dodgson."

Martin said, in astonishment, "Charles Lutwidge Dodgson? You mean *Lewis Carroll*?"

Father Quinlan untied the faded silk ribbon which held the papers together. "The very same; and we've had it authenticated, too, by the British Museum."

"But it must be worth a million dollars. An unpublished book by Lewis Carroll?"

"Well . . . another Alice adventure might be worth something. But not so many people know that Lewis Carroll was more of a mathematician than a storyteller. He wrote *A Syllabus of Plane Algebra* and an *Elementary Treatise on Determinants*, as well as *Euclid and His Modern Rivals*."

Father Quinlan turned the musty leaves of the manuscript; and there was a smell of dust and burned cream. "This is all very scrappy . . . not what you'd call a book at all. Notes, really; and some of them very disjointed. But the most interesting part about it is what he has to say about mirrors. He always believed that there was some kind of wonderland on the other side of mirrors; but his first real revelation about mirrors came early in the winter of 1869 when he became extremely ill, pneumonia probably, and he lay in bed at his home in Oxford quite close to death."

Father Quinlan looked Martin straight in the eye. "Carroll may have been delirious; but he tells in this commentary how he walked through the mirror in his sickroom in just the way that Alice did. *The glass melted away, just like a bright silvery mist.*' He found himself in looking-glass land, where everything was reversed.

"He writes here, '*Not just writing, and pictures, but*

Christian morality itself had been turned from left to right. Inside the mirror was the domain of demons, the ante-room of Hell itself.'"

Father Quinlan said, "He tried to tell his friends; he tried to tell the Bishop of Oxford. But after *Alice in Wonderland* they chose not to believe him. So he wrote *Through the Looking-Glass* as an Alice story . . . mainly because he knew that it would find the widest audience. It was a warning, expressed in childish language, in the hope that—even if adults refused to believe the danger they were in—then perhaps children would. *Through the Looking-Glass* is the single most specific warning about the return of Satan since the Revelation itself."

He handed Martin one of the pages. On it, in Lewis Carroll's own handwriting, was written 'Jabberwocky':

> *Beware the Jabberwock, my son!*
> *The jaws that bite, the claws that catch!*

Father Quinlan brought over some more wine. "Later in the book, Carroll explains away this gibberish-poem with all sorts of nonsensical definitions. But ask any *child* about the Jabberwock, and he or she will tell you about nothing except a dark wood, and a ferocious dragonlike creature, and a boy who slays it by chopping it into pieces. Alice herself says, *'Somehow it seems to fill my head with ideas—only I don't exactly know what they are! However somebody killed something.'* See what it says here:

> *"The Jabberwock, with eyes of flame,*
> *Came whiffling through the tulgey wood,*
> *And burbled as it came!*

"Then,

"One, two! One, two! And through and through
The vorpal blade went snicker-snack!
He left it dead, and with its head
He went galumphing back."

Father Quinlan smiled. "Well, it's pretty amusing stuff. But these notes aren't amusing at all. Carroll says here, *'I believe that I came as close to death as a man may go and yet return to the real world. I saw darkness; and I saw unimaginable beings; human-beings with heads as huge as carnival-masks; creatures with hunchbacks; dogs that spoke. It seems to me now like a dream, or rather a nightmare, but I am convinced that I saw Purgatory, the realm in which each man takes on his true form. In the land beyond the looking-glass, in the world of reflections, is the life after death, and the life before death. I understand now the closeness of Christianity, which teaches each man that he will have his reward or his punishment in the world beyond, and the Hindu religion, which teaches that a man will be reincarnated according to the life he has led.'"*

"But the Jabberwock?" asked Martin. "What does the Jabberwock have to do with Boofuls, and *my* mirror?"

"Absolutely everything," said Father Quinlan. "The Jabberwock is the mirror image of Satan. Carroll derived the name from Jabbok, a mountain stream of Gilead, one of the main tributaries of the River Jordan. It was in the waters of Jabbok that Satan's image was supposed to have been reflected when he fell from heaven. It may or may not be a coincidence that Carroll's doctor at the time was called Dr. James Crowe, and that the letters *c-r-o-w-e* make up the remainder of the name Jabberwock."

Martin put down his glass of wine and dry-washed his face with his hands. "God, this seems so far-fetched."

"Any more farfetched than holy water flying straight through a mirror and landing only in the reflected room? Any more farfetched than your friend Emilio disappearing into a mirror and refusing to come back? No, Mr. Williams, this isn't farfetched at all. What we are seeing here is Satan's plan for his own resurrection, as foretold in the Book of Revelation. Somehow, he possessed the boy Boofuls; and the boy Boofuls regularly held blasphemous Sabbaths at the Hollywood Divine; and he used his money and his influence to gather together the scattered remnants of Satan's physical body."

Father Quinlan tugged out one of the sheets of Carroll's notepaper, and on it was Carroll's own sketch for the Jabberwock, on which the final drawing by Sir John Tenniel had been based. A snarling creature with dragon's wings and scaly claws and blazing eyes. "You see," he said, in quiet triumph, "*the jaws that bite, the claws that catch*—and here they are." He picked up the black horny claws from the table. "Almost exactly the same; and to the same scale."

Martin said nothing. He was overwhelmed by tiredness and by the magnitude of what Father Quinlan was trying to tell him.

Father Quinlan said, "When he had recovered from his pneumonia, Carroll spent a great deal of time at the Bodleian Library in Oxford, researching the legend of the fallen devil. He discovered that, according to Jacob and Esau, who met by the waters of the Jabbok, Satan and the children of Satan can be killed only by a sword blessed in the name of God and in the name of the an-

gel Michael and engraved with the motto 'Victory Over
Ruin, Pestilence, and Lust.' Hence the vorpal sword in
the poem—V–O–R–P–A–L. And hence, I strongly suspect, the chopping up of Boofuls by his grandmother.

"They never found the murder weapon, did they?
But it must have been very sharp and very heavy. She
was an elderly woman, remember. She could have dis-
membered him only with a weapon that had considerable weight of its own, like a Chinese cleaver, or a large
two-handed machete—or a two-handed sword."

Martin lifted his hand. "All right—supposing this is
all true—supposing Mrs. Crossley killed Boofuls because she thought he was trying to bring back Satan—
how do you think she found out about it? How do you
think she found out what to do, to stop him? And
where did she get hold of a sword blessed by God and
the angel Michael?"

Father Quinlan smiled. "Every mystery has its unan-
swered questions, Mr. Williams. I'm a theological his-
torian, not a police detective. Perhaps you ought to ask
Boofuls himself."

Martin didn't answer that. He wasn't yet prepared to
admit to Father Quinlan or Father Lucas that the
curly-headed boy at his apartment was actually Boofuls. Father Lucas may have suspected it, having seen
the boy. But before Martin enlisted the help of men like
Father Quinlan, he wanted to be quite sure that he
could rescue Emilio unharmed from the world beyond
the mirror.

"You told me this was urgent," Martin told Father
Quinlan, deliberately changing the subject. "I'm afraid
I don't quite see the urgency. If we have these claws
here, and the key to the rest of the relics—well, there's

not very much that anybody can do to bring the devil to life, is there?"

Father Quinlan nodded. "You're quite right. But Satan is not to be underestimated. Neither is the prophesy that, to be given life, and to win back control over the world, Satan must be given as a sacrifice the lives of one hundred forty-four thousand innocent people."

"Is that a special number?" asked Martin.

"In the Book of Revelation, it's the number of people who defied lies and wickedness and followed the Lamb. The first fruits of God. Satan cannot live and breathe until those one hundred forty-four thousand lie massacred."

Martin raised his eyebrows. "Pretty hard to massacre that many people in this day and age."

"Hard, yes," Father Quinlan agreed. "But not impossible."

Afterward, Father Lucas walked Martin out to his car. The night was warm. Martin couldn't help thinking of the Walrus and the Carpenter. *The night is fine," the Walrus said. "Do you admire the view?"*

Martin opened his car door. A police siren echoed high over Mulholland, where it twisted through the hills. Mulholland's hair-raising curves always attracted coked-up young drivers who believed they could fly.

"What do you think?" asked Father Lucas.

"I don't know," said Martin. "I'm pretty confused, to tell you the truth."

"Father Quinlan is probably the country's greatest expert on theological legend. I know he rambles—but his research is quite extraordinary."

Martin started up his engine. "The question is, can anybody believe what he's saying?"

Father Lucas shrugged and smiled. "That, of course, is a question of faith."

"Let me think about this," Martin told him. "Call me tomorrow; maybe we can talk some more."

"Before you go," said Father Lucas, holding on to the car door, "there's one question I have to ask you."

Martin made a face. "I think I know what it is."

"Lejeune . . . that boy I met at your apartment. He does look awfully like Boofuls."

"That's why I chose him."

"It isn't remotely possible that when your young friend Emilio went *into* the mirror—?"

Martin cut him short. "Father, anything's possible."

"Well," replied Father Lucas. He made the sign of the cross over Martin's head. "If it *is* Boofuls, please take extraordinary care."

"Lejeune is—" Martin began; and then he said, "Lejeune is Lejeune, that's all. He's just a boy."

"Perhaps you should study your Bible better," smiled Father Lucas. "Mark 5, Chapter 5. *'And when He had come out of the boat, immediately a man from the tombs with an unclean spirit met Him. And Jesus was saying, "Come out of the man, you unclean spirit!" and He was asking him, "What is your name?" And the unclean spirit said to Him, "My name is Legion; for we are many."'"*

Although the night was so warm, Martin shivered. Through the oyster-shaped lenses of his spectacles, Father Lucas looked down at him with magnified, serious eyes. "He is having a little joke with us, Mr. Williams. I only wish it were funny."

Ten

Boofuls was still asleep when Martin returned to Franklin Avenue. Mrs. Capelli said she hadn't heard a sound. "There was some scratching, that's all, but it was probably the squirrels, burrowing through the trash."

Martin went quietly upstairs, let himself in, and then tiptoed along the hallway to the sitting room door. Boofuls was still huddled up on the sofa, breathing deeply, although there was an odd burning smell in the room, as if somebody had been trying to set fire to feathers or horsehair.

Boofuls was breathing deeply and regularly, and when Martin came up close to tuck him in, he remained pale-faced and still, sleeping a dreamless sleep; the sleep of those for whom reality is back to front, and who are ultimately damned.

"My name is Legion; for we are many."

Martin looked at the mirror. He could see himself

standing in the narrow band of light that crossed the room from the open door. He looked sweaty and exhausted. He wondered how the hell he had managed to get himself into all this.

He went up close to the mirror and leaned to one side, still trying to see through the sitting room door to the world where everything was different. He wondered how much of Father Quinlan's theories he ought to believe. A musty manuscript by Lewis Carroll proved nothing at all. Yet it was remarkable how closely Carroll's description of the life after death matched that of Homer Theobald, who had described "talking turtles" and people with elongated heads.

At last, Martin closed the sitting room door and went to take a shower. As he soaped himself under the hot, prickling water he almost fell asleep. He was too tired to make coffee, so he drank three cold mouthfuls of milk straight out of the carton.

In his bedroom, on the wall, the poster of Boofuls stared at him and smiled. He stood looking at it for a long time; then he reached up and ripped it right off the wall, crumpling it up and tossing it across the room.

Breathing a little too quickly, he climbed into his crumpled futon, covered up his head, and made a determined effort to go to sleep.

He dreamed of claws, scratching on polished wood-block floors. He dreamed of cats, sliding between impossible railings. He dreamed of hot breath, and flaring blue eyes, and furry things that were as long as hosepipes. He sweated, and cried out, and clutched at his bedcover, but he didn't wake up.

"Pickle-nearest-the-wind," somebody whispered. *Pickle-nearest-the-wind."*

Two things happened while he slept.

The first was that Boofuls suddenly sat up in bed, his small figure lit by the early moonlight. He stayed quite still for a long time, listening. On the far side of the room, against the wall, the mirror was cold and clear.

After three or four minutes, Boofuls climbed out of bed and padded on bare feet across to the mirror and stood in front of it with his hands by his sides.

In the mirror, the sitting room door opened, and another boy appeared, wearing striped cotton pajamas. It was Emilio. He looked white and distressed, and he couldn't stop fidgeting.

"Where's Pickle?" whispered Boofuls. "I told you to bring Pickle."

"Pickle didn't want to come."

"Pickle has *got* to come."

"Well, I can bring her in the morning."

Boofuls' eyes flared. "You'd better, otherwise you can stay in that mirror forever and ever and ever!"

Emilio said, "Please."

"Please, what?"

"Please let me out. I want to get out."

"What's the matter? You've got your grandpa and grandma, haven't you?"

Emilio's eyes filled with tears. "Yes, but they're not the same. They're *different*."

"Everything's different in the mirror."

"Boofuls, please let me out. Please."

Boofuls let out a little hissing laugh. "You'll get out when the time comes. And *if* I feel like letting you out."

"But I hate it here. It's frightening!"

Boofuls leaned close to the mirror, puckered his lips, and blew Emilio a kiss. "You'll get used to it. You can get used to anything if you try hard enough!"

"Please," begged Emilio.

"Bring Pickle in the morning," Boofuls insisted. "If you don't, you can stay there forever and ever, amen!"

Emilio covered his face with his hands and began to sob quietly. Boofuls watched him for a moment with a malicious look on his face and then went back to bed. When he looked around, Emilio had gone, and the sitting room in the mirror was empty. He smiled to himself and slept.

The second thing was that Father Lucas finished one last glass of wine with Father Quinlan and then prepared to leave.

"You have a safe at St. Theresa's, don't you?" Father Quinlan asked him. "Perhaps you'd better take these relics and lock them safely away. I don't altogether trust the cleaners here at St. Patrick's. I lost a fine briar pipe once and a walking stick with a silver top."

"That's not a very good advertisement, is it?" Father Lucas smiled. "Theological College Is Den of Thieves, Claims Holy Father."

Father Quinlan laughed, and wrapped up the claws and the hair, and carefully slid them into a padded envelope. "Here's the key, too. We don't want to lose that."

Father Lucas opened the study door. "I'm not altogether sure that Mr. Williams believes in the Book of Revelation," he remarked.

Father Quinlan shrugged. "It's rather lurid, I suppose, as prophesies go."

"That boy at his apartment . . . I'm ninety-nine percent certain that it's Boofuls."

"Yes," said Father Quinlan. "It's a pity that Mr. Williams doesn't yet feel able to take us into his confidence. Still—it's a lot to swallow, all in one go. The Revelation and Lewis Carroll all tied up together. I found it quite difficult to believe myself when I first looked into it."

"But you have no doubts now?" asked Father Lucas. Father Quinlan shook his head. "None at all."

Father Lucas said good night and left the college by the side door. He had left his dented red Datsun parked in the shadow of the chapel. He climbed in, and the suspension groaned like a dying pig. He started up the engine and was just about to back out of his parking space when he happened to glance at the padded envelope lying on the seat beside him.

Supposing he drove down to the Hollywood Divine and opened up the second safe-deposit box? The sooner he did it—the sooner he locked the relics in his safe at St. Theresa—the less risk there would be of somebody else locating them first and trying to reassemble the scattered body of Satan.

He checked his watch. It was twenty after eleven, but he was pretty sure that there would be somebody on the desk at the Hollywood Divine. After all, most of its customers didn't know day from night.

He drove eastward on Santa Monica. From time to time, he glanced at his eyes in the rearview mirror. They looked a little glassy and bloodshot, although he didn't know why. Too much of Father Quinlan's Pinot chardonnay, probably. He wasn't used to drinking. But, all the same, he was surprised how strange he felt; how detached; as if his body were taking him to the

Hollywood Divine even though his mind wasn't too keen on coming along.

Father Lucas had always liked to think of himself as traditional and pragmatic. He believed in the forces of darkness; and he believed that people could be possessed by evil spirits. He even believed that Boofuls had somehow reappeared through the mirror in Martin's sitting room—like a sort of living hologram. But it hadn't been easy for him to accept Father Quinlan's theories about the second coming of Satan. To think that Satan the king of all chaos might actually appear in Hollywood in the late 1980s *in the flesh*—well, that was one of those concepts that his well-disciplined mind was unable to encompass.

He drove along Hollywood Boulevard. At this time of night, it was at its sleaziest—the sidewalks crowded with punks and weirdos and junkies and strutting streetwalkers. One immaculately dressed black man drew up alongside Father Lucas in a white Eldorado convertible and raised his leopard-spotted fedora. "Good evening to you, your reverence. What's going down in heaven these days?"

"Good evening, Perry," Father Lucas replied. "I'll tell you when I get there."

"Don't you worry, your reverence, I'll be there first."

Father Lucas smiled. "I'm sure you will, Perry, I'm sure you will."

He turned into Vine and parked outside the Hollywood Divine. A small Mexican boy no older than eight came up to him and offered to protect his car radio. "Long gone, I'm afraid," Father Lucas told him.

"Then what about your hubcaps?"

"Take them, if you think they're going to be more use to you than they are to me."

"I don't want your hubcaps. If I was going to take anything, I'd take your whole crapping car."

Father Lucas bent down over the boy, his hands on his knees, so that he could look him straight in the eye. "If you so much as lay one greasy finger on my crapping car, I'll tear your crapping head off. And don't you ever use language like that to a priest ever again; or to anyone; ever."

The boy stared at him, wide-eyed. "No, sir. Sorry, sir. I'll take care of your car, sir."

Father Lucas made his way past the hookers and the hustlers to the steps of the Hollywood Divine. Somebody had vomited tides of something raspberry-colored all over the side of the steps, and hundreds of shoes had trampled it everywhere.

Father Lucas pushed his way through the shuddering revolving doors and crossed the dimly lit lobby. One of the Hollywood Divine scarecrows was shuffling around the perimeter of the lobby with a bottle in a brown paper bag, singing, *"You play . . . such shweet mushic . . . how can . . . I resish . . . every shong . . . from your heartshtrings . . . makes me feel I've . . . jush been kissh."*

Boofuls, thought Father Lucas. *It seems like he's everywhere. Like a storm that's brewing, and everybody can feel it in the air.*

The desk clerk was sitting with his feet on the counter reading an *Elf Quest* comic and smoking a cigarette. A half-empty bottle of Gatorade and a half-chewed hot dog showed that he was halfway through dinner. He glanced up when Father Lucas approached the desk and sniffed loudly.

"How're you doing, Father?" he asked. "Come to save our souls?"

"Would that I could," said Father Lucas.

The young man flipped away his comic and swung his feet off the counter. "Okay, then, what's it to be? Half an hour with Viva and Louise? For an extra ten bucks, they can dress up in nun costumes. Or how about a short time with Wladislaw? He's been doing great business dressing up like the Pope. The Catholic guys love it. He balls them, and then he forgives him, all included in the one price."

"Careful, Gary," Father Lucas warned him.

"All right, Father, forgive me, for I do not have the faintest idea what I do. Now, how can I help?"

Father Lucas held up his key. "The safe-deposit boxes," he said. "I understand they're down in the basement."

"That's right," said Gary, narrowing his eyes. "But it'll cost you. You're the second one in just a couple of days."

Father Lucas reached into his pocket and counted out five bills. "I'm sorry, I'm not exactly Aaron Spelling."

"Well . . ." said Gary. "Seeing as it's you." He pocketed the money, unhooked the basement key from the board, and led Father Lucas across the lobby. One of the scarecrows called out, "Bless you, Father! Bless you!" and dropped onto his knees on the filthy carpet, pressing his forehead to the floor. Father Lucas made the sign of the cross; and then followed Gary along the narrow corridor that led to the kitchens and the basement door.

Gary unlocked the door, reached inside, and switched on the light.

"Just watch your step, Father, okay? There's a whole lot of junk and trash down there. The safe-deposit boxes are way in back, by the wall. There's some kind

of an African statcher back there, they're right behind
it."

. "Thank you," said Father Lucas.

"Hey, don't mention it," Gary told him.

Gary went off; and Father Lucas climbed cautiously
down the steps into the basement. He paused for a moment at the foot of the steps, looking around. The basement was utterly silent, a grotesque landscape of
upturned chairs, hat stands, foldaway beds, and bu-
reaus. Father Lucas caught sight of the "African
statcher" and began to make his way toward it, climbing over stacks of chairs and walking along rows of
bedside tables.

Down here, he felt peculiarly shut off from the
world; and a small familiar surge of claustrophobia
rose in his chest. He didn't suffer from it very often or
very severely; only in times of stress. But there were
times when he had been forced to bite the inside of his
cheek when he was traveling in a crowded elevator, to
stop himself from shouting to be let out.

The worst thing was imagining the weight of the entire hotel bearing down on top of him, tons of concrete
and steel, all those carpets and furnishings and staircases and people.

He gripped the back of a chair to balance himself,
and hesitated for a moment, sweating. He wasn't
obliged to open this safe-deposit box. He could turn
around and go back and nobody would be any the
wiser. Yet supposing he turned around, and somebody
else got here first, somebody who was dedicated to res-
urrecting Satan? What would he think of himself then,
as the world cracked from pole to pole?

Father Lucas mopped his face with his handkerchief,
took a deep steadying breath, and then carried on,

stumbling over the furniture like a lame goat. At last, however, he reached the safe-deposit boxes. He struggled his way around the African lady with the bodacious ta-tas; and then managed to climb up on top of the stacks of boxes. He was panting hard; and he had to take off his Coke-bottle spectacles and wipe steam off the lenses. God knows, he could never go down a mine.

He found box number 531, with its lid still open. What he needed now was 135. He slid down the side of the stack of boxes and pushed the top bank sideways—finally managing to lever them out of the way using a brass pole with a board on one end pointing the way to the Starlight Bar.

He was lucky. The next bank of boxes was 1–199. The numbers were quite clear, too. He found 135, and took out the key that Martin and Ramone had discovered in the first safe-deposit box.

He was about to fit it into the lock when he thought he heard a noise on the other side of the basement. He listened, sweating. There it was again. A faint scratching sound, like rats tearing the stuffed-cotton entrails out of a couch; or somebody stealthily making his way nearer across the furniture. He listened and listened, his key still poised, but the noise wasn't repeated.

"Overactive imagination," he told himself, and inserted the key into the lock.

The lock was extremely stiff. He grunted and strained at it, and the key cut into his fingers. He wished he had thought of bringing a screwdriver and a pair of pliers, although he probably would have ended up breaking the lock that way. He twisted the key again, grunting with effort, and at last he felt it budge.

"One more try," he gasped to himself. "Come on, you bastard; open up!"

He was struggling so hard that he scarcely heard the singing. High, and clear, but oddly ghostlike, as if it could have been very close or very far away.

> *Apples are sweeter than lemons*
> *Lemons are sweeter than limes*
> *But there's nothing so sweet as the mem'ry of you*
> *And the sadness of happier times.*

He allowed himself to catch his breath; then with quivering fingers he turned the key all the way around and felt the levers in the lock slide rustily open.

The singing continued, but Father Lucas didn't hear it. He lifted the lid of the safe-deposit box and peered inside. The lighting in this part of the basement was so poor, however, that he couldn't see anything at all.

"Well, now," he told himself, "it can't be anything to be frightened of. Only claws, and tissue paper, and more of that hairy stuff."

He cautiously inserted his left hand, groping around the sides of the box. It seemed to be empty. Perhaps somebody else had gotten here first and taken the contents away. Perhaps the claws and the hank of hair were all that was left.

He reached a little farther; and then his fingertips touched something wrinkled and supple and faintly oily; like a sack of soft and heavy leather. He didn't like the feel of it at all, but he ran his hand all the way around it, trying to make out what it was. He tried to lift it, so that he could see what it looked like in the light, but it was too heavy, and seemed to be fastened to the back of the safe-deposit box.

Father Lucas took his hand out. He found his handkerchief, wiped his fingers, and sniffed them. The thing in the safe-deposit box had a curious smell; rather like machine oil lightly mixed with fish.

He bent over and strained his eyes, trying to catch even the faintest reflection from the thing inside the box. "Now, what the hell are you?" he whispered. "If you're part of Satan, I'd darn well like to know *which* part."

He was about to reach inside the box a second time when he heard a high, childish giggle. He looked up, alarmed, his heart pumping in huge, slow spasms. At first he couldn't make out where the laughter was coming from, but then right across the basement, on the far side, he caught sight of a face. Or rather, the *reflection* of a face in the tilted mirror of a discarded hotel dressing table.

Father Lucas shuddered. His eyesight wasn't very clear, but he had no doubt who it was. Those clear pale features, unnaturally white; those bright-burning eyes.

"Boofuls," he whispered.

"Hello, Father." Boofuls smiled. *"What are you doing here? Interfering? Poking your nose in where it's not wanted?"*

Father Lucas crossed himself. "Almighty Lord, Word of God the Father, Jesus Christ, God and Lord of every creature: Who didst give to Thy Holy Apostles power to tread upon serpents and scorpions—by Whose power Satan fell from heaven like lightning—"

"Father Lucas!" cried Boofuls. *"You meddled in matters which were nothing to do with you, and now you have to be punished! Look after your teeth, that's what I told you! Look after your teeth!"*

Father Lucas caught sight of a glint of glistening white down in the darkness of the safe-deposit box. He

was so terrified that he was unable to move; literally
unable to do anything but kneel where he was, open-
mouthed. His mind told him to scramble down and
run for his life, but his body refused to obey.

"Meddler!" screamed Boofuls. *"Meddler! Meddler!"*

His voice reached a pitch of unintelligible hysteria.

And then something reared out of the safe-deposit
box that was all shiny gray gristle, a thick tangled column of unspeakable muscles and naked arteries. It was
like nothing that Father Lucas had ever seen—blind,
swollen, dangling with rags of slimy gray skin, reeking
of oil and dead fish.

"Almighty Lord, Word of God the Father," Father
Lucas babbled. But then the thin skin around the top
of the column peeled slowly back, revealing row after
row of razor-sharp teeth, five, six—seven rows in all,
glutinous with fluids. Father Lucas' voice disappeared,
and all he could do was stare at this terrible apparition; trying not to believe in it, trying to tell himself
that this was only a nightmare; and that any moment
now he would fall off the safe-deposit boxes and find
himself in bed.

His nervous system suddenly reconnected itself. He
thought, *Jump!* But he was a fraction of a second too
late. The glistening gray column swayed swiftly toward him and burst straight into his mouth, smashing
all his teeth aside, dislocating his jaw, cracking his palate apart from front to back.

He couldn't scream: the thing filled his mouth. Blood
sprayed wildly across the safe-deposit boxes and onto
the basement ceiling.

Choking, he thought, *Out! Out! Got to get it out!* but it
slithered through his hands, greasy, rubbery, unstoppable.

It forced its way down his throat, tearing away his larynx. The agony was all the more unbearable because his lungs were full and yet his windpipe was blocked and he *couldn't breathe, couldn't breathe!*

He struggled and thrashed and kicked his legs; and at last he lost his balance and toppled off the side of the safe-deposit boxes onto the floor, with the gray thing's tail still protruding from his stretched-open mouth. It had a tail like a soft, collapsed sphincter, a sphincter that contracted and expanded each time the thing forced itself farther down his throat.

Something had jarred in his back when he fell. He lay paralyzed on top of a folding chair, his eyes bulging, his face blue, his mouth bloody. And the gray creature pushed its way with tearing teeth down to his stomach, ripping soft membranes into shreds—inflicting on him the greatest pain that it was possible for a man to suffer. It was worse than *seppuku*, the most agonizing form of Japanese suicide, because it came from deep inside him, and it wouldn't stop, and it scissored and wrenched and ripped at every part of his vitals.

The thing's tail disappeared into his mouth. He felt its dry palpating sphincter slide down his throat. He choked, gagged, sicked up blood and pieces of flesh. He was conscious of every expansion and contraction as the thing bulged and heaved, bulged and heaved, caterpillaring its way into his abdomen. The most terrifying thing of all was that he knew that he was already dead. Nobody could survive this ruination inside the body and survive.

He felt his stomach straining. He looked down at himself, his eyes wide. There was a moment when he felt as if his pelvis were breaking apart; and that the whole world was collapsing on top of him. The Hollywood Divine, the night sky, everything. Ton upon ton of agony and humiliation.

"O God, help me," he bubbled.

And then the gray column exploded out from between his thighs, its teeth bloody and decorated with viscera of all colors, his own torn manhood hardly recognizable among the shreds; and it stiffly swayed, nearly four feet long, the swollen member of the Lord of Darkness, mocking him, arrogant, obscene, Satan's penis between a priest's legs. Now he knew why the mirror had spat semen at him. Satan relished the sexual degradation of the clergy.

"O God . . ." Father Lucas whispered.

One by one, the rows of teeth were concealed by sliding skin. Then the gray thing dragged itself away from Father Lucas, its body rustling on the dusty floor, and burrowed itself deep beneath the stacks of folding chairs, into the darkest of corners, where it shrank into dryness, like an abandoned sack, and waited for the day that was near now; nearer than ever. The day that was almost here.

And Father Lucas' blood slid stickily across the basement floor and in between the painted wooden toes of the African statue. This little piggy had went to market, this little piggy stayed at home.

That morning, at eight o'clock sharp, Boofuls danced and sang for June Lassiter at 20th Century-Fox.

They used the set which had been built for the television miniseries *Ziegfeld Follies*, partly because nobody else was using it, and partly because it included a mock-up of a theater stage. June Lassiter sat right in front in her director's chair, dressed in an off-white suit by Giorgio Armani. Beside sat her executive assistant and the bearer of her Filofax, Kathy Lupanek, all frizzy hair and huge spectacles and radical opinions.

Morris Nathan was also present, of course; with Alison. So was Chubby Bosanquet, the Fox finance director; John Drax, the choreographer; and Ahab Greene.

Martin sat at the very back, in darkness, feeling tired and withdrawn. He was praying in a way that "Lejeune's" audition would prove to be a complete flop. If that happened—if it was obvious that nobody wanted to remake *Sweet Chariot*—maybe Boofuls would retreat back into his mirror and let Emilio go.

Some hope, thought Martin. *If Father Quinlan's theory about the reincarnation of Satan were even half true, Boofuls would make sure that, this time, he accomplished what he had been born to accomplish. No more interfering grandmothers this time. No more vorpal swords.*

At last, Boofuls appeared on the soundstage, and bowed. He was wearing a royal-blue Little Lord Fauntleroy costume that he had borrowed from wardrobe, and Martin found it totally uncanny to watch him, fifty years after his death, strutting into the spotlights as if time had stood still, as if World War II and Korea and rock'n'roll and President Kennedy and going to the moon had never happened.

"Doesn't he look *adorable*?" June cried out, and clapped her hands.

Martin felt a sinking in his stomach. She was won over already: give him five minutes and Boofuls would have her eating out of his adorable hand.

Morris said, "He's a natural; an absolute natural. Never seen a child star like him."

"And what did you say his name was? Lejeune?"

Morris nodded. "That's right. But don't you worry about his name. You just listen to him sing."

Boofuls knelt and sang "The Sadness of Happier Times." His voice was so pure and poignant that even Martin was moved. June Lassiter was unashamedly wiping her eyes with her handkerchief, and Morris blew his nose so loudly that Kathy Lupanek jumped.

When all of them were dewy-eyed, or very close to tears, Boofuls suddenly sprang up and danced the sun-beam dance from *Sunshine Serenade*. He kicked and flew and pirouetted as if gravity had no effect on him whatsoever; his blue-slippered toes scarcely touched the floor. Ahab Greene started applauding long before he had finished, and the rest of them joined him. Morris even stood up and shouted out, "Incredible! That's incredible! Would you look at that, June? That's incredible!"

Boofuls finished his dance and bowed low. Still they clapped him. At last, his cheeks flushed, breathing hard, he came down the steps at the side of the mock-theater stage and walked directly up to Chubby Bosanquet, completely ignoring June Lassiter.

"Well?" he asked in his high-pitched voice. "Will you do it?"

"Lejeune—" put in June. "That really isn't Mr. Bosanquet's decision."

"He arranges the financing, doesn't he?"

"Well, certainly but—"

"Then that's okay. I know *you* like it, Ms. Lassiter. All I have to know now is whether Mr. Bosanquet is going to come up with twenty-five million dollars."

Morris Nathan came forward and was about to lay his hand on Boofuls' shoulder, but Boofuls stepped away.

"Come on, now, Lejeune," said Morris, smiling uncomfortably. "Let's not go over the top about this. It's up to Ms. Lassiter whether Fox makes this picture or not. And it's a little impertinent, don't you think, to assume that she likes it even before she's had a chance to read the screenplay or listen to any of the songs?"

Boofuls pouted. "If I didn't think she was going to like it, I wouldn't have bothered to come down here."

June Lassiter stood up and came closer. Boofuls beckoned to Martin to bring him the revised screenplay. Martin handed it over and said, "*Sweet Chariot*, a total rewrite. Updated, dialogue altered, motivations overhauled, characterizations sharpened up."

"And what makes you think I'm going to approve it?" asked June. "Remember, it was only last week when you tried to persuade me to do the Boofuls musical; and I turned you down very, very flat."

"That was then," said Martin. "This is now."

"So tell me the difference."

Martin scruffed up Boofuls' hair. He was the only one whom Boofuls allowed to do it. "This is the difference, and you know it. He sings and dances better than Boofuls. He's going to be the greatest child star there ever was."

Kathy Lupanek pulled a so-what, child-stars-yuck kind of face. But June Lassiter gradually allowed herself to break into a smile.

"Do you know something, Martin, you're probably right. I'm going to recommend this project. Morris—you and I ought to talk some business."

Boofuls said clearly, "Mr. Nathan is not my agent."

Morris looked perplexed. "Hey, come on, now! Didn't I set up this audition for you? You *have* to have an

agent! You can't work without an agent! He's such a
mazik, this kid!"

Boofuls approached Morris and stared at him with
those welding-torch eyes. "Not a *mazik*, Mr. Nathan. A
dybbuk." Not a little devil, Mr. Nathan, but a demon
from hell.

June tried to break the tension by saying, "Lejeune,
honey—Mr. Nathan's right. You do have to have an
agent, just to protect your legal interests. I mean, if
you don't want to use Mr. Nathan, I can talk to your
parents and recommend plenty more—"

"I don't have any parents," said Lejeune. His voice
was high but expressionless.

June looked uncomfortable. "You must have
*some*body to take care of you. *Some* legal guardian."

Boofuls paused for a moment, looking around. Martin could recognize that cunning strangeness in his
face; the wolfish expression of an adult man. "My
grandmother," he said. "I live with my grandmother.
She's my legal guardian."

"Well, I'll call her myself and explain that you have
to have an agent," said June.

"I should work off my *toches* fixing this audition and then I don't even get ten percent of
thankyouverymuch?" Morris demanded.

"I'm sorry, Morris, it's Lejeune's choice," June told
him.

Morris turned on Boofuls and stabbed a stubby finger at him. "You're not a *mazik* and you're not a
dybbuk. You're the *gilgul* of my old dead partner Chaim
Selzer, that's what you are!"

Martin came forward and took hold of Morris' arm.
"Morris, forget it. I'm sorry. I just automatically assumed that Lejeune would want you to be his agent."

Alison squeezed Morris close and said, "Come on, Morry, forget it. It's better you don't represent him, believe me. If he can't be grateful for what you've done for him, Martin's right, you should forget it."

Morris tugged his large white sports coat tightly around his stomach. "Forget it, you bet I'll forget it. And *you*, Martin, you bet I'll forget you, too!"

"Oh, come on, Morry, don't be upset!" Alison cooed; but glanced across at Martin at the same time with an expression which meant, don't worry, I'll cool him down.

"All right, all right already!" Morris snapped. "I'm not upset, I'm nice! Just don't let me have to look at that kid's face again, ever! And I don't want to hear his name, neither!"

Boofuls meanwhile had eerily circled around so that he was standing in Morris' way as Morris prepared to leave. Morris stopped and stared at him. Boofuls stared back, and then gradually smiled.

"Are you *sure* that's what you want?" Boofuls asked him. "Never to see my face again, never to hear my name?"

"Got it in one, Goldilocks," Morris told him. "Now, if you'll kindly ex-*cuse* us!"

Taking Alison by the arm, Morris waddled out of the soundstage and into the sunlight.

"I didn't mean to make him cross," said Boofuls, watching him go.

June Lassiter laughed. "Don't worry about Morris. He'll get over it. Now—let's go get some coffee and cake, shall we, and talk about this musical of yours? We must talk to your grandmother, you realize that, don't you, since she's your legal guardian."

"I understand," said Boofuls sweetly, taking hold of

June's hand. Martin followed behind them, with a feeling of increasing dread. He wished to God that Morris hadn't yelled at Boofuls like that. If he had killed Homer Theobald just for touching the key to the safe-deposit box at the Hollywood Divine, there was no knowing what he might do to Morris.

Kathy Lupanek, walking beside him with her clipboard clutched to her flat chest, said, "I really hate child actors, you know? Especially snootsy-cutesy ones like Lejeune."

Martin said nothing. He didn't know how sharp Boofuls' ears were. He wasn't even sure that Boofuls couldn't penetrate right inside his mind, and hear him silently screaming, *You hideous evil son of a bitch! I'd kill you if I had half the chance, and I'd chop you up into pieces, just the way your grandmother did!*

They were back home at Franklin Avenue well before eleven o'clock. Martin wanted to go see Ramone, and so he told Boofuls to stay in the apartment and watch television.

"Can we go out later for hamburgers?" Boofuls asked him with a surprisingly childish whine.

"Sure. If you're hungry now, there's some baloney in the refrigerator, and some cake. Just don't drink the beer, that's all. You may be fifty-eight years old, but you're still under age."

Martin left the house feeling shaky and scattered and fraught. He drove badly down to Hollywood Boulevard, bumping over curbs and arguing with a Ralph's delivery truck, and when he arrived at the Reel Thing he couldn't find anyplace to park, so in the end he left the car on Leland Way, which was almost as far away as Franklin Avenue.

Ramone was leaning on the counter with his shades pushed down right to the end of his nose so that he could read the small ads in *Variety*. He stood up when Martin came in and said, "Hey, the wanderer returns! Where have you *been*, my man, I've been calling you for days! I even called round to your house this morning, around nine, and the Caparooparellis said you was away on biz-ness."

Martin wiped sweat from his forehead with the back of his hand. "When I tell you, you're not going to believe it."

"Man—I saw that snake-cat. I'll believe anything."

Martin said, "Let's go get a beer. This is not one of those things that you can tell anybody about when you're stone-cold sober."

"Okay, then. Kelly! Would you mind the store for a half hour?"

They left the store and walked out into the hot midmorning sun. Ramone said, "I asked Mrs. Capelli about Emilio; but she said there wasn't no sign."

"Was that all she said?"

Ramone nodded. "She seemed pretty uptight, so I didn't like to bug her any more."

"She didn't tell you about Boofuls?"

"No, she didn't. What about Boofuls?"

Martin hesitated. Then he said, "I promised myself I was going to keep this a total secret. The only people who know the truth so far are Mr. Capelli and myself; and Mr. Capelli found out by accident, although I guess he was entitled to know, Emilio being his grandson and everything. But—damn it—I can't keep it in any longer. I can't go around with a secret this big, especially when I have a friend like you to share it with."

Ramone stopped dead in the street, and a punk who

had been walking close behind him collided into the back of him. "Hey, man," the punk complained, but Ramone silenced him with a grotesque glare, like Mick Belker in *Hill Street Blues*. "What are you trying to tell me?" Ramone asked Martin fiercely. "What the hell has happened?"

"Lugosi went into the mirror," said Martin. "That hellcat came out."

"Go on," Ramone urged him.

"Well . . . Emilio went into the mirror . . . and guess who came out in his place?"

Ramone stared at Martin in horror. "Boofuls," he whispered. "Oh, Jesus, *Boofuls*."

Shortly before eleven o'clock, Boofuls got up from the sofa, walked across to the television, and switched it off. Then he marched smartly to the mirror, his hands by his sides, and called out, "Emilio! Emilio! Come on out, Emilio!"

There was a short pause, and then Emilio came into the reflected room. He was carrying a huge brindled cat, so heavy that he could only manage to carry it under its front legs. The rest of its body hung down, and swayed as Emilio walked, and its eyes were slitted in displeasure.

"You shouldn't carry Pickle like that," Boofuls admonished him. "She doesn't like it."

Emilio put the cat down on the floor. There were criss-cross scratches all over his small hands. "She's so *heavy*."

"She's well fed, that's why," replied Boofuls. "She eats the tongues of telltale tits; and she drinks the blood of people who meddle; and she doesn't like anybody who doesn't love her as much as I do."

"I love her," said Emilio. He looked exhausted and hungry. His T-shirt was grubby and there were crimson bruises on the side of his forehead, as if somebody had been cuffing him. *In mirrorland, everything is turned from left to right, even Christian morality.*

"She looks cross," said Boofuls. "Have you been taking care of her properly?"

Emilio nodded. "I play with her and I stroke her even when she scratches me."

"All cats scratch," Boofuls remarked scornfully.

He was just about to take another step toward the mirror when he heard footsteps on the stairs. "Ssh!" he told Emilio, and listened. Somebody was coming up to the landing. Not Martin, the steps weren't heavy enough. Not Mrs. Capelli, they were far too quick. He frowned and waited. Emilio waited, too, breathless, half hoping that somebody had come to rescue him at last.

There was a knock at the front door of the apartment; then another. Boofuls waited, not moving, not speaking. Then a girl's voice called, "Coo-ee, Martin!"

"Go back," Boofuls ordered Emilio.

"But you haven't—" Emilio began.

Boofuls snapped, "Go back! Otherwise I'll *never* let you, ever!"

Reluctantly, Emilio left the reflected sitting room and disappeared through the door. The cat Pickle, however, remained, crouched on the sofa with its front paws tucked up. "You stay there," Boofuls told it, although it obviously had no intention of moving.

Boofuls went to the front door of the apartment and opened it. Standing outside in a sleeveless T-shirt and a pair of excruciatingly tight emerald-green satin shorts was Maria Bocanegra, from next door. Her glossy black hair was wildly back-combed, her purple lips gleamed, and her fingernails were all frosted purple. She wore emerald-green high heels and she had sprayed herself with enough Obsession to overpower any aroma that dared to be subtle within a radius of twenty feet.

Miss Loud Pedal, 1989.

"Yes?" asked Boofuls, his face white with innocence.

"Well, who are *you*?" Maria smiled. "Aren't you just cute?"

"My name is Lejeune," said Boofuls. "Martin isn't here. But you can come in and wait if you wish."

"Aren't you *po-lite*?" Maria giggled. "If all men were as po-lite as you! But, listen, I can't stay! I just wanted to invite Martin to my party on Saturday. We're having a wild, wild salsa party, can you imagine that? And since Martin loves South American rhythms, well I'm sure he'd love to be there! Can you tell him nine o'clock?"

"He'll be back in just a minute," said Boofuls, straight-faced.

"Well, if you can't remember the message I'll call him," said Maria. "But I really have to fly!"

"I'm allowed to offer you a glass of wine, ma'am," Boofuls told her.

Maria was captivated. "Is that what Martin said? If a ravishing lady comes to the door, you're allowed to offer her a glass of wine?"

Boofuls nodded.

"Hm," said Maria. "How long did you say Martin was going to be?"

"Only a minute. Do come in, ma'am. I know that he'll be quite delighted to see you. He's always looking at you out of the window."

"Ye-e-es, I know that, too," said Maria. "But all right, then, just one glass of wine. I don't want Rico thinking I've been fooling around with a strange man, do I?"

Boofuls opened the door and showed her through to the sitting room. She balanced her way around on her high heels, admiring it. Boofuls stood in the doorway watching her, his hands clasped together.

"Isn't this *neat*?" Maria commented. "Very male, though. Nothing around like flowers or cushions or china ornaments. But, you know, *tasteful*. I always thought that Martin was tasteful. And that mirror's something, isn't it? Is that an antique?"

Boofuls smiled. That dreamy little smile. "It's supposed to be lucky."

"Is that right?" said Maria, peering at the mirror shortsightedly. She should have worn glasses but she was far too vain. Besides, she scarcely could have fitted them over her sweeping false eyelashes.

Boofuls said, "There's a legend that comes with the mirror that if you kiss your own reflection, you'll get everything you always wanted."

Maria laughed. "All I ever wanted was a billionaire. Or maybe a millionaire, you know, at a pinch."

"Go ahead, try it," said Boofuls. His voice was oddly echoey.

"Aw, come on," said Maria. "If I kiss that mirror, all that's going to happen is that I'm going to leave a big fat pair of lipstick lips on it."

Boofuls shrugged. "Martin kissed it, and Fox is going to make that musical about Boofuls that he's been working on for years and years."

"No kidding?" asked Maria. "They're really going to do that?"

Boofuls nodded. "Go ahead. You try it."

Maria giggled. "I feel like such a *fool*." But she waggled her way over to the mirror, and bent forward so that she was face-to-face with her reflection. "What do I do, wish first and then kiss—or kiss first and then wish?"

"It doesn't matter."

"All right, then," said Maria, closing her eyes. "I wish that I could meet a man with a net worth of one billion dollars, and by the way could he please be good-looking, too, I don't want some rich old character with a face like a month-old canteloupe."

She placed her lips against the cold surface of the mirror, her eyes still closed. Up above her, the gilded face of Pan grinned with demonic blindness.

"*Mmmff*," she said. Then—immediately—"*Mmmm-mfffffff!!!*" because she couldn't pull her lips free from the glass.

She waved her arms frantically and slapped against the surface of the mirror with her hands. *But the mirror slowly and irresistibly dragged her in, so that she disappeared inch by inch into her own reflection.* First her face, so that her head looked like a narrow football completely covered with wildly tangled hair. Then—when her head had dwindled into a dark tuft and vanished—her real neck was joined to her reflected neck like an angled pipe.

All the time this gradual process of absorption into the mirror was going on, she kicked and struggled and hammered at the mirror, reaching behind her again and again in a desperate attempt to seek help from Boofuls.

But Boofuls stayed where he was, watching her with a placid smile. He hummed to himself as she disappeared into the mirror,

Apples are sweeter than lemons
Lemons are sweeter than limes

As she was drawn right up against the mirror, Maria pressed against its surface in a final effort to save herself. The heels of her hands skidded across the glass with a rubbery sound. But the mirror's suction was too demanding for her, and her hands were drawn in, too.

At last there was nothing left of Maria Bocanegra but her ankles and her feet—two separate triangles of human flesh with high-heeled shoes at the bases of them. One foot shuddered as it was sucked into the mirror's surface; the other remained still. A thin line of blood slid down one ankle and dripped off the metal tip of her stiletto heel just before she vanished completely. It fell onto the floor and remained there to mark Maria's passing.

Boofuls approached the mirror and stared at the reflection of the brindled cat Pickle sitting on the chair. "Now, my beautiful darling," he whispered, and held out his arms.

The cat's eyes, which had been squeezed shut, now opened a fraction. Then it lifted its head and stared at Boofuls haughtily.

"Come on, my beautiful darling," Boofuls coaxed it.

At last the cat rose and stretched and yawned; and then dropped down from the chair onto the floor. It padded up to the mirror and sniffed at Boofuls. Then it sniffed at the single drop of blood that was all that remained of Maria.

"Come on, madam," whispered Boofuls; and his whisper was cross and commanding.

The cat stepped back a little, hesitated, and then sprang. It jumped straight out of the mirror into Boofuls' arms. Boofuls staggered back two or three

paces, because Pickle was so heavy, but he sank his little hands deep into her matted fur and held her up in
front of him, and he tugged and tugged.

The cat spat and hissed at him, but he held it fast,
and tugged even more forcefully. There was a tearing
sound, like a Velcro fastener being torn apart, and he
ripped the cat's stomach wide open, dividing the
shaggy fur and revealing glistening flesh, mottled in
red and purple. He paused, gasping for breath, but
then he tore at the animal again, and now something
extraordinary happened.

*A woman's face emerged from the cat's stomach; a
woman's head. She was completely bald, her eyes were
closed, and she was covered in thin slime. But she was
thin-faced, with high cheekbones, beautiful and severe;
and as Boofuls tore more and more of the cat's stomach
apart, her neck appeared and then her shoulders, and
then Pickle's head was nothing more than an ugly flap
hanging from her back, like the dried face of a fox on a
fox-fur wrap.*

The transformation was strange and prolonged. As
Boofuls pulled the body of the cat wider and wider
apart, the woman appeared with all the grace and dignity of a Chinese conjuring trick. When he dragged the
last ripped-open remnants of cat away from her ankles,
she stood naked and tall and silent, her eyes still
closed, amniotic steam rising from her shoulders as if
she had just been born.

Pickle was nothing more than an empty sack of
brindled fur, like a diseased pajama bag.

Boofuls stepped back, a step at a time, and sat cross-
legged on the sofa. "Well, madam," he said, and
smiled, and rocked backward and forward.

The woman remained still for almost a half hour.

Her eyes remained closed. Gradually, the slime on her body began to dry. She was very thin, very pale. Her skin was the color of ivory, with a tracery of blue veins branching through it. Her breasts were small and slanted, with nipples that were so pale pink that they scarcely showed. Her hip bones were high and prominent. She opened her eyes. The irises were pale amber; the pupils were wide and unfocused.

"Miss Redd," smiled Boofuls.

Miss Redd smiled back; the taut smile of somebody who has just woken up.

"We're back," said Boofuls. "Aren't you happy, Miss Redd? After all those years, we're back."

Miss Redd arched her head back and then circled it around to loosen her muscles. Then she worked her shoulders up and down. She looked around the room with eyes narrowed, trying to work out where she was; and what day it was; and what *year* it was. She was quite remarkable to look at. She could have been a *Vogue* model. There was something only half human about her; something feline and predatory; as if she had shrugged off a cat's body, but retained a cat's soul.

Boofuls came up to her and touched her thigh. "Pickle-nearest-the-wind," he said, smiling.

Miss Redd ran her long thin fingers through Boofuls' blond curls. "Never again," she whispered.

"Why don't you wash?" Boofuls suggested. "Then I can find you something to wear."

"You always were the best of boys," Miss Redd told him.

"Martin will be back soon . . . we don't have long."

"Martin?" asked Miss Redd.

"He was the one who bought the mirror . . . and brought it here. Our savior, if you like. He writes movies. He's going to help us finish *Sweet Chariot*. Miss Redd, it's happened at last. It's going to be wonderful. Fox wants to make the picture and everybody loves it and *at last* it's happened."

Miss Redd got down on one knee and took hold of Boofuls' hand and kissed it. "My Master," she whispered.

Then she bowed her head forward so that her forehead touched the wood-block floor, and repeated, "My Master . . . to whom I give my devotions."

Boofuls leaned forward and touched the base of her knobby spine with a single fingertip. He ran it all the way up her back, in between her bare shoulder blades. She remained where she was, obeisant; as if she would have stayed there even if his fingertip had been a razor blade, and he had cut her open from top to bottom.

"You are the lowliest of slaves," he told her. "You are the most degraded of bitches."

"Master," she whispered, and opened her mouth wide and pressed it against the floor, licking the bare boards on which her master's feet had trodden.

Martin and Ramone came up the stairs about an hour later. Ramone was eager to see the real resurrected Boofuls for himself. Eager, but frightened, too. This all reminded him just a little too much of what used to happen at his grandmother's house. His grandmother used to call herself a witch and mix up potions of rum and gunpowder and licorice root, potions which were supposed to cure everything from plantar warts to pneumonia.

They reached Martin's door. Ramone laid a hesitant hand on Martin's arm and said, "You'd better not be bullshitting me about this."

"You said yourself you were ready to believe anything," Martin replied.

"Well, I'm not so sure about that. I mean if I died
and I didn't realize and then somebody came up and
told me I was dead, I wouldn't go much on believing
that. I'd just as soon they hadn't told me in the first
place."

Martin was about to open the sitting room door
when somebody opened it from the inside, swiftly and
dramatically. A tall thin girl was standing there,
dressed in nothing but one of Martin's checkered
shirts, tied tightly around the waist with one of his two
neckties, the red one, which he used for interviews
with the IRS. The black one was for funerals. Around
the girl's head was a turban, wound out of a red hand
towel. Boofuls was sitting on the sofa, still cross-
legged, like a little Buddha, still smiling.

"Look who came to see me!" Boofuls cried triumphantly.

"Oh, yes?" said Martin. "Who's this?"

"It's Miss Redd!" Boofuls sang out. "I told you she'd
come!"

Martin stepped into the sitting room and looked Miss
Redd up and down. She looked back at him, her eyes
challenging him to speak. Ramone stayed where he
was, in the doorway, still wide-eyed at the sight of
Boofuls. *It was true, Boofuls was actually alive. He was
alive—and he was sitting here talking and laughing just
like a normal child.*

"How do you do?" Martin told Miss Redd. It seemed
an absurdly formal thing to say, but he couldn't think
of anything else. His mind was crowded with images of
Boofuls in 1939, hurrying into the Hollywood Divine

with Miss Redd close by his side, her black cape billowing like a thundercloud, her eyes as sharp as razors.

Miss Redd said in a faintly middle-European accent, "You rescued Walter from the mirror. We should be grateful."

It was odd the way she said "we *should* be grateful" instead of "we *are* grateful." There was a subtle implication that they should be grateful but they weren't; as if they didn't feel the need to be grateful to anyone.

Martin walked up to the mirror and stood staring at his reflection. "You came out of the mirror, too?"

Miss Redd smiled. She was exceptionally beautiful; but Martin found her too thin to be really attractive. She was right on the edge of looking anorexic—like a starving gazelle or the liberated victim of a concentration camp.

"I emerged from one stage of my life into another," she said. "You'll have to forgive me for wearing your shirt. My clothes . . . well, my clothes became lost."

Martin went over to the windowsill and poured two glasses of red wine without asking Miss Redd whether she wanted any. He glanced down into the yard, but Maria didn't seem to be around. Her sunbed was empty; her bent-back copy of Harold Robbins' *The Storyteller* was lying on the hammered-glass garden table. One of her Sno-Cones was floating in the pool. Martin handed one of the glasses of wine to Ramone and swallowed half of the other glassful himself, almost without breathing.

Miss Redd watched him without expression. Boofuls smiled and hummed "The Sadness of Happier Times."

"You're—what? Boofuls' nanny or something?" Martin asked Miss Redd.

"You could say that," Miss Redd replied.

"To tell you the truth, I don't think he really needs a nanny. He seems to be doing all right for himself just the way he is."

"There are some things which he is unable to do for himself," Miss Redd answered.

"Like what?" Martin wanted to know. "He seems to have gotten along okay so far."

Ramone said, "You came out of the mirror, too?"

Miss Redd smiled, but didn't reply.

"Well, if you came out of the mirror, you would know where Emilio is."

"Yes," agreed Miss Redd. "I would. *If* I came out of the mirror."

Martin finished his wine and set the empty glass down on the desk. "If you *didn't* come out of the mirror, how did you get here? Stark naked, walking along Franklin Avenue?"

Miss Redd continued to smile. "Emilio is quite safe," she said. "He's such a charming little boy, isn't he? Charming, but rather *grave*."

Martin said, "I've warned Boofuls about this, and now I'm going to warn you. If you so much as scratch that boy, I'm going to kill you."

Miss Redd nodded. "Well, I believe you might." She sounded just like Greta Garbo. "But it wouldn't do you any good at all. Because if you killed us, you would lose the ability to be able to bring Emilio back through the mirror. He would be trapped there forever; just as Boofuls and I were trapped."

Ramone shook his head like a dog trying to shake a wasp out of its ear. "Martin," he said, "we got to get a grip on this thing. I mean these people are walking all over you. And Jesus, Martin, they're not even *real* people!"

Miss Redd turned to Ramone and held out her hand. "Here," she said coldly. "Take hold of my hand."

Ramone hesitated, but then slowly put out his own hand. Miss Redd at once gripped him tightly and dug her fingernails into the inside of his wrist. Ramone shouted out, "Heyy! Ow! That *hurts!*" But Miss Redd continued to dig her fingernails into him deeper and deeper.

"For Christ's sake, you're real! You're real!" Ramone protested. He twisted his hand free and then angrily nursed the scratches on his wrist. "What the hell do you think you're trying to prove? You're worse than that cat!"

Boofuls laughed. Then he said, "Miss Redd is going to take care of me now. Miss Redd will feed me and dress me and take me to the studios. You have served your purpose now, Martin, and I am grateful for what you have done. But there is nothing further for you to do."

"What about *Sweet Chariot*?" asked Martin. "Supposing they want some rewrites?"

"Miss Redd will supervise the rewrites. Your task is finished."

"And Emilio?" demanded Ramone. "When are you going to let him go?"

"When it suits me," said Boofuls.

"Can you believe this runt?" appealed Ramone. "He's eight years old and he's talking like he's my father or something. You listen here, runt—"

"Ramone," warned Martin. "Don't. Right now, Boofuls holds all the aces."

Boofuls covered his face with both hands. They all watched him, saying nothing, holding their breath. When he eventually took them away again, he was smiling. Then he laughed, a high peal of laughter, bright as bells. "You all look so *frightened*!" he crowed. "You all look so terribly, terribly *scared*!"

For one unbalanced moment, Martin wondered whether Boofuls was playing them all for fools; whether he really did have power over Emilio; and whether the emaciated Miss Redd really had appeared through the mirror. But then Boofuls glanced at him quickly, and he saw the dead-certain coldness of those welding-torch eyes, and he knew that Boofuls was possessed by Satan just as surely as death sits on every man's shoulder.

Boofuls went across to Ramone and clung on to his sleeve. "You shouldn't be frightened," he told him. "You have no cause to be frightened; no cause at all; just so long as you remember how long I have been gone and why I am here; and that no man speaks against me and lives to boast about it."

Martin could see Ramone's anger rising up inside him. He could see his fists clenching and the veins in his neck swell. *Don't, Ramone, for God's sake*, he begged him in the silence of his mind.

Ramone looked across at him, and there was a look in his eyes which said, *Bullshit*, but he kept his mouth closed, and lifted his arm away from Boofuls' grasp, and gave the nearest thing to an agreeable smile that he could manage.

"Now," said Boofuls, "you promised me a hamburger, Martin. And we must take Miss Redd to buy some clothes. Miss Redd likes black, don't you, Miss Redd? Black, black, black! Black cloaks, black skirts, black silk stockings!"

Ramone came up to Martin and laid a hand on his

shoulder. "I think I'll take a rain check on the hamburger, man. Are you going to be okay?"

"Oh, I'm going to be fine," said Martin. He nodded and smiled at Boofuls. "I'm going to be absolutely fine."

Boofuls said, "Big Mac, no pickle, giant-size fries, a strawberry milkshake, and an apple pie to finish!"

"Sure," Martin agreed, but very quietly. He had just noticed the single spot of blood on the floor. It was thick, arterial blood, and it was still glistening. The most terrible part about it was not the fact that it was there, but that he didn't dare to ask, in his own apartment, in daylight, what it was.

The police came to St. Patrick's at two o'clock that afternoon to tell Father Quinlan that Father Lucas was dead.

"They found him in the basement about three hours ago. The desk clerk was so spaced out he didn't even remember that he'd let him go down there. He was pretty badly mutilated. Some crazy person, no doubt about it. But, you know, what's a fifty-five-year-old priest doing at the Hollywood Divine at that time of night? It's asking for trouble, asking."

Father Quinlan stared at the swarthy face of the detective sitting opposite and wondered how it was that such a man could be the bearer of such tragic news. He looked more like a comedian then a detective. He had a baggy face and a bulbous nose and hair that stuck up at the back like a cockatoo's crest.

"Do you know how?" asked Father Quinlan.

The detective sniffed blatantly and shook his head. "The ME's going over him now. But he was torn up pretty bad. That's why I say some crazy person. And of

course the basement's teeming with rats. They tore
him up, too, threw in their five cents' worth.''

Father Quinlan nodded. He felt curiously detached,
as if none of this were really happening. He could see
every detail of the detective's face with extraordinary
clarity. He could see the dandruff on the collar of his
tan-colored sports coat. Yet he felt as if he weren't here
at all. Not dreaming, but *absent*.

"What we can't understand is this," the detective
said. "What was he doing down in the basement of the
sleaziest roach palace in town? A priest like him?''

"Perhaps," Father Quinlan began, but when the detective quickly lifted an eyebrow, he snapped back to
alertness and continued, "perhaps he was looking for
old furniture. We always need chairs and tables, you
know, for our youth club activities, and our prayer
meetings.''

"That time of night?" asked the detective, puckering
up his nose.

"It's only a thought," said Father Quinlan.

The detective frowned for a moment and then said,
"I have to remember to pick up a rib roast on my way
home. My wife'll kill me.''

"If I think of anything," said Father Quinlan.

"Oh, sure. Call me anytime you like, this number
here. Ask for Hector. Just say Hector. Or ask for my
partner, Fernandez.''

"There's one thing more," said Father Quinlan. "Did
Father Lucas happen to have any kind of package on
him? A package of black tissue paper?''

The detective took out his notebook, licked his
thumb, and turned the pages. "Wallet, keys, loose
change, handkerchief, that was all. No package. No
package in his automobile, either.''

"Oh, well," said Father Quinlan, trying to sound as if it weren't important. "Maybe he left it at home."

"Yeah, maybe he did," agreed the detective.

Father Quinlan saw the detective to the door. The detective said, "I'm sorry I brought you such bad news. It's all I get to bring in this business, bad news."

Father Quinlan nodded and said, "Bless you all the same."

"Thanks, Father."

"And don't forget the rib roast."

"You bet," the detective said.

Father Quinlan closed the door of his study and stood for a long time without moving, stunned and saddened and frightened, too. He had not only misdirected an officer of the law, he had, indirectly, defended Satan. He had betrayed his holy trust as a priest and brought the day of Armageddon even closer.

Yet what else could he do? The police would never believe that Father Lucas had been searching for the scattered relics of the true Satan; and even if they did, there was nothing at all they could do about it. Father Quinlan would have to get in touch with Martin Williams urgently, and warn him that the claws and the hair had gone unfound—and presumably whatever was in the second safe-deposit box had been taken, too.

He picked up the phone and called Martin's number, but there was no reply. But Martin had left him his address on Franklin Avenue: perhaps he should drive up there and leave him a message. He had been thinking of calling Martin in any case. He wanted to see Boofuls' mirror for himself.

Father Quinlan scribbled Martin a letter, licked an envelope, sealed it, then raked a comb through his hair, shrugged on a crumpled linen jacket, locked up his study, and went outside to the college parking lot. It was a hot brilliant afternoon; his shadow followed him across the parking lot like an obedient black dog. He climbed into his elderly Grand Prix and started the engine.

He drove slowly and carefully. Half of the car's front bumper was hanging down and made a dull clatter as he went along. He had never been mechanically minded. Ever since he had been a young man he had been fascinated by the myths and legends of Good and Evil, the supposed reality of demons and angels. In 1954 he had been ordained to the office of exorcist, although he had only ever been called to one full-scale demonic possession—a young girl in San Juan Capistrano who had somehow managed to scorch the walls of every room in which she was locked up.

He could remember the words of the bishop's admonition even now: *"Learn through your office to govern all imperfections lest the enemy may claim a share in you and some dominion over you. For truly will ye rightly control those devils who attack others, when first ye have overcome their many crafts against yourself."*

Over the years, Father Quinlan had grown to believe in the presence of demons. Not horned and cloven-hoofed; but evil, nonetheless. He had seen their influence behind the actions of quite ordinary people; he had seen their eyes looking out from behind the eyes of politicians and financiers and movie stars and people in the street.

There was a *look* which Father Quinlan had grown to recognize. Only a demon looked at a priest in that particular way. Cold and sullen and viciously hostile. But you could see the look anywhere, when you least expected it. In the eyes of a bus driver. Behind a till at

the Wells Fargo Bank. From a scrubwoman, sluicing
the steps of a downtown office.

Through his belief in demons, Father Quinlan had
evolved his belief in Satan himself. Actually, he had
always *believed* in Satan, but now he knew for certain
that the prophesies in the Revelation were based on
verifiable fact. Satan had been defeated by the angel
Michael; but he was due to return. Not in the shape of
a man, but in his real demonic form, as the dragon of
all destruction.

And the skies would remain perpetually dark; and
the streets would run with the blood of the innocents.

Father Quinlan drove at a snail's pace along Santa
Monica Boulevard, humming nervously to himself. He
felt hot and uncomfortable because the Grand Prix's
air-conditioning had packed up, and he couldn't afford
to have it repaired. He found a crumpled Kleenex in
his trouser pocket and dabbed his face with it.

He slowed down even more. He was caught between
two trucks: an empty flatbed tractor-trailer in front of
him and a huge grinding meat truck behind him. The
noise of clashing gears and the stench of diesel added
to his discomfort. He was even more irritated when he
reached a traffic signal and found that it was impossible to pull out from between the trucks because a shiny
red Corvette boxed him in, its stereo blaring out
Beastie Boys rock.

He glanced in his rearview mirror. All he could see
was the dazzling chrome bumper of the massive Kenworth TransOrient behind him, and his own eyes. Then
the traffic signals changed, and the truck in front of
him slowly pulled away. But when Father Quinlan
tried to shift into drive, he found that his gear lever
was jammed.

The huge truck behind him blared its horn. Father Quinlan put down his window and tried to wave to the truck to move around him, but it was too close to the back of his car, and it couldn't. It blared its horn again; and this time it was joined by a chorus of horns from the traffic that was stuck behind it.

Sweating, Father Quinlan wrestled with his gearshift. *God forgive me for thinking uncharitable thoughts about truck drivers and auto mechanics.* But then the Kenworth driver leaned out of his cab and yelled, "Get that heap of crap moving, you son of a bitch!" and Father Quinlan stuck his head out of his window and shouted back, "I'm trying! I'm trying! The gearshift's stuck!"

The truck driver sounded his horn in one long continuous blast. Father Quinlan felt his temper rising. He looked at himself in the rearview mirror and his face was white and his eyes were blazing blue and it wasn't his face at all.

"You connived against me, Father," whispered the face in the mirror.

Father Quinlan stared at the face in terror. He let out a low mewl and tugged even more furiously at his gearshift. It was the child of Satan: the one who comes before to prepare the way for Satan's resurrection. He knew it; and he knew how cruel and powerful it was; and that was why he grappled with his car so furiously. *Let me get away! For God's sake, let me get away!*

Again, the truck's horn bellowed like a dragon.

"And he deceives those who dwell on the earth, telling those who dwell on earth to make an image of the beast who had the wound of the sword and has come to life."

Father Quinlan gripped his gearshift in both hands,

wrestling it forward and sideways. His face was scarlet, and sweat was trickling down the sides of his face.

"All your life you have wormed and connived against me, Father, and now is the time for you to pay. Those who use their minds to work against me must lose their minds."

There was a moment of maximum resistance. Then the gearshift clonked into drive. Father Quinlan's car lurched forward, its engine roaring, straight across the intersection, and straight toward the back of the flatbed truck that had been in front of him before, and which had now stopped for the next traffic signal.

Father Quinlan furiously pedaled the brake, but it went flat to the floor with no hydraulic pressure at all.

"Conniver!" screamed the white, white face in the mirror. *"Deceiver!"*

Father Quinlan saw the rear end of the truck speeding toward him and the second truck was right behind him and he suddenly understood that he was going to die.

He didn't even have time to think of a prayer. With a crushing, grating, screeching sound, the Grand Prix burrowed its nose deep beneath the truck's bodywork, and the aluminum flatbed sheared off its roof at exactly four feet three inches above the roadway, straight through the front roof pillars, straight into Father Quinlan's face, wrenching his head right off his neck, straight through the windows in a sparkling shower of glass, straight through the rear roof supports.

The second truck shunted the Grand Prix's rear bumper and rammed it even farther beneath the first truck, so that it disappeared almost completely.

There was a prehistoric bellow, as one of the truck's tires burst; and then there was extraordinary silence.

*   *   *

It took the wrecking crew over two hours to winch Father Quinlan's car out from under the flatbed truck. A curious crowd stood on the sidewalk in the hot afternoon sunshine, watching and waiting. There was very little for them to see. The paramedics covered the Grand Prix with a sheet and backed the ambulance up close. Father Quinlan's body was lifted out and zipped into a bright blue body bag. It was only when one of the paramedics followed the gurney carrying another smaller plastic bag that somebody in the crowd said, "Jesus, that's his head."

Martin and Boofuls and Miss Redd drove past the accident on their way back from McDonald's. Martin said, "Look at that, God, guy must've been killed instantly."

Boofuls said nothing, but smiled at Miss Redd, and reached across to take hold of her hand.

That night, Martin went downstairs to play chess with Mr. Capelli. He had been to the market with a shopping list that Miss Redd had given him. Veal, chicken, whole-meal bread, fresh fruit and vegetables. Miss Redd had announced that she was going to do the cooking: Boofuls needed his special diet. Martin was welcome to join them, she said; but Martin had no appetite for anything cooked by Miss Redd. It had been difficult enough, taking Boofuls and Miss Redd to McDonald's. To sit in his own apartment watching them eat would be like having dinner at the mortuary.

They were both dead creatures, as far as he was concerned; no matter how appealing Boofuls could be, no matter how courteously Miss Redd behaved.

Mr. Capelli looked worn out, even though his doctor

had given him Tranxene to help him sleep. Mrs. Capelli
had gone to spend the rest of the week with her sister
in Pasadena. Her sister's husband ran a successful
drain-cleaning business, Rothman's Roto-Rooter.

Martin and Mr. Capelli shared a six-pack of beer and
played chess for about an hour. The apartment seemed
empty and depressing without Mrs. Capelli. There was
no singing from the kitchen, no chopping of garlic and
onions, no aroma of bolognese sauce. Mr. Capelli
chain-smoked small cigars and wearily misplayed
most of his moves.

"This woman, then," he asked Martin, "what is she?
Is she real? Is she a ghost?"

"I don't know," said Martin. "I suppose she's pretty
much the same as Boofuls. A kind of a walking, talking
image out of a mirror."

"I got a very bad feeling about all of this," Mr. Capelli remarked, moving his queen. "I got the feeling
they're just using us, you know, for something worse,
something bad."

Martin hadn't told Mr. Capelli what Father Quinlan
had said about the second coming of Satan. He swallowed beer and moved his bishop to counteract Mr. Capelli's queen. *Satan cannot live and breathe until those
one hundred forty-four thousand lie massacred.*

Mr. Capelli said, "You know what I feel? I feel like
this is my house, but it's not my house anymore. Not
when Emilio's stuck in that mirror, and those people
are living upstairs."

Martin nodded. He knew exactly how Mr. Capelli
felt. He was glad that Stephen J. Cannell productions
had just sent him a check for four months' worth of
rewrites, because with Boofuls and Miss Redd in his
apartment, smiling, talking, prowling, planning, he

couldn't get near his typewriter; and even if he had been able to, he probably couldn't have written a single word worth squat. He was too worried about Emilio. He was too worried about what he had let loose on the world at large.

Satan? It seemed ridiculous. But Father Quinlan had believed it; and Father Lucas had believed it. Maybe one priest could be crazy; but two?

The decorated clock on Mr. Capelli's bureau struck nine. Almost at the same moment, the door chimes sounded.

"Visitors?" asked Martin. "You expecting anybody?"

Mr. Capelli shook his head. "My cousin Bernardo's coming down next week, but that's all."

"Let me get it," said Martin, and went to the door. Outside, on the landing, stood Miss Redd, wearing the clinging black-satin dress she had bought this afternoon at Fiorucci, with black stockings and black stiletto shoes. With her high cheekbones and white skin, she looked like a page torn out of a 1940s fashion magazine.

"I'm not bothering you," she said, so flatly that it was scarcely a question at all.

"What do you want?" asked Martin, closing the door behind him so that Mr. Capelli wouldn't see her.

"I wanted to tell you that Lejeune and I will be moving out tomorrow."

"Oh, yes?"

Miss Redd smiled. "I just spoke to June Lassiter at 20th Century-Fox and she will provide a private bungalow for us on the Fox lot while *Sweet Chariot* is being filmed. So—you will be pleased to know that we will not be trespassing on your hospitality any further. We leave tomorrow morning."

"What about the mirror?" asked Martin. "Are you leaving that here?"

Miss Redd said, "That's what I wanted to talk to you about. The mirror cannot be moved; not yet."

"And Emilio?"

"Emilio will be safe just as long as you do not attempt to break the mirror or get him back out of it."

"And when are you going to set him free?"

"Lejeune has made that quite clear."

"Don't call him Lejeune to me, lady," Martin retorted. "That's a poisonous and ridiculous joke. His name is Walter Lemuel Crossley, also known as Boofuls."

Miss Redd smiled provocatively. "Anger makes you handsome, did you know that?"

"It also makes me determined," Martin told her, although his voice was shaking. "And if there's one thing I'm determined about, it's getting Emilio back in one piece. Now—how long is it going to take to finish this movie of yours?"

"Fifteen weeks," said Miss Redd. "Fox is going to put everything possible into it. All the best technicians, the best lighting cameramen, the best choreographers, the best musicians. They've already chosen Marcus Leopold to direct. It's going to be a marvel."

"And you give me your solemn oath that when it's finished, you'll let Emilio go?"

"On the night of the premiere, we will let Emilio go."

Just then, Mr. Capelli came to the door. He stood and stared at Miss Redd in silent indignation.

Miss Redd said, "I sincerely apologize for all the pain we have caused you, Mr. Capelli. But sacrifices have to be made in all great causes."

"They're moving out," Martin told Mr. Capelli. "They're going to stay on the Fox lot until the picture's finished; then they promise they'll let Emilio go."

"There is one more thing," said Miss Redd. "During the production of the picture, you will not attempt to come near us; nor speak to us; and neither will you speak to anybody else about us. You will remain silent and patient, and you will guard the mirror."

Mr. Capelli said, "You, lady, are a harlot from hell."

Miss Redd slowly and elegantly blew him a kiss. "And you, sir, are more right than you will ever know."

With that, she climbed the stairs back to Martin's apartment and closed the door.

Mr. Capelli shook his head. "We should call the cops, you know that?"

"Oh, yes? And what do you think the cops are going to say? 'These people kidnaped your grandson, sir? Okay, where is he? In the *mirror*? Excuse me, sir, while I call for the men with the butterfly net.'"

"Well, you're right," said Mr. Capelli tiredly. They went back into the apartment and closed the door behind them.

"There's just one other possibility," said Martin. "I could call Father Quinlan at St. Patrick's Theological College. He's an exorcist—you know, a proper official exorcist. Once Boofuls and his lady friend have moved out—well, maybe he could try to exorcise the mirror, I don't know—maybe he could get Emilio back for us that way."

"Exorcist?" asked Mr. Capelli, shaking his head.

Martin looked up St. Patrick's in the telephone directory and then dialed the number. The phone rang for a long time before anybody answered. It was a solemn, young-sounding man.

"Can you put me through to Father Quinlan, please?" asked Martin.

"I'm sorry, I regret to have to tell you that Father Quinlan died this afternoon."

Martin was shocked. "He *died*? Oh, my God. How?"

"There was a car crash on Santa Monica Boulevard. He was killed instantly, I'm afraid."

God, thought Martin, we actually drove past that crash. "I'm sorry," he said. "I don't know what to say."

"Did you know Father Quinlan well?" the young man asked him.

"I only just met him. My name's Martin Williams. I met him along with Father Lucas."

"Oh, yes, I remember," the young man replied. "I was the one who let you in. Actually, Father Quinlan had an envelope for you in his car. He must have been on his way to give it to you. The police found it in his car, down the side of the seat. I've got it here if you want to collect it in the morning."

Martin frowned. "No, no. Open it, read it to me over the phone."

"Are you sure? It'll take me a minute to go get it."

The young priest was away for almost two minutes. When he returned, Martin heard him pick up the receiver and tear open the envelope.

"Here it is. *'To Mr. Martin Williams. You may not have heard the distressing news that Father Lucas has been murdered.'*"

"Oh, God," Martin interrupted. "I didn't know that, either. That's both of them."

"Do you want me to go on?" the young priest asked.

"Yes, please," Martin told him. Mr. Capelli was frowning at him and whispering, "What's wrong? What's happened?"

The young priest read, "'*He was found in the base-ment of the Hollywood Divine. The police think he was attacked by an addict. Somebody on angel dust perhaps. Father Lucas had the relics with him, but they are now missing. Whether you believe in the prophesies or not, it will do no harm to take all possible precautions. Re-member the prediction of the innocents, the hundred and forty-four thousand lambs of God. Try to believe! Call me when you get back. Meanwhile make absolutely sure that no woman goes near the mirror, because Boofuls will have need of his witch-familiar, Miss Redd, and the only way he will be able to retrieve her from the mirror will be by—*'"

The young priest paused. Martin urged him, "Go on, why have you stopped?"

"Well, are you really sure you want to—? I mean, it's kind of *odd*, isn't it, to say the least? Father Quinlan was always known as something of an eccentric."

"Please," Martin insisted, "will you just finish read-ing the letter?"

"All right, sir, if that's what you want. Where was I? Oh, yes—'*the only way he will be able to retrieve her will be by trading one life for another—the way he did with the cat—and with your young friend Emilio. The witch-familiar will protect him and succor him until the day when he can revive his satanic parent. Witch-familiars usually have ancient and ribald names like Blow-Kate and Able-and-Stout and Pickle-nearest-the-wind.*'" The young priest coughed in embarrassment.

"Please," Martin begged him. "This may sound like nonsense to you but it makes a whole lot of sense to me."

"Well, there's only one more paragraph," the young priest told him. "Father Quinlan says, '*Remember Alice,*

*read it carefully; and remember, too, that only the child
can destroy the child, and only the child can destroy the
parent.'"*

Martin asked, "Is that all?"

"That's all," the young priest told him. He sounded
more officious now that he had done his duty to Father
Quinlan.

"I'll come by and collect the letter in the morning,"
said Martin. "Perhaps you can keep it safe for me."

The young priest hesitated, and then he ventured, "I
don't mean to speak ill of the dead, Mr. Williams, but
you do realize that most of the time Father Quinlan
was out on a limb, so to speak? I mean theologically.
The church these days doesn't recognize the old biblical legends as strict fact. The Revelation in particular.
I mean movies like *The Omen* have set us back decades.
We can't have people believing in Satan, not these
days. There are so many other problems for them to
deal with. Unemployment, debt, divorce, drug addic-
tion, street crime, isn't that enough to worry about
without worrying about the fiery dragon of the Revelation?"

Martin was silent for a moment. Then he said, "With
all due respect, hasn't it ever occurred to you that all of
those contemporary evils you're talking about—divorce and debt and mugging and everything—hasn't it
ever occurred to you that these evils are nothing more
than the modern face of the same old fiery dragon?"

The young priest said stiffly, "Well, sir, I don't really
think that this is an appropriate time to get into a religious discussion. You can collect your letter at the
secretary's office. And—sir—I do not believe in Satan,
nor ever will."

"Your choice," said Martin, and put down the phone.

Mr. Capelli looked up from their chess game. "What's happening?" he wanted to know.

Martin came around and stood beside him. "We're on our own," he told him. "It's you and me and Ramone, because nobody else will believe us."

Mr. Capelli said, "You've got something to tell me, don't you? Sit down, let's hear it. Tell me the worst. Come on, I'm an old man, I can take it. And aren't we friends? And by the way, I just took your bishop."

Eleven

PRINCIPAL PHOTOGRAPHY STARTED on *Sweet Chariot* in the second week of September. Fox took a full-page advertisement in *Variety*, trumpeting, "Pip Young, Geraldine Glosset, Lester Kroll, in Sweet Chariot, an angelic musical, words and music by Art Glazer and Michael Hanson."

"Pip Young" was June Lassiter's inspired new name for Lejeune, the Fox board having decided that Lejeune was too foreign-sounding, especially for a boy with such a clipped foreign-sounding accent. Actually, Boofuls' accent wasn't foreign at all, it was simply fifty years out of date.

Martin kept in touch with *Sweet Chariot*'s progress through Morris; and through Kathy Lupanek, with whom he had made a special effort to be friends. He had even taken her out for lunch at Stratton's and brought her flowers. Kathy Lupanek had spent two hours telling Martin about her abused childhood. Martin had sympathized.

Back at Franklin Avenue, week after week, Martin and the Capellis lived a life of empty restlessness, waiting for *Sweet Chariot* to be shot and edited and scored and premiered. As far as Martin was concerned, time inside the house seemed to stand still, while the days rushed silently past outside his window, a speeded-up movie of clouds, sunsets, thunderstorms, smog.

He tried not to watch the mirror. He took his typewriter into the kitchen and kept up his income by pecking out rewrites for *Search for Tomorrow* and *The Guiding Light*. But every now and then he would find that he had dried up; and that he had been staring at his keyboard for almost a half hour without writing a word. Then he would walk into the sitting room and stare at his reflection in the mirror and whisper, "Emilio? Where the hell are you, Emilio? Are you alive? Are you dead?"

But there was nothing. No answers, no apparitions, nothing but a cold and clear reflection of the world as it was.

Sometimes Ramone came by, and they would sit on the sofa and look at themselves in the mirror and drink a couple of bottles of wine. To begin with—when Martin had told him all about Father Quinlan and his threats about the Revelation—Ramone had been all for smashing the mirror to pieces. "Just break the bastard to bits, why don't we?" But the days went by, and he became calmer and more philosophical, and maybe Father Quinlan had been nothing but an oddball, after all.

One morning soon after Boofuls and Miss Redd had left the house they saw police next door. Maria Bocanegra had disappeared; nobody knew where. At first her landlady had assumed that she had gone home to her parents in San Diego, but then a month later her parents had arrived to visit her. Her clothes were still strewn around her room, her bed unmade, her lipstick still open and melted across her dressing table. Her father had declared, "It's a total mystery, like that ship with breakfass on it and no people, the whassname, the *Marry Sir Less*."

They saw nothing at all of Boofuls and Miss Redd. Nobody was allowed anywhere near them, except at specially selected press calls, to which Martin was conspicuously not invited. Martin tried to call Boofuls on the telephone three or four times, but each time he was told that "Mr. Young is not accepting any calls, I'm sorry." One Thursday afternoon, drunk on California Chablis, he had driven around to Boofuls' bungalow and yelled out, "Boofuls! You bastard! You listen to me, you bastard! I want Emilio back!" He had been escorted off the Fox lot by two tetchy security guards, and June Lassiter had called Morris Nathan and told him to keep Martin Williams at least a mile away from Century City at all times; in fact, he wasn't even allowed to turn into Avenue of the Stars, on pain of never writing for 20th Century-Fox Television ever again, *ever*.

Martin bitterly wondered which was worse: Armageddon or never writing for 20th Century-Fox Television again.

Meanwhile, taking Father Quinlan's advice, he read and reread *Through the Looking-Glass*, and he studied the letter which Father Quinlan had been trying to deliver to him on the day he was killed.

"Only the child can destroy the child, and only the child can destroy the parent." What the hell did that mean?

Ramone remarked, "My old man, he was always saying that I was going to be the death of him. Maybe *that's* what it means."

In the first week of November, Mr. Capelli came stamping up the stairs and walked into Martin's kitchen without knocking. He was holding up a folded-back copy of *Variety*. He slapped it with the back of his hand and dropped it on the kitchen table. Martin had been typing out some new dialogue for *As the World Turns*, and he froze for a moment, trying to remember the end of the sentence he had been writing.

"It's there!" Mr. Capelli declared. "Premiere date! There it is! November 12! That's when I get my Emilio back!"

Martin picked up the paper. Another full-page advertisement. "20th Century-Fox announces the world premiere of *Sweet Chariot*, an angelic musical starring Pip Young, Geraldine Glosset, Lester Kroll . . . unprecedented simultaneous premieres at Mann's Chinese Theater, Hollywood Boulevard, as well as Lux Theaters, Union City Theaters, Hyatt Theaters . . . altogether four hundred movie theaters throughout the United States . . . plus special international openings in London, Paris, Madrid, Rome . . . Absolutely no previews."

Martin slowly shook his head. "Did you ever hear of anything like this? Simultaneous openings throughout the world? They're really going to send out four hundred prints before they have any idea whether anybody's going to *like* it or not?"

Mr. Capelli didn't answer, but tapped the paper with his finger. "That's the date, November twelfth. That's when I get my Emilio back."

Martin pushed back his chair and went across to the

telephone on the kitchen wall. He punched out Morris
Nathan's number. "Morris. . . ?" he said at last. "Yes,
it's Martin. Listen, did you see how Fox is going to
launch *Sweet Chariot*?"

"I saw it," said Morris. "And if you want my candid
opinion, I think they're out of their tree. They've kept
this whole picture secret. Nobody's seen any rushes;
nobody knows whether it's good, or half good, or terrible. Still, they want to burn their fingers, who am I to
tell them what to do? They're taking a hell of a chance.
June told me the final production cost was $32.4 mil-
lion. So I said, what's this, *Heaven's Gate* with music?"

"And what did she say?"

"She said, wait and see, that's what she said. And I
said, just remember, I didn't have anything to do with
this. If you lose $32.4 million because of some un-
trained juvey, don't come whining to me."

"Do you know whose idea this was? This simultaneous premiere?"

"The kid's, or that nanny of his, who do you think?"

"And they gave in to him? June Lassiter gave in to
an eight-year-old kid?"

"They had to. That's the way I heard it, anyway.
They were three quarters of the way through shooting
the picture and the kid appears in ninety percent of the
scenes and sings every single song, and then he turns
around and says they have to open worldwide in four
hundred theaters and that's it, otherwise he walks.
They could have sued him, but what for?"

"Okay, Morris, thanks," said Martin.

"Did you finish that rewrite yet?" Morris demanded.

"Oh, sure, I'll run it up to you later this afternoon."

Morris cleared his throat. "You're a good writer,
Martin. One of these days you're going to be a better
than average writer."

"Morris, you're an angel."

"Don't talk to me about angels."

The night before the premiere, Martin stood by his open window, looking out over the lights of the Hollywood Hills. Ramone turned the corner of the street and came walking toward the house, brandishing a large bottle of red wine. "Hey, *muchacho*, fancy a little nerve suppressant?"

Ramone came upstairs and they stood side by side, drinking wine and feeling the cool night air blowing on their faces. Ramone lit a cheroot and blew smoke, and the smoke fled around the corner of the house as if it were trying to escape from something frightening.

"Sometimes I don't know why I stay in this town," said Ramone. "It's tatty and it's tawdry and where the hell are its *values*? Sometimes I feel like finding myself a small place in Wyoming and raising horses."

"You'd hate that," Martin remarked.

Ramone nodded. "You're right, I would. Shit."

They drank in silence for a long while, and then Ramone said, "What are you going to do if he doesn't let Emilio go?"

Martin shrugged. "I haven't thought about it. I don't think I've even *dared* to think about it. He promised, after all."

"I was thinking about it this afternoon, though," Ramone went on, "and I couldn't quite get the whole deal to balance in my head."

"What do you mean?"

"Well . . . what I'm trying to say is, as far as we know, Boofuls can't stay in the real world, can he, unless Emilio stays in the mirror-world? So the only way that Emilio is going to get free from that mirror is if Boofuls goes back into it?"

Martin nodded. "I guess that's true."

"Right," said Ramone, "but what I'm saying is—if this mirror-world is as disgusting as it appears to be from where *we're* standing, why should Boofuls agree to go back at all? I mean, *I* wouldn't, if I were him, would you? I'd say forget it, no matter what I promised. Unless—and this is what I was trying to get my brain around—unless he doesn't *need* to go back, once this movie's been premiered. Do you see what I'm trying to get at? Maybe there's something in the movie, maybe the movie changes things. Maybe Boofuls is going to become *real*, once people have seen his picture on the screen, and the reason he wants a worldwide premiere is that the more people who see it, the more real he gets. I don't know. This whole thing's got me baffled. I really hate to think, Martin. It's bad for my sinus. But this thing's making me think."

Martin swallowed wine and nodded. "I don't know, Ramone, maybe you're right. Boofuls was real anxious to start remaking *Sweet Chariot*—right from the moment he stepped out of the mirror."

"So it was important to him, right?" said Ramone.

"That's right; it was crucial."

"And if it was crucial, if it was life and death, maybe it was more than just a comeback, right?"

"Well, maybe it was and maybe it wasn't," said Martin. "It depends whose comeback you're talking about."

"You mean—"

"Ramone, for Christ's sake, I don't know *what* I mean. But maybe this movie is like an up-to-date equivalent of the rituals in the Bible, the rituals that are supposed to resurrect Satan. I've been reading it and reading it and I *still* don't understand it, but the

Bible talks about the great red dragon with seven heads and ten horns, and how his tail swept away a third of the stars from heaven and threw them to earth. But who the hell knows what it's all supposed to signify, because I don't?"

Ramone turned around and stared at the mirror. "Maybe we ought not to wait. Maybe we ought to try getting Emilio out of there now."

Martin shook his head. "Too dangerous. Boofuls said we might kill him."

"Well, he *would* say that, wouldn't he?"

"Supposing we did kill him?" Martin retorted. "Would *you* tell Mr. and Mrs. Capelli?"

Ramone thought for a while, then chucked the last of his wine down his throat and wiped his mouth. "Let's watch some television. I'm tired of thinking."

Up at his house on Mulholland Drive, Morris Nathan was working late, reading over the boilerplate of a television contract with MTM. He sat in his study under a circle of light from his desk lamp, a cigar perched in the ashtray beside him. Alison didn't allow him to smoke anywhere else in the house.

He was almost finished when the doorbell rang. He took off his reading glasses, tightened the belt of his peacock-blue bathrobe, and walked through to the Mexican-tile hallway. Alison was just coming down the curved stairway, dressed in nothing but a loose pink T-shirt with *Andy Warhol 1928–1987* printed in red over her breasts, and a red silk scarf knotted around her hair.

"It's okay," said Morris. "It's Benny Ito, he promised to call by this evening. And in any case, I wouldn't let you answer the door dressed like that."

"Dressed like what?" Alison protested. "I'm not dressed like anything."

"Exactamundo," Morris agreed.

The bell rang again. Morris pressed the intercom button and said, "Who is it?"

"It's Benny, Mr. Nathan. I brought the stuff you wanted."

"Come on in, Benny."

Morris opened the door and a young Japanese with a spiky black haircut and a black cotton jumpsuit came into the hallway, carrying a large padded envelope under his arm. "Here you are, Mr. Nathan. None of it's terrific; just outtakes. But you can't get near to the finished footage with a Sherman tank."

"You promised me a complete print," Morris protested.

"Believe me, I tried. But the Fox lot is up to its ass in security guards. And they won't deliver the prints to the movie theaters until one hour before they're due to start screening. That's what Walt Peskow told me, anyway, and he should know."

Morris opened the envelope. Inside was a single can of movie film. He prized it open and looked inside disparagingly. There couldn't have been more than three hundred feet of stock in it, little bits and pieces spliced together to form one single reel.

"You expect five hundred dollars for this *chazzerei*?"

Benny shrugged and sniffed and shifted his weight from one foot to the other. "Maybe two-fifty."

"Two-fifty? Half? For what? For not even half of a movie?"

"Hey, come on, man, the risk was the same. I could have lost my job."

"For this, you should have lost your balls."

Nevertheless, Morris reached into the pocket of his bathrobe and took out a thick roll of twenty-dollar bills, neatly held together with a rubber band. He stripped off two hundred dollars and handed it to Benny Ito without a word.

Benny counted it and said, "Two hundred? Is that it?"

Morris slapped him on the back and guided him toward the door. "There's an old saying, Benny. Half the failures in life are caused by pulling in your horse, just when he's leaping. You know who said that? Well, neither do I. But you just did it. Good night."

He closed the door, locked it, and then walked back across the hallway with the can of film. Alison had been watching him from the staircase. "What's that, Morry?" she wanted to know.

"The one and only piece of *Sweet Chariot* that isn't in the vaults of 20th Century-Fox. It's not what I wanted. This is all *shtiklech und breklech*, and I wanted the whole damned movie. But at least we'll have some idea of what June Lassiter got for her $32.4 million, and if it looks like a real stinker we'll make absolutely sure the press get to see it first thing tomorrow morning."

Alison came down the stairs, her breasts double-bouncing under her T-shirt. "I wish you hadn't," she told him.

"You wish I hadn't what? You wish I hadn't gotten hold of this footage? Did you think I was going to let that eight-year-old *faigeleh* treat me like a dumb stupid idiot, introducing him to June Lassiter, here you are, June, look at this hotshot kid, June, and what happens, all of a sudden I'm not his agent at all. Do you know what they *paid* that kid to appear in *Sweet Chariot*? Nine hundred eighty thousand dollars! And do you know what ten percent is of nine hundred eighty thousand dollars?''

Alison stared at Morris for a moment, dumbfounded. Then she whispered, "No. I flunked math at school."

Morris put his arm around her and led her through to the sitting room. "Let's just say that 'Pip Young' or 'Lejeune' or whatever he calls himself has cut me out of enough profit to keep myself in new Ferraris for the rest of my natural days."

"I thought you said you didn't like Ferraris."

Morris went across the room and flicked two switches on the wall. With a low hum, a movie screen unrolled itself from the ceiling, and a 35-mm projector rose out of the middle of the coffee table. He pressed another switch, and the beige velvet drapes jerkily closed themselves, all the way around the room.

"Do you want to pour me a drink?" Morris asked Alison as he took the movie out of its can and began to thread it into the projector.

Alison went over to the liquor cabinet and fixed them both an old-fashioned. Then they settled down together on the beige velvet couch, and Morris pressed the switches to dim the lights and start the movie running.

On the screen, there was a brief flicker of numbers; then without warning the face of Boofuls appeared, slightly unsteady, slightly out of focus, but staring intently into the camera.

Morris watched this impatiently for a moment, sipping his drink, and then said, "What the hell is this? Two hundred dollars I paid for this! A screen test!"

Alison patted his arm. "Wait a minute, there's probably more."

"There'd better be probably more," Morris declared. "Otherwise Benny Ito is going to suffer good, believe me!"

He was just about to switch the projector off when the voice of Boofuls came out of the stereo speakers, high and clear.

"You said you never wanted to see my face again, didn't you, Morris? You said you never wanted to see my face and you never wanted to hear my name."

Morris stared at the screen in shock and then turned to Alison. "Did you hear that? He's talking to me personally!"

Alison said, "Morris, switch it off, please!"

"But he's talking to me, out of the screen, just like he's here! What the hell is that Benny trying to pull? A joke, already?"

"Morry, *please*—" Alison begged him. "That boy Lejeune—he's *bad*, Morry, he's *evil*! There's something about him! Martin thinks so, too!"

"A *kaporeh* on Martin! Listen to this! Did you ever see such cheek? Benny must have gotten together with the kid and filmed this on purpose!"

"You said you never wanted to see my face again, Morris, never ever! Well, now your wish has come true! And you said you never wanted to hear my name again, Morris, and you shall have that wish, too!"

Morris stood up and switched off the projector. "Did you ever hear such garbage?" he asked Alison. "Two hundred dollars I paid for that! I'll strangle that Benny Ito, with my bare hands!"

Alison finished her drink.

"How about another?" Morris suggested. "Then we'll go to bed. I finished that contract for MTM."

He went across to the liquor cabinet, turned his back to Alison, and poured out whiskey.

"Are we going to the premiere tomorrow?" Alison asked him. "I bought this beautiful gold dress today at Alluci's."

Morris reached for two cocktail stirrers. "Spending my profits again, hunh?"

"Oh, it's beautiful," said Alison. "I'll try it on for you when we go upstairs. It has a very low front, very daring, but a fantastic bow on one hip, and it's kind of split down the same side, all the way to the hem. It's very sexy but it's very chic."

Morris turned around, a drink in each hand. "Everybody's going to be looking at you, hunh?"

"Oh, Morry, you know it's all for you."

"No point in doing it for me," said Morris; and for the first time Alison caught the odd, tight tone in his voice. She turned and looked at him and at first she couldn't understand what he had done, but as he shuffled nearer with the two drinks, grimacing as he came, she suddenly realized in utter horror that Boofuls' mocking prediction had come true, and that Morris had fulfilled it.

A sharp cocktail stirrer protruded out of each of Morris' eyeballs. He had prodded one directly into the iris of each eye, as far as it would go, blinding himself instantly. Now he was groping his way toward Alison with thin glutinous runnels of optic fluid dripping down each cheek.

Alison screamed. A high-pitched genuine theatrical scream. "*Morry! Oh, God, Morry! What have you done! Morry, your eyes!*"

Morris hesitated, stumbled, and dropped both glasses of whiskey. One of them rolled on the carpet, the other caught the edge of the coffee table and smashed.

"It was the only thing I could do," he said in bewilderment. "It was the only thing I could do."

Alison stood up, but she was so appalled that she

couldn't go near him. "Morry," she wept, "take them out, Morry. Please, Morry, take them out! I'll call for the ambulance, please, Morry. *Please!*"

Morris groped forward, trying to follow the sound of her voice. "Alison, honey, I—" But then he stopped and turned his head around, as if he were listening to something. And at that moment, the projector clicked and whirred into life once again, all by itself, frightening Alison so much that she screamed and screamed and this time she couldn't stop.

Boofuls' face appeared on the screen yet again, that white, expressionless face, and his voice whispered from the speakers. *"You have one of your wishes, Morris. You will never see me again. What do you say, Morris? What do you say? Don't you ever say thank you when somebody gives you what you want?"*

Morris bent his head slightly forward and took hold of the sticks that protruded from his eyes. Shuddering, gasping, he drew them out, and when he did so a large clear glob of fluid swelled out of the puncture holes that he had made in each iris. Alison's screaming quietened to a high, endless whimpering, but she couldn't take her eyes away from him, she couldn't move, she couldn't do anything to help him.

And all the time the high, childish teasing of Boofuls continued to pipe from the movie speakers, and Boofuls' bright face continued to stare at them out of the screen. *"You couldn't be nice, Morris, you couldn't be nice! You couldn't be sugar and spice. Now you'll get it, whatever you want, blind as a bat and deaf as a post!"*

"Shut up! Shut up! For God's sake, shut up!" Alison screamed, and rushed across to the movie screen and tugged at it and tore at it until it came rumbling down from the ceiling. Then she turned to the speakers, and

lifted them up one after the other, and smashed them against the coffee table.

The projector, however, continued to run, and Boofuls' flattened-out face appeared on the back of the white-leather couch, silently mouthing the same words over and over. Alison hysterically threw herself at the couch and tried to drag the image of Boofuls off the leather with her fingernails.

Morris meanwhile had sunk slowly to his knees onto the white carpet. Between the finger and thumb of each hand, he held up the two cocktail stirrers.

"Alison, honey, I couldn't do anything else. There wasn't any choice, honey-pie."

Alison threw back her head and sobbed, one harsh, strangulated sob after the other. "Oh, God, Morry, what are we going to do? What are we going to do?"

But Morris couldn't hear her. Morris' head was filled with the lisping monotonous voice of Boofuls, like an old silk dress being dragged across a floor, saying, *"You never wanted to see me, Morris; you never wanted to hear me. I can give you your wish, Morris! I can give you your wish!"*

Morris slowly raised the two cocktail stirrers and blindly prodded them against his cheeks until he found his ears. Then he inserted the points deep in each ear, so that he could feel them pricking painfully against his eardrums.

Alison had stopped sobbing and was messily wiping the tears from her face with her hands. "Oh, God, Morry," she told him. "I'm sorry. I couldn't stand to see you that way. I'd better go call for an ambulance."

She turned, and there he was, kneeling on the floor with his hands up to his ears, and a cocktail stirrer in each hand. His injured eyes were closed, so that he

looked almost normal, and there was an expression on
his face of curious calm.

"Morry?" she questioned him. Then she saw the
cocktail stirrers. *"Morry!"*

With a small suppressed gasp, Morris pushed the
points of the sticks straight through his eardrums,
puncturing both of them at once. He stayed quite still
for a moment, holding his breath, and then he gave
each stick an extra twist, so that his tympanic membranes would be completely torn open.

Alison, trembling, picked up the cordless telephone
and dialed 911. "Mr. Nathan's house," she whispered.
"That's right, Mulholland Drive. Please, quickly."

Then she put down the phone and went over to Morris and knelt down in front of him.

"Oh, Morry," she said, and held him tightly in her
arms, her deaf and blinded husband, and rocked him,
and swore to herself that if she never did anything else
in her life, ever again, she would have her revenge on
Boofuls.

The morning of the premiere of *Sweet Chariot*, the Los
Angeles basin was filled with thick sepia smog. Because of its elevation on the lower slopes of the Hollywood Hills, however, Franklin Avenue was clear of
pollution, and when Martin looked out of his kitchen
window he felt as if were staring out over some strange
and murky Sargasso Sea.

He drank two cups of hot black coffee, ate a little
muesli sprinkled with wheat germ, and then dressed in
a white T-shirt and khaki slacks and went downstairs
to see if Mr. Capelli would like to take a walk down to
Hollywood Boulevard.

"A walk?" said Mr. Capelli. "You mean that thing

when you put one foot in front of the other and don't stop till you get home again?"

They walked arm in arm, not saying much, but friends, brothers in crisis. They went downhill on La Brea; and then east on Hollywood Boulevard as far as Mann's Chinese Theater, where half a dozen workmen were dressing the marquee for tonight's opening. A huge 3-D billboard had been erected with a fifty-foot acrylic painting of Boofuls, flying up through the clouds with a sweet smile of innocence. That scene came from the very end of the picture, when God decides that the young street Arab has done enough good deeds to redeem himself, and accepts His errant son into the Kingdom of Heaven.

Martin and Mr. Capelli stood in front of the theater for a long while, watching the electricians connecting the klieg lights. Mr. Capelli said, "You know something, I saw the Kliegl brothers once, when I was a kid. They were arguing in the street about something really technical, like carbon arcs or something. And one of them said to the other—well, I don't know which one it was, John or Anton—but he said, 'If it wasn't for me, movies wouldn't even *exist*.' And the other one said, 'Maybe that would have been a blessing.'"

Martin smiled. "You actually saw that?"

Mr. Capelli nodded. "That was a long time ago. Maybe things were more innocent then."

Martin said, "I don't think things have *ever* been innocent, Mr. Capelli."

Mr. Capelli squeezed Martin's arm. "I guess you're right, Martin. I wish you weren't."

They went into Maxie's for a cup of coffee. They said very little; but then they didn't need to. They were both thinking about Emilio.

When they returned to Franklin Avenue (both perspiring, because the morning was growing hot now), they saw a pale blue Rolls-Royce Corniche convertible parked outside. The license plate was 10 PC.

"That's Morris Nathan's car," said Martin in surprise. "I thought Morris wasn't speaking to me—not after I went around to the Fox lot and tried to tell Boofuls what a bastard he was."

"Just so long as he doesn't keep that heap of imported junk cluttering up my driveway," Mr. Capelli complained.

"Mr. Capelli, that's a Rolls-Royce Corniche!"

"Listen, Martin, one day you'll learn. *All* automobiles are a heap of junk. What are they, plastic, chromium, foam rubber, bits and pieces. This one is a heap of *imported* junk, that's all."

"But you love your Lincoln."

"Sure I love my Lincoln. Do you know why? I always kid Emilio it turns itself into a robot, you know, like Transporters."

"Transformers," Martin corrected him; but kindly.

"Sure, that's right, Transmorfers. He loves it. He keeps telling me, Granpa, I saw it happen, I saw it change. The wheels turned into hands and the hood turned into a hat and the trunk opened up and two legs came out, and who knows what?" There were tears in Mr. Capelli's eyes. "Martin, he's just a little boy. I love him so much. Can't we get him out of there?"

Martin said soberly, "Boofuls did promise. So did Miss Redd."

Mr. Capelli shook his head. "Those people," he said. "Those people."

When they entered the house, however, they were surprised to find not Morris but Alison, sitting on the stairs in a tight white cotton suntop and a wide 1950s skirt and strappy high-heeled sandals, waiting for them.

As soon as she caught sight of Martin, she came up and flung her arms around him and burst into tears.

"Hey," said Martin. "Hey, what's happened? Alison? What's happened?"

"It's Morry," she wept. "Oh, Martin, it's Morry."

Mr. Capelli laid a hand on her shoulder. "Hey, now, don't get upset. Look at you, you're all upset! And look at me, I'm all upset, too!"

Martin asked Alison, "What's happened? Alison! Is Morry okay?"

Alison choked out, "He's *blind*, Martin. He's blind! And he did it himself, with two cocktail stirrers, just like that! And then he stuck them in his ears and made himself deaf!"

"What?" said Martin. "Are you kidding me, or what? Morris *blinded* himself? He *deafened* himself? Alison— he works in the movies!"

"Is that all you care about?" Alison screamed. "He's my husband! I love him! He gives me everything! And now he's blind and he can't ever *see* me again, and he's deaf and he can't ever *hear* me again!"

Martin held Alison close. Mr. Capelli, despondent, sat down on the stairs. "I don't know, what the hell. You sometimes wonder if it's worth living."

Martin said, "Come on upstairs. There's another bottle of Chablis in the fridge. The very least we can do is get drunk."

Alison drank two large glasses of cold Chablis one after the other and then told Martin and Mr. Capelli everything that had happened last night, the way that Morris had pierced his eyes and ears. "I couldn't do anything to help him," she said; and the tears ran freely down her face. "I broke the screen, I broke the speakers, but it didn't make any difference."

Martin said, "I'm sorry. I'm so sorry. Whatever arguments I ever had with Morris."

Alison wiped her eyes with a crumpled tissue. "Morry never did anything worse than speak his mind. Nobody deserves to be blind and deaf, just because they spoke their mind. You know, Morry was always speaking his mind, and he was rude sometimes, but he never deserved that."

"But you really believe that Lejeune did it?" Martin asked her.

Alison nodded. "I wouldn't have come here otherwise. It was *his* face, it was *his* voice. And you remember what he said to Morry, when he was auditioning at Fox? When they had that argument? *You never want to see my face again, you never want to hear my name.* Well, that's just what he said on the movie. Exactly that—like he was talking to Morry face-to-face."

Martin said, "I'm sorry, Alison. I'm really sorry. But there's nothing I can do. I tried to get to Lejeune, but they wouldn't let me."

Not long afterward, Ramone appeared. He stood in the doorway with his thumbs hooked through the belt loops of his jeans, looking like Carlos Santana on his weekend off. Martin told him, "There's nothing. There's no news."

"Maybe you should switch on the television," Ramone suggested. "They're showing an hour-long program, 'The Making of *Sweet Chariot*,' just about now. Channel Four."

"I don't want to watch that," said Mr. Capelli. "Maybe I'll get some pizza."

"Pepperoni, deep-dish, with extra chilis, mushrooms, onions, and sweet corn," said Ramone, easing himself onto the couch.

Mr. Capelli stared at him in astonishment, but Martin gave him a nod to tell him that Ramone never took anybody for granted. "I'll have whatever," he told Mr. Capelli.

Alison said, "I'll pass. I'm sorry. I don't feel very hungry."

For some reason, all four of them turned toward the mirror, where the gold-painted face of Pan grinned at them in silent triumph. They looked like a group portrait printed on sun-faded paper: an evanescent photograph of four people who had been brought together by pain and friendship and circumstance, and who would soon have to face the most harrowing experience of their entire lives.

As if to mock them, the mirror seemed to darken and dim, until they could hardly see their faces in it at all.

Mr. Capelli watched the mirror for a moment, and then angrily and with great determination went off to buy some pizzas.

Just before six o'clock that evening, Martin said, "Come on, I can't stand waiting around here any longer. Let's go down to Mann's and see the damn thing for ourselves."

"You go," said Mr. Capelli. "I'll wait here. Just in case—you know—Emilio gets to come out of the mirror."

"I'll stay, too," said Alison. "You don't mind if I stay?"

"Sure, go ahead," Martin told her.

At that moment, however, Ramone said, "Look, on the television, there it is!"

It was a CBS report by Nancy Bergen, transmitted live from Hollywood Boulevard. In the background they could see the crowds of fans already assembling— even though the first stars weren't expected to start arriving for at least an hour—and the huge triumphant marquee picture of Boofuls.

Nancy Bergen was saying, "—motion-picture event of the decade—unknown child star discovered by June Lassiter at 20th Century-Fox—extraordinary natural talent for song-and-dance—won him the lead role in a thirty-five-million-dollar remake of a musical that was actually never made in the first place—or at least never completed—*Sweet Chariot*—"

Martin put in, "Notice how she hasn't mentioned Boofuls, not once. He's still bad karma in Hollywood, always will be."

Ramone said, "Bad karma? He'll be catmeat if I ever get my hands on him."

Nancy Bergen went on, "—such confidence in *Sweet Chariot*'s success that they are holding simultaneous premieres throughout the United States and Europe— which means that in London they're holding their first screening in time for an early breakfast, and in New York it's going to be a one-o'clock-in-the-morning affair—so sought after have the premiere tickets been, however, that—"

"You want some more wine?" Alison asked Ramone.

"Oh, sure, thanks, just a half glass," Ramone told her.

"—thousand people will see *Sweet Chariot* simultaneously—"

"How many did she say?" Martin asked.

"What?" said Ramone.

"How many people did she say would be seeing *Sweet Chariot* tonight?"

Ramone shrugged. "I don't know, man. I didn't hear. Must be quite a few thousand."

Martin quickly pressed the remote and flicked the television from station to station, but none of the other channels were carrying reports about *Sweet Chariot*.

Martin told Mr. Capelli, "Give me the phone book."

"Sure," said Mr. Capelli, "but what's the problem?"

Flicking quickly through the pages, Martin found the number for CBS Television News. "I thought I heard Nancy Bergen say a particular number, that's all. It rang a bell."

He picked up the phone and dialed CBS. The switchboard took endless minutes to answer, and then endless more minutes to connect him with the news desk.

"Chuck Pressler," announced a laconic voice.

"Oh, hi, sorry to bother you," said Martin. "I was watching Nancy Bergen's report on the *Sweet Chariot* premiere. She mentioned how many thousands of people were going to be watching the first screening simultaneously. Do you have that figure there? I missed it."

There was some shuffling around, and then the laconic voice said, "I don't have that information here right now. Nancy's going to be back later tonight, around eleven o'clock. You could try calling her then. Or tomorrow morning maybe."

Martin put down the phone and dialed 20th Century-Fox. This time there was no answer at all. "Damn it," he said. "Come on, Ramone, let's get down there and ask Nancy Bergen for ourselves."

They left Mr. Capelli and Alison at the apartment

and jogged down La Brea in the sweltering evening heat. When they reached the intersection with Hollywood Boulevard, they found that it was already crowded with thousands of fans and sightseers, and that there were police trestles all around the Chinese Theater. Inch by inch, sweating, alternately elbowing and apologizing, they forced their way through to the front of the lines, as close as they could to the CBS outside-broadcast truck. It took them almost ten minutes to get there, and when they did they found two cops standing right between them and the CBS crew.

Martin glimpsed Nancy Bergen, with her brushed blond hair and her shiny cerise evening dress, and shouted out, "Ms. Bergen! Ms. Bergen!"

The girl standing next to him scowled and said, "That was right in my goddamned ear, you freak."

Martin ignored her, and cupped his hands around his mouth, and yelled, "Ms. Bergen! Over here!"

At last, catching the sound of her name amid the bustle, Nancy Bergen turned around and frowned toward the crowd. Several of them waved, and she smiled and waved back. The noise around the theater was already tremendous: talking and laughing and shuffling of feet, and even when Martin bellowed, "Ms. Bergen!" one more time, she turned away because she obviously hadn't heard him.

Martin checked his watch. There were fewer than eleven minutes to go before the premiere. The first guests were already arriving, and there was a long line of shining limousines all the way up Hollywood Boulevard. With a cheer from the crowd, the klieg lights were switched on and stalked around the night sky on brilliant stilts.

Ramone said, "Why is this so *important*, man? I'm getting my feet jumped on here."

"Listen," Martin told him, "I want you to create a diversion so that I can get under the police trestle and across to the television truck."

"Create a diversion? How the hell do I create a diversion?"

"Well, go farther down the line there and try to push your way through."

"Oh, that's great, and get myself arrested?"

"Pretend you're sick, then. Pretend you're just about to have a heart attack."

"That's right, and get myself carried off to the hospital."

"Well, think of *something*, for God's sake. I have to talk to Nancy Bergen, and I have to talk to her now!"

Ramone rubbed sweat from the back of his neck and nodded, "Okay. But you'd better have a damned awesome reason for doing this, *amigo*."

"Have faith, will you?" Martin told him.

Ramone jostled his way through the spectators who were crowding the police trestles until he was twenty or thirty feet away. He bobbed his head up and down a few times and then turned toward Martin and made a circle between finger and thumb, *Watch this, buddy*. Then he suddenly started flailing his arms and shouting out, *"Thief! Thief! You stole my wallet! Thief!"*

Everybody around him backed away. Either he was crazy and he was going to attack them, or else he wasn't crazy and somebody was going to be accused of taking his wallet, and either alternative was about as attractive as catching AIDS.

At first, the two police officers didn't see him, they were too busy standing in camera shot and trying to look groomed and tough, but then two or three girls stumbled and fell because of the commotion that Ramone was causing, and they hurried down the police line to see what was happening. Martin immediately ducked under the trestle, dodged around the back of the CBS truck, and approached Nancy Bergen from behind. She was listening to her producer talking to her over her earphone, and saying, "Yes, Farley; okay, Farley; but they won't be arriving for at least five minutes."

As soon as she had finished, Martin tapped her politely on the shoulder.

"Ms. Bergen?"

She stared at him blankly. That hostile don't-bother-me stare that he had seen on the faces of so many TV personalities when the grubby public came a little too close.

"Listen, you don't know me, Ms. Bergen, my name's Martin Williams."

"You're right," she said, marching back toward the television truck. "I don't know you."

"Ms. Bergen, I'm a screenwriter, I wrote most of the *Sweet Chariot* screenplay. Actually, I updated it from the original. They probably haven't given me credit on the screen, but—"

"—but now you're angry as all hell and you're going to sue. Well, believe me, Mr. Wilson, it happens all the time, and if I were you I'd save your money. The only people who make money out of law are lawyers. I've been there, I know."

"Ms. Bergen, I'm not complaining about that. But there's a whole lot more to this production than meets the eye."

Nancy Bergen's red-haired personal assistant came

up with a glass of Perrier water, a clipboard, and a lit cigarette in an aluminum-foil ashtray. Nancy swallowed two mouthfuls of water, propped the cigarette in the corner of her mouth, and began to scribble notes on the clipboard. "Do you have something to tell me, Mr. Wilson? Otherwise I'm going to have to say *hasta luego*, you know?"

"Do you mind if I ask you a question first?"

Nancy Bergen continued to scribble, ignoring him.

Martin said, "You mentioned that x-thousand people were going to be watching this premiere simultaneously all over the world."

Nancy Bergen stopped scribbling, handed the clipboard back to her assistant, dropped her cigarette back in its ashtray, blew out smoke, and said, "One hundred forty-four thousand, why?"

Martin took a deep breath. "I'm going to sound like some kind of religious nut when I tell you this."

"Then don't tell me. Hank, do you have that radio mike ready?"

"It's ready, Nance," said a thin, shaven-headed man in a sweaty T-shirt.

But Martin said, "One hundred forty-four thousand, that's the exact number in the Book of Revelation, the exact number of innocents who follow the Lamb—the exact number of people who have to be sacrificed so that Satan can come alive again."

Nancy Bergen beckoned one of the CBS sound men. "Harvey, will you escort Mr. Wilson back to the barriers for me?"

Martin insisted, "Ms. Bergen, I don't think you understand what I'm saying here. That boy Pip Young isn't Pip Young at all."

"Mr. Wilson, I already know that. His real name is

something Lejeune. Now, please, I'm going tonto here as it is."

"Ms. Bergen, Pip Young is Boofuls! The real Boofuls! The real murdered Boofuls, come back to life!"

A big blond man with biceps like Virginia hams and a sweatband around his forehead laid his hand on Martin's shoulder and whistled through ruined nasal cavities, "Come on, man, let's be friendly here, hunh?"

"Boofuls was possessed!" Martin shouted. "That was why his grandmother killed him! Boofuls was possessed by Satan! But he escaped! He went into the mirror! But now he's back and everybody who sees this movie is going to die! Ms. Bergen! Listen! One hundred forty-four thousand innocent people are going to die!"

Nancy Bergen was already out of earshot, preparing her first star interview. A gleaming black Fleetwood had just pulled into the curb, and the door was opened so that Geraldine Glosset could step out onto the sidewalk in a clinging white dress splashed with diamanté. The crowds roared and whistled and screamed, and the klieg lights crisscrossed the evening sky as if it were wartime.

Martin struggled and kicked, but the big blond man twisted his arm around behind his back and hop-skip-jumped him back to the barrier. "Ms. Bergen!" Martin screamed at the top of his voice. "He's bringing back Satan, Ms. Bergen! He's bringing him back *tonight*!"

Several of the crowd turned to stare at Martin pityingly. The big blond man lifted him clear over the police trestle, said, "Pardon me, lady," to a woman who was pressed up against the barrier close by, and set Martin down onto the ground.

"Now, you listen, friend, you stay there, otherwise I swear to God you will never walk again."

Martin was sweating and shaking and all fired up. All the same, he nodded and said, "Okay, okay," and rubbed his twisted wrist, and tried to look as if he had been effectively warned off. The big blond man returned to the CBS truck, glancing fiercely back at Martin from time to time, but all Martin did was smile and nod, okay, already, I'm behaving.

Ramone came pushing his way back through the crowd to join him. "Well?" he demanded. "Did you get what you wanted?"

Martin took hold of his arm. "It's true, it's one hundred forty-four thousand."

"You've lost me, man."

"That's why they're holding all of these premieres all at once, all over the world. That's why they've never showed the movie to anybody before. There's something in the movie—I don't know, something in the way it's made, something in the screenplay, some subliminal message, maybe. All of those people who see it tonight are going to be killed."

"You're putting me on. One hundred forty-four thousand? What the hell for?"

"Because tonight is the night, trust me. Tonight is the night that is prophesied in the Revelation. The night that Satan comes back to life, the real dragon, for real, and if you and I don't do anything about it the sun isn't going to come up again tomorrow, nor ever."

Ramone stared at him. For the first time, Martin could see that his friend didn't believe him. And for the first time he could hear the sound of his own voice and he sounded as if he were raving.

All around them, the screaming and the applauding of the crowd sounded like a thunderous landslide as a sapphire-white limousine appeared, bringing Pip Young, a.k.a. Lejeune, a.k.a. Boofuls.

"Ramone," said Martin, "you and I have been friends for a very long time."

Ramone nodded. He looked exhausted, battered, almost sad.

"Believe me, Ramone, you've seen the mirror for yourself. These terrible things haven't been happening for nothing. They've been happening for a *reason*, Ramone, and the reason is it's *time*. It's time for Satan to come back to earth, it's time for the dragon. It's all in the Bible, in the Revelation, but what it says in the Revelation is that Satan's going to come back and then be defeated for good. That's why he's used Boofuls. Boofuls has made damn sure that he doesn't get defeated. He's going to come back if we let him and this time he intends to stay."

Ramone lowered his head. "I don't know, man. I used to believe in Satan when I was a little kid."

Boofuls emerged from his limousine and stood alone for a moment on the crimson-carpeted sidewalk. He was wearing a white suit with silver-sequined lapels, and his hair was shining and curly. Close behind him came Miss Redd, pale-faced, with scarlet lips, in her sweeping black cape.

As Boofuls walked up toward the theater entrance, the crowd let out an extraordinary moan of delight, and two girls in glittery cocktail-waitress costumes came tottering up on stiletto heels to present him with cellophane-covered bouquets. Boofuls accepted the flowers gravely, then passed them back to Miss Redd, who in turn passed them back to the chauffeur.

Martin tugged at Ramone's sleeve. "Right now, I don't care whether you believe in him or not. I want you to help me, that's all. *I* believe in it, and that'll be good enough for the two of us."

"So what are you planning on doing?"

"I don't have any idea. But the first thing we have to do is get ourselves into this premiere, and see what Boofuls is planning to do."

Ramone said, "You and me, in sweaty old T-shirts, we're going to get into the most glamoroso premiere of the decade?"

Martin looked down at himself. "I guess you're right. Damn it. Maybe we can sneak into the back."

"Do you see those cops?" said Ramone. "How the hell are we going to get past those cops?"

"Mandrake gestures hypnotically," replied Martin bitterly. "Instantly, our heroes are clad in immaculate tuxedos."

"Hold up just one moment," Ramone told him. He dug into his back pants pocket and produced his keys. "I believe our problems are ov-ah."

He grasped Martin's arm and together they struggled back out of the crowd. It took them almost five minutes to reach the opposite side of Hollywood Boulevard, but once they were clear of the police lines they were able to dodge and shuffle their way along quite quickly. They reached Ramone's store, the Reel Thing, and Ramone unlocked the front door, switched off the burglar alarm, and let them in.

"What's on your mind?" Martin wanted to know.

Ramone took him across to the side of the store, where there were rails of old movie costumes. Right in front, with a label on it, was the painter's smock that Spring Byington had worn in *You Can't Take It With You*. Ramone, however, was rummaging around at the far end of the rails, and after a few moments he triumphantly came out with two immaculate tuxedos.

"If you're the same size as William Powell, this'll fit," he told Martin.

"You're as crazy as I am," said Martin.

"I don't think so. Now, listen, I have shirts, too, and neckties, and evening pumps. Go into the back and wash up and I'll have it all laid out for you, better than a valet."

Martin went through to the back of the store, splashed his face with cold water, and combed his hair. By the time he returned, Ramone was already half dressed. "Believe me," said Ramone, "you and me are going to look like a couple of swells."

Within ten minutes, they were leaving the store, dressed this time in tuxedos. Martin's vest was far too tight, and so he had ripped it up the back. Ramone's pants flapped around his ankles. But in the crowds and the excitement, they hoped that nobody would notice.

"God help us," said Martin.

"He will," Ramone reassured him. "He will."

Their timing was almost perfect. They managed to push their way through to the front of the crowds just as the last official limousine was pulling away, and the police were dragging a trestle to one side. Martin elbowed his way around the end of the trestle, and slipped behind two policemen into the roped-off area reserved for celebrities and guests. Bud Zabetti from Columbia Pictures noticed him and waved, obviously unaware that he had no invitation, and that was enough of a credential for a beady-eyed security guard to turn away satisfied, and let Martin and Ramone shoulder their way into the throng of people in the theater lobby.

The lobby was hot and crowded and smelled strongly of Giorgio. Martin gradually eased his way through the crowds, nodding and smiling to people he knew. At last he approached the magic circle: June Lassiter, in a striking but somewhat extraordinary directional evening dress, more like a turquoise kite than a dress; Lester Kroll, all wavy gray hair and protruding upper teeth, and heavy gold rings on his fingers that had been given to him by various boyfriends; Geraldine Grosset, always smaller than she looked on the screen, tiny in fact, in a black gown with a gold spray over one shoulder; some starlet who was showing her naked body through a gauzy white dress; Miss Redd; and in the epicenter of this small tornado of Hollywood influence, Boofuls himself, with noticeably staring eyes, gleeful, pale, sucking in every moment of adoration as if he needed it to stay alive.

Martin came right up to him and stood beside him and said nothing; but at last Boofuls turned and saw him. He registered a split second's surprise, then looked away.

"You're not actually supposed to be here," he said. Martin was appalled at the way Boofuls looked. For the first time, he really looked *dead*, like a boy who had been killed and then resurrected. There was paint and powder on his face, as if he had been prepared by an unskilled mortician for viewing by his relatives.

"You could have sent me an invitation," Martin told him. "After all, I wrote sixty percent of the dialogue."

Boofuls smiled to Esther Shapiro. "It'll be out on VCR before you know it. Then you can watch it all you want."

Miss Redd touched Martin's hand with her own hand, as cold as chilled chicken. "I think Pip would prefer it if you left now, Mr. Williams."

Martin ignored her, and leaned toward Boofuls, and said, "It's tonight, Boofuls, isn't it? It's tonight."

For the first time Boofuls looked up at him directly. His eyes were rimmed with red. "I don't know what you're talking about, Martin. Go on, now. Go home. You'd be better off watching this on television."

"Tonight's the big night, when you and Miss Redd plan to off one hundred forty-four thousand innocent people, all at once, so that you-know-who can come back."

"You're mad," said Miss Redd in a low, harsh voice that was more like a man's than a woman's.

"We'll see," Martin retorted. "But let me tell you something, Boofuls. Mad or not, I'm going to do to you what your grandmother did; and that is to chop you up into more bits than anybody will ever be able to put together again. And this time there won't be any mirrors around to save your soul."

"Martin," said Boofuls, "I'm trying to save you. I'm trying to do you a favor."

"I don't want any favors from you. I just want this madness called off, is all. One hundred forty-four thousand people, Boofuls. Think of the slaughter. Think of the grief. And what have they ever done to you?"

Boofuls took two or three deep breaths, feverish, unhealthy, like a child in a sickroom. "I'll tell you what they did to me, Martin. They brought down my father; they brought him down; and my father has lived a life of exile and agony ever since."

"Maybe he deserved it," Martin replied.

"Oh, no," said Boofuls, vehemently shaking his head. "Nobody deserves a punishment like that. Nobody deserves an exile that never ends. In the end, everybody deserves forgiveness, no matter how great their misdemeanor."

"And this is the answer, to sacrifice all these people?"

"Martin," June Lassiter interrupted, "are you monopolizing our star? Come on, Pip, we have to get upstairs to our seats."

But Boofuls beckoned Martin closer, and touched his shoulder, and whispered, *"And I looked, and behold, an ashen horse; and he who sat on it had the name Death; and Hades was following with him. And authority was given to them over the fourth of the earth. To kill with sword and famine and with pestilence and by the wild beasts of the earth."*

Martin, in spite of himself, shuddered. "Boofuls," he said; although he was quite aware how pathetically ineffectual he sounded. "Boofuls, for Christ's sake, don't do it."

Boofuls laughed. "I liked you, Martin, from the moment I first saw you. I think I always will. But go home, now. There is nothing else that you can do. And don't ever ask me anything, for *Christ's* sake."

"I can bring this mirror down here and damn well force you back into it."

"You'll never be able to lift it. You know that."

"I'll try, God help me."

For a fleeting moment, Martin thought he saw Boofuls flinch, as if the prospect of Martin trying to move the mirror somehow disturbed him.

"Leave the mirror where it is," Boofuls told him. "If anything happens to it, then Emilio will die. Do you want Emilio to die?"

Miss Redd now swept herself protectively in between them. "Enough," she said, staring at Martin with glittering eyes.

Martin tried to step around her, but she seized hold

of his left hand and dug fingernails into it. The pain
was sharp and intense; just like being scratched by a
cat's claws. Martin whipped his hand away and it was
bleeding.

"Is anything wrong here?" asked Lester Kroll, benev-
olently tilting his way over. He smelled strongly of
whiskey. "It's time we took our seats, isn't it? Come on,
Pip, you young pipsqueak."

June Lassiter came up to Martin and said, "I don't
know how you managed to inveigle yourself in here,
Martin, and I don't think I want to find out. But since
you're here, and since you wrote so much of the picture, and since poor Morris is in such a bad way . . .
well, you can have a couple of seats at the back."

"You're a princess, June," said Martin, trying to tug
his vest straight.

"Think nothing of it," June told him. "You're a good
writer; and now you've gotten Boofuls out of your system, maybe you'll turn out to be a *great* writer. Tell me
one thing, though."

"Anything."

"Where the hell did you get that tuxedo? It looks like
it came off the city dump."

Martin looked down at his drooping elephant's-ear
lapels. "You wouldn't believe me even if I told you."

After a few minutes, Martin and Ramone were beckoned through the crowds by Kathy Lupanek and
shown to two seats right at the very back of the theater. The auditorium was already packed, and there
was an endless cascade of excited conversation, as well
as the usual coughing and shuffling and waving and
women calling out, "Aaron, *darling*! I didn't know you
were here!"

"Long time since I sat in the back row," Ramone remarked. "And I never sat in the back row with a *guy* before!"

At last, the theater lights dimmed; and a single spotlight fell onto the stage in front of the drapes. There was a roll of recorded drums, and then Boofuls appeared, in the white suit that he would be wearing toward the end of the film, when he was pleading with God to let him be an angel. The audience roared and cheered, and one after another they got out of their seats to give Boofuls a standing ovation. "And—Jesus—they haven't even seen the movie yet!" marveled Ramone.

"The power of publicity," Martin remarked, standing up so that he could get a better look at Boofuls, but not clapping.

Boofuls raised his arms and eventually the clapping spattered away to nothing and everybody sat down. He paused for a short while, not smiling, but bright-eyed, and then he said, "You don't know how happy you've made me. I hope only that I can make *you* just as happy in return."

The audience applauded him some more. Again, he gently silenced them.

"Once upon a time," he said, and his piping voice sounded weirdly echoing and distorted through the loudspeakers, as if he were talking down a storm drain. "Once upon a time there was a boy; and that boy was a legend in his own short lifetime. Once upon a time there was a musical; and that musical was never finished.

"The story of that boy and that unfinished musical is too tragic for us to think about tonight. Instead, let us celebrate another boy, and a musical that has been finished. A boy, and a musical, which all of us who worked on *Sweet Chariot* have grown to believe will change the world."

A large woman in a tight black dress who was sitting just in front of Martin leaned over to her red-faced companion and whispered, "Cocky little so-and-so, isn't he? Just like Vernon was telling us. Do you know he wouldn't even let the *producer* see the whole picture. And they went through seven editors. Seven!"

"Ssh, Velma, he's magic," her companion replied.

"Magic, my ass," Velma retorted.

Boofuls left the stage and went to sit between June Lassiter and Miss Redd. The audience cheered him so vociferously that he had to stand on his seat and wave to them. At last the drapes swept back, and the audience fell silent, but there was a low murmuring of excitement all around.

Then the first chords of music sounded; and New York appeared on the screen; and the audience settled down.

Martin stared at the screen for over an hour without moving or saying a word. He was completely hypnotized. The music was so ravishing; the dances were so dazzling; the photography was unlike anything he had ever seen before. And right from the moment when he first appeared on the screen, Boofuls wrung his emotions in a way which Martin wouldn't have believed possible.

Martin hated this boy; he absolutely detested him. Yet when he was kneeling on the sidewalk trying to save the life of a dying friend, Martin found that his eyes filled up with tears and his throat choked up. He looked around the theater and saw that everybody was weeping, *everybody*, including Ramone, and that some women were so upset that they were hiding their faces in their hands.

When the musical reached the moment when Boofuls has to choose between staying with his mother and becoming an angel, and sings a song while his mother goes about her daily chores, unable to see him, the grief in the audience became almost uncontrollable. Martin found himself smearing tears away from his eyes with his hand; and several people were sobbing in genuine grief.

> *"Mother . . . how can I leave you*
> *Even when the angels are calling?*
> *Mother . . . how can I turn away*
> *Into the rain that will always and always be falling?"*

Martin turned from Ramone to wipe his eyes. But, as he did so, to his bewilderment, he caught sight of Boofuls and Miss Redd hurrying hand in hand toward the theater's side exit. And when he saw that, the melodramatic spell that *Sweet Chariot* had been casting over him was immediately and unexpectedly broken. He said, "Ramone! *Ramone!*" and Ramone looked at him tearfully. "Ramone, something's going down here, something bad."

"Man, this movie makes me feel so goddamn *sad*," Ramone said chokily.

"No," said Martin. "It's more than that. It's like mass hysteria."

He looked around at the weeping, distraught audience. Their wet cheeks glistened in the half darkness. Some of them were covering their faces with their hands and sobbing as if they were totally distraught.

At last Martin began to understand why Boofuls had allowed hardly anybody to see the completed picture,

and why he had insisted on its being premiered simultaneously throughout the world. It wasn't just a brilliant
and captivating musical. It was a hymn to human tragedy. In a particularly subtle and convincing way, it
dramatized not hope and faith and human optimism,
like most musicals, but utter despair. It highlighted the
inevitability of death and the uselessness of life. The
only way to true fulfillment was never to be born at all.

Martin also began to understand why Mrs. Alicia
Crossley had felt it necessary to slaughter Boofuls before he had been able to finish the original version of
Sweet Chariot. In some extraordinary mesmerizing
way, *Sweet Chariot* was capable of drawing its audiences into a whirlpool of helpless emotion, like
drowning moths being sucked down a drain, and Martin began to be desperately afraid of what was going to
happen next.

"Come on," he told Ramone. "Let's get the hell out
of here."

"I want to see the end," Ramone protested.

"Out!" Martin snapped at him, and grabbed hold of
his sleeve.

Ramone struggled and argued, but then one of the
ushers shone a torch at him and said, "Out of there,
please, sir. You're disturbing other folks' enjoyment."

At last, still grumbling, Ramone allowed himself to
be escorted out to the lobby.

"That movie is like some kind of drug, almost," Martin told him. "Can't you feel what it's done to your
emotions? It's washed you and spun you and hung you
out to dry! God knows what's going to happen to the
rest of that audience."

Ramone took two or three deep breaths, then stared
at Martin as if he had never seen him before. "That

was terrible," he said, and he sounded genuinely shaken. "I feel like I have a hangover. Man, I felt so *miserable*."

"That, I think, is the whole idea," said Martin. "But Boofuls and that lady friend of his weren't going to stick around and get miserable with the rest of us."

"They left?"

"A couple of minutes ago."

"So where do you think they went?"

Martin said, "I have a very good idea. But first I want to go home. I have a feeling that it's time we went looking for Emilio."

They were only halfway across the lobby when they heard a high, agonized screaming sound: so high at first that it didn't sound human. They stopped and stared at each other; then they turned back toward the movie-theater doors. There was another scream; and then another; and then a terrifying howling and a noise like wooden buckets being knocked together.

One of the ushers, white-faced, said, "Is that the sound track, or what?"

But then Martin went up to the swing doors and tried to push them open and there was a heavy collision of bodies on the other side, and more screaming, and he couldn't push them more than an inch or two.

"Man—what in hell's happening?" gasped Ramone.

A cop came running through the lobby, followed by two more. Martin said, "I can't get the doors open, it seems like there's a whole lot of people pushing against them on the other side."

The cops pushed with him, but there was a dead weight behind the doors which they couldn't budge. The screaming inside the theater grew louder, and there was more thumping and scrabbling and knocking.

"Upstairs!" shouted one of the cops. "Jack—you take the side!"

The first cop bounded up the stairs to the theater balcony. Martin and Ramone followed him, panting with fear and effort. The noise inside the building was almost unbearable. It sounded like hell itself. There were no intelligible cries for help: only a muffled, brutish moaning, and endless screaming, and that terrible hollow knocking. The cop reached the doors to the balcony and instinctively drew his gun. Then he kicked the doors open and dodged to one side. Well—for Christ's sake, who knew *what* mayhem was going on in there. A fire, a riot, a sniper. It could be anything. Already Martin could hear police sirens warbling in the street outside.

There was a second's pause. Then the cop yelled out, *"Freeze! Police!"* But it was only fear that had made him shout out. The woman who suddenly appeared in the open doorway was no threat to anybody.

Martin whispered, "Oh, God. He's done it."

Ramone crossed himself and shook his head, but couldn't speak.

The woman was blond, and might have been pretty when she first arrived at the premiere. But now it was impossible to tell. Her face was smashed as if it had been hit with a hammer. Her hair was stuck up with blood like a cockatoo's crest; one of her eyes was gone. Her white jawbone protruded through the raw flesh of her cheek, a mush of broken bone, and Martin could even see a gold tooth. She had been wearing a green silk evening dress and a white mink stole. The dress had been torn down to her waist at the front, baring her breasts, and the mink stole was nothing more than a bloodstained rope.

She swayed for a moment and made a crunching, bleating noise for somebody to help her; but as she staggered forward, Martin saw that her right arm had been torn off at the elbow, literally torn off, leaving a dangling loop of bloody muscle, and that the woman was bleeding to death right in front of them. She collapsed and slid down the side of the door, leaving a wide smear of blood.

"Ambulance!" the cop shouted out. "For God's sake, get an ambulance!"

"Ramone," said Martin tensely; and stepped past the fallen woman while the cop yanked off her bloodstained panty hose so that he could improvise a tourniquet. The woman's smashed-up face was pressed close to the carpet. She didn't even murmur. Martin felt bile surge up inside his throat, but he had to swallow it down.

Ramone peered into the darkness of the theater. The screaming and the moaning had subsided a little now; but they could still hear tearing noises, and there was still an occasional drawn-out shriek of agony.

"You don't *have* to go in there," Ramone told Martin, serious-faced.

"Yes, I do," said Martin. "I started all this. I let Boofuls loose."

"Man, it wasn't your doing," Ramone replied. "There was Satan in that mirror and Satan would have found a way of getting out of there one day, no matter who bought it. If anybody let him out, Emilio did."

Martin hesitated, and swallowed once more, and then said, "I still have to go see what's happened."

The cop shouted, "Medics! Where the hell are those

medics?" and then to Martin, "You can't go in there, mister. I don't want any more casualties than we got already."

Martin ignored him and stepped through the half-open doors into the semidarkness of the theater balcony. Followed closely by Ramone, he walked along the back row of seats and then stood looking down at the whole interior of the theater.

The movie had finished, the screen was silvery blank, and the theater was suddenly silent. A battlefield after a battle. Hundreds of people were strewn across the seats, and almost all of them were dead. The smell of fresh blood and opened-up human bodies was so sweet and hot and pungent that Martin had to press his hand over his nose and mouth.

Gradually, the theater lights brightened, and police and paramedics appeared at the various entrances around the auditorium. They stood, like Martin and Ramone, in silence. There was nothing else they could do. Mann's Chinese Theater had been full to capacity this evening with nearly one thousand five hundred of Hollywood's glitterati, and now they were all torn to pieces.

"I wouldn't of believed it," Ramone whispered. "If I hadn't have seen it with my own eyes, I wouldn't of believed it."

Martin cast his eyes around the theater. A director from 20th Century-Fox Television with whom he had once had lunch at the Fine Affair lay sprawled just in front of him, his mouth wide open, his shirtfront crimson with blood. His head was a mass of blood and bruises. His wife lay beside him, almost naked, her hair torn from her scalp, one of her legs twisted underneath her.

A world-famous cinematographer, who two years
ago had won an Oscar for his vivid scenes of death and
destruction in Vietnam, stood half propped, armless,
like a grisly Venus de Milo, against a tangle of bodies.

In every aisle, bodies in evening dress lay heaped,
and blood soaked in dark tides into the carpet. The
stench was intolerable—bile and blood and partially
digested dinners. And everywhere, in every direction,
there were heaps of jewelry, furs, silk, and glistening
heaps of soft intestines. A massacre, in black-tie.

"What did they *do*?" Ramone asked hoarsely. "What
happened to them?"

"They clawed themselves to pieces, that's all," said
Martin. His voice in the huge auditorium sounded
small and flat. "They went mad with grief. Mad with
despair. Mad with whatever, I don't know. You saw
how upset they were, all that crying. They've been
trampling on each other, look, strangling each other,
tearing each other's arms off. And all that knocking,
they were hitting their heads against the seats and the
walls."

Ramone said, "I can't take any more of this, man. I
never ever seen *one* dead person before, except for my
grandmother. I can't take any more."

It was then, however, that the movie screen flickered
and came to life. A faint faded image of Boofuls, triumphant. Martin turned to face it and stared at it as if
Boofuls were speaking to him personally.

And he said this: *"And He was asking him, 'What is
your name?' And he said to Him, 'My name is Legion, for
we are many.' Now there was a big herd of swine feeding
there on the mountainside. And they entreated Him, saying, 'Send us into the swine so that we may enter them.'
And coming out, the unclean spirits entered the swine*

and the herd rushed down the steep bank into the sea,
about two thousand of them; and they were drowned in
the sea."

Boofuls slowly smiled; and then laughed; that high-
pitched laugh that to Martin was now so familiar.
Then his face faded from the screen and he was gone.

They jogged all the way back to Franklin Avenue, strip-
ping off their tuxedos and their vests at the corner of
La Brea, and throwing them into the dust. They said
nothing. They were too shocked, too breathless, and
they knew that if they didn't hurry they could be too
late. Lightning danced in the distance, over the San
Gabriel Mountains; and thunder bellowed all across
the Los Angeles basin, as if madmen were shouting at
each other from different rooms of an echoing old
house.

When they reached Martin's house they found Mr.
Capelli waiting for them at the front door. "I heard on
television, some kind of disaster. Everybody killed. I
thought maybe you got killed, too, and then what was I
going to do?"

Martin tugged the front of his shirt out of his waist-
band and bent forward so that he could wipe the sweat
from his face on it. "I guess we were lucky. But first,
listen, we have to get Emilio back."

Mr. Capelli clutched his arm. "You can't! What are
you doing? You heard what Boofuls said. He could die
if we try to get him out."

"Believe me," said Martin, "if we don't try to get
him out, he's going to have to stay there forever. I don't
think that Boofuls ever had the slightest intention of
letting him out."

"But he said, if we tried to get Emilio out, he could die!"

"Unh-hunh, suddenly, I don't think so," said Martin. He felt shocked and off-balance; but at the same time he felt a strong certainty that he understood now what Boofuls was up to; and how Boofuls had deceived them all. Boofuls was utterly unscrupulous, because he was the son of evil incarnate, and not a single word that Boofuls had ever told them had been anything but self-serving trickery. He had prevented them from rescuing Emilio partly by real occult power and partly by bluff. At least, that was what Martin now believed.

And even if Boofuls had been telling the truth—even if Emilio really would be in mortal danger if they tried to rescue him out of the mirror—what in the end was the life of one small boy, when one hundred forty-four thousand had already been massacred?

They went upstairs to Martin's apartment. Through the open door on Mr. Capelli's landing they could hear Tom Brokaw saying, "—a worldwide disaster—latest counts indicate that as many as one hundred thousand people may have died—not only here but in London, Paris, Stockholm, Bonn, and Madrid—"

Martin reached the top of the stairs and opened the door of his apartment. Mr. Capelli lifted up one hand as if he were waving to him from a great distance. "Martin—he's just a boy, think about that."

Martin said, "That's why we have to get him back, Mr. Capelli. He's just a boy, yes. But he's an innocent boy. He's the boy that Boofuls traded places with so that he could organize all of this killing. Boofuls is the son of the devil, Mr. Capelli; the actual son of Satan. But you remember what Father Quinlan said: *'Only the child can destroy the parent.'* And do you know what that means to me? It means that Emilio is capable of wasting the devil. In fact, he could be the only person who can."

"I just want him back," said Mr. Capelli with considerable dignity, his back as straight as if he were wearing a corset.

"Mr. Capelli," said Martin, "we'll do our best."

He opened his apartment door and went inside, with Ramone following. Alison was in the bathroom, and she called out, "Martin? Is that you?"

"In here," Martin called back.

Ramone breathed out and said, "Man, those people . . . all those dead people . . . that had to be worse than Hiroshima or something." He sat down on the sofa and held his head in his hands. "Man, that was the worst thing I ever saw."

"Are you okay?" Martin asked him.

"What do you think?" Ramone retorted. "Okay? How can I be okay? I'm going to have nightmares about that for the rest of my life."

Martin went across to the windowsill and opened the bottle of red wine. He poured Ramone a generous glassful, and then one for himself. Then he sat on the edge of the desk staring at the mirror at the opposite end of the room.

"That's one son of a bitch," Ramone remarked, staring at the mirror, too.

"But not unbeatable," Martin told him.

"Oh, no?" said Ramone. "We can't move it, we can't break it, we can't do nothing except sit here like the Two Stooges and wait for it to ruin our lives."

"We can go into it," said Martin with determination. "We can go into it, and we can get Emilio back. And

then, by God, we can use Emilio to get rid of Boofuls
once and for all."

"You're really going to try?" asked Ramone.

"Yes," said Martin, although he was almost frightened to hear himself say the words out loud, "I'm
really going to try."

He stood up, and at that moment Alison came into
the room, white-faced. "Martin? Ramone? Thank goodness you're all right! We were watching the premiere
on television and when they said that everybody was
getting killed—!"

Martin held her in his arms for a moment. "It's okay;
we're fine. Well, fine isn't the word for it, but we're still
alive."

"What *happened*? They were saying on the news that
everybody just went crazy."

Martin nodded. "That's just about what happened,
yes. But I have the feeling that something even worse is
about to happen. It's pretty hard to explain, but Emilio
is the key to it. We have to get Emilio back."

Alison slowly turned and stared at the mirror.
"When you say something worse—?"

"I mean much worse. Like the sun never coming up,
ever. Not in our lifetime, anyway."

"And we have to get Emilio out?"

"That's right. We have to go into the mirror, if we
can, and find out where he is, and bring him home."

Alison hesitated for a moment, but then she said,
"Let me come with you."

"Hey, come on, you're loco," said Ramone.

"But I have *some* psychic sensitivity, don't I? I mean,
not very much. But maybe it could help."

Martin shook his head. "I can't let you take the risk."

"Then what are you going to do? Go on your own?"

"I don't know," said Martin. "I guess I am." He reached out and touched the surface of the mirror. It was cold, hard, as impenetrable as real glass; but he had the feeling that if he closed his eyes and simply *walked right through it* that it would dissolve, just as the looking-glass in *Alice* had dissolved.

"Well, I think two heads are better then one," Alison argued, "especially when it comes to anything occult."

"For instance?" asked Ramone.

"For instance, if you manage to get into the mirror, how are you going to get out again? Have you thought about that? Emilio can't get out. How will *you* be able to?"

Martin said, "Trust to luck, I guess."

"Oh, yes, and be trapped in the mirror forever, just the way that Boofuls was?"

"Well, do you have any bright suggestions?" asked Martin.

"I don't know. It may not be foolproof, but you could use a rope when you go into the mirror, just like they did when they went through the spirit-world in *Poltergeist*, because let's face it, that mirror is a spirit-world, right? And if you have a rope, somebody on this side can haul you back onto this side of the mirror if you get into any kind of trouble."

"Well . . . that kind of *sounds* like some kind of sense," Ramone admitted. "Nutty, but sense."

"Oh, sure," said Martin, who was still uneasy about the idea of taking Alison with him into the mirror. "And where do we find enough rope?"

"No problem," said Ramone. "I have about a thousand feet of nylon diving rope in the back of my store. I can go get it, easy."

Martin thought for a while and then nodded. He

couldn't think of any other way to guarantee their safe return to the real world. "Okay, then. If you can go get the rope."

"You'll be just like divers," said Ramone. "I'll stay here, holding on to the other end of the rope, and if you get into any kind of trouble, you can tug on it, and I can haul you in."

Ramone went off to find his diving rope. Meanwhile Martin poured Alison a glass of wine. "Maybe I should change into something more practical," she said. She was still wearing her tight white elasticated suntop and a wide 1950s-style skirt. "Do you have a jogging suit I could borrow, something like that?"

Martin took her into the bedroom and rummaged through his closet until he found her a loose gray sweatshirt with a pull-cord neck and a pair of white cotton shorts that had shrunk the last time he washed them.

She crossed her arms and tugged off her suntop, baring the largest breasts that Martin had ever seen. They bounced independently, as if they had a life of their own. Then she stepped out of her skirt; under which she wore a plain white thong. Martin watched her as she buttoned up his shorts and slipped on his sweatshirt, and knew exactly what it was that Morris had seen in her. The tragic part about it was, Morris would never see her again.

"Something's happening, isn't it?" asked Alison as she brushed her hair in front of the mirror. "Something really serious?"

Martin swallowed wine. "Yes. I guess you could call it Armageddon."

"That's the end of the world, isn't it?"

"Just about. It could be worse than the end of the world."

"Worse?" frowned Alison.

Martin shrugged. "Somebody once defined Armageddon as all the most distressing things that you can imagine happening to you, all at once, forever. To me, that sounds worse than the end of the world."

Outside, the sky crackled with fibers of lightning, and there was a smell of burned oxygen on the wind. Dogs began to bark, all over the neighborhood, and cats yowled and howled as if they were in heat. Down on Hollywood Boulevard, the klieg lights had been doused, but the ambulance lights still flashed and the sirens still wailed, and the desperate shouting of medics and firemen echoed from one side of the street to the other. Martin turned away from the window and tried not to think about the heaps of mutilated dead he had seen in Mann's Theater.

Martin switched on the television. There was a special report from London, showing fleets of ambulances outside the Empire, Leicester Square, ferrying bodies to hospitals. Sandy Gall the newscaster was saying, "—already laying blame on the highly emotional content of the film. Dr. Kenneth Palmer of the Institute of Social Studies drew parallels with the mass suicide in Jonestown of the followers of religious fanatic James Jones; and of incidents in Africa in the 1880s when whole tribes battered themselves to death in the belief that it was the only way for them to get to heaven. The Home Secretary, however—"

"Look at that," said Martin. "One hundred forty-four thousand people have killed themselves, all at the same time, all watching the same movie, and the news media are trying to rationalize it already. If you ask me, being rational is going to be the death of the human race. It's about time we started believing in the inexplicable. Or maybe it's already too late."

* * *

It took Ramone almost twenty minutes to come back with the rope. He was sweating and out of breath. "It's like a riot down there. Thousands of ambulances, thousands of police cars, TV trucks, you name it. And thousands of sightseers, too. People who get a kick out of seeing their fellow citizens lying dead."

A police helicopter flew low overhead, followed by another, and then by a deep, reverberating grumble of thunder. "I think we'd better hurry," said Martin. "We may not have too much time left. In fact, we may be too late already."

They tied one end of the rope around the steel window frame opposite the mirror. "I just hope this damn window holds," Martin remarked. "I don't want to yank on the rope when I'm in mirrorland and end up with a six-foot window in my lap."

While Martin and Ramone prepared the rope, Alison stood in front of the mirror and called softly and coaxingly to Emilio. If she could persuade him actually to come into the sitting room, that would make their bizarre task a hundred times easier. But the door of the reflected room remained closed, and no Emilio peeped through it, and there was nobody in the mirror except themselves—Martin, Ramone, and Alison.

At last, Ramone was satisfied that the rope would hold. "Believe me, an elephant couldn't pull this free."

"Thanks a lot," Alison retorted with a nervous laugh. "I've been trying to lose weight."

Martin and Alison looped the rope around their waists, as if they were mountain climbers. "Just remember," Ramone reminded them, tugging at the knots to make sure they were firm, "any trouble, and I'll pull you back. All you have to do is yank on the rope."

Martin took a deep breath and glanced toward the mirror. "All this is supposing we can get into the mirror in the first place."

"Faith, man," said Ramone, laying a hand on his shoulder. "Everything in this whole wide world requires faith."

Martin nodded. He reached out and grasped Alison's hand. "Let's do it," he said, and together they stepped toward their own reflections in the mirror.

They waited. They felt none of the irresistible suction that had pulled Lugosi into the mirror, and which had almost taken Emilio and Martin and Ramone all at once. Martin looked at Alison and said, "I hope to God we're not making fools of ourselves."

"Faith," Ramone exhorted them.

"What good will that do?" asked Alison.

"I don't know, but why don't you close your eyes and kind of *imagine* you can walk through the mirror. Then, when I count to three, take a step forward and just keep on walking."

Martin gripped Alison's hand tight and closed his eyes. He tried to remember the words in *Through the Looking-Glass:* "And certainly the glass was beginning to melt away, just like a bright silvery mist."

"Are you okay?" he asked Alison without opening his eyes.

"I'm fine," said Alison.

"I'm leaning forward," said Martin. "I'm going to press my forehead against the glass. You try doing the same."

The glass felt flat and cold against his forehead, and pressed his spectacles against the bridge of his nose. But he tried to use its coldness to imagine mist, instead of glass. *It's possible*, he told himself, you've seen it happen for yourself. A ball can bounce in and out of

mirrorland. A cat can jump through. Even a boy can
walk into a reflected room and out again. If all that can
happen, you can step through, too.

Lewis Carroll had done it—*"it seems to me now like a
nightmare . . . the land beyond the looking-glass, in
which each man takes on his true form."* It's possible,
it's been done, I've seen it done, and now I'm going to
do it.

He thought he heard Ramone saying, "One . . ." But
then Ramone's voice slurred and twisted, and Martin
was being wrenched forward, toward the mirror, head-
first, so violently and so suddenly that he lost his grip
on Alison's hand.

He tried to reach her, he tried to cry out, but it was
impossible. He was being pulled forward so strongly
that he couldn't do anything at all but squeeze his eyes
tight shut and contract his muscles and pray that he
wasn't going to be pressed to death.

He knew, however, that he was being pulled through
the mirror into the reflected room beyond.

It was the strangest experience. One moment he felt
as if he were being stretched out, impossibly thin. Then
he felt as if he were being compressed, impossibly
squat. And all the time he could feel the mirror's surface drawing him in, as if it were mercury—a deep liquid chill that swallowed first his head and then his
body and then gradually enveloped his legs.

He believed for one whole second that he was dead;
that the mirror had killed him. But then he opened his
eyes and he was standing in his own sitting room, with
Alison beside him. The only difference was that he was
now facing the window, instead of the mirror. And
when he turned around, to look at the mirror, there
was no reflection either of him or of Alison. Only
Ramone now existed both in reality and as a reflection.

"*Madre mia*, you did it," Ramone exclaimed. "You walked right through the mirror. You walked right through it, just like it was a door."

Martin looked down at the rope that was attached to his waist. Instead of appearing through the mirror behind him, it was now fastened to the reflected window in front of him. "Is the rope following us?" he asked, turning around to face the real Ramone.

"The rope's just fine. Why don't you try walking forward a little, let's see if it pays out from here."

Martin took two or three steps across the unfamiliar, back-to-front sitting room, and Ramone called out, "That's okay, that's terrific. The rope is following you into the glass."

Alison took hold of Martin's hand. "I can't believe this is happening, this is just too strange for words."

Martin went across to his desk and picked up a copy of *Variety*. The headline read, Sweet Chariot Rolls Tonite, and underneath, the entire text was in reverse. He looked at Alison and saw that she was a mirror image of herself; that her hair was parted on the opposite side, and that her wristwatch had changed from her left wrist to her right. He checked his own watch. The second hand was sweeping around the dial counterclockwise.

"We don't have too long, if this thunder and lightning is anything to go by," Martin told Alison. It was thundering just as violently in the mirror-world as it was in the real world. "Let's go see if Emilio's downstairs."

He turned to Ramone and called, "Ten minutes! Give us ten minutes! Then tug on the rope a little, just to remind us!"

"You got it!" Ramone shouted back.

Martin crossed the sitting room and opened the door,

with Alison following closely behind him. It was odd to open the door the other way around, with the hinges on the right instead of the left. The corridor that led to the front door of his apartment looked the same, however. Martin even noticed the small rectangular mark in the plaster where he had dug in his screwdriver to kill the cat. Exactly the same, except that it was on the opposite wall.

He glanced into the kitchen. Everything appeared to be identical to the real world, apart from the lettering on the spice jars,—Ṡalt, Ṗepper, Ṫhyme, Ṁarjoram, Ȯregano—and the newspaper lying on the table, *Los Angeles Times*. "So far so good, as they say in the adventure stories," he told Alison. More thunder shook the evening air; and somewhere they heard the rattle of shingles falling from a roof.

Still trailing the rope, Martin and Alison went to the front door of Martin's apartment and opened it up. The stairway was gloomy, but it didn't look any different from the stairway in the real world. Except—Martin lifted his head and sniffed. There was something different about it. There was no smell. No garlic, no herbs, no subtropical mustiness. In fact, no smell at all.

"What's the matter?" asked Alison, coming up close behind him and touching his shoulder.

Martin shook his head. "Nothing, not yet. But there's no smell. Normally this place smells like La Barbera's."

Alison sniffed, too. "I guess it's because we're inside the mirror. Have you ever pressed your nose to a mirror? Cold, no smell."

Cautiously, they made their way down the stairs. Their rope zizzed on the top stair as it paid out behind them; their only connection with the real world. They reached the landing and stood outside the Capellis' front door. The card next to the bell read ilʃǝqɒƆ, in sloping handwriting.

"Okay, I'm going to ring the bell and see if Emilio's in here," said Martin. "But there's one thing you have to know. People in the mirror-world may sometimes look weird. You know, really grotesque. That's because they take on their real shape—their physical looks and their personalities combined. At least, that's what Father Quinlan said; and Lewis Carroll, too."

Alison nodded mutely. Martin pressed the doorbell.

Twelve

RAMONE SAT on the sofa, gripping the rope in one hand and a glass of wine in the other. He didn't feel at all happy, watching the rope disappear a little at a time over the gilded frame of the mirror and into nothing at all. He could see his reflection, holding the rope, and his reflection didn't look happy, either.

He jiggled his foot and whistled "Samba Negra." Outside the house, the thunder still collided, and spasmodic bursts of dazzling lightning pierced the venetian blinds. He heard more sirens, down toward Hollywood Boulevard. There was a smell of Apocalypse in the air, an end-of-the-world atmosphere, ozone and fear and freshly spilled blood.

Ramone stood up, still holding the rope, and went across to the windowsill to pour himself another glass of red wine. He parted the slats of the venetian blind, and down in the street he saw a woman running, not jogging, but really running, as if all the devils of hell were after her. A flash of lightning illuminated her face and it was grim and white, like one of those Japanese Noh masks.

Disturbed, Ramone closed the slats again and turned back toward the mirror.

To his surprise, Martin was standing in the room, right in front of the mirror, smiling at him.

"Martin! For Christ's sake! You trying to give me a heart attack or something?"

Martin said nothing, but approached him slowly, rubbing his hands together, still smiling.

"What happened?" asked Ramone. "Where's Alison? Did something go wrong? You took your rope off."

Martin said, "Nothing's wrong. Everything's fine."

"Did you find Emilio?"

"Emilio? Oh, no. No, not yet. But I guess we will, given time."

Ramone peered at Martin closely. "Man, are you all right? You sound really strange."

Martin smiled. "Strange?"

Ramone glanced over his shoulder toward the mirror. "Are you sure everything's okay? What's Alison doing? Did you leave her in there, or what?"

Martin put his arm around Ramone's shoulders. "The thing is, Ramone, we found out a couple of things while we were inside the mirror. We found out that you can live your life according to a whole lot of different values. You can live it meekly, you know, doing what you're told all the time, loving your neighbor, paying your taxes; or you can live it to the full."

Ramone was completely bewildered. "Man, I thought you were looking for Emilio."

"Well, we were," Martin admitted. "But—what—

he's only a boy, after all. And what's one boy, in the great glorious scheme of things?"

Ramone turned his head in an effort to free himself from Martin's embrace. It was then that he saw Martin's wristwatch, on his *right* wrist, with a second hand that went around counterclockwise. He jerked around to stare into Martin's face, and he suddenly understood that Martin's hair was parted on the opposite side, and that the mole on his right cheek had somehow switched sides.

"Man, you're not—" he choked out.

But then Martin's eyes flared blue, incandescent blue, and his arm gripped Ramone tightly around the neck, so fiercely that Ramone heard something snap, a bone or a vein or a muscle.

"Get off me!" he screamed. "Get off me!"

Martin hugged him closer and closer, still grinning, his eyes flaring so brightly that Ramone had to squeeze his own eyes shut.

He struggled blindly; and it was probably just as well that he didn't see Martin's mouth stretch wider and wider, and his jaw suddenly gape. Inch by inch, something protruded out of Martin's mouth. Not his tongue, but the slimy top of another head, pinky gray and wrinkled, which gradually forced its way out from between his teeth, rolling back his lips, compressing his nose and eyes and forehead into a grotesque little caricature of himself, like a Chinese monkey.

The head which emerged from Martin's mouth was another version of Martin, smaller and less well formed, but its pale eyes burned fiercely blue, and its mouth was filled with sharp savage teeth, dripping with glutinous saliva.

Ramone, fighting, kicking, opened his eyes. He stared

for one terrified second, and then he let out a bellow of desperation.

Martin's second head stretched its mouth open with a sickening gagging noise and bit into Ramone's face. The lower teeth buried themselves in his open mouth; the upper teeth crunched into his eyebrows. The creature's jaws had a grip like a steel hunting trap; and when Ramone tried to force his hands into its mouth to prize it loose, its teeth were so sharp that his fingers were cut right down to the bare bone.

In a final convulsive effort to break free, Ramone twisted his body first one way and then the other. He couldn't see what effect this had—the creature's gaping mouth completely covered his eyes—but this twisting did nothing but drag the head further and further out of Martin's mouth, on a long slippery pinkish neck that seemed to disgorge forever.

Ramone dropped to the floor, rolling wildly from side to side, but the snakelike head refused to release its grip. Instead, it began to ripple all the way along the length of its neck, as if its muscles were building up strength for one last terrible bite.

Ramone thumped on the wood-block floor, like a wrestler pleading for mercy. One thump—two, three—and then the creature's neck bulged once, in a hideous muscular spasm, and its teeth crunched through flesh and bone, right into Ramone's sinus cavities, biting his tongue through at the root, chopping his optic nerves; and then tugging backward, taking the whole of his face with it.

The creature began almost immediately to slither back into Martin's open mouth. Within six seconds, only the top of its head showed. Within seven, Martin's mouth had closed and returned to its normal size.

Within fifteen seconds—by the time Mr. Capelli had
puffed his way up the stairs to find out what all the
thumping and the thrashing was about—Martin had
disappeared.

Mr. Capelli knelt slowly down beside Ramone's savaged body. There was extraordinarily little blood; but
the bite in his face was so terrible that Mr. Capelli
could do nothing at all but cross himself, and cross
himself again, and then turn to stare at the mirror.

Martin rang the doorbell again. At last, they heard
footsteps, and a muffled voice called out, "Who is it?"

"It's me, Martin, from upstairs. I was wondering if
Emilio was home."

There was a pause, and then bolts were slid back,
and the door was opened. At first it was difficult to see
who was standing inside. The hallway was very dark
and there didn't seem to be any lights anywhere. Martin was aware of something huge and nodding and
draped in black. It looked almost like a large parrot
cage covered with a black cloth.

"Emilio went out," the muffled voice told him.

It was then that the lightning flickered again, and
Martin realized with a thrill of dread what he was
looking at. It was Mrs. Capelli, wearing a black mantilla on her head. But her head was huge, a cartoon
head; like the drawings of the Duchess in *Alice in Wonderland*. Her face was enormous and waxy-colored; the
face of a long-suffering Italian matriarch. Her mantilla
was decorated with thousands of jet beads; and she
was draped with jet necklaces and pinned with jet
brooches; a mother in mourning for the old country,
and for lost innocence, and for long-buried relatives.

This nodding huge-headed monster was Mrs. Capelli

amplified five-hundredfold. Her physical appearance exaggerated by her inner self.

Martin heard Alison gasp just behind him. But he was determined to find Emilio. He was determined to destroy Boofuls. And even though his voice was shaking, he managed to ask, "Do you know—do you know where he went?"

Mrs. Capelli shook her huge birdcage head. Her jet jewelry clattered.

"It's important," Martin insisted. "I really have to find him."

Mrs. Capelli stood silently for a moment and then turned back into her apartment. However, she left the door open, as if Martin should wait for a reply. Martin stepped gingerly into the apartment after her, following the huge swaying bulk of her mantilla.

She went into her parlor, across the patterned carpet. As she passed in front of the mirror on top of the chest of drawers, she changed, without warning—her huge swaying head dissolving like a conjuring trick back to its usual size, her mantilla swallowed up like smoke. It was only when she reached the far corner of the parlor, out of sight of the mirror, that her head expanded, and her black-bedecked mantilla returned.

Martin reached back and grasped Alison's hand. "You see that? When she walks in front of a mirror, she's normal."

Alison said, "Yes, you're right. I get it now. Anybody looking into the mirror from the real world—they wouldn't see anything strange."

They followed Mrs. Capelli to the kitchen. It was here that they saw another apparition, even stranger. A bloated white-faced man—more like a huge jellyish egg than a human being—sitting at the kitchen table.

Martin was reminded of Humpty-Dumpty in *Through the Looking-Glass:* "The egg got larger and larger, and more and more human. When she had come within a few yards of it, she saw that it had eyes and a nose and a mouth."

There was no nursery-rhyme amusement in this creature, however. Illuminated only by intermittent flickers of lightning, he was soft and bulging, with black, glittering eyes, and he breathed harshly and softly, as if his lungs were clogged. He turned and stared at Martin with suspicion and contempt.

"Whaddya wan'?" he demanded in a thick stage-Italian accent.

"Mr. Capelli?" said Martin. "I'm looking for Emilio."

"Why for?" Mr. Capelli wanted to know. "He's-a play someplace."

"Mr. Capelli, it's crucial. I have to find him."

"Do I know you?" the egg-shaped creature wheezed. Something approaching recognition glittered in one of the eyes which swam on his featureless face.

"Martin, Mr. Capelli. Martin Williams. Emilio and I have always been friends."

"Martin Williams?"

"That's right, Mr. Capelli, Martin Williams. I live upstairs."

"Ah . . ." said Mr. Capelli. He thought for a moment his eyes opening and closing like mollusks. Then he coughed, and cleared his throat, and flapped one pale flipperlike hand toward the door. "He went to the market. Maybe with one of his friends. To buy coffee and candy. Now, leave me alone."

Mrs. Capelli stood silently in the corner, watching them with a face as huge as a white upholstered chair Martin said nothing, but took hold of Alison's arm and piloted her back out of the apartment. He closed the door behind him and stood on the landing trembling, taking deep breaths, one hand against the wall to steady himself.

"Do we really have to go outside?" Alison asked him.

Martin said, "There's no alternative."

"But if the Capellis look like *that*—"

"There's no alternative, we have to find Emilio."

Paying out their rope behind them, they went downstairs to the front of the building. The sky was inky black now; the wind was up; and the palms were rustling and rattling. "The market's this way," said Martin. "I think we're going to have to get rid of this rope. Maybe I'll tug it a couple of times, just to let Ramone know that we're okay."

He yanked at the rope twice and waited; but there was no answering pull from Ramone. Martin hesitated for a moment, wondering if he ought to go back and tell Ramone that they were venturing out without the rope, but then a deafening barrage of thunder changed his mind. This was the night that Satan was coming. There was no time to spare.

Quickly, they untied the knots around their belts, leaving the rope lying coiled on Mr. Capelli's driveway. Then they hurried along Franklin Avenue toward the market, crossing La Brea and heading toward Highland. Martin found himself wildly disoriented, because the glittering lights of Los Angeles were on his left side now, instead of his right, and traffic was driving on the wrong side of the street. Neither of them looked too closely, but the drivers and passengers of some of the passing cars appeared to be peculiarly deformed, hunched figures in silently rolling vehicles.

The wind blew stronger. They felt rain on their faces.

Across the street, a tall man with a head like a sheep hurried home with armfuls of groceries. His yellow eyes gleamed at them furtively, then turned away.

The market was right on the intersection of Franklin and Highland, its windows brightly lit. Martin began to jog as they approached, and Alison jogged to keep up with him. Even before Martin had crossed the street, he had glimpsed Emilio at one of the checkout counters, waiting to pay. That dark, tousled head; that small, pale face.

"There!" Martin exclaimed in relief. "Look, there he is!"

Emilio wasn't difficult to pick out. He was the only person in the market who wasn't distorted. The cashier behind the register had a long rodentlike face with the skin texture of a withered carrot, and was tapping at the keys of the cash register with a long claw. Right behind Emilio waited a woman with a tiny head and a vastly swollen body, her small face nothing but a tight cluster of scarlet spots. As Martin and Alison reached the window and looked around the market, they saw nightmarish creatures moving up and down the aisles, some of them crawling like spiders, others with huge nodding heads like Mrs. Capelli, others who were more like dogs. They were seeing firsthand the world that Lewis Carroll had written about in *Through the Looking-Glass*—the world which he had been able to describe only in a children's fantasy, because of its unbelievable horror. It was the world in which people appeared as they really are; and that was more than the Victorian imagination would have been able to accept.

As the creatures in the market passed the curved security mirrors at the far corners of the aisles, their appearance momentarily changed, and they took on a semblance of their everyday selves, except that their faces were swollen by the distortion of the mirrors, and their bodies and legs were shrunken like dwarves.

"Oh, my God," murmured Alison. "It's like some terrible kind of zoo."

But Martin was set on getting hold of Emilio. He banged on the window; and banged again; and at last Emilio looked up and saw him. The little boy's face— at first despondent—broke into a wide smile. Martin beckoned him frantically to leave the market and come on outside.

Emilio dropped all of his groceries and came running out of the store and into the street. Martin opened his arms for him, and they hugged each other tight.

"You came!" sobbed Emilio. "I didn't think you ever would! I thought I was stuck here forever and ever!"

Martin wiped Emilio's tears away, and affectionately ruffled his hair, and then stood up. "It's time to go back," he said. "I don't think anything bad is going to happen to you if you step back through the mirror. But we have something important to do. Something dangerous."

Emilio trotted along beside him as they made their way back toward the Capellis' house.

"Will you do it?" Martin asked him. "You're the only one who can."

"I'll try," Emilio panted.

The wind was howling so strongly by the time they reached the house that they could scarcely walk against it. Sheets of newspaper tangled around their ankles and dry palm leaves whipped at their faces. The streets were almost deserted; but Martin could hear the howling of the fire sirens over the wind, and the distant shouting of a huge crowd, like a distant ocean lashing against the shore.

Martin picked up the loose end of the rope that they had left lying in Mr. Capelli's driveway and wound it over his elbow as they went back into the house. Emilio tugged at Martin's sleeve and said, "I don't have to go back to *them*, do I?"—meaning the mirror-Capellis. Alison put her arm around him and smiled. "No way, José. You're staying with us."

They climbed the stairs, with Martin still winding in the rope. The door marked Ɔapelli was slightly ajar, and the sound of extraordinary garbled opera music was coming out of it, like a record being played backward. Alison ushered Emilio quickly past the door, although Emilio couldn't keep his eyes off it. God only knew what grotesque memories he would retain of what had happened there; of what distorted monstrosities he had seen; man in all his glory.

Martin had almost reached the head of the stairs when his own apartment door opened. He stopped, his heart bumping. Alison said fearfully, "Who is it?"

The door hesitated, then opened a little wider.

"Who is that?" called Martin.

His question was answered almost at once. Out of the door came Martin himself, followed by Alison. Their own reflections, identical in every way, but somehow invested with an independent life of their own. They stood at the head of the stairs side by side and looked down at Martin and smiled benignly.

Martin felt a terror unequaled by almost anything he had experienced in the days since he had first opened his eyes and seen Boofuls standing over him. If he had encountered Boofuls at the head of the stairs, or Miss Redd, or that vicious cat Pickle, then he probably

could have coped. But to come face-to-face with himself, smiling so blandly, that was more than his nervous system could cope with. "Oh, God," he whispered.
"Oh, God, that's the end of it."

Alison stood white-faced, paralyzed with fear.

"What's wrong, Alison?" taunted her mirror image.
"Don't tell me that *you*, of all people, are afraid to look
at yourself?"

Martin's mirror image smiled, and took the hand of
Alison's mirror image as if they had been secret friends
for years. "What a daring fellow you are, Martin! Into
the world of mirrors, just to save your five-year-old
friend."

Martin's mirror image came down two or three
stairs, until he was standing directly in front of him.
"You always had big ideas, didn't you? Little man, big
ideas. Well, I guess that we can forgive you. Every
man's entitled to dream. And your best dream was
Boofuls. *Boofuls!*, a musical by Martin Williams. Look
what it led to! It changed the world, didn't it?"

Martin hoarsely said, "Get out of my way."

"Oh, come on, now, Martin, you're talking to yourself. The only person in your way is *you*."

Martin felt the blood drain out of his head. His
mouth was dry, and he was close to collapse. But
something told him that his mirror image was speaking the truth. The only person standing in his way was
him. His vanity, his ambition, his carelessness, his bad
tempers. Indirectly, *he* had caused the deaths of all
those one hundred forty-four thousand innocent people.

In the Bible, James had said, *"For if any word is a
hearer of the word and not a doer, he is like a man who
looks at his natural face in a mirror; for once he has*

*looked at himself and gone away, he has immediately for-
gotten what kind of person he was."*

Now, however, Martin knew what kind of person he
was; and he knew that it wasn't this smug, smiling
character who was standing in front of him now.

"Get out of my way," he repeated. He felt his
strength returning. He felt his confidence surging back.
"Get out of my goddamned way!!"

Instantly, as fast as a cobra, Martin's mirror image
threw back its head and stretched open its mouth. Out
from its lips poured the slippery pink head with snapping teeth, its eyes blazing bright blue. Martin dodged,
ducked back, but the creature's neck swayed around
and its teeth snagged at his shoulder, tearing his shirt
and furrowing his skin.

Alison screamed; and Alison's mirror image
screamed, too, not in fright but in shrill triumph. But
Martin scrambled back down the stairs, missing his
footing and tumbling down four or five of them at
once. And as the snapping head came after him, he
looped the rope around its neck and yanked it viciously
tight.

The head choked and gargled, its eyes bulging. At the
head of the stairs, Martin's mirror image gargled, too,
and fell onto its knees. Whatever this vicious head was,
it was deeply connected to the innards of Martin's mirror image, and if he could manage to strangle it, he
could strangle his mirror image, too.

Martin pulled the rope tighter and tighter. The blazing blue eyes began to dim and to milk over. Saliva ran
from the sides of the creature's lips; then bloody saliva;
then blood. The head shrank and shriveled, almost like
a collapsing penis, and then dropped against the stairs.
Martin's mirror image came after it, head over heels;

and the hideous body lay jammed against the side of the landing.

"Now," said Martin to Alison's mirror image, looping the rope again and mounting the stairs, "how about you?"

But Alison's mirror image drew back her lips and hissed at them and then ran down the stairs, pushing all three of them aside, and disappeared into the street.

Alison hugged Martin tight. "You did it. You're beautiful! You did it."

"Come on," Martin urged her. "I'm just hoping to God that we're not too late."

They went into Martin's mirror-apartment, closing the door behind them. Then, with each of them holding one of Emilio's hands, they approached the mirror.

"Ramone's not there," Martin frowned. "Look—the rope's there. But no Ramone."

"Let's just get ourselves back," Alison begged him.

Hand in hand, they closed their eyes and pressed their foreheads against the cold glass of the mirror. *I can do it*, thought Martin. *I can step through glass. All I have to do is take one step forward, and I'll be there, back in the real world.*

He felt that sensation of being drawn out thin; and then compressed. His ears sang, and his heart thumped; and for one long, long moment he believed that he was dead. *I'm dead*, he told himself; and then he opened his eyes and he was standing with Emilio and Alison, back in his real sitting room.

"We made it," he said. "And, look, what did I tell you, Emilio's fine. Boofuls was bluffing us all along."

Alison looked around, worried. "No sign of Ramone. He didn't seem like the kind of guy who would get up and leave us, just like that."

"Maybe Mr. Capelli knows," Martin suggested.

Emilio piped up, "Where's Grandpa? Where's Grandpa? Is Grandpa here?"

Martin bent down and picked Emilio up in his arms, and together they went down to Mr. Capelli's apartment. They rang the doorbell, and Martin could feel Emilio tense up. Without saying a word, he pointed to the name card on the door. *Capelli*, not illǝqɒↃ.

Mr. Capelli opened the door almost at once. He was about to say something—but then he saw Martin and Alison, and best of all, Emilio.

He couldn't speak. He clutched Emilio close to him, and the tears ran down his cheeks. Martin and Alison waited, and all Martin could say was, "He's fine, Mr. Capelli. He'll have one or two nightmares, I guess. But he's fine."

Mr. Capelli finally put Emilio down, but still held him close. "I have bad news," he said. "Your friend Ramone."

Martin felt cold. "What happened? Did he have to leave?"

Mr. Capelli said, "No, I'm sorry. It was very bad, very dreadful. I heard him banging the floor upstairs, I went up as quick as I could."

"And?"

"Something from the mirror, I suppose," said Mr. Capelli. "His face—all of his face. It was chopped away, like *bitten*, you know. I could hardly bear to look. I think he must have died straightaway. The ambulance came to take him; the police will come later. They are so busy with all of those poor people who died at the Chinese Theater."

"Bitten?" said Martin; and all he could think of was the chilling pink head which had poured out of the mouth of his own mirror image, with razor-sharp teeth.

"It was very dreadful," said Mr. Capelli. "I'm sorry. It was very bad."

Martin covered his eyes with his hand. For a moment, he felt close to crying. But no tears wanted to come. Not yet, anyway. First of all, he had to deal with Boofuls.

"Mr. Capelli," he said, "I'm going to ask you a favor."

"What favor?" asked Mr. Capelli, with his arm tightly around Emilio.

"I want you to let Emilio come with us; just one last time."

Mr. Capelli slowly shook his head. "I may be old, my friend, but I'm certainly not stupid. This boy has been through enough."

High above the house, thunder cracked; so violently that plaster sifted down from the ceiling.

"Mr. Capelli, if Emilio doesn't come with us now, believe me, the sun may never rise again."

It took Martin almost ten minutes to change Mr. Capelli's mind. Meanwhile, the storm outside rose even more violently. Two palms were uprooted, with a noise like tearing hair, and fell across the street; and the water in Maria Bocanegra's swimming pool frothed and splashed. The wind began to pick up so much speed that it screamed through the telephone wires: a high, tortured scream like desperate souls. Lightning branched everywhere, striking the twin towers of Century City and the Bonaventure Hotel downtown.

"Martin," Mr. Capelli argued, "he's all I have. Suppose something should go wrong?"

"Mr. Capelli," Martin insisted, "this world is all any of us have. I don't want to risk Emilio's life any more than you do. But the way I see it, we don't have any choice."

"A curse on you for buying that mirror," said Mr. Capelli bitterly.

"Yes," said Martin. "A curse on me."

Mr. Capelli sat with his hands clasped together for a very long time, thinking. At last he said, "You can take him. All right? I agree. You can take him. But you guard him with your own life. Your own life, remember. And one thing more. You break that mirror before you go. You smash it."

Martin said cautiously, "I'm not so sure that's a good idea."

"Smash it," said Mr. Capelli. "Otherwise, you can't take Emilio nowhere. Do you think I'm going to sit here, while you're gone, and any kind of monster could come jumping out? I saw what happened to your friend Ramone. You should count your lucky stars *you* didn't see it. Half his face, chomped!"

"Mr. Capelli—" said Martin; but Mr. Capelli was adamant.

"You smash that mirror. Otherwise, forget it. It's brought too much trouble already. And, besides, I don't ever want Emilio going back there. Or even to *think* about going back there."

Tired, shocked, still sick with grief for Ramone, Martin eventually nodded. "I'll smash the mirror, okay? Will that make you happy?"

"Not happy; but better."

Alison waited with Mr. Capelli while Martin went back upstairs to his apartment. Halfway up the stairs, he stopped, and leaned against the wall, and covered his eyes with his hand. *God, give me the strength to carry this through. God, help me.* He waited for a short while, to allow himself to recover, and then he climbed the last few stairs.

He opened the door of the sitting room and there was the mirror, with its gilded face of Pan, still there, still mocking him. The room felt very cold. It was like stepping into a meat market. It was so cold that the surface of the mirror was misted, almost opaque. But Martin ignored the mirror and closed the sitting room door behind him and walked across to his desk. He opened the drawer where he kept his tools and took out a hammer.

"This is it, you bastard," he said out loud. "And Mrs. Harper had better forget about her second installment."

With one sweep of his hand, he wiped the clouded surface of the mirror and then swung back the hammer.

And stopped, frozen.

Because he wasn't there. There was no reflection of him swinging back the hammer. The room in the mirror was empty.

He stepped up to the mirror, his heart beating in long, slow bumps. He touched it. Then he understood what he had done. He had killed his own reflection. He could never appear in a mirror again.

He stood still. He felt an extraordinary sense of loss, like the boy Daniel who stole the sacred harp and lost his shadow.

Then he heard Alison calling, "Martin?" and he swung back his arm and hit the mirror dead-center.

The glass smashed explosively. Huge shards dropped from the frame and clattered onto the floor. And the

face of Pan on top of the frame roared out loud, scaring
Martin so much that he jumped back two or three
paces and almost fell over the sofa.

"God protect me," he whispered, and stepped back
up to the mirror again and hammered the face right off
the frame, onto the floor. He beat it and beat it until it
was nothing more than a smashed-up heap of gilt and
plaster.

He stood up, breathing heavily. Now it was time to
go for Boofuls. And now he needed a weapon with
which to kill him. *A sword blessed by the angel Michael*,
Father Quinlan had told him. But where the hell was
he going to find a sword? And even if he did, how was
he going to get it blessed?

He was about to turn away when a flicker of lightning illuminated the room and flashed from a long
shard of mirror glass. It was nearly four feet long, and
slightly curved, like the blade of a saber. Martin knelt
down and carefully picked it up. He tested the edge
with his finger and immediately cut himself, so that
blood welled up and ran down his wrist. This would
do. This would be his holy sword.

He rummaged in his drawer until he found a roll of
insulating tape. Then he wound it around and around
the end of the mirror-sword to make a safe handle. At
last he lifted it up and swung it around. It made a
thrilling whistle as it swept through the air. Boofuls
was going to regret that he had ever stepped out of that
mirror.

He held the sword by the blade, the way that he had
seen knights hold their swords in storybooks, and he
closed his eyes.

"God, bless this weapon, if You can. Or at least give
me the strength and the intelligence to use it well.
Thank You."

Then, with the blood that ran from his cut finger, he smeared onto the mirror-sword's blade the letters V–O–R–P–A–L.

He walked downstairs. Alison and Emilio and Mr. Capelli were waiting for him on the landing. "It's broken," he told Mr. Capelli, and he lifted up the mirror-sword.

"What in the name of God are you going to do with *that*?" Mr. Capelli demanded.

"Make amends, I hope," said Martin. Then, "Come on, Emilio, let's go find that playmate of yours."

> *He took his vorpal sword in hand:*
> *Long time the manxome foe he sought—*

They drove in Martin's Mustang across to Vine Street. Alison held the sword while Martin drove: Emilio sat in the back. The wind was still fuming across Los Angeles, and lightning was crackling from one side of the valley to the other, like the roots of giant electrified trees. There was hardly anybody else around. A few cars crept along the freeway, but it seemed as if most people had decided to stay home. A wild, dark night, thunderous with impending doom.

They reached the Hollywood Divine hotel. Martin parked on the opposite side of the street and they all climbed out of the car. Half a dozen hookers still strutted up and down outside, but otherwise the sidewalk was deserted.

"Hey, young boy," one of the hookers called to Emilio, "want me to pop your cherry?"

Martin pushed his way into the hotel lobby, with Emilio and Alison following. The usual collection of drunks and scarecrows were still there, but the young desk clerk was nowhere around. The lobby was gloomy and sour and smelled of urine and burned copper. Martin paused and listened, and he could hear a faint rumbling somewhere in the building, more of a deep vibration than a noise, and the sound of voices, chanting.

"Upstairs," he said. "The Leicester Suite."

Alison said, "Martin, I'm frightened. This is it, isn't it? I mean, this is really *it*?"

"Come on," Martin reassured her. "At least we've got God and all his angels on our side."

"I wish I could believe that."

"Martin—" she said.

He looked at her. He had a feeling that he knew what she was going to say.

"Not now," he told her gently. "Let's get this done first."

They climbed the marble stairs until they reached the mezzanine. On the far side of the landing, the double doors of the Leicester Suite were wide open; and from inside a fitful flickering of pale light illuminated the paneling and the drapes. The vibration was even stronger now, even deeper. Martin hefted the mirror-sword from one hand to the other and then said, "Here we go."

They walked into the Leicester Suite. Three or four men in tuxedos were standing by the inner doors, but nobody made any attempt to stop them; or even to look at them. They were all staring in awe at the horrific spectacle which filled the high-ceilinged room.

When Martin stepped into the room and looked up at it, he almost felt like dropping to his knees. It was one thing to be told of Satan in storybooks. It was quite another to find himself standing in front of the Great Beast itself.

The room was dark, lit only by two wavering candelabra. Kneeling on the floor with their heads bowed were fifty or sixty of some of the most famous actors and actresses and directors and producers in Hollywood. Even in the darkness, Martin recognized Shany McKay and Derek Lorento and Harris Carlin and Petra Fell. Even Morris Nathan was here, at the very end of the front row, his head bandaged, leaning on the arm of his old friend Douglas Perry. It was like a Who's Who of Hollywood, all in one room.

At the very front of the kneeling celebrities, with his back to them, stood Boofuls, quite naked, his arms outstretched. His back was narrow and white-skinned, his blond curls flew upward as if he were standing in a fierce wind. Beside him, in her swooping black cape, stood Miss Redd, her hands pressed together in prayer.

In the shadows at the very far end of the cavernous room, Martin saw something stirring. Something huge, and leathery, and inhuman. He heard its claws shuffling on the marble floor, he heard its dry dragon wings rustling. It was the color of death: yellowy gray, its skin crazed with wrinkles. Its skull was wedge-shaped, with curled horns like an aging ram, and its eyes were narrow and dull and infinitely evil.

It stood three times as tall as a man, its head swaying slowly from one side to the other, surveying without emotion those who had been vain enough and proud enough and weak enough to raise it at last from its endless sleep.

"Is it real?" whispered Alison. "It can't be real."

Martin swallowed. "It's real," he said, and then swallowed again.

"It's the devil," murmured Emilio.

"And there's Morry," said Alison in disbelief. "Right at the front—there's *Morry*!"

Martin tried to restrain her, but Alison hurried forward and took hold of Morris' arm and shook it. "Douglas," she said, "why is Morry here? He should be back in the hospital!"

Martin came after her. "Alison, for God's sake!" But Miss Redd had already turned around and seen them, and she touched Boofuls with her long clawlike hand, and Boofuls turned around, too.

Deaf and blind, Morris turned his bandaged head. Douglas Perry said brusquely, "I asked Lejeune, and he promised that Morry would be given his sight and his hearing back if I brought him here."

"From *him*?" Alison almost shrieked. "From the *devil*?"

It was then that Boofuls walked up to them—naked, smiling, beatific. "Hello, Martin. So you came to pay homage?"

"I came to give you what you damn well deserve," Martin told him.

"Too late." Boofuls smiled. "I have brought back my father from his exile, and he lives. You and Alison and young Emilio can provide him with his first feast."

Behind him, the immense dragon-creature arched back its withered neck and let out a harsh gargling sound.

Boofuls said, "He is back now, to rule his rightful domain. All praise. And all praise to those who found his scattered body, piece by piece, and brought it here so that I could breathe life back into it. These actors and directors spent millions of dollars finding the last few pieces of my father's body . . . some were found in

Europe, others were found in Arabia. And then all that was needed was the great sacrifice—one hundred forty-four thousand innocents, whose souls gave my father new life."

Martin lifted the mirror-sword. "I'm going to do now what your grandmother should have done, all those years ago. So if you've got some prayers to say, you'd better say them."

Boofuls laughed. "Do you think that *you*, of all people, can ward off the realm of endless night? The sun will refuse to rise tomorrow, my friend, and it will never rise again, and the world will die in chaos and darkness and storm and cold. The time was promised in the Bible, my friend, and the time is now!"

Behind Boofuls, the bulk of Satan suddenly and thunderously spread his wings and opened his jaws in a screech of triumphant fury. Dust and decayed fabric were stirred up into a whirlwind, and the devil clawed his way toward Martin with its eyes staring and his teeth bared. Boofuls lifted both arms, and stepped aside, and sang out, "A feast for my father, that's what you'll be!"

Martin was so frightened that he could hardly think how to make his arms move. But he managed to lift the mirror-sword and swing it around and around so that it whistled cleanly through the dust and the murk, and gleamed like a helicopter blade above his head.

Satan lunged his head forward, and the tip of one of his horns caught Martin in the chest. Martin heard two ribs crack and felt a sharp, agonizing pain. Satan's head swayed around again and grazed against his shoulder. For a split second, he had a close-up of that watery, evil eye, and gingery fur that was thick with maggots; and when he breathed in he breathed the nauseating stench of excrement and dead meat.

Satan was playing with him, enjoying his fear, relishing his pain. Martin rolled aside and shouted out, "*Bastard!*" and took a swing with his mirror-sword at Satan's neck. But Satan rolled his head away, with fumes pouring from his nostrils, and Martin lost his balance, stumbled, and dropped the mirror-sword on the floor.

"A feast for my father!" screamed Boofuls, dancing up and down. "A feast for my father!"

Martin felt one broken rib grate against the other. He tried to turn himself over and pick himself up, but Satan's wing was already flapping over him like a circus tent in a storm, and Satan's reptilian head was already diving toward him with its fangs agape.

"Oh, God, help me!" he yelled.

And it was then that Emilio ducked quickly under Satan's brushing wing and picked up the sword marked *vorpal*. The glass blade was almost as tall as he was; but he grasped the insulating-tape handle in both hands and ran three or four paces forward, and just as Satan turned his head sideways to grip Martin with his teeth, Emilio jabbed it straight into the devil's eye.

It was so sharp that it slid all the way in, and it's point came gleaming out of the back of the devil's withered neck.

Martin had his eyes shut. He didn't see the sword run in. But he heard Miss Redd scream; and he heard Boofuls shouting in dismay; and then he opened his eyes again and saw Satan rearing up, up, up, leathery trunk on leathery pelvis, wings stretched taut in agony, dust and maggots showering down from his shaken fur.

There was a moment of deafening silence. Everybody in the room rose from their knees and stepped backward in awe. The dragon that was Satan stood immensely high, his head arched back, the mirror-sword glittering out of one eye. *Remember that only the child can destroy the parent.*

Then the dragon collapsed. He literally fell apart, limb from limb, claw from finger, bone from bone. His skull dropped from his neck and rolled across the floor with a hollow sound like an empty barrel. His wings folded and dropped. Within a few minutes, there was nothing left of his leathery eminence but all the fragments that had been so painstakingly and expensively collected over so many years by the vainglorious Satan worshipers of Hollywood. A pall of stinking dust hung over him for a while, but gradually sifted and settled.

Boofuls stood quite still, with his eyes wide open.

"What have you done?" he said. *"What have you done!!"*

Without a word, Martin limped over to the devil's skull, placed his foot against it, and tugged out the mirror-sword. Then he turned back to Boofuls and faced him, the sword lifted over his right shoulder, ready to strike.

"The son of Satan," he whispered.

Boofuls said nothing, but continued to stare at him, wide-eyed. Miss Redd, a little farther away, weakly mouthed the word "no."

Martin swung the mirror-sword with all his strength. It flashed through the air and sliced Boofuls' head clean off his neck. The bloody blond head bounced across the floor. The small naked body stood in front of Martin for a moment, its neck pumping out squiggles of blood, and then it fell stiffly sideways, as if it were a tailor's dummy, and dropped to the floor.

Shaking, half berserk, Martin advanced on Miss Redd.

"You will never kill me with that," she spat at him, backing away. "I am quite different."

"I know that," said Martin. He tossed the mirror-sword aside, and it dropped to the floor and smashed into half a dozen pieces. "But Father Quinlan told me to read my *Alice* carefully, and that's just what I did."

Martin stepped forward and gripped hold of Miss Redd's cape. *She shook the Red Queen backwards and forwards with all her might.* He shook her violently, until she screamed. But he kept on shaking her and shaking her, so that her head was hurled from side to side, and her whole body was jerked around. *The Red Queen made no resistance whatever: only her face grew very small, and her eyes got large and green: and still, as Alice went on shaking her, she kept on growing shorter—and softer—and rounder—and—*

Martin was holding nothing but an empty black cape. He dropped it, exhausted, just in time to see a brindled cat dodging off into the darkness of the Leicester Suite, and jumping up onto the drapes, and disappearing.

"That was Pickle!" said Emilio in astonishment. "Martin—that was Pickle!"

Martin looked at his bloodstained hands; then at Alison; then at the decayed ruins of the angel whom God had banished from heaven forever. "Yes, Emilio," he said. "That was Pickle."

Together, Martin and Alison and Emilio turned away and walked through the silent assembly of actors and directors. Morris blindly called out, "Alison!" but Alison ignored him and took hold of Martin's hand. Martin in turn took hold of Emilio's hand.

"*Alison!*" called Morris one last time; and that was the last word that echoed in the Hollywood Divine.

They buried Ramone next to his mother at Forest Lawn. It was a windy summer's day. Afterward, Martin took them to lunch at Butterfield's. Alison and Emilio, Mr. and Mrs. Capelli. They were all too hot, dressed as they were in black.

Alison looked at Martin for a long time. Then she said, "I'm going away tomorrow."

"Oh, yes?" Martin had been hoping they could spend the weekend together.

"Acapulco, just for a couple of weeks."

"Hey, Acapulco, that's nice," said Mr. Capelli.

"By yourself?" asked Martin, trying to sound off-hand.

"Well," admitted Alison. "There's this guy I met . . . he's an independent producer. He has this house in Laurel Canyon. I mean you wouldn't believe it! Nine bedrooms, *two* pools!"

Martin nodded. "Quite a guy, by the sound of it."

Alison reached over and squeezed his hand. "You're not upset?"

"Upset? Why should I be upset?"

But then Emilio came around the table and laid his hand on Martin's shoulder and said, "It's okay, Martin. You can play with me."

They demolished the Hollywood Divine on the last day of November that year. As the wrecking crew brought down the great domed roof of the Leicester Suite, a brindled cat was watching from across the street, its eyes narrowed against the sunlight and the dust.

The cat was still watching as a passing derelict sifted through the rubble that had spilled into the street, attracted by something bright.

The derelict picked up a squarish fragment of mirror, turned it this way and that, and frowned into it. Then he buffed it up on his sleeve and dropped it into his pocket.

He shuffled southward on Vine Street, with the cat patiently following him.

GRAHAM MASTERTON

- ☐ 52187-0   DEATH TRANCE $3.95
- ☐ 52188-9   Canada $4.95

- ☐ 52183-8   THE MANITOU $3.95
- ☐ 52184-6   Canada $4.95

- ☐ 52185-4   NIGHT WARRIORS $3.95
- ☐ 52186-2   Canada $4.95

- ☐ 52193-5   THE PARIAH $3.50
- ☐ 52194-3   Canada $3.95

- ☐ 52199-4   PICTURE OF EVIL $3.95
- ☐ 52200-1   Canada $4.95

- ☐ 52181-1   REVENGE OF THE MANITOU $3.95
- ☐ 52182-X   Canada $4.95

THE BEST IN HORROR